Sam Bowring is a television writer, playwright and stand-up comedian. His previously published works include two books for children, *Sir Joshua and the Unprofessional Dragon* and *The Zoo of Magical and Mythological Creatures*. He lives in Sydney, Australia.

THE BROKEN WELL TRILOGY

Prophecy's Ruin

COMING IN 2010

Destiny's Rift
Soul's Reckoning

PROPHECY'S RUIN

TWO HEROES, ONE SOUL, AND ALL THE WORLD TO CONQUER

SAM BOWRING

orbit

ORBIT
Published in Australia and New Zealand in 2009
by Orbit
(An imprint of Hachette Australia Pty Limited)
Level 17, 207 Kent Street, Sydney NSW 2000
www.orbitbooks.net

National Library of Australia
Cataloguing-in-Publication data

Bowring, Sam.
    Prophecy's ruin / Sam Bowring.

    1st ed.

    978 0 7336 2433 9 (pbk.)

    Bowring, Sam. Broken well trilogy; 1.

A823.3

Text design by Bookhouse, Sydney
Typeset in 12/17 pt Adobe Garamond Pro by Bookhouse, Sydney
Printed in Australia by Griffin Press, Adelaide

Hachette Australia's policy is to use papers that are natural,
renewable and recyclable products and made from wood
grown in sustainable forests. The logging and manufacturing
processes are expected to conform to the environmental
regulations of the country of origin.

*To my father Ian, who started reading fantasy
to me when I was young and impressionable,
so whose fault this all is.*

PART ONE

The Blue-Haired Boy

I very occasionally wonder what direction my life's path would have taken had my birth not been foretold a hundred years before I actually emerged from my dead mother's womb. If the prophets had not given all the necessary directions as to how I could be recognised, and what I would be, I fancy I would not have the same view now as I do from my windows. If, if, if . . . if there was any point dwelling on things unchangeable.

Instead, a century ago, on a certain day at a certain time, every single prophet in the world stopped what they were doing and saw my future. Forks were dropped clattering to plates, conversations halted mid-sentence, the dreams of the sleeping were pushed aside and the same vision clouded every set of eyes. What they saw: a man with blue hair who possessed the power to end the war. For which side? Unclear. How? They couldn't say. The only other thing they knew (the way we just know things in dreams sometimes) was that I would be born within the next hundred years.

In beginning this tale, I choose the hour of that birth. I call it 'that' birth because I do not exactly think of it as being 'my' birth, as you may grow to appreciate. Be that as it may, my prophecy was alive in the world, and a race between shadow and light was being run.

And it was a dark and stormy night. Of course.

Moments of Fatherhood

A man stood in a hut in the forest, staring into a mirror. Lines scored his face like tributaries, feeding the purple delta beneath his eyes. He'd torn at his bushy brown beard, and tears had fallen heavily, like the rain that would come. He heard the screaming again, a high-pitched wail he'd been powerless to stop; it spiked out of memory to stab at his heart.

'What is it?' he asked his reflection. 'What has happened?'

His eyes focused, and in the mirror he saw behind him reflected that which was real. Twisted sheets, sprawling limbs, blood. Her hair shining too vividly for her to be dead. His wife, Mirrow.

An unbidden image flashed into his mind: a shovel-load of dirt hitting her face. He lashed out against it, shattering the mirror. If only the pictures in his mind's eye could be smashed away so easily.

He sat down next to Mirrow's body. Pushing her hair back from her pointed ears, he remembered when it had been blonde, not this freakish blue. He forced his eyes further down the bed to the baby she had died expelling. The child they had hoped for these last three years. She had been so happy to discover she was pregnant.

'Little man?' he whispered, reaching out to touch the baby's foot.

The baby did not stir; it just lay still, breathing quietly, eyes closed. It was a strange way for a newborn to behave, and the man did not know what to do. In his heart he believed the child would die, but his mind danced around this belief as though it were a pit full of spikes. He did not know how he would cope with double grief. He probably wouldn't.

'You just rest,' he said, patting the boy. 'You just sleep, little man. So you can wake up healthy.'

He was almost scared to touch the boy, scared his shaking hands might clumsily break whatever sinew kept the child tied to life. Why did the boy have blue hair too? Why had his wife's turned such a colour? Again he saw dirt, her face, and he knew that leaving the terrible duty undone was driving him insane.

He found himself standing outside the hut with a shovel, asking himself where she'd like to be buried. His gaze fell on the flower garden. It was the place.

His shovel bit the soil.

Clouds gathered in the fading light and a sprinkling of raindrops heralded the storm. It could have been raining fireballs for all he cared. When it was done, he climbed out of the grave and leaned on the shovel. For a merciful time his mind went blank. Around him the storm whipped into a fury, and it took a thunderclap to stir him. The grave was beginning to fill with water. Maybe, when he put her down there, the water would cover her and he wouldn't have to shovel dirt onto her face after all? He almost laughed.

'How dark the day,' he shouted at the trees, 'when one must hope for such things! How could you let this happen? She loved you as much as I loved her, and still you let her die! Do you hear me, Vyasinth? One of your fold comes home!'

With the weight of grief making it hard to breathe, he re-entered the hut. No change with the boy, and certainly no change with his wife. Unable to bear the sight of her lying there, he bore her up and out of the hut, into the driving rain. Over the grave, he rested his face against the cold skin of her neck. 'Mirrow,' he choked raggedly. By the time he lowered her in, the rain had cleaned her body of blood. A long time he looked upon her, burning her features into his mind to scar them there forever. Then he began to shovel dirt.

With the grave filled, he promised that tomorrow he would bring the boy out and they would say goodbye together. 'And when he's old enough, I'll tell him of you, Mirrow. Everything about you. You will not fade easily from our lives, I swear.'

If he lives, came the treacherous interior voice.

Corlas remembered the prayer she had asked him to repeat if ever she died. It had always made him angry when she brought it up, and he would gruffly inform her that she was *not* going to die with him around to protect her. 'You cannot take on every danger with an axe, my woodsman,' she'd reply. He hated that she'd been right.

The prayer was in the same language as her songs, and he'd learned the words surprisingly easily. Mirrow had always maintained that it was because of his Sprite ancestry, but he had never truly believed her. How could he? He didn't see meaning in the way a leaf twirled to earth, or hear voices in the trees, or see faces in streams. He didn't remember generations of ancient peoples who had gone before him – blood memory, as Mirrow called it. 'The Lady told me I am almost pure Sprite,' she'd said. 'I've many of the old talents that are lost to our kind. Perhaps with you it was only a very distant relative who had Sprite in them and so it is not so easily seen. Yet you are Sprite nonetheless.' And he would smile and remain silent, because he knew the idea pleased her.

Summoning it from memory, Corlas spoke the accursed prayer. The wind howled, sharing his despair, and earth blasted from the top of the grave. The trees surrounding the clearing shook violently, twigs and leaves ripping free. Sticks and stones took off from the ground and Corlas heard the *whiz* of objects hurtling by his ears. Underneath the wind came the whispering of unearthly voices. A chill seized him as he realised that the spirits of the wood were all around, churning the air. The fear faded, however, as, although the wind roared loudly, he didn't feel the slightest breeze. And then, for a moment, he thought he saw her. In the fork of a tree by the clearing's edge, some twenty paces above the ground, she stood watching. Taller than a mortal woman, with arms like branches and fingers like twigs, her face was impossible to make out in the dark. A voice spoke to him clearly above the others, seeming to come from all around . . . and he understood that the forest loved Mirrow as he had, and that her spirit was safe. Then the Lady was gone, replaced by whipping branches and rustling leaves, and he wondered if he had seen her at all.

Shivering, he went back inside. There, he stared at the bed for a long moment. Then he glanced from left to right. As he tore the sheets off the bed, confusion fast became horror.

The child was gone.

~

Corlas clutched his beard. Had he gone mad with grief? How could a child vanish? Had he moved the child and not remembered? Surely that wasn't possible.

It was a small hut that Corlas had built, just one room with simple furnishings – a bed, table, rug by the fireplace, and the cot he had made for the new arrival. It took only a moment to sweep it with his eyes and find no sign of the child. He kneeled down and looked under the bed.

Amber eyes stared back at him.

Corlas fell backwards in surprise. Under the bed, on hands and knees, the child was alive! The boy regarded him curiously, with open, seeing eyes. Corlas stared back in disbelief. He didn't know a lot about babies, but he certainly knew they did not see and crawl and . . . *climb off beds?* . . . when they were but hours old. The child had blue hair, the same shade that Mirrow's had turned with her pregnancy. Was it the work of spirits or demons? No, surely not. Corlas had grown to trust Whisperwood since he'd come to live here and he didn't think it would allow such a thing.

The child burped, and giggled at its own wit. Suddenly Corlas relaxed. This child was no demon spawn. *This was his son.* He blinked as the thought sank in, then reached under the bed to seize the child under his chubby arms and hoist him out. Standing, he awkwardly arranged the baby against his chest, staring down in wonder. The child, unnaturally aware, stared back at him.

'A son,' Corlas breathed. He rocked the baby, who cooed gently. Corlas smiled, cracking the lines of grief on his face. Happy tears fell, and splotches of dried blood on the child's skin ran afresh. 'A son,' he repeated. 'I have a son!' He held the baby aloft and shouted the words. The baby looked a little worried and Corlas laughed with joy.

Setting the boy carefully on the bed, he busied himself stoking an almost faded fire back to life. The room began to warm, and Corlas heated water in an iron pot. He bathed the child, rinsing his downy blue hair.

'I thought you might escape me, boy,' Corlas said. 'You lay so still.'

His drowsy eyes slid closed, and he dreamed of his wife. Most his time with Mirrow had seemed like a dream anyway.

His eyes opened. He was sitting on the banks of a clear stream just outside Whisperwood, against a willow tree in the shade. The heat was slow and thick, and running water the only sound. For the first time in a long time, he was at ease. The ache of the wounds given to him at the Shining Mines had finally begun to fade.

Movement by the water caught his attention. On the forest side of the stream, someone emerged from the trees. She kneeled by the water, singing in a language Corlas hadn't heard before, but which resonated with him somehow. It was beautiful. Her wild hair shone gold in the sunlight, her small ears were pointed. She ran her hands through the water, fingers slim and graceful. She looked up and saw him watching. He felt awkward, a hulking battle-scarred warrior sitting in the shade, staring silently at a beautiful girl. He thought she would run and was filled with sadness. Instead, she smiled in greeting.

'Are you from the healers' valley?' she called.

'Yes,' answered Corlas. The word floated by itself, oafishly alone.

She jumped to her feet and began to wade into the stream with no regard for her dress. He tried to rise, but his body creaked, and before he knew it she was kneeling at his side.

'Don't get up,' she said. 'You've been hurt.'

'Some months ago now, miss,' he said, dumbfounded by how bold she was. 'I'm almost healed.'

Her blue eyes were shot through with orange flecks and turned up slightly at the corners. He realised she had Sprite in her blood, and a strong dose at that.

'The wounds, yes,' she said. She touched him where his flesh was tender, and his surprise doubled. 'But not returned to vitality, I think. You should spend some time in the wood – you'd quickly return to your full self.'

'What do you mean?' he said.

She laughed heartily. 'Why, because of your Sprite blood of course! The wood looks after its own.'

He chuckled, though confused. 'I have no Sprite blood, miss.'

At this she laughed even louder. 'You don't even know that you have Sprite blood?'

'I don't see how I could,' said Corlas. 'I have none of the marks. Though you do, stronger than I have ever seen.'

'Seen? Seen?' she repeated, eyes flashing. 'Do you mean pointy ears and twice-coloured eyes? I am talking about the blood underneath your skin!'

She reached up to put her hands on his forehead. He froze, unwilling to move lest he startle her.

'*There* it is,' she exclaimed. 'Bubble, bubble. You need to learn to look underneath the surface, my fine fellow.'

She leaped to her feet. 'I think you should come for a walk in the wood!'

Corlas was enthralled. Right then he might have joined her if she'd announced she was walking to the moon. She grabbed his arm to haul him to his feet, and he rose clumsily, still marvelling at her forwardness.

'Are you not afraid to go walking alone with a strange man?' he said.

'Alone *and* with?' She chuckled. 'You make no sense. Besides, you are not just a human man. I certainly wouldn't allow one of *them* to catch sight of me by the stream.'

He allowed himself to be led into the water, the flow soaking his trousers.

'And I never,' she whispered in his ear, 'would let one hear me sing that song.'

'What did it mean?' he asked. 'Your song?'

'Don't you remember?' she said.

'I have not heard it before.'

'Not with your ears.' She smiled and thumped him on the chest. 'But maybe your heart remembers.'

She sang again, and something within him stirred.

They walked into the forest, which he hadn't left since.

The Lady Vyasinth wafted through the trees above the hut. She would have to become more involved again, she knew, as she had been when Mirrow was very young. Back then Vyasinth had appeared to the girl almost every day, to look after her and teach her the ways of the Sprites. Mirrow had been supposed to pass the knowledge on to her children, a plan which, sadly, had died with her. Vyasinth now regretted having ignored Corlas, offended by his refusal to believe what he was. She would have to put her qualms aside, unless she wanted the child to grow up in ignorance, as good as an end to all her hard work. Yes, she would speak to Corlas, but not now, not yet – for there were strangers in the wood, presences that pricked at her far-reaching awareness. *Why are they here?* she thought, even though she knew the answer, knew with a horror like an inversion of the joy she'd felt when Mirrow's hair had turned blue with her pregnancy. Arkus and Assedrynn coveted that which was hers.

Her ire increased as she thought of those two. Everything was their fault! How she longed for the days when there had been only one type of magic in the world – Old Magic, as it was now called – which had existed when the two gods had ruled together. Arkus, God of Light, and Assedrynn, God of Shadow, had once lived in duality and balance – night and day, water and fire, certainty and uncertainty, truth and dreams. There had been only one Great Well, where all souls journeyed upon death to become part of a collective. That had changed when the gods had gone to war. They had closed their domains to each other, and come to one final agreement that made it possible for one to destroy the other: to break the Great Well. Each god had drawn out his own aspect from the Well, shattering the duality that had previously existed. The souls of those not fully dissolved had suffered the most, their very beings wrenched apart. Vyasinth remembered vividly their cries.

After that, the Old Magic had no longer worked. Instead each god created a new Well of his own, in his own domain, so that the souls of his people would go to him alone. With shadow and light thus divided, a creature could be born only of one or the other. Born of light returned to light in death, and born of shadow returned to shadow. Vyasinth had seen it as a violation of the natural order and, unlike the other minor gods, had refused to side with either Arkus or Assedrynn. As punishment they had banished her here, to Whisperwood; meanwhile, her people suffered greatly.

The Sprites weren't like the luckier creatures of the land who had more easily survived the division of magic. The Zyvanix wasps, for example, had always built their hive cities in the arid plains of the north. Their neighbours, the Varenkai, were bronzed farmers, growing food under the sun in open fields. These were folk of the light, and Arkus had always been their god. The Varenkai's pale cousins, the Arabodedas, lived by the sea in the cloudy south; here, deep water offered up food and life and icy winds drove their robust ships. There were the Vorthargs who dwelled in caves, and the Graka who lived in the storm-laden Bentemoth Mountains. These were all folk of shadows, and their god naturally became Assedrynn. They had made the transition quickly, instinctively.

The Sprites, however, were folk of the forest in whom Old Magic was strong – after all, trees keep their roots in shadow and leaves in the light, relying upon a balance of both. Robbed of balance, the Sprites had died in their multitudes. Only those living in Whisperwood survived, for with Vyasinth's presence it became the only place in the world where Old Magic could still exist. The survivors weren't many, and had been forced to interbreed with Varenkai, so their blood had thinned over generations. Soon there had been no true Sprites left, only half-breeds or less, beings who could survive outside Whisperwood. As they had spread out into the land, all vestiges of culture had been lost and no more souls returned to Lady Vyasinth and the Well that was Whisperwood.

In Mirrow, Vyasinth had sensed, for the first time in centuries, almost pure Sprite blood. She had decided it was time to rebuild; her sorrow finally replaced with purpose. She had called Mirrow to the wood, and time had even brought her a suitable mate. When Mirrow's hair had turned blue with her pregnancy, Vyasinth had guessed that the child would be born special . . . and maybe she could even hope for more than simple rebuilding. Maybe she was to be delivered a champion.

It was then that she had decided to give Mirrow the Stone. She had never told her that it was special, created when the Great Well was broken, retrieved by Vyasinth before she was cast down into the world. It would make a fitting weapon for a blue-haired hero.

And yet others had discovered him too. Now, despite what they had promised her, Arkus and Assedrynn trespassed in her domain.

A Converging in Whisperwood

Battu's consciousness dissolved from his body and melted down the sides of Skygrip Castle like black butter. He trickled down stairwells and spread over balconies, seeped through cracks and curled around doorways. Sometimes it was useful to travel so slowly and widely. With his awareness diffused, he gathered impressions of all that he touched. In his broadest moments he could *feel* the castle itself, as if he were a glove over an enormous hand.

Skygrip rose a league into the sky, a cyclopean tower of black stone. At the top rested a globe of rock twice the width of the tower that supported it, from which four stone spikes reached up to the sky. From between the spikes rose a thick stream of vapour like a slow-moving hurricane, feeding upwards into the Cloud. The Cloud, which covered all of Fenvarrow and kept it safe in shadow.

Skygrip had been built by Kryzante, the first Shadowdreamer. Legend said he had carved the castle from a single piece of rock, once called Mount Mokan. What power must he have possessed to shear the slopes from a mountain? To carve the tower and its sceptre peak, to hollow the corridors and caverns within? *He must have had help from the gods*, thought Battu. *Curse their arbitrariness.*

He reached the fortifications at the base of the castle and gathered himself together. From there he sped north over the mountain's old foothills, through the capital city of Mankow in the blink of an eye, and out across the Ragga Plains. Beyond the ringlet of the five goblin cities he found the bulk of his gathering army. Thousands of soldiers marched the earth flat. Teams of engineers moved between smoking war engines. Battu was pleased by the convincing display – it looked very much as if he was preparing for war. The Throne of Kainordas could not help but take notice, even if he suspected it was nothing but an enormous diversion.

Onwards he travelled, to rockier lands. Here a fine mist hung suspended in the air and made the Stone Fields slick. Battu slipped easily through a cobweb of cracks, covering an expanse of nothing much but rock and twig, and came to rest at the edge of his realm.

The border divided the world into perfect halves, from east coast to west and further out to sea. Above Battu the Cloud ended, and during the day a wall of light fell unhindered to earth. The border was harder to see under the moon, but was there nonetheless – a darker line across the ground where the Cloud's shadow fell.

Only a few shadow creatures made their homes this close to enemy lands. There were huge malformed moths, which sometimes crossed over in pursuit of the moon. There were quick and viscous shadowmanders – lizard-like things that hunted across the border. Battu noticed one now, a blood red flash that slipped from rocks and darted into Kainordas, becoming briefly visible as it wrestled a brown beetle. A second beetle scuttled away in alarm, and the mander leaped to kill it too – though it only brought one back to Fenvarrow to eat. It seemed that shadowmanders killed creatures of light more instinctively than hunger dictated. Battu admired them. *If only they were bigger.*

Other common but more pathetic denizens of the border were spirit creatures known as the Trapped. These were creatures once born of light, which were now consigned to a different life. Leftovers from the Shadowdreamer Assidax's war, shaped by the constant panic of being so close to their homeland and yet unable to cross the threshold, they were the slightest of the undead. *The best to be said about Assidax*, thought Battu, *is that she'd caused the enemy such heavy losses.* Those who had been resurrected by her would never find their way to Arkus's Great Well, even once their bodies had rotted off their souls. They were shadow creatures now, and they would go to Assedrynn.

The Trapped sensed Battu's presence in the shadows and drifted clear of him. One made the mistake of flashing past and he seized it instinctively, as a cat would snatch a flashing object. The thing twisted pitifully in his ethereal grip.

Who were you?

The Trapped couldn't remember. Its weakness filled Battu with disgust and he focused his power to destroy it. Somehow it felt what was coming and writhed eagerly. It wanted peace so desperately, it would gladly go to the Well of its ancient enemy. If Battu had been in his body, his stomach would have turned. He pushed the wretched thing away, denying it the mercy it sought, and it wailed soundlessly in despair.

Battu spread out along the border like oil on water, searching for a point of safe access into Kainordas. There was none to be found. Despite the storm in Whisperwood, here the skies were clear and the moon shone brightly. He didn't dare travel into Kainordas on such a night. There was too much risk that a shadowline would break and cut him off from his journey home. He would have to rely on other eyes to know what went on in Whisperwood tonight. He sped along the border with another destination in mind.

Alone in his tent, the goblin Turen pored over his maps, wondering where to strike next. As he stooped to place pins in likely targets, chill water from the ice lantern above dripped onto his neck. He straightened to rub it over his tar black skin, welcoming the cool sensation.

Around him were camped several hundred goblins and Arabodedas – the pale men of the south. This was one of six such encampments along the border, all of which had been making forays into Kainordas. Turen's command had tallied the worst of the damage so far, and he meant to keep it that way.

A dry, deep voice spoke behind him. 'Commander Turen.' Fear flushed him with adrenaline, but he managed not to start. In the darkest corner of the tent rose a darker shadow, a man-shaped void with uncertain edges.

'My great lord,' said Turen, bowing. 'You honour me with –'

'Report,' said Battu.

Turen swallowed, forcing himself to raise his eyes and meet a stare he could not see. 'I've placed scouts and archers along trade routes to Holdwith. We don't venture within a league of the fortress, but instead harry their patrols and shipments. Six days back they sent forth a sizeable force to scour the countryside, but we retreated across the border and suffered few losses.'

'New prospects?'

'The outlying village of Lerinsk is heavily guarded, but I'm confident I can lead a sneak attack against it. I would aim to cull the guards without entering the village, but that would look like an aborted attempt to penetrate.'

'Do it,' said Battu. 'The Throne's gaze must be retained.'

'Very good, my lord.'

Battu's shadow wavered in some unseen wind. 'I am combining your encampment with those of Golt and Salindy,' he said. 'You'll be in charge.'

Satisfaction suffused Turen, but again he held his emotions tight. 'As you wish, my lord. Thank you.'

'I am not overly pleased with Salindy's efforts thus far,' said Battu. 'And although I want no undue risks taken, in battle there will always be risk of some kind.' His shadow grew larger, creeping up the walls of the tent. 'Feel free to risk her.'

'I understand, lord.'

'Reinforcements will arrive shortly, and war engines from the ringlet. Marshal them as if we are planning for full-scale invasion. Continue to harass in the meantime.'

'Yes, lord.' Turen's curiosity fought with caution and he dared to venture a question. 'My lord, may I ask . . . do we have the child?'

'Soon,' said Battu.

With that, the Shadowdreamer receded like smoke flowing backwards. The tent's shadows returned to their normal selves. Turen stood a few moments longer just to make sure, then let out a long breath. He turned to his maps and stuck a pin into Lerinsk.

Elessa Lanclara broke free of an entangling vine and slid down an embankment. She was a slightly plump young mage with a fair complexion, blond hair and sapphire blue eyes. She wore a white dress of office that had seen better days. As she reached the slippery rock of the gully below, Dakur was waiting to steady her. He was a blade, assigned as her personal guard – a stocky fellow of medium height, with tanned skin, short, dark hair and a square jaw. He wore thick trousers and boots, and a leather vest that did little to keep the rain from his shoulders. At his side hung a long sword with a bronze hilt. The two of them were Varenkai, humans of Kainordas, land of the light.

Once Dakur was certain Elessa had her footing, he turned to frown at the stream that gushed through the gully. It flowed high and fast in the storm, but Elessa knew he worried about things more dangerous than currents. There were many reasons why Whisperwood was known not to be a welcoming place.

On either side of the gully towered the tall grey trees that populated the wood, their crisscrossing branches waving in the wind like a spider's web. On the gully floor, pale rocks shone where moonlight found them, and reflections of the running water danced across their faces. Elessa shivered, and not because of the rain. She wasn't quite ready to believe the stories about this place, but nonetheless moved a step closer to Dakur. Maybe she just didn't *want* to believe them.

'I could float us across,' she suggested.

Dakur scratched at the beginnings of stubble. 'No,' he said. 'We don't know who else is running about in this accursed wood. You should save your power.'

'My power won't be worth much if I'm at the bottom of a stream being chewed to bits by a fisherman's bane!' Elessa snapped.

A half-smile flashed across Dakur's face so quickly she wondered if she'd imagined it. 'We'll cross by foot,' he said. 'I'll stand upstream. If anything happens, float yourself out of danger before you worry about me.'

'Dakur –'

'Banes prefer still waters anyway, I think. We should be safe.'

Locking hands around each other's wrists, they stepped into the stream. Instantly they were up to their waists in rushing water, struggling against a forceful flow. Elessa scanned for movement upstream, but the water churned too violently to see anything beneath the surface. The undercurrent dragged at her dress and things unseen brushed her legs. She hoped they were leaves and twigs.

Moments later they emerged on the opposite bank, scrabbling across rocks until they stood beneath trees. Elessa realised she was still holding Dakur's wrist and sheepishly let go. She pulled up the soaked sleeves that clung to her arms and they slid right back down.

Despite the determined expression she wore, she was scared. She glanced at Dakur – thank the light he was with her! If he hadn't been, she didn't know what she would have done. Found the courage to go on anyway, she suspected begrudgingly. *Damn it all!* she thought, suddenly angry. There should have been another mage here, and an experienced one at that, not a fledgling like herself! She squeezed water from her hair.

She'd been serving at Indereen, her first posting as an overseer. She'd barely knocked the dust from her bags when a dispute had erupted with the neighbouring town, Ridgeway. The people of Indereen had been clearing a group of crystal trees – so called because their leaves were transparent and brittle like delicate glass. During the clearing, many of the leaves had been shaken free, to drift spinning in the breeze, down the valley into Ridgeway. The leaves had razor-sharp edges, and the streets and surrounding fields of Ridgeway had been covered in dangerous shards. One small boy had lost an eye to a floating leaf. The dispute had been heated on both sides.

In the middle of Elessa's mediation, a loudmouthed healer had arrived at the town inn. He'd boasted of how he'd travelled alone into Whisperwood – a foolishness compounded when he'd strayed from the path to scour for rare herbs. He'd happened upon a couple living in the wood, something which was strange enough in itself. Stranger still, the expecting mother's hair had turned blue with her pregnancy. The healer speculated excitedly to anyone who would listen that surely this meant the woman would give birth to a blue-haired child, the mark of the prophesied child of power.

The standing orders from the Open Halls were very clear when it came to the prophecy. The hundred years since its foretelling were almost up. Any hint, rumour or even lie regarding a child with blue hair was to be investigated immediately, and Elessa knew the Halls had chased many of late. Nothing she'd heard of sounded as plausible as the healer's theory. She'd questioned him herself and it was *very* difficult to lie to an overseer. It had instantly become her bound duty to ascertain the truth of the claim. She had left Indereen immediately, sending out messages to other mages nearby. None had yet joined her.

If indeed she discovered a child with blue hair, she would take it as quickly as possible to the Halls – no matter what the parents wished. Despite the potential presence of the enemy, it was this thought that worried Elessa the most. *Surely,* she thought, *the parents will see that a child destined to break the balance between shadow and light will be hunted by the forces of evil. It* must *be protected from the Shadowdreamer.* She almost lost her footing as she clambered across sprawling roots. *And surely they must already love their child and not want anyone to take it away. As should be their right.*

She silently prayed that the Shadowdreamer had no knowledge of this blue-haired woman. Reports said Battu had instigated a series of skirmishes along the border. Many conjectured they were the precursor to a full-scale invasion, stronger than when Battu had attacked the Shining Mines four years before. Mages and soldiers had been sent to the border in droves, which had made it difficult for Elessa to find support along the way. She hoped Battu was distracted with his warmongering and his gaze was far away from this place.

She knew it was a foolish hope. Battu's net reached far and wide.

She wondered whom he had sent.

Slashing through the undergrowth, Rhobi's mood grew fouler as steadily as time passed. He was drenched, but it wasn't that that angered him – in his homeland, the cold and damp were as common as air. No, it was his commander who made him grind his claws inside his fists, raking furrows into the skin of his black palms. Hiding his hatred had become almost impossible.

Tyrellan was his commander's name, but if Rhobi had his way it would never be written on any gravestone. The thought made him grin in the dark, and rain pooled atop his black lips. Maybe he could control his hate after all; he just had to remember that Tyrellan was as good as dead.

The rain slated at all angles through the forest canopy. A few paces ahead Tyrellan pulled back a large fern, flinging droplets on himself but making little difference to his already wet stare. He remained silent as he stared off through the trees, his orb eyes as black and still as deep water.

Rhobi struggled to hold his tongue, but his patience evaporated faster than a teardrop on a fire. 'Anything there?' he asked, barely managing to keep terseness from his voice.

Tyrellan ignored him completely. Rhobi scowled, his claws curling around the pommel of the sword at his side. He longed to unsheathe it, to ram it into Tyrellan's back and deliver a blow that would leave him enough time to realise from whom it came. That was important – Rhobi didn't want Tyrellan's soul floating away before he had a chance to gloat.

Rhobi was from a noble family, one of the highest amongst the Black Goblins. Despite this, Tyrellan extended him a lack of regard he'd never experienced before. *You imagine yourself protected by a hierarchy of titles, Tyrellan*, he thought. *You underestimate the hierarchy of blood.*

Still, Rhobi knew he had to pick his moment wisely. He'd wait until they got the child safely away from the wood and then, on the journey home, Tyrellan would die. All the glory for the mission's success would go to Rhobi. Fazel wouldn't care. Fazel didn't care about anything and had no need for glory.

'What do you see, Tyrellan?' said Fazel now.

Rhobi glanced at the mage curiously. Only a few had ever seen Fazel's face, and Rhobi knew that if they ran into opposition tonight, he would be one of them. Rain rolled over the brown cloak that enveloped the mage, his hooded gaze turned downwards, as ever.

Tyrellan turned his head slightly at Fazel's question. 'There's a light,' he said. 'Not far.'

You never ignore Fazel, thought Rhobi. *And he's nothing but bones and rot. Soon enough, you will be too.*

For a moment the wind picked up, whipping Rhobi's stringy hair into an orgy of snakes, ripping apart falling raindrops and turning them to spray. The gust passed on, howling through the trees like a maddened spirit. Rhobi shivered.

Fazel sighed.

~

Battu travelled back to Skygrip quickly, speeding up the tower to the sceptre peak, to the long window that ran the length of the throne-room wall. The throne room itself was long and rectangular, the roof but ten paces high. At one end was a dais on which stood Refectu, throne of the Shadowdreamers. Beside the throne was an arch veiled by a curtain of shadow, the entrance to the Shadowdreamer's private study. Opposite the dais was the throne-room entrance, a simple doorway leading to a winding corridor. The rest of the room was largely featureless. The walls were smooth though not flat, as ripples and imperfections showed in the surface of the rock. Cut into the walls were alcoves in which stood goblin guards, their faces shadowed beneath heavy helms, still as statues.

Battu's body remained where he'd left it, gazing out the window over Fenvarrow, and for a moment he stared himself in the face. Then he drained into himself, like water filling a bottle, until he was contained in his own flesh. It always seemed a little tight after travelling as a flowing shadow.

He was a large man, broad of chest, with a head that seemed too big for his body. Silken black hair hung from a flat skull, down past his ears and longer at the back. His broad nose sat above thick pale lips, and his eyes were tiny creased pits. A dark cloak billowed around him, its movement independent of any breeze. It seemed to meld with the shadows, the edges of the cloth indistinct and shifting. He blinked his earthly eyes, feeling again the cold breeze that came through the window, leaving the ledge shiny with a coat of condensation.

Battu hadn't returned for the use of his own eyes, however. It was Fazel's gaze he sought, the one undead created by Assidax who remained under Shadowdreamer control.

Assidax, a powerful necromancer, had cut further into Kainordas than any before her. She had been able to animate undead legions from bloody battlefields even as the fighting continued. Every death fed her army, tipping the balance inexorably towards a shadow victory. Battu had seen glimpses of those battles in the shadowdream – Kainordas soldiers frozen in terror as their once-comrades rose from the earth as new opponents. As land had fallen under Assidax's control, the Cloud had grown to cover it. She had aimed to cover all Kainordas, but had made it only as far as Kahlay. In a desperate push the Kainordans had beat her back, and at the end of her reign, Fenvarrow was no larger than at the beginning. Remnants of her necromancy still remained, undead creatures over whom control had been lost.

When Battu had received his orders from the gods, he had put together special strike squads to move around Fenvarrow destroying undead wherever they found them. It seemed the gods preferred to add these souls to the Great Well than to leave them wandering about trapped in bones. The only ones Battu had left untouched were those pathetic souls on the border, for they made the Kainordans fear to cross.

Fazel, the mage, also remained, for he was unique amongst the creatures Assidax had created. She'd tied his soul to the throne Refectu, bound it with twines of shadow, enslaving him to whomever sat there. It was well that, in this at least, Assidax had shown foresight. Fazel made for a most powerful minion.

Now, Fazel had a bug-eye implanted in his skull, a magical parasite through which Battu could see what Fazel saw. Battu regularly put them into his servants, or sent them flitting randomly into Kainordas in the hope that they would find an unknowing and useful host. The bug-eyes were bred in vats deep in Skygrip, and Battu was never satisfied with how many he created. He sought always to widen his network of spies, willing or otherwise.

One of his eyes unfocused as its vision was replaced by what Fazel saw in Whisperwood, far to the north. The undead mage was plodding at his usual pace. He never made any more effort than necessary in carrying out his instructions, and seeing what Fazel saw usually served only to frustrate Battu. Fazel's hood hung low and he looked at nothing but the ground in front of him. Sometimes Battu had to watch for hours before Fazel would glance up. He was sure the mage seized upon every small rebellion that the strict confines of his servitude allowed. Fortunately, he did not have to wait long this time before Fazel raised his eye.

The two goblins – Tyrellan and the other one – were walking through trees ahead. Just visible through the driving rain and dense foliage was a light. Battu saw it for only a moment before Fazel's gaze became downcast once more. It was long enough for Battu to learn what he wanted. His minions in Whisperwood were drawing close to the prize.

～

'Curse this rain!' growled Dakur. 'I can't see a damned thing!'

'We're still west of the path, aren't we?' said Elessa. 'We must be close, unless that healer got his directions wrong. Or maybe he "tested" some of his herbs and imagined the whole thing.'

Dakur smiled to himself. He knew Elessa must be terrified – the soft-faced girl had only just finished her training a few months ago and, while she was a talented mage, she had little real experience. Yet here she stood in much-feared Whisperwood, dress soaked through, hair slick against her skin, brave-faced and determined.

He cast his eyes about. 'I can't tell. It's darker than an Ebon's arsehole out here.'

Elessa bit her lip. 'We're running out of time, I think. We must hurry.' Then she blinked. 'Dakur!'

'What?'

'I saw something. A light! Just for a moment, but I saw it! Come on!'

She ran off ahead, and a moment later he saw it too, twinkling through the trees. The wind picked up, prickling him with leaves and twigs, making him shiver. There was something of *presence* about it, and Dakur felt like an intruder discovered.

'Infernal forest,' he muttered to himself and hurried to catch up to Elessa.

The wind passed on.

Corlas went to his son, who was sitting up in the cot looking troubled.

'Don't fret, little man,' he said. 'It's only a storm. We're safe in here tonight.'

His eyes came to rest on Mirrow's pendant, lying atop the table. She'd taken it off, along with everything else, for the birth. She'd wanted to have the child outside, before the trees, but when the trouble began he'd moved her back into comfort and warmth. He wondered now if he should have moved her at all, and the thought twisted painfully in his gut.

The pendant hung on a chain of black gold and was the size and shape of a small rock. What was remarkable was the strange pattern that shifted about its surface, a coalescence of greys, blues, black and white, tinges of orange and yellow. It was not colour so much as light, shining from within the stone. The Lady had given it to Mirrow when she'd been small, and she'd worn it every day he'd known her.

'Here, little man,' said Corlas, slipping the chain around the boy's neck. The boy held up the stone for inspection and was instantly entranced. 'Bit long on you now, eh? You'll grow into it. Now you'll always carry something of your mother with you.'

There was a knock on the door.

Corlas was so startled he almost jumped. Of those few strange souls who dwelled in the wood, none would come calling in a storm like this. Quickly he took his axe down off the wall.

'Who is it?' he called.

'Representatives of the Open Halls!'

An old worry, long forgotten, slammed to the front of his brain. Surely they couldn't have tracked him down here? Surely they didn't care enough about one man's desertion after all this time had passed?

Maybe they were lying.

'Go to the window!' Corlas shouted, pulling back the curtain.

Two bedraggled forms appeared beyond the rivulets of rain: a woman in a white dress with hair plastered to her scalp, and a man with a sheathed sword wearing the badge of a blade. They were telling the truth, it seemed, but why were they here? If it was him they had come for . . .

Still holding the axe, he unbolted the door and stepped backwards. It banged open in the wind, sending rain flying into the hut. The woman and man ducked inside, obviously relieved to be out of the storm.

Corlas gestured at the fire. 'Warm yourselves,' he growled.

The two moved to the fire, but the woman seemed anxious and kept sending glances at his son. Corlas did not much care for the scrutiny in her eyes.

'Why are you here?' he demanded. 'Have you wandered from the path?'

'Yes,' said the woman. 'But with a purpose. My name is Elessa Lanclara and I'm a mage of the Halls. This is my personal guard, Dakur.'

Dakur nodded.

'Why do you come to my home?' said Corlas. 'We do not tend to get travellers through these parts. At all.'

Elessa glanced at Dakur, who was matching Corlas's stony expression. 'Would you mind if I looked at your newborn?' she asked.

'Indeed I would,' said Corlas, knuckles whitening on the axe. In truth, he hoped he would end up trusting this Elessa enough to let her inspect the baby. There *was* something strange about him, and she was a mage . . . as well as a woman. 'Your purpose first,' he counter-offered.

Impatience crossed Elessa's face. 'We're in danger here,' she blurted. 'All of us. The child especially.'

'What?'

'The Shadowdreamer seeks your child. His forces approach even as we speak. We must move from here, now!'

Corlas rolled his massive shoulders. 'I have heard tales less wild that turned out untrue,' he said. 'And if any shadow creature tries to harm my boy, it will feel my axe just the same as you.'

'You fool!' hissed Dakur. 'Can you not see what your child is?'

Corlas glanced at the cot. The boy was staring through the bars with wide eyes.

'Untrusting of you, I think, like his old man,' Corlas replied.

'Have you never heard the prophecy, woodsman?' said Dakur. 'Concerning the birth of the child of power? The one who will upset the balance between good and evil?'

Something stirred in Corlas's dormant memories of nights spent in taverns, drinking and gambling, talking of greater things and rubbish.

'The child who will be born with *blue hair*?' prompted Dakur forcefully.

Corlas shook himself. Those nights had been many years ago and he recalled them little. 'I do not concern myself with popular superstition,' he replied levelly.

The woman was staring distantly out the window, biting her lip. She did not seem to be paying attention any more.

'Popular superstition?' said Dakur with a scowl. 'It has been written so for a hundred years! You cannot –'

'Quiet, the both of you!' Elessa snapped, her voice charged with such power that Dakur and Corlas instantly fell silent. She was still a moment, head tilted, eyes glazed. Then: 'It's too late,' she said. 'They're already here.'

It Never Rains

'Stay here!' Elessa ordered. 'I can't fight magic and protect you from it at the same time. If I'm defeated, you two will be all that stands between the shadow and the child.' She stopped Dakur's protest with blazing eyes. 'I will call for you if I need you, Dakur. *Watch over the child*. And you, woodsman,' she added, turning to Corlas, 'you are going to wish you'd fled with us when you had the chance. If it comes down to the bones, you'd better understand that the future of this child is one that will affect the whole world, not just your little home in the forest.'

'You think that understanding will lend me courage?' said Corlas with a glower. 'When my child is more important to me *than* the whole world!'

'Work with Dakur,' snapped Elessa, opening the door of the hut. 'Remember, it is *we* who are your allies.'

She closed the door behind her and took a deep breath, surveying her surroundings. The hut lay at one end of a large clearing bordered by grey trees that were whipping in the wind. The driving rain hindered her sight, so she searched with the same magical awareness that had first alerted her to the presence of the shadow.

They would have the advantage, for the sky was filled with clouds, making it a shadowed night. The low rumble of thunder reached her ears and for a moment her spirits lifted. Maybe she would fight in the company of lightning.

Her search stopped at a place on the far side of the clearing. There was a void there that her senses could not penetrate, large enough for one mage, or two standing together.

If it is two, she thought, *we are lost.*

At least she could make out those who accompanied the magic wielder – ugly little humanoids, about a pace tall, with large heads and tar black skin.

Two Black Goblins, she whispered in Dakur's mind.

They were watching from the trees and she could almost feel their eyes prickling her skin. The opposing mage, or mages, were strangely silent. Elessa had been taught to expect all sorts of taunts and threats from hostile shadow mages, yet none came.

She waved a hand about her body, casting a ward of protection. An aura of light suffused her, but a moment later she gasped. It felt as if a monstrous claw had clenched shut over her body, dug its nails underneath the protective shine and ripped it savagely away. A shell of light fell to the ground, still shaped in her image, and quickly faded. Elessa steadied herself. The counterspell had been powerful and surprising, but she recovered quickly. If only Fahren were here . . . but he wasn't. It was just her, a court-bred mage with no battle experience, fighting for all the folk of Kainordas.

'Well, so be it!' she muttered to herself. 'Then I *refuse* to die tonight!'

As if to reaffirm the thought, her mind's eye flashed up an image of Kessum, the cheerful young noble who always smiled when he caught her gazing at him. Kessum, who'd sent her a shining heart flower and a note on the day she'd departed for Indereen. Her courage flared. She did not intend for that to be the last silly, warm little moment in her life.

She strode forward, again waving a hand over her body to re-ignite the protective ward, this time on guard for any spells from the trees. A figure emerged at the end of the clearing, stepping from between trunks onto a coiled root. It was tall and covered by a brown, hooded cloak. Only a hand was visible, resting at its side – and Elessa saw that it was skeletal. A moment later the figure's voice echoed in her head.

My name is Fazel, he said. *And I see that you are powerful for one so young.*

Elessa was surprised by the civil greeting, though she didn't let it show. *Yes*, she replied, *and you will taste that power if you do not leave this place.*

The voice in her head gave a bitter laugh. *Ah. I appreciate your spirit. But I have been a mage for longer than you, I think.*

The figure raised the bony hand to its hood, grasped the folds and brought them slowly back. Elessa drew a breath. She had never seen one of the undead before and her gentle soul was mortified by the abomination before her. What flesh remained clung to his skull in rotten grey clumps, so an approximation of the face that once had been still showed through. Elsewhere mottled bone lay exposed, or dry skin cracked like bark. A single bulbous eye stared out from beneath a torn eyelid and drooping brow. He still retained some facial hair – both eyebrows, one side of a moustache, a string or two of beard. His neck disappeared into the cloak as a twisted mass of tendons and bone.

'The years have not been kind,' he said, his true voice carrying across the clearing – all too human for the curdled lips it fell from. 'My dear girl, you cannot hope to best me. You are only a child, and I . . . I have *more* than a lifetime's experience, and the night is on my side. Have you not heard of me?'

'No,' said Elessa, her own voice carrying through the pelting rain. 'And it wouldn't matter if I had.'

'No?' said the creature. 'I'm certain that Fahren wouldn't advise you to sacrifice yourself and your two men in a pointless fight against me.'

Elessa tensed at the use of her master's name. Had Fahren met this Fazel? Maybe this was the taunting he'd warned of? Maybe the creature was trying to unnerve her so it could launch another surprise.

Fazel's voice hardened. 'Surrender the child to me,' he said, 'and I promise you shall live to see the sun rise again.'

'And see it rise over a worsened world, atrocity?' she yelled back, and poured all her fear into an attack. Reaching out with her power, she seized Fazel and lifted him into the air. His cloak whipped about his flailing limbs as she spun him wildly, then brought her fist down hard. Fazel hurtled to the ground with a crunch and lay, stunned, in the dirt.

Pity, came his voice. *Now there's no time to wish you luck.*

❧

Dakur stood at the window, sword drawn, trying to see through sheets of water. He was her guard, damn it, and it wasn't going to take much provocation for him to abandon the hut, whatever her orders were – especially if the dark mage's companions entered the fray. He might not be able to protect Elessa from bolts of energy, but he could certainly beat back blades.

'So tell me, *friend*,' said Corlas, still standing in front of the cot with his axe ready, 'what is your plan for my son if we survive this?'

'He'll be taken to the Open Halls,' said Dakur, not turning from the window, 'where he'll be safe from the shadow and can be raised in the light. And then, one day, he will claim the south from the Shadowdreamer.'

'Oh, of course,' said Corlas. 'And his father? Where does he fit into all of this?'

Dakur remained silent.

'*Where?*' bellowed Corlas, startling Dakur.

'I don't know,' said Dakur, turning to hold Corlas's gaze. 'That will be for Throne Naphur to decide.' He frowned suddenly at the man. Was his face familiar?

'I see,' said Corlas, and when Dakur turned away again, he ran his fingers up and down the axe handle. 'Mirrow, my heart,' he muttered to himself, 'you were right – you cannot take on every danger with an axe.' His eyes narrowed on Dakur's back. 'But there are some, my love. There are some you can.'

Fazel lay in the mud, his broken bones painfully mending. He'd been caught off guard, having underestimated her willingness to attack.

Well, well, he thought, *must be getting old.*

Elessa launched another attack, but this time his defences went up and her power slammed into his. He grunted as he struggled to his feet, joints creaking and exposed muscles flexing. His admiration for the girl went up another notch – she had followed up on her success without hesitation.

The air around him began to thrum. Light shone from Elessa's body, illuminating her determined face as she sent power towards him. He directed his own back towards her. Light and shadow crashed against each other like breaking waves and Elessa screamed. *More despair than pain in that scream*, he thought. He was too strong for her and she'd know that now. It would be all she could hope just to keep him at bay. He sighed.

He sent a tendril of darkness creeping towards her like a floating serpent. It eased forward steadily, worming its way through her glimmering defence. Sweat beaded on her forehead as she struggled to halt its advance. The serpentine shadow hovered before her, then darted in to touch her stomach. There was a flash of blue energy and she went flying, her muscles contracting to squeeze her bones, her lips pulled back in a silent scream. She hit the ground in a twisted, shaking heap, gasping for air through constricted lungs.

Come on, girl, Fazel thought. *Get up.*

She flooded her body with light, which he knew would hurt her, but would also nullify any shadow energy it touched. He raised his hand for a spell that would pop the organs from her body, but it crackled into the ground where she had been but a moment before. She had managed a dodge spell, and reappeared a few paces from where she'd been, her defences shooting up again.

Good girl, thought Fazel, smiling grimly as he sent a new wave of power crashing against her. *Just win, girl. Win.*

Crouching beside Tyrellan on a gnarled branch at the clearing's edge, Rhobi watched the battle raging. He'd never seen conflict between such strong mages and was fascinated. Elessa and Fazel staggered around each other, emanating light and shadow as their hands spewed forth power.

'How long do you think we'll have to wait?' he asked.

Tyrellan did not take his eyes from the fight. 'Fool,' he muttered, not with venom, but as if it were simple fact. 'Do you suppose the day is already won?'

Rhobi glared at him.

Tyrellan turned to meet his eyes. 'Mages have their uses,' he said. 'Does that void us of ours? You,' he said, jabbing a black claw at Rhobi, 'skirt the perimeter of the clearing. Stay out of sight. Get to the hut.'

'While you sit safely in the trees?' Rhobi asked, scowling.

'I'll draw out the mage's guard, which means attacking her with steel. If you think *you* can launch a physical attack on one of her magical prowess and survive, be my guest. I'll fetch some marshmallows to toast over your charred remains.'

Tyrellan seized Rhobi by the throat, pinning him against the tree trunk. Rhobi's eyes bulged as his legs kicked the air. Tyrellan pulled up close, speaking softly in his ear. 'I normally don't brook recalcitrance with such good grace.' He glanced back to the battle while

Rhobi scratched at his grip, fighting for breath. 'But you're about to prove yourself useful whether you like it or not.'

He released Rhobi, who scrabbled for purchase on the slippery branch as he gasped.

'Forgive me, First Slave,' Rhobi croaked.

He prayed that Tyrellan would survive this night and leave the pleasure of sliding a knife between his ribs to Rhobi alone. Never had he been so affronted. Tyrellan had gone too far! He massaged his neck, wondering if he would bruise. Perhaps Tyrellan had earned himself a painful death. He could drug the bastard, tie him up, then eke out a slow revenge . . .

'What would you have me do, First Slave?'

'Get to the hut,' repeated Tyrellan. 'Wait until I draw out the Varenkai blade, then get inside. Deal with the woodsman, nab the child. *Do not harm it.* Get it away from this clearing, then head south as quickly as you can. Get out of the forest tonight. We'll catch up once there's no one alive to follow. Understood?'

'Yes, First Slave,' growled Rhobi.

He slipped off the branch into the darkness below, landing without breaking a twig. As he headed for the perimeter, he tried to exorcise the blissful image of Tyrellan begging for his life and concentrate on the job at hand.

Tyrellan smoothed a hand over his hairless scalp and thought about changing his vantage. Higher or lower, that was the question. Wherever it was, he needed to be able to get away from it *fast* once he had acted. Did he, even with his superb night vision and finely tuned reflexes, trust a drop from a tall treetop through these windy, rainy, branch-infested surrounds? And if he didn't place the drop right, with a tree between himself and the mage, he would be falling exposed in the air, an easy target.

He fingered one of the daggers hanging from his belt. He would try for a killing strike, of course, but at this distance, through the wind and rain, he was doubtful. Even if he landed one, it was unlikely to deliver the instant death necessary to avoid a backlash.

He would just have to be very careful.

Before Fazel rose a translucent conjuration of a sunwing – a legendary warrior of Arkus. It was a golden-skinned humanoid, with oversized oval eyes and large, languidly beating butterfly wings. Through its insubstantial form Fazel could see Elessa, her brow deeply furrowed in concentration, her lips moving with incantation. The sunwing flipped a shining arrow from its quiver and notched it to a bow. It drew the arrow back, sighting Fazel.

The spell was a powerful one and Fazel was impressed. He dared to hope. He was gravely disappointed when he saw how easy it would be to counterspell. The girl was expending too much power to properly attend to her defences.

Fazel waved a skeletal hand and from the shadows beneath the sunwing erupted a darker visage. Cavernous black jaws exploded upwards, molten mud falling from a fish-like head with burning red eyes. Fazel's counter-creature clamped shut over the sunwing, leaving only one wing exposed, which continued to flap uselessly. As the sunwing was dragged downwards, both enchantments faded, leaving no sign in the earth of their passage.

Elessa staggered backwards, tears of frustration streaming down her cheeks. It had taken all she had to force the sunwing through the mage's defence, yet he'd squashed it like a bug. Now she felt the merciless push of his power once again.

'Damn you!' she screamed, her dress flapping in the wind. 'Back to the grave!'

She *pushed* with all the strength she could muster and for a moment the shadows about her receded.

Dakur, she sent to the blade, while she could, *he's too powerful. Escape with the child.*

I am your guard!

Escape with the child, curse you!

I will not!

'No!' she shrieked as another serpent head uncoiled before her face. It reared forward and she knew it was a death strike.

Lightning cracked the sky, and briefly the clearing was brightly illuminated. In that split second, the advantage was hers. She drew hard on the light, channelling a burst of power towards Fazel, destroying the snake head and piercing his defences with blazing yellow beams. He howled as skin, cloth, flesh and bone sizzled and smoked. The air suddenly stank.

She waved her hand and a glowing sword appeared, solidifying in her grip. She drew close enough to strike and aimed a downward swing at his head – but he'd seen her coming and threw up his hands. The blade deflected, sliding down the length of his arm instead, shearing off a sheet of bone.

Fazel swung his other arm, hitting Elessa in the mouth with a bony smack.

Almost, girl, came his voice in her head. *Almost.*

Perched so high in the swaying tree that the trunk was no more than a handspan wide, Tyrellan watched for an opportunity. With one arm hooked around the trunk, the other twirling a dagger between his fingers, he seemed an extension of the tree itself. A shadowed branch and a single deadly dancing leaf.

Rhobi should have reached the hut by now, was probably waiting in the trees that bordered it. Far beneath, Elessa and Fazel forced each other back and forth across the clearing. *By the Dark Gods,* Tyrellan thought, *she must be talented to have survived him this long.*

Tyrellan knew enough about magic to prevent him flinging the blade while the mages were warring at their strongest. That would be when all kinds of defences were raised, and a lone physical attack from an unprotected source would result in almost automatic death for the dealer. He needed to wait, wait until she was hurt, confused, down from an attack. He needed to wait until her defences had been broken.

He did not have to wait long.

A twisting root shot from the ground, wrapping itself around Elessa's leg. She hacked it away with her conjured sword and immediately two more took its place. They were thorny, puncturing her flesh as they wound about her. She disintegrated them with bolts of power, but knew she was only attacking the limbs of the spell, not the heart. More roots snaked up, binding her more quickly than she could hack or fry them.

She knew she took a risk in diverting enough power from her defence to kill the spell, but she also knew she had no choice. With a few well-directed bolts of energy she managed to free a single leg, then stamped it on the ground. A gaping crack ran out from her foot, exposing a mass of roots all split in two and squirming like beheaded worms.

Fazel wasted no time. With her power diverted, he shot bolts of blue energy at her. Several sizzled to nothing in her aura of light, but one penetrated all the way and cracked against her shoulder. The strength of it flattened her, leaving her in the mud fighting to think straight.

From high above came the flash of a turning blade. She heard a wet slap as the dagger buried itself in her side. She screamed, instinctively directing a stream of molten fire towards her new enemy with one hand while strengthening her defence against Fazel with the other. Her power surged, fuelled by rage, pain and fear. Then, as she gasped and drew the dagger from her flesh, a voice echoed in her head that fuelled her with hope as well. *Hold fast, Elessa Lanclara*, it said. *Reinforcements are at hand*.

It was another mage of the Halls, not far away!

Dakur saw the dagger hit Elessa and that changed everything. No longer was this a fight of magic alone.

'What a fool I've been!' he muttered as he thrust the door open to run out into the storm. 'Tarrying inside like a snail in its shell!'

He darted into the trees at the side of the house and began to make his way around the perimeter of the clearing, keeping well hidden from the eye of the undead mage.

'Forgive me, girl, I should not have listened to you!'

He slowed, moving stealthily from tree to tree, pausing with his back to each one, listening for any sounds of approach – though the storm would mask all but an ogre's footsteps. Had Elessa's fire scorched the goblin who had let the dagger fly? Was there just one of the little bastards running around out here, or two?

He started as Elessa's voice echoed in his head. *The one who attacked me is just ahead of you.*

The blade glanced through the trees at the continuing battle, worried that Elessa's communication with him might have cost her, but she seemed strangely empowered for all her hurts.

Look to yourself, he communicated back, but was thankful for the warning.

Tyrellan rested a moment. The liquid fire had not sprung from Elessa's hand to him instantaneously, but rather had issued like a jet of water. Changes in her aim had to travel along the stream, so the whole thing had arced just a step or two behind him the entire way.

He had abandoned his perch as soon as the dagger had left his fingertips, swinging around the tree to place it between himself and the mage, then dropping straight down. As he dropped he'd heard fire hit the tree on the other side and follow his trajectory down the trunk. About halfway down, he'd caught hold of another branch and swung off in a new direction, hot cinders falling after him on the backs of raindrops. He'd leaped and swung from tree to tree, the stream of fire trailing after him. He knew he'd be dead the moment he paused.

He hit the ground running, burning droplets smattering his back as the fire engulfed a branch behind him. He dived away, always focusing on putting a high root or fallen log between himself and molten death. The whole trial had lasted seconds, but for him the time stretched like sap.

Finally he'd heard the magic hiss out behind him. He'd slowed his pace and curved back towards the clearing. His back stung, but the rain soothed it. Perhaps it wouldn't scar. Tyrellan had never understood fools who showed off battle scars like trophies. Only the most formidable passed through a lifetime of danger unscathed.

He hadn't seen whether or not his attack had drawn out the blade – or in which direction the man had gone. He reached the perimeter of the clearing and slipped into the lee of a rock, peering towards the hut. Either the guard was still inside or he'd already left; there was no way yet to tell.

Tyrellan bared his fangs and rested a moment.

Rhobi watched the blade burst from the hut and run into the forest. He passed so close that Rhobi could have leaped onto his back with a knife. But since the blade was going after Tyrellan, and Rhobi didn't care which of the two ended up dead, he didn't see any need to intercede. Instead he turned his attention to the hut.

Entering by the door was out of the question. It was surely bolted, and getting through would take time and place him in the open. Breaking a window, while quick, would alert both the woodsman inside and the Varenkai mage. The chimney? He peered up at it and saw smoke. He had no desire to dry off *that* quickly.

Damn this.

It was going to have to be a window. At least there was one on the tree side of the hut. Hopefully the mage would be too caught up in her own troubles to pay attention – and anyway, would she dare attempt an offensive when he was so close to the child?

Rhobi picked up a rock, tested its weight and stared at the window. He could see nothing inside save a wall dappled by firelight, the edge of a bed and the opposite window. He decided to try to smash out both windows with one shot, giving himself double exit points.

He hefted the stone and sent it flying, shattering the windows almost simultaneously. Would the woodsman even know from which direction the stone had come?

What a talented fellow I am, Rhobi thought with a grin, and somersaulted out of the storm.

As he whirled through the smashed window, he felt the waft of a great axe head swing just beneath him. He landed on the hut floor and leaped backwards in one fluid move, a dagger jumping into each hand.

Opposite him stood the woodsman – a hulk of a Varenkai with torn hair and beard. From under thick brows, enraged eyes met his, while behind the man the child wailed in its crib.

'Why, you almost had me landing in two pieces,' said Rhobi. 'Didn't your bitch of a mother teach you how to treat a guest?'

Before he'd finished speaking he was hurling one of the daggers at the man's chest, but Corlas was ready. He flicked the axe head to intercept and the blade clattered harmlessly to the floor. Rhobi gave a nod of appreciation and drew his sword.

'When I'm done with you,' rumbled Corlas, 'it won't just be the rain you're dripping with.'

He bellowed, swinging the axe before him in great sweeping arcs. It was a fearsome sight, and for a moment Rhobi was worried. Then he saw something so simple it made him chuckle.

In a lightning move he dropped to his knees, gripped the rug in both claws and yanked with all his strength. Corlas's feet shot out from underneath him and, arms flailing, he fell. There was an almighty *crash* as his head cracked the floorboards.

Rhobi moved forward cautiously. Blood was creeping over the splintered wood beneath the man's skull. The goblin smiled, and bent to retrieve his dagger.

Outside, the wind picked up with a great howl. The walls of the hut shuddered and Rhobi paused. Had he just heard voices? He shrugged, and lowered the dagger to slice the man's throat. A second later he was almost knocked from his feet as roaring wind poured through the smashed windows. It drove into his clothes, pushing him, now pulling, churning like a sea of malice. Rhobi spun at a whisper in his ear, to be greeted by a slam of air to the face. Stricken by a fear that went straight to his soul, he fought the urge to flee screaming into the night.

He forced himself towards the cot, the gale now pressing solidly against him. He reached out for the bawling child, muscles straining, eyes watering. A vase flew over his head and smashed against the wall.

'Damn you!' he shouted, gritting his fangs and lunging forward to scoop up the baby. He struggled to the door and strained against the door knob, but the surging air kept it closed. He screamed defiance at the wind, and voices screamed in return. Rhobi's bladder emptied into his pants. Strengthened by fear, he wrenched the door open, bundled himself and the child through, and collapsed into the natural storm on the other side.

The door slammed behind him with such force, he was surprised it didn't fly off its hinges into his back.

Elessa advanced, drilling Fazel with so much power that he slid backwards, his bony heels leaving grooves in the mud. She felt good, almost giddy. She laughed. What had changed?

She had been treading the edge of despair the entire battle, expecting to be dead at any moment. The dagger blow had pushed her over that edge and she had hung from the cliff by a thread. With nowhere to go but up, she had been filled with a determination she'd never felt before. Now, she manipulated her power with skill and precision, tapping reserves she hadn't known she possessed. Bringing her hands together as if squashing an orange, she compressed the air about Fazel's skull. There was an audible *crack* as a hairline fracture appeared across his forehead, and he clutched at it, howling. Elessa increased the pressure and the jagged rent grew.

The throbbing in her side was strong and she glanced down at the dagger wound. Blood stained her sodden dress all the way down her leg. She waved a hand over the wound, setting a magic bind to stop the blood flow. Proper healing would have to wait until later.

Somewhere behind her, the hut door slammed. A Black Goblin stumbled into the storm with the crying babe. He seemed dazed and she vaguely wondered if he'd been injured. She sensed Fazel shake free of her crushing spell, and caught his thought urging the goblin to run for the trees.

I think not.

Sending twin bursts of golden energy towards the clearing's edge, she disintegrated the bases of two trees, toppling them towards the undead mage. Fazel spun to face the oncoming trunks, his rotten brow creasing in concentration, and Elessa was able to turn away for a moment. She weaved her hands through the air, her fingertips leaving glowing trails, until she held a mesh of light. Her hands shot forward, launching it at the goblin. The goblin's eyes opened wide as he saw it coming, and he dropped the child to flee. The net hit his back and slammed him to the ground beside the stunned child, its glowing ends sinking into the earth and pinning him there.

Elessa turned back to see one of the trees sailing towards her like a colossal javelin. With an almighty *push* of power she sent it off course. It rotated on its axis and one of the larger branches almost took her head off. As she dodged, her wound bit her savagely and she clutched her side, gasping in pain. A splintering met her ears as the tree crashed through the middle of the hut.

Fazel faced her, the other tree rotating massively in the air above him. She backed away towards the child, who lay in a pool of mud. Fazel loosed the other tree towards her. This time Elessa *pushed* it upwards, so that it passed above the treetops at the clearing's edge and soared off into the storm.

'That's going to surprise someone,' came Fazel's voice, along with a harsh rasp of laughter.

He advanced, keeping the distance between himself and Elessa equal as they moved towards the child. He smiled at her – a disturbing sight.

'I'd wager Fahren has never seen you so in tune,' he said. It sounded to Elessa almost like admiration.

'Flatter me all you like if you need the delay to recover your strength,' she replied.

She'd surprised herself with these verbal retaliations, having always been a shy and softly spoken girl. Now her tongue felt as sharp as her anger.

She was nearing the child, which he wouldn't risk harming with an attack. She could feel him weaving some kind of magic in the air about her, but it was so subtle she could not identify its target. She restrained herself from going on the offensive. She was so close to the child, so close . . .

Confusion came over her. She should have arrived at the child and netted goblin by now. She glanced around and saw that she had almost backed herself against the hut. Her gaze flicked forward again, her eyes narrowing. She'd been tricked.

Now she knew what the subtle magic had been, and something Fahren had once said echoed in her thoughts: *Don't forget that little spells sometimes win big fights.*

It only takes the smallest mouse to slip under the greatest door.

Clenching her fists, she shattered Fazel's spell. It was just a simple illusion, to disguise the child and goblin as two more puddles on the ground. She, on the lookout for bolts of crackling death, had backed straight past them.

'Almost,' said the undead mage. 'Almost had you there, Elessa Lanclara.'

They came to a halt and stood watching each other. The child and the struggling goblin lay between them, at equal distance from both.

Each knew the fight would end here, one way or another.

The baby watched, not comprehending the fierce battle raging about him, yet mystified by the power that charged the air. He was cold and wet, but that wasn't important. He gazed at the lady in white, and the pain he saw on her face worried him. She looked nice and soft, and he hoped she would pick him up and snuggle him, take him back inside. He cooed at her, but her face was a mask of concentration and she didn't notice. Then he looked at the strange one, who didn't look nice and soft at all, but the strength of magic that emanated from him was fascinating.

Around the baby's neck, the pendant thrummed.

Spells and defences crashed against each other, and in the middle of the interlacing forces lay the child. If she could just get him into her arms, Elessa could retreat towards the approaching reinforcements.

She tried to levitate him towards her, but instantly Fazel shot out an opposing pull. She'd been prepared for a tug of war, but her grip on the child felt surprisingly insubstantial. She poured power into the effort, but it seemed to *disappear* as it met the child – as if the undead abomination was somehow managing to nullify it. Yet she seemed to be thwarting him somehow, for while she couldn't get a hold on the boy, Fazel seemed not to have one either.

About the child's neck, the colours of the pendant flashed excitedly. He shifted in discomfort.

Fazel sent another blanketing wrap over the boy and again felt it vanish from his control. He could not establish even the weakest fleeting hold! Never in all his years had he met with magic such as this. What was the girl doing? If she'd erected some kind of shield around the babe, he should have been able to sense it. How was she draining away his power?

Hope flared within him. Elessa had found a way of negating him, and because he genuinely could not think of anything to counter it, he could continue struggling to grasp the child without breaking the rules of servitude. He increased his efforts to strengthen his grip, hoping it was part of her plan.

The child opened his mouth and screamed, cutting through the storm with pure terror.

'Let him go!' Elessa shouted.

The screaming grew louder.

The child thrashed in the mud, his limbs twisting as if in the throes of a violent seizure. His scream rose and fell with the wind, continuous and seemingly without need of breath. Then, with a final gasp, his back arched and his muscles went taut and stiff. When his eyes opened, agony and fear danced through them hand in hand. About his neck, the Stone shone strangely in the grey light of evening.

Great pressures imploded inside the child, forming two sinkholes of terrible force. Both wrenched at him with equal strength, at his body, his mind . . . at his soul. Both *pulled* at him from within. His component parts strained in their places and began to come loose, his very being ripped to pieces. Some parts went into the dark sinkhole, others took off into the bright light. Through the madness, his tortured mind wailed with thick, distorted horror as it came apart at the seams. Then suddenly, mercifully, his consciousness shattered and he was gone.

A shock wave of power erupted outwards, jolting Elessa and Fazel backwards, jarring their teeth and fizzing in their sinuses. It was a power neither recognised, and it had little regard for their defences. An object shot out of it – the Stone – and sizzled away to land somewhere outside the clearing. Then, as the white noise ringing in their ears subsided, they heard the sound of crying.

It had two voices.

In a smoking crater blasted free of puddles, the ground spitting with residual charge, they lay together, side by side, wailing to the sky.

Two boys with blue hair.

fire and Lightning

From the trees above, she watched it all, a great rage burning inside her. This had never been her purpose in giving the Stone to Mirrow! It had been supposed to serve her people, many years from now, as a weapon. Instead, it had ripped the boy apart, just as Assedrynn and Arkus had ripped apart the souls in the Great Well. And those two, curse them, were openly interfering. This place was her sanctuary – they had no right! Yet they were strong, as they had always been, and they ruled the skies above. Clouds were sent to cover the moon; lightning flashed down to light up the world. She had done what she could against them, but it hadn't been enough. The spirit wind she had sent after the goblin in the hut had drawn their combined attentions and they had sent her whirling, dispersed. The old agreement held little sway, it seemed. Now all she had the strength to do was watch.

How had these interlopers even found out about the child she had created? It had never been her will that the child's hair turn blue, but when it had she had thought it a sign that her cause was good. She had certainly never intended to fulfil someone else's prophecy. With cold realisation, she understood that she had created champions *for* her enemies! The child who should have been born of Old Magic was sundered, divided into light and shadow. For the second time in her long existence, the Lady Vyasinth saw a breaking of balance.

Swords clashed again, and Dakur cursed – this was taking too long. It had been minutes since Elessa had cried out for aid, but this Black Goblin was proving a formidable opponent. Only last year Dakur had won the Spring Tournament, beating the former titleholder decisively, and it had been easier than this. This little bastard was quick.

He'd dodged Dakur's initial surprise swing – if indeed it had been a surprise – spinning out of the sword's path like a whirligig. He was all claws, gleaming fangs and a treacherous flashing blade wielded with such fluidity that it would have been awe-inspiring to watch had Dakur not been so focused on keeping it well away. The goblin fought in a confusing flurry, ducking and weaving, gliding in and out of Dakur's reach, sometimes disappearing behind a tree or rock only to leap out again from an unexpected direction. More disturbingly, the creature fought in total silence, never a grunt or a threat or a laugh. Just the unknowable stare of his orb-like eyes.

Dakur deflected defensively, waiting for an opportunity to lash out in return. So far his offensives had met only empty space, his opponent preferring to wheel out of the way than actually meet his steel. Their swords only connected when the goblin attacked. It was infuriating.

The creature leaped up onto a rock and Dakur avoided lunging at him, waiting instead for the inevitable disappearance into the undergrowth. Instead the goblin sprang at him bodily, batting Dakur's blade aside while in the air and crashing against his chest, knocking him down. The goblin dropped his sword to grab Dakur's sword arm and pin it to the ground, using his other to slip a dagger from his belt. As the dagger flashed down, Dakur's free hand shot up to catch it a handspan from his throat. For a moment they lay locked, the goblin so close that Dakur could smell his earthy breath. He tried to twist his sword arm free, but the goblin dug his claws in harder, forcing Dakur to drop his blade. He gritted his teeth as he pushed back on the dagger.

'Strong for a little fellow, aren't you?' he grunted.

In a painful movement, he wrenched his pinned wrist free to crack the goblin across the jaw, spattering the black chin with his own blood. The force of the blow knocked the creature off him, dagger and all. Dakur rolled for his own sword but the goblin leaped on his back. He elbowed the creature viciously in the face and staggered to his feet, sword in hand. With a bellow he spun around.

On the low-lying branch of a tree some paces away, the goblin sat watching, his sword stuck upright in the wood beside him.

'What are you waiting for?' Dakur said. 'Had enough, have you?'

The goblin slowly uncurled a claw. Dakur frowned, but looked down to where the goblin pointed. As his gaze fell, he let out a cry of surprise. Protruding from his belly was the hilt of a dagger.

Giddiness swept over him. He fell to his knees, pawing at his ruined stomach in disbelief. Then, with a bark of anger, he yanked the dagger free, raising it for retribution.

The branch was deserted.

There was a soft footfall on the leaves behind him.

Elessa was tiring and the wound in her side was agonising. Whenever she moved, pain coursed up her abdomen. Despite her magically stemming the blood loss, the wound still needed to be attended to and Elessa knew that time was running out. She thought of Kessum, and the shining heart flower, and how she had planned to send him one in return when she got back to the Halls. And so she would! She would not die tonight!

At her feet the babies bawled. She hadn't believed her eyes upon seeing the pair of them, but there wasn't time to think on it now. Her opponent still faced her, and his body mended itself, whereas hers would not survive another of his spells. Miserably she felt her power failing, felt his darkness penetrating her defences in many places. She pushed it back, but it was like pushing back a glacier. Slowly and surely, it came. Death came.

And then . . .

Tyrellan crept to the tree line. The blade had taken longer to kill than he'd anticipated and he had no idea of what had occurred between Fazel and the Varenkai bitch in the meantime. He was vexed to see that Fazel had not disposed of her yet, but it didn't look like long now. She was hunched over, no doubt due to the dagger wound, and her outstretched arms shook with effort. Fazel, however, looked just as he usually did, and Tyrellan could see his dark magic creeping towards the girl, snuffing out her light as it went.

Just one final light to snuff out, he thought.

And then . . .

Forks of electricity cracked down from the sky, striking treetops around the clearing, sending flaring branches to earth. Strike after strike, one after the other in quick succession. Tyrellan scowled, the lightning gleaming off his fangs. This *reeked* of interference. The higher powers were taking an interest. Strike after strike . . .

With the clearing lit up like white day, the girl straightened. Her arms steadied, her hands moulding power drawn from the light, and a ball of flame collected at her fingertips. Between lightning flashes the growing fireball bathed the clearing in its own orange illumination, lending strength unto itself. A few moments on and it was huge, the heat so intense that Tyrellan caught a waft of it in the wind.

With a defiant cry, Elessa splayed her fingers and released. The fireball roared towards the undead mage, expanding as it went. Fazel raised a hand to ward it off, but the ball changed neither direction nor velocity. Just before it hit him, he flung his arms wide. It was a gesture of embrace.

The fireball carried his burning corpse across the clearing where it exploded against a tree, sending out a cloud of sparks and ash.

Fazel's words reached Tyrellan as his body became a conflagration: *Tell your master that I did my best.*

And after that a joyous laughter, fading into silence. The rain reduced the flames to tongues and charred bones fell to earth.

Thunder followed the lightning. The rain began to clear.

Battu flinched as the oncoming flames consumed his view and snuffed out Fazel's sight. His real sight took over, blazing out the window, as if sheer force of will would allow him to go on seeing what occurred in the north. It did not. The bug-eye in Fazel's head had been incinerated along with its host.

Why were there two babies? Damn it all, wasn't anything ever simple? Did it have something to do with the Stone? He had recognised it for what it was, and harboured vague suspicions about what had happened . . . but now was not the time for theories. He could see no way to retrieve the Stone, and even if there was a way, there seemed no point. The damage was done.

Instead Battu cast around for other useable creatures, and found one so perfect he almost disbelieved it. One of the blade reinforcements who hurried through the wood towards the clearing was ignorant of the bug-eye in his skull – and Battu knew in that moment why he sent out so many of the creatures. Impatiently, he waited for the man's sight to become useful.

All Elessa wanted was to lie down and sleep. Every vestige of her power had gone into the fireball, and another casting would knock her unconscious, if not kill her. More than anything, she needed another mage to help her heal. How far away were the reinforcements?

She could no longer sense them. Pain stabbed her side again and she threw up.

Lurching forward into the smoking crater, she foggily remembered the child's transformation. Two babies in the hole, both with blue hair! The closest turned a cherub face towards her and cooed. She wasted no time, moving forward to gather him up. How could a baby weigh so much? How would she manage the other one too?

The goblin she had netted rolled into the crater with a hiss, coming to rest next to the second baby, a dagger in his hand. So, her net had failed. Not surprising.

The goblin stared at her sideways, breathing hard, but apart from that he was still. So was the child in his grasp, she noticed, staring impassively up at the sky.

Elessa knew she had to move if she was to have any chance at all. The reinforcements would have to track down the second boy themselves. She backed away. As she did, another goblin emerged from the tree line across the clearing.

She turned and fled into Whisperwood.

An Early Birthday Present

Rhobi didn't know Tyrellan was there until he felt the boot in his side.

'Get up, you fool.'

'Is she gone?' snarled Rhobi. 'Perhaps the only thing saving us from bolts of fire is my close grasp on this child?'

'Nothing will save you from a dagger up your arse if you don't do as you're told.'

Rhobi stood.

'Why are there two boys?' Tyrellan asked.

'There was only one in the hut,' said Rhobi. 'After that I was pinned down by the Varenkai. There was an explosion of some kind. I didn't see what happened. And now, two boys.'

Tyrellan shifted his gaze from the pale baby to the direction in which Elessa had fled. 'She won't get far,' he said. 'I don't think she has much more magic in her tonight.' He seemed to reach a decision. 'Take this one and travel south. Retrace our journey here. I'll make a try for the other. But I have a feeling,' he flexed a claw and turned to Rhobi, 'there may be others in the woods tonight. Either way, I'll rejoin you shortly. Do not deviate from the course I've given you.'

As Rhobi stared into the bottomless orbs of the First Slave's eyes, the cruel features somehow made worse by their flat neutrality, he wondered if he would ever have the courage to follow through with his murderous musings.

Elessa stumbled over a root, her vision blurring out of focus. Her soaked dress clung to her like a second layer of skin, her body racked by an involuntary shivering that tore at her wound. The tips of her fingers were numb and she had to fight just to keep the baby in her grasp.

'Please,' she choked. 'Please be close . . .'

The baby squirmed and cried out. With the storm subsided, the sound rang crystal clear.

'No,' she whispered. 'Don't start that.'

The baby's cries echoed through the trees like a beacon. Elessa stumbled again and this time she did fall, her arms clasped protectively around the boy. She hit the ground with a grunt.

They were partway up a rise littered with pale rocks and topped by a great tree. She managed to crawl up the slope using one hand, holding the babe against her with the other, and propped her back against the tree trunk.

As she drifted out of consciousness, the image of a shining heart flower filled her mind.

Tyrellan slipped through the trees, following the sound of the crying child, sending glances at the sky. There were only a couple of hours of darkness left, so he needed to be quick if he was to find safe cover before daybreak. On the way north Fazel had hidden their true natures with illusion. Now they would have to travel by night, or at least heavily disguised, lest they be hunted by every northerner who spied them. Hopefully Battu's false invasion was keeping Kainordan eyes focused on Holdwith, as they had planned. Soldiers and mages would be called away from their posts, giving them fewer to avoid on the journey home.

He spied the girl, lying slumped against a tree at the top of a rise. She was dead or dying, for her eyes were closed and the child had slid from her grasp almost completely. Tyrellan produced a dagger and padded silently towards her. He could hit her, dead or not, from this distance and put an end to all doubt. Raising the dagger, he noticed her hand twitching. A wavering thread of light crept from her palm to entwine her fingers. Her eyes half-opened, watching him from beneath tangles of hair. For a moment neither moved nor spoke. Then:

'Go away,' said Elessa.

'You're dying,' Tyrellan observed.

'If you come any closer, I'll outlive you by a few moments yet.'

Tyrellan slid the dagger back into his belt. 'You have no magic left in you tonight, Varenkai,' he said. 'I know enough of the stuff to see that. One more spell will finish you.'

'As you say,' murmured Elessa, 'I'm dying. So it hardly matters, does it?' The light around her fingers pulsed and Tyrellan eyed it warily. Elessa's eyes glazed over and she shifted her head slightly. 'Mages are almost here,' she whispered. 'And soldiers. Can you hear them?'

Tyrellan could. Someone was hurrying through the woods, not far off.

'A stalemate then?' he said. 'Personally I'd try to kill me, if all it cost you was a few extra moments of pain. I'm Battu's First Slave, someone dangerous to your people, who may return to cause further grief.' Tyrellan waited, unblinking, as the sounds of approach drew nearer. 'And revenge would be yours,' he added, 'since you have me to thank for that wound.' He bared his fangs at her.

Elessa's dimming eyes grew angry and the light at her fingertips flared. Tyrellan tensed, ready to spring away – but a moment later the mage relaxed.

'I don't think so,' she said softly. 'You escaped me once before, and I am weaker this time. Go away, goading little goblin. Leave me in peace.'

Shouts echoed through the trees.

Elessa smiled wanly. 'You have no time.'

Tyrellan scowled. He was so close, yet he dared not tread any closer. If only he could have waited out her death – but she was right. His time was up. He edged away, and as he went she closed her eyes – but the light didn't stop playing through her fingers.

'May Assedrynn take you for his slut,' he snarled. Then he turned and fled.

Death's embrace tightened, and memories floated by. Her childhood, growing up in Open Halls, her father when he was home from travelling, Fahren's lessons . . . and one particular moment bobbed to the surface.

She had been fourteen.

A warm breeze was blowing into the study. Fahren stood at the window with a brittleleaf roll, brown smoke oozing about him. The breeze ruffled his long blond hair as he gazed over the land with crystal blue eyes.

Elessa sat cross-legged on the floor with a book in her lap. It was a strange book, full of odd spells that made no sense. Fahren never objected when she pulled it off the shelf, but he never suggested her reading it either. She liked it for its colourful pictures. She looked at one now: in a gnarled chair slumped an ancient woman whose bony fingers clutched the armrests. Standing behind the chair was a warrior in golden armour, his head covered by a spiked helmet, and behind *him* was the sun. From the woman's breast came a glowing stream, and where it ended was a large butterfly, patterned so beautifully that she'd remembered it ever after.

Underneath the picture were spidery words: *The Legacy Spell.*

'Ah, my curious one,' said Fahren, looking over her shoulder. 'That is not a spell that need concern you for some years, I pray.'

'What is it?' she asked, fascinated, resting her fingers on the people in the picture. 'Who are they?'

Fahren sank onto the rug beside her, his robe spilling around him in a blue and gold puddle. 'The old woman is a light mage, and she's dying. See? The Sun God Arkus stands behind her in both his classic forms: a mighty warrior, the defeater of darkness, and as the sun itself – the greatest source of light. He's reclaiming her life force to take it to his Well, as he does with all creatures of light when they die. But look – see the stream of energy ending in this butterfly?'

'Yes.'

'The mage is casting a legacy spell. As her life force leaves her body she diverts part of it, something she can only do as it's draining out of her. That part is cut off from the rest and moves on, becoming her legacy – something she leaves in the world as she passes. It is tied to the object or place on which it's cast, never moving far from it. In this case she has shaped it into a butterfly, though the form is up to the individual. It only takes a small amount of life force to create, not enough to mar her return to Arkus . . . but it is permanent.'

'Permanent?'

'Yes. Once left behind, it cannot be destroyed, or spelled away.'

'Why?'

Fahren smiled warmly. 'A difficult thing to describe, my girl. Maybe when you're older.'

She pouted. 'I'm old enough now!'

Fahren chuckled.

'Our souls, Elessa, return to Arkus's Well when we die. The legacy spell is a way to leave part of ourselves behind in the world – cut off, then, from the light forever. It becomes something else: neither light nor shadow, but energy without denomination. And neither light nor shadow has the ability to affect it any more, because it exists outside their rules.'

'Oh,' said Elessa. She thought a moment and Fahren let her. Then, 'So it's an invincible magic?'

'It is, I suppose,' said Fahren. 'But, as I said, it can only be left behind in small amounts. That, also, I do not understand. Perhaps it is because the gods will always reclaim as much as they can of their creatures' spirits, or simply that one's life force does not divide readily. I don't know.'

Elessa looked at the picture again.

'It's a very beautiful butterfly,' she said.

Tyrellan paused as a voice sounded in his head.

Hello, First Slave.

It was the mage. She'd opened a mental connection with him for some reason.

Aren't you dead yet? he asked, moving on, a dark shape slipping between the trees.

In a moment. I just thought I'd let you know – I plan to have my revenge after all.

Oh yes?

Yes. I'm giving you an early birthday present.

Tyrellan choked, his claws going to his throat. He felt as if he'd swallowed something.

What have you done?

Why, little goblin, laughed the voice in his head, *I've made you the cocoon. I thought you might like to know what it feels like to create something beautiful.*

WHAT HAVE YOU DONE?

You have to wait until your birthday to open it. She chuckled softly and the connection was gone.

Tyrellan felt his throat again, but whatever was there had slipped downwards. He could feel something in the pit of his stomach – something foreign and wrong. Something magic.

For the first time in a long time, Tyrellan felt very uneasy.

Through the trees they ran, two mages streaking ahead of the soldiers who followed, fleet on magic-aided feet.

They'd felt surges of power in the forest but a short time ago and knew a battle had taken place. They did not know the outcome, but they heard a child crying. Was it with allies or enemies? With reckless haste they went, anxious and uncertain, until they came to a rise in the forest floor.

Elessa lay against the tree, her white dress stained with blood and dirt, torn in many places. Her hair fell forward over her slumped head, her face was downturned towards her lap, where the source of the sound that had spurred them on continued to wail at the sky. A baby, with blue hair.

With great reverence and respect, they lifted him from the dead woman's arms.

Dawn approached and, a league south of Whisperwood, Rhobi hid inside a cluster of bushes. The thick leaves and low earth were the best protection from sight he had come across since leaving the forest. Truth be told, he wasn't much of a navigator. With the burden of the child, and the sky lightening in the north, he hadn't dared to press on further.

He sat against a low-lying branch that ran parallel to the ground, twirling a dagger as he stared at the child. The baby, for his part, didn't pay Rhobi any attention. He simply lay there, staring up at nothing.

Rhobi didn't know much about babies, and certainly not Varenkai babies. The only thing he'd thought to do was build a fire, which he now wished he hadn't placed right in the centre of the available space. As a source of warmth and light, it offended his sensibilities.

'You'll have to get used to the damp and cool soon enough, little Varenkai,' he sneered at the child.

That, however, was a concern for the Shadowdreamer, and in the meantime the last thing Rhobi needed was for the stupid creature to get sick and die on the way home. He hadn't reached his current rank by taking chances.

He heard a twig crack and his head snapped towards it. Just a bird. If it had been Tyrellan, Rhobi mused, he probably wouldn't have heard a thing.

Ah, Tyrellan, he thought. *Your guts will hit the ground before you do. How the glory will be mine when I return the sole survivor of this mission, bringing the Shadowdreamer his treasured prize. I don't see how he could refuse to make me First Slave.*

When would he kill Tyrellan? His finger stroked his dagger absently, almost obscenely. Part of him knew it would be better to wait until they were almost over the border. Whatever else Rhobi thought of Tyrellan, his commander was a survivor, and united they stood a better chance of returning home. He also knew that Tyrellan might kill *him*, especially if he suspected the hatred that brewed in Rhobi like fermenting poison, as he surely must by now. If Tyrellan was in any way suspicious, he'd think nothing of murder to quell his doubts. Also, Rhobi didn't know how much longer he'd be able to control himself. Tyrellan might do something to push him over the edge, and the idea of a head-to-head confrontation made him greatly afraid. There were reasons why the First Slave had lived so long with his title. There were reasons why hardly a creature living in Fenvarrow didn't treat him with fearful deference.

So, Rhobi was decided. He would find the first opportunity after Tyrellan rejoined him, something very low risk. A dagger while he slept or walked ahead. No drawn-out death. Although Rhobi lusted for it, he'd leave nothing to chance. As he thought about it, he knew he was right. Tyrellan wouldn't leave anything to chance either, would he?

No, he would not.

A dagger wheeled out of the bushes and sank into the side of Rhobi's neck. He gasped wetly as Tyrellan stepped from the foliage, watching him impassively. The First Slave bent down in front of his soldier, batted Rhobi's bloodied hands away from the wound and wrenched the weapon free. Rhobi stared back with hateful eyes, a black stream pumping from his neck. He tried to speak, but the blood filling his mouth made for a burbled mockery of words.

Tyrellan arched a hairless eyebrow. 'Yes?'

Rhobi fumbled for one of his own daggers with shaking hands.

'This?' asked Tyrellan, reaching to draw a dagger for him, then plunging it through the other side of his neck. He withdrew his hands and rested them on his knees.

'Next time,' he said, 'serve the darkness half so well as you serve yourself and you may not return to it so quickly.'

Rhobi gurgled and died.

Tyrellan wiped the daggers on his tunic, taking Rhobi's to replace the one he'd flung into Elessa. He scowled at the fire. Smoke would be seen for leagues in these flat grasslands, and they were still close to Whisperwood.

He set about piling earth on the flames, sending glances towards the baby boy. Who was watching him.

It was fortunate that the Halls wouldn't know, for a while at least, that this second child existed. Without witnesses to tell them otherwise, they'd assume that their blue-haired boy was the only one. Nevertheless, Tyrellan was bothered. He had a good working knowledge of magic, despite not being able to wield it, but he had no idea why there were two boys. It was a puzzle, he decided, for the Shadowdreamer. He simply had to deliver the boy he did possess.

The fire was out. Tyrellan understood why Rhobi had lit it, but his subordinate was far too limited in his thinking. While he found such physical contact deeply offensive, Tyrellan knew that the best way to keep the boy warm without alerting others to their presence was to huddle against him while they slept. Not that Tyrellan ever really slept.

With nothing to do save wait for the cover of night, he turned his attention to the child. The boy lay still, but strangely alert. His eyes followed as Tyrellan crouched over him, brown pupils set in the clearest whites the goblin had ever seen. His blue hair was a limp mess of strands atop his head, and his skin was almost ivory. Tyrellan reached down to poke him in a stomach devoid of the usual chubby fat. Suddenly the boy smiled and caught Tyrellan's poking claw with a tiny hand. Tyrellan started.

Many shadow creatures were pale in their looks. The Arabodedas, hard men of the south, had skin pale from generations spent in the absence of sunlight. This boy was even paler than they were, though his face seemed to hide a darkness behind it, like a mask. Tyrellan grew lost in admiration, even forgetting for a moment the disturbing sensations the cursed mage-bitch had left in his gut. It was a strange thing, that a creature born so far from Fenvarrow would have such a dark aura about it. It had troubled Tyrellan that his master sought a child who should, by rights, have been strong in the light. He'd assumed Battu intended to turn the child somehow into a creature of shadow. Now he had a feeling that this babe needed no such conversion.

Tyrellan decided the boy was blessed, and thus his safeguarding was a grave honour and responsibility. He silently swore to watch over the boy always, protecting him as he grew to power.

In Whisperwood, at the base of a blackened tree, ashes stirred as if there was a breeze. Floating low across the ground, they began to collect around pieces of scorched bone.

Through Dead Eyes

Borgordus was the northernmost of the five states of Kainordas. A fertile region of hill, farm and wood, it was said that here the sun passed closest to the land, as it rose from behind the Morningbridge Peaks. It was also here that the Thrones kept their stronghold, the Open Halls.

The Halls were built on a green plateau above the capital city, Kadass. Both Halls and Kadass were enclosed by stone walls: two great circles connected by a corridor that provided protected passage in a time of war – though no enemy army had ever penetrated that far. The Halls themselves were a collection of white buildings great and small, but all constructed without roofs. In buildings over a storey high, many of the outside walls were missing as well. These skeleton structures were open to air and light and the lazy breezes that rolled in from the Shallow Sea. An ancient enchantment diverted rain from falling into these roofless dwellings, and a form of subtle magnetism kept anyone from falling from high open places or exposed stairwells. The only way to fall was to be pushed, or to leap deliberately. The Halls were quiet too, for the enchantment stopped sound floating freely out of rooms for all to hear, and blurred the vision of anyone who tried to peer directly into another's home. The High Mage Fahren called the enchantment the 'Essence of Walls'.

To the west stood the Open Castle, a huge block some thirty levels high. It wasn't a beautiful building by any means, looking from a distance like a white brick riddled with holes. Inside, however, was plenty of colour and garish excess, and a bustling menagerie of brightly feathered courtiers and nobles. On the castle's roof was the Sun Court and the great seat of the Thrones, Borgordusmae.

To the south of the Halls stood the barracks, surrounded by training fields for soldiers. In the east, student mages were schooled at the Academy of the Sun. Overlooking it was the Open Tower, which was missing so many of its outer walls it looked as if it should topple. The Tower was home to many mages, including the High Mage Fahren, whose chambers lay at the very top, the highest point of the Halls. It was here that Fahren tossed and turned, water squeezing from between clenched eyes. He jerked awake, forehead slick with sweat. Outside, the sky was lightening.

'Elessa,' he murmured. She'd always been one of his favourites – a bright student, and a beautiful girl. Now he was certain she was dead, certain that the dream of a terrible battle in Whisperwood had really happened. 'Forgive me,' he said, horrified by what she had gone up against. Having faced Fazel himself once before, part of him also glowed with pride that she'd bested him.

Fazel had been a great man once. Born a Varenkai, he'd loved life and the light and performed many great deeds. Many had wanted him to be High Mage, but

Fazel had never accepted the title. He'd served under the Throne Siante, during the time that Assidax had been Shadowdreamer. Fazel had hated what Assidax had achieved in the south, and eventually had journeyed to find her. Arrogant and brave, he'd believed he could defeat her in her own realm – but when the two had fought, Fazel was slain. Assidax's terrible gift for necromancy meant she'd been able to bring Fazel's spirit back whole and bind him to her as a shadow creature. Unlike many of the undead, he'd retained his intellect, but was powerless to act on it. He become a slave to the Shadowdreamers, locked in servitude to those he'd always loathed the most. Fazel hoped Elessa had truly killed him, for his was a soul that needed to be put to rest. Poor Elessa . . .

Later, thought Fahren. Springing from bed, he dressed hurriedly in his blue and gold robe and left his quarters. Tall and spry, he bounded down the Tower stairs three at a time, a clashing mix of age and youth. He had wrinkles, but they were well defined, as if they'd always been part of his face. His hair and beard were long and full, a vibrant blond untouched by grey. His crystal blue eyes shone clear, and there were still women who vied for their attention. As he ran, he thought about what he had dreamt and had to force his feet to keep moving lest any single realisation stop him in his tracks. *It couldn't be,* he thought. *It couldn't be that.*

Mentally, Fahren was well prepared for the coming of the child of power. The prophets had known the child would be born within a hundred years of their collective vision, and that hundred years was almost over. But what had happened to the boy to split him in two? It was something to do with that stone around his neck, Fahren was sure.

'It has to be,' he muttered. 'The Stone of Evenings Mild.'

Legend said that when Arkus and Assedrynn had joined forces one last time to destroy the Great Well, the Stone of Evenings Mild had been created at the point where they had focused their power. It was a way for them to stay unified even as their magic separated. The Stone, then, was capable of uniting shadow and light to the same purpose; something impossible since the demise of Old Magic. Used in reverse, it might also be capable of separating Old Magic into its opposite parts – and that, Fahren theorised, was what had happened to the child. From around the child's neck, the Stone had channelled the *pulling* spells of Elessa and Fazel into one force, drawing the child into the Stone and breaking him into shadow and light.

Questions without answers burbled through his mind. Was this breaking part of the prophecy, or had the child's potential been destroyed? Were *both* children now capable of breaking the stalemate? That seemed pointless, for it would only instil another level of balance. Fahren believed the long war existed because shadow creatures were stronger in Fenvarrow, just as the creatures of light were stronger in Kainordas – thus each had a defence stronger than their attack. What did it mean if both boys could counteract that? Or was one great, the other weak? Why had the original child been born with Old Magic? Where had the Stone appeared from?

At least one thing was certain: Fahren wanted the shadow child *and* the Stone brought to him as quickly as possible.

At the bottom of the Tower he composed himself. The air was warm and the gardens quiet with a sense of serenity he did not feel. He trod paths that were pale in the early morning, his robe swishing around his sandalled feet. Towards the Open Castle he went, expecting to find the Throne Naphur asleep in his rooms. Instead, as he approached the castle, the Throne appeared striding towards him, fully clothed and surrounded by guards. A squat man, but broad-shouldered and muscular, Naphur was bronze from his many days holding court under the sun. Hair grew upon him in unruly abundance – his chest hair in particular refusing to stay tucked beneath the neckline of his cream silk shirt. A red cape hung from his shoulders, and around his head was a circlet of gold with an image of the sun set at the front. Gold 'rays' spread up from the sun, over his forehead and into his closely cropped brown hair, where they moulded perfectly to his scalp. The circlet was the Auriel, crown of the Thrones, and it hadn't left Naphur's head since he was twenty-two.

'Fahren!' said Naphur. 'What are you doing? Have you had further news from the front?'

Fahren fell into step beside his ruler. 'The front, my Throne?'

'Yes, the front!' said Naphur. 'Battu is marshalling war machines. All this increased activity we've been experiencing along the border – he's been testing our defences. We're certain he plans to invade again! Gerent Ratacks and his cerepans are assembled in the barracks to discuss our recourse.'

In that moment Fahren saw it clearly. Battu must somehow have known where and when the child would be born, or else his servants could not have been there at the precise moment. More importantly, how long had he known? Long enough to create an enormous distraction to draw Kainordan troops away from their regular postings? To clear the land of threats to his returning minions?

'Where does he concentrate his forces, my Throne?'

'In the southeast. We think he sets his gaze on Holdwith.'

Not the Shining Mines then, the target of his last invasion? No, of course not, for the Mines were due south of Whisperwood, right in the path of his servants.

'My Throne,' said Fahren, 'there is something even more pressing we must discuss.'

'More pressing?'

'Naphur,' said Fahren, 'the child of power has been born.'

Naphur frowned, then looked startled, then scowled and shook his head. 'Magic,' he spat.

As they strode towards the barracks, Fahren described his dream – from the moment Elessa had stepped from the hut, until the reinforcements arrived too late. He spoke of the separation of the child and his theory about the Stone. Naphur was annoyed by that, as he always was when magic complicated things.

'And this "invasion" of Battu's,' continued Fahren, 'I don't think it's real.'

Naphur drew to a stop. 'What do you mean, it isn't real?'

'It's to focus our gaze elsewhere, so Tyrellan can escape with the child.'

Naphur frowned. 'I cannot ignore armies collecting on my border, whatever motive put them there.'

'Of course,' said Fahren. 'But you cannot ignore the other concern either. Send out patrols south of Whisperwood, put the area on high alert.'

'I'll do what I can,' said Naphur, glancing impatiently towards the barracks. 'But why do you worry so greatly? By the sounds of it, we have the right child under our control. He should be here in a matter of weeks, and surely it's a good thing that all the shadow has been blasted out of him.'

'I've no idea what it means, my Throne,' said Fahren, 'but the future of Kainordas depends upon our actions. We need to do whatever we can to get the Stone and the other boy. Will you promise me that you will take this seriously?'

The Throne look somewhat abashed – he'd never really forgotten that Fahren used to rap his knuckles as a boy. 'I'll do what I can,' he repeated. 'Soldiers will be sent to comb the clearing in Whisperwood for the Stone, and I will deploy extra patrols from the Shining Mines. Will that satisfy you?'

'It's a start,' said Fahren.

'I'll have birds sent presently. As for now, my officers await. We'll speak again soon.'

Fahren watched the entourage head off down the path. Naphur would do what Fahren asked, but Fahren doubted he grasped its significance. Naphur was a soldier at heart, and would fight this in his own way, even if that was exactly what the enemy wanted.

Today Fahren would be sending out birds of his own.

Each breath he took was another painful cobblestone on the slow road to consciousness. Dimly he began to smell wet wood and bracken, hear birds in the trees, feel a throbbing at the base of his skull . . . and then, rudely, he was awake. He opened his eyes with a moan.

A couple of handspans above him was what looked like the rippled bark of a tree trunk. How could it exist at such an angle, given he was lying down? He felt groggy and disoriented. Where was he? He shifted his weight and felt planks beneath him – the floor of his hut, but covered in splinters and branches. Everything was creaking. The tree trunk above him was stuck through his hut like a spear through a pig. The events of the previous night rushed back to him like scenes from a nightmare.

His boy!

His pain forgotten, Corlas rose from under the tree and stared about his broken home. Against the wall the cot lay in pieces, but there was no sign of his son. Bellowing angrily, he ran out into the clearing.

Sunlight shone merrily on ruination. The grass and earth were churned to sodden clumps. A gaping crack rent the ground. Trees around the clearing were burnt, broken or missing. Wood was everywhere, from tiny chips to massive branches. As Corlas took in the wreckage, the breeze brought him the stink of death. Fearing to find his son, he searched. The only body he found was the blade from the Halls, Dakur. Corlas left the corpse in the trees and returned to the clearing, a grief beyond madness shining in his eyes.

He fell to his knees on the destroyed flowerbed that housed his wife's grave, plunging his fingers into the mud. This time yesterday his wife had been alive, giving birth to a child they both already loved, in the home they'd built together. Today he could not recognise where she was buried, their home was destroyed and his son was gone. Corlas did not even know who had taken him.

A seizing, choking pain gripped his chest, and he hoped that it would crush his heart and he would die.

When he came back to himself, he was standing in the trees with his axe in his hand. He didn't remember getting it, but there it was. He glanced around – the clearing was behind him, as if he'd been walking away from it. Certainly he could not go back there yet, if ever. He stumbled away into the trees, and eventually fell, and slept where he landed. Sunlight began to burn his back, but above him the branches seemed to move closer together and blot it out. A soldier and mage passed him nearby, and grass grew around him to shield him from their searching gazes.

When Corlas awoke it was night. He broke free of the grass easily, without really wondering where it had come from, and hauled himself up against a tree trunk. He stared at the sky and thought not much of anything. Eventually he slept again, and dreamed torturous dreams of his wife that made him howl on awakening.

The next day, a baby deer walked out of the trees and simply lay down in front of him. Corlas knew he must force himself to eat, for it would be an insult not to. A small part of him was comforted that the wood still looked after him despite the loss of his Sprite wife. As he built a fire and spit, the rumbling in his stomach made him remember he was still alive.

The deer had begun to smoke when suddenly he heard voices carrying through the trees. He froze – who had come? Moving swiftly and quietly for such a large man, he stole towards the clearing, going low to the ground behind a log. Beyond, outside his hut, a troop of blades was working back and forth over the ground with rakes. Anger rose hot in him and his fingers itched on his axe. When would the violation end?

'Spread out!' yelled the penulm, the second in command. 'The High Mage said it landed outside the clearing! You,' she singled out a droopy-nosed fellow and pointed to where Corlas lay watching, 'get over there!'

Corlas crawled backwards and slipped into the shadows at the base of a tree. The droopy-nosed fellow appeared where Corlas had been moments before and started raking the undergrowth unenthusiastically.

'Three years of service,' Corlas heard him mutter. 'Would a bit of excitement be too much to ask? Yes, apparently. What's your next assignment, Gudgeon, they ask. Well, it's raking through leaves for bits of old jewellery! Pretty impressive, hey ladies?' The blade spat and leaned on his rake. 'You would think,' he went on, 'that with Fenvarrow looming on the doorstep, I'd finally get to see some action. You would think!' He slammed his rake back into the ground, digging into roots.

Corlas caught a growl before it made it past his lips. How dare this man treat the forest with such disrespect.

Gudgeon paused, then raised his nose into the air, giving a long sniff. Corlas wondered what he was doing, but then he too smelled it – off a way into the trees, his deer was cooking well.

'Now there's a thing,' said Gudgeon, narrowing his eyes. 'Smells like someone's stolen off for a snack when they should be working.' He put the rake against a tree.

'Damned if the price of my silence ain't going to be a tasty leg or two.'

The blade moved off into the trees, following his nose.

They even want to steal my lunch, thought Corlas, and almost found it funny.

Gudgeon became irritated that the illegal picnic wasn't closer. There was something sinister about Whisperwood and he quickly discovered that he didn't like being alone in it. People told stories about the place; stories that hadn't seemed so worrying when he'd been working alongside a full troop of soldiers in a sunny clearing. It was said you could hear the whispers of the dead flying about the trees at night, and the streams in the north were full of fisherman's banes.

'Gudgeon, you fool,' he muttered to himself, 'you're inventing fancies. There's nothing out here but birdsong.'

The scent became stronger and he heard the crackle of flames and melting fat from around a tree. 'Ah ha!' he exclaimed, leaping out to surprise his soon-to-be-co-conspirators, then glanced around in confusion. Before him was a badly angled spit holding a deer above a fire, but there were no other blades in sight.

Something hit him in the back of his head and he blacked out.

A splash of cold water woke him, and he choked on the gag in his mouth. Attempting to raise his hands, he found them tied behind his back. Before him crouched a massive man, staring from under heavy brows and unkempt lengths of ratty hair that might once have been curly. His rippling torso was bare and covered with scratches and scars, and he wore only a pair of frayed trousers. In his hands he held a great axe, and the smear of blood on its blunt end told Gudgeon what had hit him.

'You are forgiven for trying to cry out when you woke,' growled the man, 'but will not be again. Understand?'

Gudgeon nodded an affirmative, and the man pulled the gag out of his mouth.

'Who are you?' Gudgeon asked shakily, his head pounding.

For some reason this seemed to amuse the man, for a flash of teeth showed through the tattered beard. 'Who am I?' he repeated. 'I used to live in the clearing that your comrades now search. I had a home and a wife there. My name is Corlas. Of the bloodline Corinas.'

Gudgeon stared hard at the man. He'd seen a portrait of Corlas Corinas in the Halls, as had every soldier who'd eaten in the barracks mess there. It could be this man bore a passing resemblance, but Gudgeon couldn't see much beneath the hair and grime. Certainly it was impossible to reconcile the image of the great warrior Corlas with this animal. Probably the bastard was mad.

'It matters not if you doubt me,' said Corlas. 'What do you search my clearing for? I have nothing left to take.'

A thought struck Gudgeon. If this wild man lived here, perhaps he'd found the pendant. Maybe Gudgeon could buy his way free.

'A pendant!' he said. 'A precious stone hanging on a black chain. It will fetch a great reward for the man who finds it. A great reward! Have you seen such a thing?'

Corlas stared off into the distance. 'It was my wife's,' he said eventually. 'Then my son's. Now, like them, it is lost.' He twisted the axe in his grip. 'Why do *you* search for it?'

'They didn't tell us,' said Gudgeon, hoping the man was lying about the pendant's loss. 'But I do know that if you can find it, the Throne will pay dearly to possess it.'

'I told you, soldier,' Corlas said, 'it is gone. Where is my son?'

'What?'

Corlas backhanded Gudgeon across the face. He yelped, and Corlas seized his throat, constricting the next cry so it came out as a squeak.

'Do not call out. I'll ask again. My son. He was here with me in this wood. A mage arrived with a soldier. They wanted my boy. Then shadows came creeping. As all fought over him, I was knocked unconscious.' He drew close. 'Who has the boy with blue hair?'

He released Gudgeon's throat and the soldier sucked in air, glaring with angry eyes. When he could wheeze out words again, he said, '*You* claim to be father of the false child of power?'

'Who took him?' Corlas said, raising his hand again.

'We did!' said Gudgeon. 'The light took him, though I've heard only rumours. I didn't even know this wood was where they found him.'

'Where did they take him?'

Gudgeon could feel a tooth coming loose in his gums and spat out blood. His mind raced – how could he appease this man? 'Mages were spotted carrying him through Redbrook, but . . . he died.'

'*What?*'

Gudgeon worried he'd made a terrible mistake, but he couldn't turn back now. 'A chest fever, they said. He died in his sleep.'

Corlas's knuckles went white on the axe and Gudgeon whimpered. Instead of hitting him, Corlas laughed humourlessly.

'Dead, is he? We'll just have to see about that. Tell me why you called him the false child of power.'

'Well,' Gudgeon said, 'he can't be the child of power if he's dead. I also heard that his hair was dyed.'

'Dyed?' said Corlas. 'I see.'

He tapped Gudgeon on the forehead with his axe and the man fell unconscious once again. 'I am sorry, blade,' he rumbled.

Corlas moved to the smoking deer and tore a leg from it, eating without tasting as a fire built in his belly. He knew his son's hair had not been dyed, so they had to be hiding him because they believed him to be the child of power. There was only one place they would take him. Corlas finally had what he needed – a direction.

He left the fire and the unconscious soldier. The man would suffer no permanent damage, and would soon be able to call out to his comrades. Although Corlas's thoughts ran red whenever they turned to the Halls, he could not blame an individual blade. The soldier was simply following orders, as he'd done himself for many years.

One day, Mirrow, he promised. *One day I will return. But until I have our son again, there is only one thing I choose to take with me.*

He twisted the axe in his grip.

～

Vyasinth watched from on high, displeased by the soldiers scurrying about her domain. What they searched for was gone, carried away in a charred grip, and still they disturbed the earth.

At least the man whom Corlas had caught could serve some use. Foolishly, Corlas had left him alive, but that was something she could fix. Underneath Gudgeon, the earth caved in and slowly he sank into it. Leaves settled over his disappearance and tiny shoots began to grow.

Vyasinth wondered if Corlas could ever prove a worthy champion. The Sprite blood in him was old and buried, and he'd never even believed that he had it. She hadn't intended him to be anything more than a mate for Mirrow. Now he was her only hope.

Return with the child, Corlas, she bade him, *and you will not find Whisperwood so lightly defended against our old opponents. This I swear.*

A bright speck in the corner of his awareness rose and fell on high thermals and finally Fahren accepted that he couldn't concentrate on his book. The bird's pleasure at being aloft washed through him and for a moment he forgot his anxiety over the news it carried. Affinity with animals had always been one of Fahren's strengths. In his younger years, when he'd served at Holdwith, he'd tracked animals of Fenvarrow to make friends with them and use them as spies. The only ones he'd failed to charm were the shadowmanders, so surprisingly hateful in their dark little hearts.

Currently most of his animals were messengers, and he'd sent out many birds in the past few days. South they had flown, to mages and cerepans and anyone who owed Fahren a favour, but all were distracted by the threat of invasion. Day after day passed without word of Tyrellan.

Fahren also kept close watch on the baby being brought to the Halls. Stupidly, his mages hadn't thought to hide the boy as they'd passed through a village on the journey home. Fahren had ordered they return to the village and falsify the child's death, giving out that he'd been a fake and that his hair had been dyed. It was common sense to carry something so important in secret, and his underlings were going to rue their thoughtlessness – if he didn't simply wipe their memories.

Getting up from his table, he walked to the edge of his study where, between shelves, a missing section of the wall allowed him to stare out from the top of the Open Tower. The sundart dived towards him, its golden wings spread full span. A beautiful thing it was, always Fahren's first choice when delivering messages to pretty ladies. It landed on his outstretched hand, chirping as he stroked its wings. He unclasped the note attached to its leg and unrolled the tiny coil of paper. Breathing out slowly, he put down the note.

The Stone had not been found.

Thy Enemy's Enemy

The forest's edge came abruptly, a line of tall trunks like a grey fence. They overlooked the Grass Ocean, a region of grassland that stretched all the way to the Great Rass and Dragon's Sorrow rivers. The day was hot, the dry air smothering the land like a blanket, the grass bowing many heads under a lazy sun. Somewhere a solitary bird chirped half-heartedly, as though making up its mind whether or not to sing.

Suddenly it stopped.

From inside the forest came the sound of footsteps, crunching towards the tree line.

Corlas blinked as he stepped into the sun, shielding his eyes as they adjusted. How many years since he'd left the forest? His life beforehand seemed like a dream.

As he began to stride purposefully north, a beady gaze followed him from shady branches. The creature focused on Corlas's thoughts, so intent that they pulsed clearly in the psychic landscape. The man went to find his son, a boy with blue hair, who'd been taken away to the Open Halls.

The carcass of the bloodied songbird slipped forgotten from the creature's claws.

Battu halted halfway up a staircase. One of his spies was sending him a psychic message, somewhat frayed around the edges for the distance it travelled. The spy was watching a wild-looking man who stalked away from Whisperwood carrying a fearsome axe. Suddenly Battu understood what his spy understood – this man was the child's father and went to find the boy who had been taken by the light. Was there some way to turn this to his advantage?

Well, he thought, *the weaver will follow and I will know soon enough.*

Right now he was more concerned with Tyrellan. Through the eye of the unknowing blade, he had seen the female mage dead with one of the mysterious babes in her arms, which meant Tyrellan must have escaped with the other. Tyrellan, however, had disappeared, and Battu hadn't been able to scry him out. He both admired and damned the goblin's ability to hide, leaning towards damnation as time passed.

Meanwhile, his army continued to gather, as did the Throne's forces, at Holdwith. This was concerning, as there was always a chance the Throne would decide to take the offensive. Though Battu would love to wage outright war, that had never been part of the plan. He had his orders, received from the Dark Gods all those years ago, and already he had taken liberties.

Where was Tyrellan?

Ahead, at the top of the spiral staircase, was a door behind which his answer might lie. Plucking a key from his robe to undo the lock, he listened for a moment to the roar of the Cloud on the other side. He still felt the

old excitement when he came here. There was no way
to tell what he might experience in the shadowdream.
Perhaps he would float in ecstasy, or be inundated with
despair. He might see the future, the past, or things that
never were and never would be. And though the dream
ran thick through the walls of Skygrip, it was here on
the roof that entering it was most overwhelming.

He opened the door.

In the centre of the roof, between the four great
pinnacles, a curling stream of grey-black vapour rose
into the sky. It moved upwards slowly, thundering like
a distant sea, feeding into the boiling Cloud high above.
This was the birthplace of the biggest shadow in the
world, one that fell on land and sea, on past and future,
even on possibility.

Battu stepped into the vapour and felt the updraught
of the Cloud's passage, the soft caress of floating
moisture. He kneeled on the cold stone from which
the Cloud emanated and breathed in a darkness
that suffused his body and mind. He began to float,
indistinct, in a place where time and space held no
sway. A great void surrounded and carried him, though
it did not take him to anything, nor did it bring him
from anywhere. Distantly he heard the sound of the
world from conception to end, but avoided listening
too closely. He spread outwards without purpose until
he had almost spread too far. *Be a leaf in the stream*,
Raker had taught him, *not the stream itself.* He reined
himself in, and then he began to chance upon other
leaves, drifting . . .

. . . *dark shapes slip through dark water, circling
a kill, which darts back and forth desperately. The
anticipation of blood, flesh between the teeth, means*

the sharks won't, can't, hold back much longer. No, thinks Battu, draw away . . . this is not the time for pleasant distractions . . .

. . . a young man sits by a stream, feet dangling in the water, listening to the sound of insects chirping. He has pale skin and eyes like midnight lakes and wears the blackest gloves Battu has ever seen. Battu has never known calm such as he sees on the young man's face. Someone comes to sit beside him, runs her hand through his long blue hair . . .

. . . Fahren is angry, raises a warning hand. Battu pulls back the hood of his cloak and the old man's eyes widen in surprise and recognition . . .

. . . a field of tiny flowers, white. Battu walks across it, the sun shining brightly on his back, the grass soft under his bare feet. In the sky, golden birds circle and play, catching flies in a warm breeze. What is he doing here?

. . . an orange puffer fish swimming in a dark sea. It gets tangled in a net, extends its thorns to protect itself and they catch in the weave. It begins its final journey, to Battu's table . . .

. . . Tyrellan, but younger than he is now. The goblin sits hunched by a cliff overlooking the Black Sea. Someone approaches and he moves behind a rock, stringing an arrow to his bow. His brother arrives, calling for him. Tyrellan puts an arrow in his back, sending him off the edge of the cliff. Tyrellan stands, walks to the edge to look down . . .

. . . a scar-faced man, Raker, stands on the roof in front of the Cloud. He turns to eleven-year-old Battu and smiles fiercely. Battu thinks he is ugliest when he

smiles. Raker tells him to come and see, to touch the
Cloud, to get lost in it ...

... Raker again, this time fighting for his life. He's
wounded already, for Battu has caught him off guard.
His eyes are full of rage, but Battu sees he is genuinely
surprised at this betrayal. Battu learns a valuable lesson
about trust ...

... and Tyrellan again. The goblin crouches amongst
bushes, a child with blue hair tightly strapped to his
back. He hides from the day, and a group of soldiers
on horses, a Varenkai patrol riding past. The move on;
failing to spy him.

Battu flooded back to his body, rolling out of the
Cloud to gasp in cold air.

Tyrellan was coming home.

That evening, on a bare patch of earth between trees,
Corlas fed sticks to a fire. He'd built it without thinking,
for there was nothing to cook and no need to see the
empty, miserable world around him. Though this was
a land he'd once fought for, he felt little connection to
it now. It was tainted by those who ruled it, those he'd
once served but who had stolen his child and left him
for dead. Weariness closed his eyes, but anger kept him
awake.

'Sleeping so soon?'

Corlas leaped to his feet, axe at the ready. Hopping
about at the edge of the firelight was a little bird.
Corlas's movement startled it and it cocked its head
at him warily. A moment passed and it returned to its
fossicking. Corlas glanced around but no one else was

there. Had he imagined that singsong voice as he'd been falling asleep?

'Who's there?' he demanded of the darkness.

'Just us,' came the voice.

Corlas spun about, but again there was nothing there save the bird. It scratched the earth and gave a low chirp.

Sitting down heavily, Corlas buried his head in his hands. Had he lost his mind as well? Would there ever come a time when he had nothing left to take?

'Why do I bring such despair, Varenkai?' came the voice.

'Silence!' bellowed Corlas. 'You do not exist! Leave me be!'

'But I hate to see someone alone in such a state.'

The voice was so close that Corlas's head jerked up. At his feet stood the bird, unafraid. It was sparrow-sized but far more colourful, with wings of scarlet, a yellow breast and a bright blue tail. It had eyes like beads of blood. Corlas blinked at it.

'Did you . . . speak?'

'I've been speaking for some time.'

Corlas stared in shock.

'I'm sorry if I scared you,' said the bird. 'I have that effect on people sometimes. Most birds don't talk, I do realise that.'

'You . . .' Corlas licked cracked lips. 'You are real?'

The bird gave a chirp of what seemed to be amusement. 'I certainly hope so! Did you think you were imagining me?'

'Indeed,' said Corlas slowly. 'And still I am not convinced. My mind has been . . . overloaded of late. I fear I may have dropped it altogether.'

The bird seemed to think about this, then launched off the ground to alight on Corlas's arm. Corlas flinched as it tightened sharp little claws on his skin.

'There,' said the bird. 'Does that feel real?'

Corlas was dumbfounded. The bird did seem real enough.

'What are you?' he asked.

'A friend. Perhaps one more significant than my appearance suggests.' It seemed to sigh. 'Not many of my kind are left these days, but long ago we were the Sun God's messengers. We lived in his Garden and filled it with song. So prized by Arkus were we that he bestowed upon us the power of speech and allowed us to fly free into the skies of the world. Wherever we go, we bring his light, and when we feel the presence of one who lives without it, we are driven to help. And I have not felt misery such as yours for a long time. I don't know what ails you, but, if you wish it, I will travel with you for a time. Perhaps I can help?'

Corlas laughed bitterly. 'What help is a tiny bird?'

The bird scratched its head idly with a claw. 'Companionship is not measured by size or shape, and it can be good to talk if one is troubled. Perhaps you will tell me what has befallen you?'

Corlas's faced darkened.

'Something I've learned,' the bird said, 'is that if one hoards his feelings like gold, he can expect to collect interest. And, like wealth, too much misery can drive a man insane. Perhaps your heavy mind would lighten if you shared its load?'

Corlas closed his eyes as sadness welled up within, like water pushing against a dam. Perhaps he did need to talk to someone. *Yes,* came soft words somewhere in his mind, encouraging, understanding. *Speak.*

The dam burst and words gushed in a torrent. Corlas told the bird everything: about the death of his wife, the birth and theft of his son, the days or weeks following as he'd roamed the wood, forcing himself to keep on living, to put food in his mouth and lie down to sleep, instead of climbing a tree to throw himself off. Then the soldiers had come looking for the pendant, bringing with them the information he'd needed – the whereabouts of his child. At the end of the deluge his voice was hoarse. Only then did he realise he had been shouting in anger.

'Those are terrible things to happen to a person,' said the bird, full of compassion. 'Terrible things. You poor fellow.' Its eyes flickered. 'Did the soldiers manage to rob you of the pendant as well? After they had taken everything else?'

'I do not know where it went,' murmured Corlas. His bleary gaze shot up. 'I do not care! It's my son whom I travel to find, not a piece of jewellery!'

'Of course,' soothed the bird. 'Of course. I didn't mean to upset you.'

Be calm, came an urging in Corlas's mind, quietly enough to seem his own. His breathing slowed and he calmed. It had been cathartic to yell and scream, to pour out his unspoken troubles.

'We should talk some more,' said the bird, 'but for now I think it's time you rested. You're very tired, and I did interrupt you going to sleep.'

Corlas was indeed tired, and growing more so by the second. The bird flitted off his arm and landed on the ground. 'Do you have a name, little bird?' he asked.

'Of course,' said the bird, the fire reflecting in its blood-drop eyes. 'It's Iassia. What's yours?'

'Corlas,' said Corlas, and slept.

'Well, Corlas,' said Iassia, 'it looks like we might travel a way together, you and I. Perhaps quite a way.'

Iassia chuckled softly to himself as he sent out thoughts towards Battu. *Prized by Arkus indeed* . . .

It was true that weavers had been created by Arkus long ago in his Garden of Paradise, but the rest of the story was a bit more complicated. It seemed that Arkus, in his vanity, could not stand to make anything simple, so he'd given his birds power and intellect despite the mundane nature of their intended function. He had expected them to be happy flitting prettily from tree to tree, entertaining others with their songs and playful natures. Iassia wondered how a god could be so stupid.

Back in the days before the gods went to war, Assedrynn, Lampet, Elsara or any of the Dark Gods had often visited the Garden – and in fact Arkus had created a great lake there to make them feel more at home. Assedrynn had enjoyed speaking with the weaver birds, and saw potential where Arkus saw only pretty plumage. He had also noticed that, as the birds grew ever more bored, some of their tricks and jokes took on a nastier flavour. As disagreement erupted between Arkus and Assedrynn, the birds continued to do what was in their nature. As they carried messages, they encouraged misinformation between the gods and told Assedrynn things that Arkus would not have wished him to know. *We were brash,* thought Iassia, *but we were created brash.*

War began, and no longer did Assedrynn visit the Garden, so the respect he had paid the weavers went too. The birds grew restless, their tricks more malicious. One weaver, whose common name was Osesha, managed to ruin a burgeoning love pact between two of Arkus's retinue, and Arkus was enraged. He called together all the weavers and warned them that their games had gone too far, that they were expected to entertain and amuse, not to harm. As further warning, he destroyed Osesha. The birds were silent before his wrath, but they remembered what Assedrynn had said about the importance of being true to one's nature. They were affronted that Arkus saw them merely as jesters. No one mourned the death of Osesha, as weavers are entirely selfish creatures, but Iassia remembered the great fear and hatred the act had produced in them. As soon as Arkus was gone, their thoughts began to fly between the trees in a whirlwind debate. For once, the weavers were united. They would abandon Paradise.

At the Garden's gate they had found the Guardian, one of Arkus's strongest servants, whom they knew would not allow them passage. While no single weaver could affect such a powerful mind as his, collectively they dealt him an onslaught of confusion and terror, driving him insane in a matter of moments. He left his post to rage into the Garden, mad and destructive. With the gate abandoned, things that had no place in Arkus's Paradise began to drift through. Against this backdrop of growing chaos, the weavers made good their escape into the world. *That was a fun day,* thought Iassia.

Knowing that Arkus's anger would be great once he discovered their treachery, the weavers fled to the newly created Fenvarrow. They could not find Assedrynn in the mortal world, but they did find Kryzante, then the High Priest of Assedrynn, who would later become the first Shadowdreamer. Kryzante had offered the birds a bargain: if three would serve him until the time of his death, he would perform the rituals needed to convert the weavers' magic into shadow and so hide them from Arkus. The weavers agreed. Kryzante warned the birds that though their souls were now hidden, if someone summoned Arkus's attention by using a weaver's true name, Arkus would be able to recognise his wayward servant. Such a weaver would not enjoy its return to Paradise.

Paradise, thought Iassia derisively. *Another arrogance of Arkus to call it such. Give me a world full of puny minds to torment – that's paradise.*

He twittered again as he watched over the sleeping form of Corlas.

Battu sat back in Refectu with building satisfaction. Not only was Tyrellan safely on the way to Skygrip with the child, but the weaver bird had had some stunning luck. Discovery of the child's father might prove useful in itself, but there was something even more incredible about Iassia's new friend. Beneath the man's overgrown hair and beard, beneath the dirt-encrusted skin, Battu had recognised a face he'd never expected to see again. He'd forced himself to forget his assailant at the Shining Mines, the warrior who'd dealt him a grievous blow yet slipped through his clutches unscathed. Though he'd

desired revenge, Battu had had the sense not to tear up
Kainordas looking for a single man. Yet here the man
was again, this time the father of the prophesied child.

Perfect.

A plan began to form, one that married purpose with
revenge, and the longer the dark lord thought about it,
the wider the smile stretched across his face.

Fate's Children

Tyrellan strode across the Stone Fields, satisfied that he was back under the Cloud. Battu's distraction had worked well: on the journey home, enemy patrols had been thinner than usual. He'd managed to go undetected until the very last stretch, which had been across wasteland with little cover. Risks had been taken and he had been spotted. No matter. No Varenkai force would ever catch him in his homeland, if they dared to cross the border. Most Kainordans were too terrified by the presence of the Trapped, though there was little the floating spirits could do to harm them. Weak-willed fools.

'Tyrellan.'

The goblin halted as a shifting man-shape rose from the rocks before him. 'My lord Battu,' he said, bowing his head. From his back the babe looked on with wide eyes.

'I'm glad to see you back,' said Battu. 'You've been longer than expected.'

'I was forced to move quietly, lord. And the babe needed to be fed.'

'Is there a murdered wet-nurse somewhere on the trail behind you?'

'No, but many farmers wondered why their cows gave no milk the morning after my passing.'

The Battu shape wavered in an unseen wind. 'What of the other who was with you?'

'He was killed, lord.'

'Ah,' said Battu. 'I shall have an escort sent from Logale.'

'They will only slow me.'

'See that they don't. I'll take no chances with the child's safety. There will be a whelkling waiting to bring you to Skygrip.'

Battu's shadow loomed forward, losing all human shape, surrounding the boy like the fingers of a claw. The boy looked back curiously, without fear, meeting Battu's inspection with one of his own. Then Battu withdrew and was gone.

For the first time in weeks, Fahren felt calm. The boy had arrived, safe and well, and now slept in a cot in Fahren's quarters at the top of the Open Tower. His long blue lashes caressed chubby cheeks, his blue hair grown into a mess of curls.

The door to Fahren's chambers burst open and in strode the Throne, highly agitated and puffing hard. The Tower steps were unforgiving when one was in a hurry.

'What is it?' said Fahren.

The Throne didn't answer, but moved to the cot. 'So,' he said, 'this is the child of power? He doesn't look very scary.'

'He's three weeks old.'

The Throne grunted, glancing around distractedly. 'What is it, Naphur?'

'Battu,' snarled Naphur. 'He's disbanded his troops and war engines. He doesn't mean to attack.'

Fahren felt his heart sink. That could only mean one thing – the goblin had reached Fenvarrow. The other baby was as good as lost, at least for the moment.

'So,' said Naphur, keeping his voice steady, 'it seems you were right, High Mage. It was a feint, massive and costly, but a feint nonetheless.'

'And so,' said Fahren, 'you are finally curious about what we possess? And what the enemy now possesses?'

The Throne nodded. 'What do we do with him?'

'Keep him safe, and watch him grow. The Shadowdreamer must not find him, so his identity will be kept secret.'

'His hair is blue,' said the Throne.

'A simple enough enchantment can take care of that. It's his eyes I wonder about . . .'

'His eyes?'

'You will see when he's awake, Throne. They are amber flecked with gold. The child must have some Sprite in his ancestry.'

'Really? He's a Sprite?'

'No, he is human. There are some who still carry an aspect of that ancient bloodline, but it's always weak. Besides, I think the physical characteristics are all that's left to him. Any Old Magic would have been destroyed when he was separated from his shadow self.' Fahren frowned. 'I've been wondering endlessly if this is all meant to be, if each side is meant to have a champion

– it does not seem chance that he was born with Old Magic *and* the only artefact in the world capable of separating him into shadow and light.'

'I only heard "no",' said Naphur.

'I shall leave his eyes, but change his hair,' sighed Fahren, used to Naphur's refusal to even attempt understanding of things magical.

'What of the parents?'

Fahren took a moment to think about that. 'Most likely they are dead. My dream showed nothing of them, and nothing's been found since.'

'Very well, we shall assume them dead. You will be the boy's guardian, responsible for his upbringing and education. He shall remain under your roof, so to speak. That is what you want?'

'Yes, my Throne.' He was glad to hear Naphur finally treating the matter with the seriousness it deserved.

'And what of Battu's child?' asked Naphur.

'I don't know,' said Fahren. 'I'm uncertain of many things. Perhaps both sides have a champion, perhaps just one, perhaps neither.' He sighed. 'I shall need time to ponder, and I may not have an answer until it is delivered to us by fate.'

Naphur's jaw tightened.

'I am worried,' continued Fahren, 'that I haven't sensed anything of magic in him yet.'

'Who's to say there'll ever be any?' said Naphur. 'To blazes with magic. Maybe he'll be a great warrior.'

'He *is* the child of power,' said Fahren flatly.

'There are all kinds of power.'

'Your problem, my good Throne, is that you see what you want to see. And though I agree that there are all kinds of power, our world is so governed by magic . . .

I don't see how someone without the gift can possibly hope to change it.'

'I hope you appreciate that I find that insulting, even though you're wrong,' said Naphur. 'As the Throne of Kainordas, I don't have to be magical myself to command *you* to go off and fight the Shadowdreamer, do I?'

Fahren leaned back in his seat. 'I suppose not.' He sighed. 'Well, for now there is only one thing to decide.'

'What's that?'

'A name, my friend. We should not let wider concerns distract us from the pleasant trivialities of life. The boy requires a name. Something unassuming. I suggest we have some wine while we argue about it.'

Fahren filled two large goblets, and they sat watching the baby in the cot, bickering with each other until the sun began to set. Eventually they came to an agreement.

'Bel,' said Fahren, placing a hand on the brow of the sleeping boy. 'Your name will be Bel.'

The child stirred in his sleep.

A knock at the door made Lalenda start and look up from her book. Books were the only escape from the stark room where she spent her days alone. She was reading about a human girl child, the same age as her, who got up to all kinds of mischief. It was a happy, funny story, although sometimes the thought of such freedom made her weep. When she dreamed of it, waking was all the worse.

Nervously she got off her bed and went to the door. Outside stood a fat Grey Goblin. From the goblin's short breaths, Lalenda could see that the journey into the depths of Skygrip had taxed her.

'There a portal door round 'ere?' the goblin demanded.

'Yes,' said Lalenda, staring out from under strands of black tousled hair. 'Away up the passage by the crystal fountain. It connects to the upper castle.'

'Old fish-head be damned!' muttered the goblin. 'I couldn't find the blighter. 'Ad to come down all them stairs!'

Her tone seemed to imply that this was Lalenda's fault. Lalenda wondered who old fish-head was.

'You Lalenda?' continued the goblin.

'Yes, ma'am.'

''Is lordship wants to see you immediately. You'd better 'urry, as I took so long to get 'ere.' Her message delivered, the goblin turned to huff off down the corridor.

Dread filled Lalenda. Since the boy had arrived yesterday with Tyrellan, she'd hoped Battu would forget about her for a while. If only she could make him understand about prophecy, but she didn't dare try. Her visions seldom concerned Fenvarrow on any broad scale, nor Battu's future as its ruler.

She went to her dressing table with its cracked mirror, the only furnishing in the room besides the bed. Once, while Lalenda had been sitting at it, she'd had a flash of its former owner – the wife of an Arabodedas counsellor, smearing her lips blue. Now the mirror stood covered in dust. In an attempt to make herself presentable, she tied back her long hair, then rubbed a washcloth over her cheeks to wipe away dust arisen from old pages.

'I tie ribbons in my hair, which the wind catches and makes me dance,' she said.

She turned away before she saw tears.

Lalenda forced herself down the narrow corridor. Every few paces was an alcove containing a bust of some Shadowdreamer past, softly lit by a glowing block of ice set into the wall behind. Their stony faces loomed over her, for Mire Pixies were a short folk, and at six years old she stood less than a pace tall.

Her skin was the same colour as the mud of the swamp where she should have been growing up. Her lips, hair and curving lashes were black, and she had large eyes of cobalt blue – a rarity amongst her people. Most of the time her small mouth hung pensively downturned, pointing away from her upturned nose. Her fingers were tipped with retractable claws, though she'd filed them back so as not to damage the pages of books. Two crystalline wings folded tightly across her back.

She tried to take another step but her legs refused. To her side was an alcove containing the Shadowdreamer Raker, whose bust, for some reason, was not lit. The darkness in his alcove seemed like sanctuary and, without thinking, she slipped into it to crouch in hiding. Time passed. At her knees a pool of tears silently grew.

Lalenda wished she hadn't been born a prophet. Sometimes it seemed she spent every moment wishing it. It had ruined her life, bringing her to the castle at an age when other Mire Pixies were still being taught the mysterious ways of Swampwild. Children she'd known would be flitting through willow trees, chasing fireflies or teasing humptoads.

Her thoughts turned, as they often did, to her mother. Before she'd come to Skygrip Castle, she and her mother had been each other's only family. Her father, killed when she was barely flying, was but a face and a voice and a single burning scene seared into memory by pain.

It had disturbed her parents to see their daughter so, pulling on her father's arm with fear written so plainly on her face – not yet able to talk but wordlessly begging him to stay. What possessed the child?

'What is *wrong*, my little Lalenda?' her father had asked. He had knelt before her, cupping her face in his hands, and she had clasped firmly to his wrist. Into his arms he'd gathered her, but she maintained her grip. 'I won't be gone long, willow princess.' His special name for her. She remembered that too.

Then he'd pulled away. By the time she'd scratched and bitten her way free of her mother, he was already flying. As he'd disappeared into a grove of willows, she'd known it was the last time she would see him alive.

A few hours later his body was found, claws extended, caught in the tendrils of a demonflower. Her brethren had burnt it out, and her father's body with it. Lalenda stood nearby, clutching at her mother's leg, finding it difficult to breathe. She had seen this already, in a vision that had come from the future. A vision she had been unable to communicate. She had been too small.

After that, Lalenda had stayed silent long past the time she was first due to speak. She'd wake bawling in the night, and her mother was almost thankful, for it was the only time her daughter responded to her any more. Her poor mother, whose grief had increased as she understood that the death of her husband had also killed her child's happy, giggly nature. But as time passed they grew closer again and helped each other heal. When Lalenda finally did choose to speak, she spoke well.

About a year ago, word had got out amongst the community about Lalenda's gift. Eventually it reached the ears of the Swampwild Counsellor. Discovery of a prophet was never overlooked, and soon enough Black Goblins arrived. Her mother tried to stop them, but was struck and knocked out cold. Lalenda had been taken to Skygrip to become one of Battu's prized possessions.

With the coming of the child of power so close at hand, Battu had taken a keen interest in her. Since Tyrellan had gone, she'd been summoned to the throne room even more frequently, asked questions to which she had no answers. The more she learned of Battu, the more afraid she grew. The dark lord's moods were erratic, his temper quick and sometimes deadly, and he was as paranoid and cunning as a thief with money.

She had, at least, already proven herself useful to him. It had been two months since she'd foretold the location of the child's birth. Battu had immediately dispatched Tyrellan to fetch it.

In the meantime, it was unwise to keep the dark lord waiting. Lalenda stood, wiped her eyes, straightened her skirt, and moved off down the passage.

Battu did not enjoy having a crib in the throne room. It looked ridiculous, somehow insulting, standing there by itself in the middle of the otherwise empty space. He would have to assign some chambers to the child immediately.

The pale boy stared up at him, meeting his eyes with what seemed like interest. Battu frowned. The previous

Shadowdreamer, Raker, had discovered Battu at a young age, had raised him and taught him – and what had that got Raker? A knife in the dark and spells to follow. Would this child do the same to him?

'Shadowdreamer?' came Tyrellan's voice.

Battu was annoyed to have his thoughts disrupted. This was why he didn't keep advisors. In Raker's day, the throne room had thrummed with nobles and counsellors, but Battu had put a stop to that. Battu liked to stare out his long window in thought, and in silence. Of all who served him, however, he trusted Tyrellan the most. He found himself compelled to put up with the goblin's interjections, even to try to keep him *content*. Tyrellan was a vigilant pair of eyes around the castle, one who took the safety of the Shadowdreamer very seriously – perhaps something left over from his days as security chief. Tyrellan had been the one to journey into the Midgeon Hills to enslave the ancient Golgoleth Ghost that now guarded Skygrip's front door. He'd captured the ghost's amulet, which kept it tied to this world, and personally set it into the archway above the castle's main entrance cavern. Most importantly, without Tyrellan, Battu would never have risen to power, nor kept it.

'What?' he growled.

'The Mire Pixie is here.'

'Ah,' said Battu, turning. He hadn't noticed her come in, so tiny were her footfalls. She even walked as if scared of attracting attention. He smiled thinly. 'Lalenda.'

'Yes, my lord?' she said, quaking.

Battu waved a hand lazily towards the crib. 'The product of prophecy,' he said. 'Take a look.'

Lalenda ventured forward to look through the crib bars, and gasped at the ivory boy. 'He's . . . he's beautiful.'

The comment seemed to draw Tyrellan's attention for a moment, but he quickly returned to his impassive gaze. Unexpectedly, the baby smiled at Lalenda, and she smiled in return. Battu could not remember seeing such an expression on her face in all the time she had been at Skygrip.

He whacked the side of the crib, knocking the smiles from both their faces. Tyrellan's lip curled in a snarl, but he smoothed it away before the dark lord saw.

'Now, girl,' Battu continued, 'I have some questions.'

'I will try, my lord,' she whispered.

'Mmm,' said Battu. He paced around the crib like a hulking bear, wrapped up in his swirling black cloak. He began to speak of the events in Whisperwood, asking Lalenda if she could explain them. She could not.

He asked if there were supposed to be two boys, as the prophecy had spoken only of one. Was the child in the crib the child of power? Who was the child who'd been taken north? Lalenda could not say.

Battu came to a stop before her, penetrating her with his deep, pitted gaze. 'It wasn't easy, Lalenda,' he said, 'taking Refectu from a Shadowdreamer too complacent to raise a hand against our enemies.' His features twisted in hatred. 'The gods should have been pleased with his demise. How could I have known?' he muttered, almost to himself. 'And the dream has become even more ambiguous of late. It shows me nothing of my future. Do I have reason to be concerned, Lalenda?'

Lalenda was too terrified to blink. Battu stamped his foot, making her jump.

'This boy!' he hissed. 'He is to end the war.' His hands shot out and clenched her shoulders. 'Is he destined to become the Shadowdreamer?'

'I . . . have seen nothing, my lord.'

'Do I raise a usurper to my own throne?' Battu demanded, shaking her so hard that her teeth snapped. 'You must have seen something! *Anything!*'

All she could do was shiver uncontrollably.

'What good is a prophet,' he roared, lifting her into the air, 'who knows nothing of the future!'

He drew back a hand, blue energy collecting across his fingertips. Lalenda cried out, and in his crib the boy twisted, echoing her cry.

Tyrellan glanced at the child sharply, saw his eyes widen in distress over what was happening. Was it possible the saviour child did not want Battu's rag doll harmed? Perhaps he was simply reacting to violence and shouting, but Tyrellan did not think so. The boy had seen worse than this on their journey home and not uttered a sound.

'My lord!' Tyrellan said. Battu turned slowly to his servant, fingers still poised with blue energy crackling. Tyrellan bowed deeply. 'Forgive me, lord, but I have heard that prophets grow more in tune with their gifts as they grow older. Perhaps in time she will prove useful.'

Dazedly Lalenda stared at him, no doubt wondering why he had intervened. She went still in Battu's grip as the dark lord decided what to do. Suddenly he dropped her, and instinctively she spread her wings for the fall.

'Get out!' Battu bellowed. '*OUT!*'

She scrambled to her feet and ran headlong from the chamber. Battu stood breathing hard, his jaw set as he considered the boy. Tyrellan watched him carefully, quietly, a finger playing atop the hilt of a dagger in his belt. If Battu raised a hand to the child . . .

'Is this my fate then?' Battu said finally. 'That I have strived to bring this boy to us, to raise him in my castle, teach him as my heir . . . only to bow to him in the end?'

Tyrellan knew how jealously Battu guarded his power. Even if the Dark Gods themselves ordered him to, Battu may not willingly give away Refectu. The boy would remain in constant danger as long as Battu thought he represented a threat to his rule. Tyrellan flexed his jaw, choosing his words carefully. 'He was born to serve the shadow's will,' he said. 'But we do not need chaos or unrest. I do not imagine it is his destiny to overthrow you.'

'No?' said Battu, running a hand along the crib.

'He's to lead our armies into Kainordas. For a push like that, we'll need unity in Fenvarrow. A hero on the frontlines with a strong leader behind him. If you teach him well, my lord, you will foster his loyalty and respect.'

Battu pondered this. 'Maybe so.'

'You are also in a position to learn how he can be controlled. If he's to be your instrument, you must familiarise yourself with him.'

'My instrument . . .' echoed Battu. 'Yes. Maybe that's what they meant when they said I'd be rewarded for all my years of patience.'

'Lord?' said Tyrellan.

Battu waved a hand dismissively 'None of your concern.'

Tyrellan watched his master depart. He knew Battu understood that he couldn't kill the child – such a crime would be punished forever in the afterlife. Nonetheless, Battu could act rashly when in a rage. How long would Tyrellan have to monitor his master's fears? It would be better if he didn't have to remove Battu; Fenvarrow needed him while its true leader grew strong.

A Rush of Blood

Corlas sat on a hill under a tree with arms resting across his axe handle. In the valley before him stood a farmhouse: painted bricks, and smoke wisping from the chimney. In the yard were carrot tops, tomato plants and a henhouse probably full of eggs. In the past two weeks it was the closest he'd come to settlement, having steered clear of roads, towns and farms. During that time he'd eaten little and now his hunger bit him painfully. He'd steadfastly ignored it, for his true pain was above and beyond all earthly concern. To attend to hunger seemed somehow like stooping.

'You're hungry, aren't you?' came Iassia's voice on his shoulder.

The bird had been with him since they'd met, his only source of comfort. Iassia had helped him through days when it had been so hard to rise, almost impossible to put one foot in front of the other.

'Do you read minds now, little bird?' rumbled Corlas.

The bird twittered in amusement. 'It doesn't take a mind-reader to hear the growls of your stomach.'

Corlas grunted.

'Your goal beckons so strongly,' mused the bird, 'it's no wonder all else has faded to irrelevance. But, Corlas, you are still a man, with day-to-day concerns. To acknowledge your hunger may be to accede to that also. It can be hard to admit it to oneself after such troubled times, but life goes on.'

Corlas frowned. From the start the bird had been able to read him so perceptively. This time Iassia had echoed his own thoughts almost exactly. Yet Corlas could not go down to the farm. He would either have to steal or beg, and he was not a man for either.

'You wouldn't have to beg,' said Iassia. 'Look at all that unchopped wood out the back there. You could offer your axe in return for a meal.'

Corlas turned the idea over in his head, but there was something else that kept him from going down there. Now that he'd returned to the world, he felt apart from it. These were not his people any more. These were enemy lands.

'They are simple folk, Corlas,' came Iassia's voice. 'Don't let your anger at those in power trickle down to them. They are but farmers living as best they can. It wasn't their decision to take everything from you.'

Corlas shut his eyes, remembering the farm where he had grown up. To his younger self, a soldier's life had seemed glamorous and worthwhile, better than scraping a life out of the dirt. Now the dirt seemed more honest, or at least less ignorant. As a soldier, Corlas had been an unthinking instrument. These people were merely working to live. Somewhere inside himself, dully and emotionlessly, Corlas forgave the farmers.

'Aye,' he said. 'These people are not my enemies. There is no shame in asking them for work. Will you accompany me?'

'I think not,' said the bird. 'Talking birds tend to complicate things.'

Corlas started down the hill just as someone emerged from the henhouse. She was a young woman, strong and vital, who stopped short and clutched her basket when she saw him. He realised what a frightful visage he must make, tattered and filthy, especially with the monstrous axe swinging at his side.

'Greetings, madam,' he called out. 'I mean no harm, and will leave if you wish it. I am simply a traveller with an empty belly. I thought perhaps my axe and I could see to your woodpile in exchange for a meal?'

The woman seemed to relax somewhat at his polite tone. She glanced at the woodpile then back to him. The farmhouse door banged open and a little girl with curly brown hair came barrelling out.

'Back inside, Essie!' snapped the woman.

The girl stared wide-eyed at Corlas, then slowly did as she was told. Corlas suddenly doubted the farmwife would let him anywhere near her family.

'I see you have a small one,' he said, 'and would be understandably concerned about strangers in the home. I will bother you no more, madam.'

'Wait,' she said, and came closer the fence. 'What's your name?'

Corlas's tongue stuck in his mouth. Not wishing anyone to mark his passage, he didn't want to give his real name. The first thing that came to mind was the name of the blade whose bones lay rotting back in the wood.

'Dakur.'

'Well, Dakur,' she said, 'my husband told me this very morning he'd chop the wood himself.'

'I see.'

'In fact he tells me that every morning. The man thinks he can be a keeper and still play farmer too.'

She studied his face as she made this remark, presumably because she wanted to see that he'd registered her husband's profession. A criminal wouldn't deliberately enter a peacekeeper's home.

'In his compulsory years of keeping, or by choice?' asked Corlas.

'By choice.'

'Ah. That is well. No risk of being sent away from his family then.'

At that she smiled, and he nodded thankfully as she opened the gate.

An hour later the wood was chopped and Corlas felt almost cleansed of dirt for all the sweat that had rolled off him. The woman, Frera, appeared from the house with little Essie at her side. Corlas was touched to be invited in, and sat at the table trying to contain his hunger as bread, cheese and fruit were placed before him. He forced himself to take proper bites instead of cramming full his mouth.

'Where are you headed, Dakur?' asked Frera.

'Towards Kadass,' said Corlas. 'I hope to find work there.'

'Ooooooh,' said Essie. 'Kadass! I never been to Kadass!'

'Have you not?' said Corlas, amused by her bright eyes. 'It is a busy place. There are folk from all over Kainordas.'

'Are there Saurians?' asked Essie.

Corlas chuckled. 'Some. Mostly they prefer their deserts, but some do venture south.'

'I never seen a Saurian! What are they like?'

'Well, they sssspeak funny,' said Corlas, and Essie giggled.

The door opened and in walked a muscular young man dressed in the leather uniform of a peacekeeper. He stopped immediately when he saw Corlas.

'Who's this?' he demanded.

'Don't be rude, Chavus,' said Frera, rising. 'This is Dakur. He chopped the wood for us, and now we're having a meal.'

'I was going to chop that wood,' said Chavus, not taking angry eyes from Corlas. 'You should know better than to bring strangers into our home, Frera.'

'Chavus!' said Frera, shooting Corlas an apologetic look.

Corlas rose with stormy eyes. The softening effect of little Essie on his spirits had been instantly expelled. It seemed that soldiers in uniform brought him nothing but trouble these days.

'I am no longer welcome,' he said. 'I shall see myself out. Thank you for the meal, Frera.'

Against Frera's protests, he went to the door and let himself out. Behind him he heard the sound of heated words. As he headed for his axe, left leaning against a log, the farmhouse door banged again.

'Not so brief, stranger,' came Chavus's voice. 'I'd have your purpose here.'

Heat rose in Corlas. 'My purpose is none of your concern.'

Chavus faltered under his glower, but the expression was quickly replaced by the pride of a man with something to prove. Corlas recognised it well, and found it entirely misplaced.

'It is indeed my concern,' said Chavus, hand going to his sword hilt. 'I've been ordered to keep an eye out for suspicious fellows such as you, for there have been strange happenings in the south. You will answer my questions, man. It's the law.'

'Not my law,' said Corlas.

Chavus's eyebrows shot up. 'Then you admit to being aligned with the shadow?'

'No,' said Corlas, 'I do not.'

'You will come with me to my headquarters,' said Chavus, levelling his sword at Corlas's chest.

'Keeper, I mean neither you nor your family harm. You would do best to put away your sword and allow me on my way.'

'I'm giving the orders here!' snapped Chavus.

Corlas stooped to pick up his axe.

'Stop!' shouted Chavus. 'Stand still!'

'Out of my way,' said Corlas. 'I am going to leave.'

'I think not!' said Chavus, and lunged.

Corlas sidestepped and Chavus overextended. Corlas swung the axe, blunt end first, into Chavus's stomach. The man doubled up on the ground with eyes watering. From the farmhouse window came Frera's cry.

'It is all right, Frera!' called Corlas. 'He's only winded. I will leave you now.'

Quickly he made his way to the gate. A shout sounded from behind and he spun, surprised to see Chavus back on his feet and charging him down. Instinctively he brought up his axe, batting the sword away. Chavus came onwards, swinging wildly, and Corlas was forced back under a rain of blows. The look in Chavus's eyes was determined, righteous – he truly intended to do Corlas harm. Each shuddering jolt on his axe jarred Corlas's teeth in his clenched jaw. His blood began to sing its old song, forgotten for many years – the song of battle. Fire exploded in his heart and bubbled up his arms, calling them to action. It was like his old soldiering days, when he would lose himself in the fight. Others called it going berserk, but to Corlas it was like entering a vivid dream where a single, simple truth held sway – kill, or be killed. Time seemed to slow and every sense heightened. The heft of the axe in his hands, rough wood against his skin. The sweat running down his face, salty in his mouth. The light flashing off the axe head as it turned in the air, the hairs on his arms rustling as he swung. The roar of his own voice above the sound of blood rushing in his ears. A pinprick of white-hot rage burning in his centre . . . or was it fierce joy? He hadn't felt so alive since Mirrow had died.

Then for a time everything went blank, until another sound trickled into his consciousness. He blinked, coming back to himself. Only moments had passed, but for Corlas it seemed like waking from a long sleep. Crying sounded at his feet, and slowly he looked down. Frera was sprawled by her husband's side, sobbing as she tried to stem the blood flow from his ruined chest, turning her hands to gloves of scarlet.

'Stupid boy,' muttered Corlas, dazed.

Frera turned her eyes upwards; they blazed through her tears. 'Curse you!' she screamed. 'May the Dark Gods take you!'

'Frera . . .' choked Chavus, his eyes beginning to mist. 'For goodness sake . . . get back in the house!'

A child was crying too, and Corlas saw Essie at the farmhouse door, clutching her dress to herself in fear and anguish. He backed away.

'Forgive me,' he mumbled, and ran.

Corlas awoke, and couldn't remember feeling more drained. Sitting up, he became aware of all the aches and pains his body had developed from nights spent on hard ground. Dread filled him as he heard Frera's shrieking once more. *It's not my fault,* he thought. Did he believe that? Maybe he could have disarmed Chavus, or fled, if the blood frenzy hadn't taken him. No, Chavus had brought it upon himself by backing Corlas into a corner.

There was a rustle as Iassia alighted on a branch nearby. 'They turned east,' he said, of the soldiers who'd been looking for them since yesterday. The bird had been scouting a wide circle, giving Corlas ample time to move if trouble came his way. 'We should press on.'

'Why?' growled Corlas. 'Now I am no better than those who destroyed *my* family.'

The weaver chirped sympathetically. 'You must stay the course. The events at the farmhouse were not of your making. You must still right the wrongs committed against you.'

'But I have no plan,' said Corlas. 'I have steamed ahead with no idea of what to do once I reach the Halls. I cannot take on every soldier in Kainordas once I get there.'

Iassia cocked his head. 'I have a plan,' he said. 'But I must have the truth from you if it's to work. I've gathered, from things you've said, that your career in the military was quite successful before you left it?'

Corlas went silent. Had he spoken to the bird about that? He couldn't remember. He'd been such a mess, and had ranted and raved in the bird's presence often. Probably something of his past had come out sometime.

'I was an officer in the army,' he said eventually.

'Of any note?'

'My full name is Corlas Corinas.'

The bird seemed surprised. 'Corlas Corinas? The great commander of the Shining Mines?'

'I was not the commander,' said Corlas with a scowl.

'But you are well known for your actions there,' said the bird. 'This is good – it fits well with my plan. You must assume this identity again.'

'If it will get me back my son,' said Corlas, and shrugged. Then he half-smiled. 'But what is your plan, oh little wise bird?'

'One step at a time,' said Iassia. 'First, we must strike a bargain, which is the way of my kind. If I am to help you, you must promise me something.'

'What?'

'Sometime, in the future, I may call on you to return the favour. You must then do something I ask of you. I may never ask anything,' he added in a casual tone, 'but if you agree, I have the power to bind you to your promise. It is a trick granted to my race by Arkus in his benevolence.'

Corlas frowned, mulling over his choices. If the bird could help him, what was the harm in having to collect a few worms for it sometime in the future?

'Seems like a fair trade,' he said. 'I will strike you your bargain. Perform your trick.'

'One more thing. The bargain is between us alone. You may not speak of our association to others. The "trick", as you call it, binds you to that as well. My kind must remain secret so we can continue our good work.'

Corlas grunted, but nodded. Iassia flew onto his head and he felt an odd sensation, almost like a knot being tied in his mind. Iassia gave his skull a sharp tap and hopped back to the ground.

'Did you feel that?' he asked.

'I felt . . . something. It went away quickly.'

'Wonderful,' said Iassia happily. 'Then we are bound as allies. Now, let's work out how to get back your son.'

In the weeks that followed, Corlas and Iassia continued towards the Open Halls. With the bird's help Corlas was able to avoid pursuers, and after a time it became clear they'd escaped altogether. Thoughts of Frera and Essie troubled him, but Chavus should have remembered his family before setting himself against Corlas's axe.

He no longer took such long, undeviating strides, and his eyes went in other directions than north. The anger that had driven him relentlessly was no longer a shield from his grief and he began to feel a purer, more profound sadness. Iassia proved a comfort, and the two talked long as they walked, or camped at night.

Eventually they came to the Great Rass, a white, swirling river on the border of Centrus, and crossed into the hilly grasslands of Borgordus. They came to a town with a quarry, where even someone as raggedy as Corlas was able to make coin splitting rocks. He bought new clothes to replace his rags, and a razor and comb. When they moved on, he felt more human than he had in a long while. There was food in his belly and clean cloth on his back, and he'd worked honestly for both.

They travelled on until, one day, Corlas found himself only a league from the capital.

Iassia considered the distant ward stone standing at the top of a steep rise. It stuck out of the grass like a limestone monolith, giving off an almost imperceptible light. Part of a larger circle, it was a marker in an otherwise invisible border all around Kadass and the Halls. If any creatures of the shadow tried to pass the stones' perimeter, they would meet with resistance and a silent alarm would be sent to nearby military mages. Lightfists, Iassia recalled they were named, his feathers fluffing in distaste. He couldn't risk going any further.

'My friend,' he chirped in Corlas's ear, 'I fear our time together is at an end.'

Corlas transferred the colourful bird from his shoulder to his hand, holding him before him. The clumsy movement irked Iassia, but he did not let it show.

'I thought that may be so,' Corlas said, for Iassia had never accompanied him into civilisation before. The man's brow furrowed and Iassia sensed his thoughts. He was anxious about re-entering Kadass and the Open

Halls. These were places of his youth, where many would remember him. Also, he was trying to figure out how to thank Iassia. Internally, Iassia was amused. The man would not thank him if he knew Iassia's true purpose, or that the bird was bored to blazes with having to sympathise with his plight.

'No need for thanks, Corlas,' Iassia said. 'Helping is its own reward.'

'I would thank you anyway,' said Corlas. 'I would be lost but for you. If not in body then in heart. So thank you, little wise Iassia.'

'Well, this is not a final goodbye,' said Iassia brightly. 'I may find you again, when you are free with your boy – why, I'd like to meet the lad who caused all this fuss! And perhaps one day I will call on you to repay the favour you still owe me. Who knows?' The bird was silent a moment and then, very seriously, he said, 'Corlas, do not rush towards your goal. Remember your boy will be closely watched, perhaps disguised, and it may take time for the right opportunity to present itself. Gain the trust of those in the castle. Be patient. In time, your son will know his father.'

'For his sake I will be patient,' replied Corlas.

Iassia sensed the man making a sincere effort to commit to his words. 'Very well,' he said. 'Then take my blessings with you. I'll pray for your success. Goodbye, Corlas Corinas.'

With that Iassia launched into the air, rising quickly on the warm breeze.

'Goodbye, little bird,' said Corlas.

Tyrellan Paints the Town Red

Tyrellan went to his cupboard, which was taller than he had use for. His quarters were large and he didn't like them, but they went with the title of First Slave. He'd preferred his smaller rooms further down the hierarchy. These larger ones simply meant more space for the same few things, more places to have to hide weapons, and more air for the ice to cool. They weren't efficient.

He took a goblet and bottle of wine from the cupboard, then sat in a wooden chair before the iceplace. He rarely bothered with the luxury of dark ice, although he was more than entitled. Tonight, however, he was dimly aware that he should do something special for himself and so a luminescent blue cube stood in the iceplace. Its light illuminated the edges of objects, and it sent out cold wafts like ghosting fingers across his skin. Scowling, he gave up trying to find enjoyment in the sensation. Instead he unstopped the bottle and filled the goblet. Sipping, he felt the wine trickle down his throat, felt the toxins worming their way through the tiny tracks of his body, into his blood where they danced and destroyed. It dulled his senses after only a sip and he didn't care for that at all. 'Filth,' he said, putting the goblet down. Let the idiot masses have their common joys. They weren't for him.

He placed a claw on his stomach. The strange sensation left there by the accursed light mage had become more noticeable by the day. Now it almost felt like something was wriggling in his belly. Also the mage had mentioned his birthday and . . .

Today was his birthday.

Probably no one alive knew it, but Tyrellan didn't think that would matter to whatever foul magic had been planted inside him. He'd asked Battu about it, but Battu hadn't sensed anything out of the ordinary and had dismissed him. The thought of the Shadowdreamer letting potentially dangerous enemy magic go unchecked behind his lines angered Tyrellan.

The feeling in his gut leaped upwards. He lurched from his seat, knocking the wine to the floor. The *wrongness* inside drove him close to panic. A part of him wondered why he could still breathe when his senses were telling him something too big was forcing its way up his throat. He fell to his knees and threw up.

What had that bitch done to him?

The thing was almost in his mouth. He felt stalk legs reach out of his throat and grasp his tongue, pulling up the body behind. He shoved his hand into his mouth to tear the thing free, but there was nothing to grasp. He gagged as his claw hit the back of his throat. He clenched his jaw shut despite his disgust. Could he trap the spell there? If so, Battu might still be able to do something about it. Whatever was inside him seemed to lose form again and the *wrongness* streamed up his nasal cavity, out his nostrils. It was so quick he didn't have time to pinch his nose.

A glowing light spilled onto the floor before him and collected together. It formed and reformed into the same shape – that of a butterfly. The lines grew more distinct, the shape more stable. The butterfly raised a wing and, as it moved, the glow was replaced by solid colour. The effect spread over its whole body as it hardened into reality. The butterfly waved its antennae and tested its wings, which were as large as hands.

What was the nature of this spell? There had to be more to it than the creation of an insect; that was hardly fitting revenge for a dying mage. He suppressed his inclination to stomp on the creature, suspecting a trap. Instead, he took a step back and examined it. Its wings were pure white, their edges sky blue. Two large false eyes, one on each wing, had centres of the same blue and were ringed by concentric circles, yellow then scarlet. From the outer scarlet circle crooked lines ran down the wing, as though the colour had been painted on and then drizzled. Its body was as white as the wings; the legs and antennae, a chrome blue. It typified everything Kainordas folk found beautiful – all colour and garish excess without subtlety, like a whore displaying her wares. The sight of it filled Tyrellan with loathing.

The butterfly beat its wings and launched into the air. As it began a lazy circle of the room, Tyrellan reached warily for his sword. The butterfly flapped towards him and Tyrellan backed away, uncertain of what threatened him or how he should react. He snarled and swung the blade, hoping to scare the thing away. The butterfly kept coming and he swiped at it viciously. The blow landed across the insect's abdomen, but instead of slicing through, the blade bounced as though hitting stone. The butterfly didn't appear to notice, staying on course as if nothing had happened. It was almost upon him! He backed away, swinging again, each blow meeting with the same resistance. Finding himself backed against the table, he dropped the sword to seize a chair, swung it with all his strength. The chair splintered to shards in the air and the butterfly continued unhindered.

Despairing of weapons, Tyrellan tried to snatch the creature, but his hands could not even stop its wings from beating. It powered through his grip and landed on his shoulder. Horrified, he tried to push it off. The weight was no more than any butterfly, but the creature was as immovable as if frozen in time.

Tyrellan leaped wildly, trying to shake it off, and landed hissing in front of the mirror. He drew a dagger and tried to pry it away, but only succeeded in cutting his own skin. He flung the dagger away, then turned and sprinted towards a wall, shoulder charging with all his strength. He bounced backwards with fangs gritted in pain. The butterfly pulled its legs free from where they'd been driven into his shoulder by the impact, less yielding than the flesh beneath them. It began to clean black blood from itself.

Tyrellan fought to regain self-control. It wasn't the pain that bothered him; it was having this *thing* on him.

'Maybe you won't like the cold,' he muttered, 'if indeed you're a creature of light.'

He retrieved his dagger, went to the iceplace and stabbed out a chunk of ice. Dark ice was so cold that it burned, but even when he set the chunk to the butterfly's back, it took no notice. Tyrellan cursed and flicked the ice away.

Without warning the butterfly fluttered from his shoulder and back across the room. For a moment Tyrellan stood still, watching it. Then, warily, he edged to the door. As his claw touched the handle the creature circled back towards him, but he was through in a flash and slammed the door shut. He went swiftly down the shadowy stone corridor.

Behind him sounded a crash, and he spun to see the door hanging off its hinges. The butterfly flapped lazily towards him down the passage.

He turned and sprinted with grim determination. At the least he should be able to outrun the revolting thing! He felt the beating of wings on his neck and the creature alighted once more on his shoulder. Tyrellan hissed in frustration, slowing to a walk. He bared his fangs at the butterfly.

'Don't get comfortable,' he said.

The ancient throne Refectu seemed to spill out of the wall behind it, as if the shape of a throne had been pushed through molten rock then set. It was a part of the castle itself, made when Skygrip had been hewn from the mountain. Across its surface ran complex carvings, an entanglement of living things from all over Fenvarrow: the wing of a Graka, claw of a Mireform, petals of a demonflower, tusk of a Vortharg, branch of a weal tree, and hundreds of others all entwined. They spilled from the throne onto the wall behind, running out like ripples across water. To the eye they seemed frozen, but over time they moved, slowly as light travelling around a sundial. Faces turned and sank back into the stone; leaves twisted in an unseen breeze; mouths

opened and closed with unheard words. They were not
solid carvings, but reflections of the land the Cloud
covered. It was said that during the rule of Assidax, as
she expanded the Cloud across Kainordas, all kinds of
light creatures had appeared there too.

Battu drummed his fingers on a row of fangs that
had been erupting out of the armrest for some hours.
He understood what it was like to get caught up in a
blood frenzy – his time with the sharks had made sure
of that – yet still it was infuriating. Corlas had been
a Varenkai hero, had even fought Battu himself! Yet
here he was killing dumb farmers, running the risk of
execution. Such an end would not serve Battu's plan
at all. If Corlas was going to get himself safely inside
the Open Halls, Iassia was going to have to prove his
worth twice over. Battu drummed his fingers even
harder, jabbing the sharp ends of the armrest fangs in
under his nails.

Tyrellan strode into the throne room – almost angrily,
it seemed to Battu. Did Tyrellan dare to openly display
anger towards him? A moment later the thought was
forgotten as a colourful butterfly sailed in after the
goblin. It followed Tyrellan across the room, landing on
his shoulder as he came to a stop and bowed.

'By the Dark Gods!' exclaimed Battu in genuine
surprise. 'What is this creature, Tyrellan?'

Tyrellan remained bowed, his voice sounding as if
his fangs were bared. 'I don't know, lord. It appeared
just now in my chambers – birthed, I suspect, from the
magic implanted within me at Whisperwood. I cannot
kill it, and it will not leave my side.' Tyrellan raised his
head. 'Help me, Shadowdreamer.'

Battu reached out with his finer senses, just as he'd done when Tyrellan had first announced the 'enchantment' he'd felt in his belly. As before, he sensed nothing. He moved down the dais steps to consider the butterfly more closely. 'What a grotesque creature,' he mused, reaching to touch it. Instead it launched from Tyrellan's shoulder and flitted around Battu, coming to rest on Refectu.

'In Kainordas they would call it beautiful,' said Tyrellan, scowling. 'Yet everything it has to offer is available at first glance. It is vulgar.'

'I never took you for an aesthete,' said Battu.

He scratched his chin, wondering what to do. He couldn't disenchant something he couldn't sense, so he opted for brute force instead. Extending a finger towards the butterfly, he raked it with blue lightning. The butterfly stayed right where it was, wings opening and closing slowly, ignoring the magic that passed over it. Battu made a fist and compressed the air about the insect with enough force to crush a skull to dust. The butterfly was not bothered. Suddenly Battu understood.

'Ah, Tyrellan,' he said. 'There's nothing I can do.' Muscles twitched in the goblin's face. 'You say the light mage cast this spell on you while she was dying?'

'Yes, lord.'

'It's a legacy spell.' Battu chuckled. 'The whore cast her legacy spell on you.'

'I am pleased my lord is amused,' said Tyrellan flatly, 'but I do not understand.'

Battu raised a hand towards the archway entrance. 'Let us walk,' he said.

As he led Tyrellan from the throne room, the butterfly flew to join them. They passed the recess where the

Castle administrator, Turry, sat with scrolls and ledgers piled about him, and came to the alcoves containing busts of past Shadowdreamers. Battu halted before one that wore a twisted half-smile partially displaying her sharpened teeth, with stone dreadlocks framing her narrow, snake-like eyes. It, like the other busts, was incredibly lifelike.

'Assidax in her youth,' Battu muttered. 'I'd have liked to meet her. She gave Kainordas such a great deal of trouble . . . and was, apparently, a vigorous lover, if you could match her.' He broke from his reverie and turned to Tyrellan. 'This bust is the result of Assidax's legacy spell. In fact, every bust here is the legacy of the Shadowdreamer it depicts.' He pointed to an empty alcove. 'That's the place I have picked out for my own.'

Battu opened his palms to Assidax's bust, discharging such a massive burst of energy that it blew chips out of the wall . . . but left Assidax undamaged.

'You see?' he said. 'To leave one's image behind like this is traditional for Shadowdreamers. Even Raker,' he nodded to where the scar-ridden Raker stared out from his alcove, 'managed to leave one, despite the fact that I obliterated his body completely. The legacy spell is one that can be cast even from death, as the spirit is departing.' Battu sneered at his former master. 'Not that I begrudge him his memory as I did his life, but I couldn't remove this statue of him even if I wanted to. A legacy spell cannot be destroyed. You could take a hammer to this bust for days and the only thing you'd break would be your wrists. Even if Skygrip itself were somehow reduced to rubble and these floors collapsed beneath us, I have a feeling these statues would remain where they are.

'Unfortunately, Tyrellan, this light mage cast her legacy spell on *you*. I've never heard of it done this way before, and whether she attached her legacy to your body or your spirit I cannot say. Perhaps this butterfly will perch forever above the grave you sleep in. Perhaps it will follow you even into Assedrynn's Well. Whatever the case, you two are going to be close companions.'

Tyrellan stared out the corner of his eye at the butterfly on his shoulder. 'Surely there must be a way. You cannot accept this travesty within your own walls.'

'Ah, First Slave, is that a hint of desperation in your voice? I never thought I'd see the day. Who knows – perhaps the shadowdream will reveal something to me. Now come. I have a task for you and your new-found friend.'

Usually Tyrellan left Skygrip by a lesser door, but today he went to the main entrance cavern. The cavern was immense and circular, ringed by towering statues of Fenvarrow heroes and mythical creatures, some of which almost reached the roof, some fifty paces up. Between the statues were tunnels, above which hung cruelly spiked grates. If ever the enemy breached Skygrip, the grates could be lowered, creating further barricades against invaders. Other safeguards were the slots cut into the walls higher up, behind which were hidden passages from which archers could pelt arrows. At the north end of the cavern were huge hardwood double doors, thirty paces tall and wide, to the side of which stood a massive iron cogwheel. Turning it to close the doors took twenty guards, so the doors stood open most of the time, as they did now, letting in the grey light of day. There was little danger in leaving them so, since Skygrip was surrounded by a fort wall, on which guards kept constant vigil. Not to mention the powerful Golgoleth Ghost that manned the entrance itself, always ready to make a quick meal of the unwelcome – or anyone else it could get away with. Tyrellan thought he heard the ghost hiss at him as he passed, and he snarled in return. As he walked out, he ignored the guards staring at his new insect companion.

He made his way to the fort armoury, a long flat building. The stop wasn't part of his task, but fortunately he could combine Battu's orders with his own purposes. Inside the armoury was a storeroom where Jacix, the head armourer, kept all the choicest weapons. Tyrellan surveyed the racks of deadly tools, tapping his belt buckle thoughtfully with a claw.

'Er . . .' said a voice beside him. Jacix had sidled in nervously and was now staring at the butterfly. 'Can I assist you, sir?'

Tyrellan glanced at him. It was not yet time to make his example. Instead he smiled, such a rare and unnerving sight that Jacix took a full step backwards. 'I'm going into Mankow,' Tyrellan said. 'I need weapons.'

'Of course, First Slave. Do you require aid in your selection, or shall I leave you?' It was obvious from Jacix's tone which option he preferred, but Tyrellan didn't answer. Jacix quickly followed his gaze. 'Ah,' he said, moving to the sword Tyrellan was eyeing. 'This would be a good choice. Fresh from the forge.'

Jacix took the sword off the rack, turning it in his hands for Tyrellan's benefit. It was longer than the one Tyrellan carried, with razor-sharp teeth on one side of the blade. Tyrellan thought it a cumbersome, stupid weapon, but it would appear fearsome to others and that was what he needed. He nodded, and Jacix busied himself finding the sword's scabbard. In the meantime, Tyrellan picked up a small triple crossbow.

'Ah,' said Jacix proudly, noting Tyrellan's selection. 'May I invite the First Slave to test that out?' He gestured to the other side of the room where three dummy soldiers stood lined against the wall, straw poking out of their stuffed heads.

Tyrellan tested the weight of the bow, then aimed it at the dummies. On pressing the trigger three steel bolts sprang out of their grooves, one flying straight and two whistling off at diagonals. The bolt that flew straight lodged in the middle dummy's head, while the others clattered against the stone wall.

Jacix cleared his throat. 'Not the most accurate weapon, of course,' he said. 'One would have to be standing the right distance from one's marks in order to hit them all. But in close quarters, with enemies standing in proximity, this weapon could easily bring down more than one.'

Tyrellan nodded, and Jacix quickly replaced the steel bolts. Tyrellan hooked the crossbow onto his belt and, satisfied, left the armoury and the cringing Jacix to make his way to Skygrip stables. Today he wished to be as visible as possible and a long-legged horse would serve that purpose.

Soon he was riding through the outer gate of the castle walls, the guards having raised the portcullis quickly upon seeing him. They stared as he rode silently past, whispering to each other about their superior's new adornment. Tyrellan bared his fangs, but remained facing forward. *Soon*, he promised himself. Soon they would cease to stare.

Pebbles rolled away from the horse's hooves on the loosely paved road running down the foothills of the mountain that Skygrip had once been. Tyrellan noted the conditions – he would have to assign some workers for repairs. It did not reflect well on the Shadowdreamer if the main road to his castle was unsound.

Around him the earth was fertile, with trees and bushes plentifully populating the thick blue grasses. At the bottom of the foothills was the Fenvarrow capital, Mankow, stretching out in ramshackle glory on an old flood plain through which no river ran any more.

Tyrellan entered the city by the south gate. On either side buildings sprawled messily, most constructed from stone and wood, some with dried mud and thatch. There appeared to be no order, the wealthy living alongside the poor. Taverns, brothels and drug dens were all doing a steady trade as night approached, and glowing ice lanterns began to appear. Food vendors trundled carts along the road, and from a distant tavern piped the discordant music of a Graka band playing their knobbly wind instruments. Everywhere he went, people turned to stare and point at the colourful butterfly on his shoulder. He buried his rage just under the surface, letting it build, all the while taking a deliberately long route to the centre of the city. He turned into a side alley, heading towards the Mireform's Maw, the tavern where, according to his spies, Heron had been staying. It paid to keep a watch on people and, with luck, she would still be there. At worst it was a starting point for the search.

The tavern was three storeys high and tucked up tight against the buildings beside it. Verandahs off the rooms above overlooked the street at slanted angles. On the third storey an old Mire Pixie leaned against the railing, smoking a pipe and considering Tyrellan curiously. From inside he heard all the regular tavern sounds – laughing and shouting, the clinking of glasses, the clatter of dice. He dismounted and tied his horse to a railing, then walked up to the front door and into the building.

The doors swung shut behind him. To his left was the bar, attended by a fat Arabodedas woman of middle age. Filling the narrow room were a number of round wooden tables, most of them occupied. To the side was a staircase disappearing up to the higher levels. A large iceplace on the opposite wall was glowing with a generous slab, and above it hung a painted carving of a Mireform's head baring its teeth in a savage tableau. The denizens of the tavern – mostly men and goblins – glanced over to see who had entered. Tyrellan stared back, quite a sight with the fearsome collection of weaponry hanging from his belt and the butterfly on his shoulder. Silence fell. Evidently some recognised the First Slave, while others were merely taken aback by his appearance. All were quick to turn away from his steely black gaze.

The butterfly launched itself to do a loop of the room, coming to rest on the bar before the bemused Arabodedas woman. Tyrellan followed it to the counter where he sat on a stool. 'A mug of whatever you drink here,' he said. As the bartender nodded and moved away, conversation began to filter back into the room. Tyrellan could hear that most of it now concerned him and his strange familiar.

The woman plunked a mug of something brown in front of him and he flicked some coins onto the bar. As he raised the mug to his lips, the butterfly returned to his shoulder. Someone in the corner snickered.

Not long now.

'Don't, Deeter,' someone whispered. 'It's the First Slave.'

Deeter, apparently too full of alcoholic bravado to heed his friend's warning, sidled up to the bar next to Tyrellan. 'Ho there!' he announced, spit flecking his rubbery old lips and black Arabodedas beard. He waved a hand towards one of the tables. 'My friends tell me you're the great Tyrellan, the First Slave.'

Tyrellan tapped the mug with a claw and inclined his head. 'That's right. And you, if I'm not mistaken, are Deeter the sot.'

'Ooooooh!' said Deeter, rocking back on his heels in amusement. 'I should be offended, but you have me pegged. Listen there, Mr Slave – we was wondering something, if you aren't too busy.'

The bar had gone silent again, and Deeter was talking loudly enough for everyone's benefit. Tyrellan forced a smile, trying his best to appear friendly. 'Yes?'

'Well, ya see . . . the terrible Tyrellan we heard of, he don't quite fit yer description. See, we never heard of him going around with a sweet little butterfly sittin' on his shoulder.'

Tyrellan waited a moment, taking note of the stifled laughs and nervous tension in the air. Then he swivelled on his stool, butterfly and all, to face Deeter directly.

'It's true, Deeter,' he said, also loud enough for all to hear, 'I've only just recently acquired this creature. A mage of the Halls gave it to me while she lay dying by my hand. It is a curse I will never be rid of, but it changes nothing.'

'Is that right?' chortled Deeter. 'Well, p'rhaps you'll allow me to buy yer new friend a drink? Barkeep – a thimble of your finest sugar water!'

He thumped the counter with a laugh that set the whole bar laughing too, people banging their mugs on tables in appreciation of the joke.

Tyrellan did a quick head count, then turned back to the fat barmaid, who was also grinning in amusement. Her grin froze as Tyrellan punched a dagger into the folds of her neck. As she toppled backwards from the counter, he turned to the startled Deeter and caught his jaw in an uppercut that blanked his eyes and sent him crashing to the floor. Twisting from his stool while drawing the fanged sword, Tyrellan ran it through a seated goblin at the nearest table. Another dagger left his hand and hit the goblin's companion, who was scrambling to his feet. Angry shouts went up.

Tyrellan smashed the sword through a chair that was being raised against him, then kicked a table savagely so it slid into those who rose behind it, knocking them to the floor. He flipped the table over onto their struggling bodies and leaped on top of it, up and down and up and down until all struggling ceased. As he did this, an Arabodedas rushed towards him with sword drawn, and a Mire Pixie flew through the air with claws extended. The pixie fell immediately with a dagger in his eye, and the sword of the other was deflected with a clang.

Tyrellan smacked the man in the side with the fanged edge of his blade, raking flesh as he withdrew it.

As he leaped off the bloody mass of limbs and wood, a mug glanced his skull and he reeled around, hurling his sword and pinning the thrower against the wall through his stomach. Only three remained standing, keeping well away from Tyrellan with weapons drawn, eyes full of hate and fear. Two, a goblin and a man, stood close together. Tyrellan flipped the triple crossbow into his hand at an angle that compensated for the height difference of his targets. The bolts whistled and his targets fell, steel protruding from their skulls. Tyrellan drew the last dagger from his belt and twirled it in his fingers, staring hard at the remaining man. The butterfly flapped back onto his shoulder.

The man was backed against the wall, his sword held wavering before him. He was only young, his features soft, and he stared in horror at the carnage around him – the blood-spattered walls, the smashed furniture, the man pinned upright through the belly with limbs twitching. A puddle of urine collected at his feet.

Tyrellan raised the dagger for him to see clearly and the young man whimpered in terror. Then Tyrellan slipped the blade smoothly back into his belt.

'I am First Slave to the Shadowdreamer,' he said. 'It is certainly unfortunate that I've been cursed to carry this insect, given to me as I performed my duty to the dark. It is unfortunate, but it changes nothing. From now on, any who think to joke about it, to comment on it, even to *look* at it, will receive as swift a death as I can manage – and you have seen what I can manage. *Stop looking at it!*'

The dagger left his hand as suddenly as it had reappeared there and the man cried out as it thunked into the wood by his head.

'Now go!' roared Tyrellan. 'And warn all of my words!'

For a moment the man was too afraid to move. Then he rushed to the door, dropping his sword to scrabble at the knob with sweaty hands.

Tyrellan turned and walked up the stairs.

Arriving on the first level, he rapped on the closest door. No one answered. The whole tavern would have heard the fight and be lying low.

'If I have to break down this door,' called Tyrellan, 'you will not live to regret it!'

'What do you want?' came a quaking voice.

'Does Heron still live in this tavern?'

A sense of self-preservation in the unseen occupant kicked in quickly. 'On the next level. Second door on the left.'

Tyrellan gave the door a sharp kick to scare the coward inside, then continued up the next flight of stairs. In a silent hallway he found Heron's door unlocked. On pushing it open, his nostrils were assailed by the stench of liquor, vomit and sweat.

Apparently Heron had heard none of the ruckus downstairs. The crone lay face down and passed out on her filthy bed, an unlabelled bottle of black liquid still clutched in her spidery hand. Her hair was a tangle of damp grey strands sprayed over her bare back, and a wooden bucket of congealing sick lay on the floor beside her.

Tyrellan scowled. He went to her cupboard, found a sack, and bundled her clothes into it. There was no jewellery, nor anything else of value – she must have sold it all. He reached down to shake her shoulder.

'Get up, old mage,' he said.

She groaned, but gave no further response.

He rolled her over and propped her up, wrapped a cloak around her naked torso, ignoring her feeble protestations. Then he hoisted her up and over his shoulder – she was light, the pasty old stick – and bent his knees to pick up the sack. Finally he turned and walked from the room with the unconscious mage dribbling down his back.

A Hero Returns

The throne Borgordusmae had a great gold triangle as its back, almost twenty paces tall and wider at the top. It caught the sun and shone it over the court, the level of its brightness dependent on the mood of the Throne himself. Once, when Naphur had been in a great rage, Borgordusmae had shone with a brilliance that had never been forgotten – especially by the treacherous man quailing at his feet.

Today, though the sun was blazing in the sky, Borgordusmae merely glowed warmly. Naphur sat as relaxed as possible, listening to the Citizen Prime for Kadass going on about some new lake he wanted to build. His muscular body only just fitted into the seat. He often wondered why whichever ancient magic bugger it was who'd created the damn thing had given it such a towering back, such huge armrests and sides, and yet such a constrictive seat. *Addle-brained wizards,* he thought. *No grasp of the important things. A cushion would have been nice too.*

When a messenger came running, interrupting the Citizen Prime with her surprising news, Borgordusmae flashed brilliantly. 'What did you say?' asked the Throne, leaning forward intently.

'The news, my lord,' the messenger said, 'is that Corlas Corinas, long-missing commander of the Shining Mines –'

'Yes, yes, I know who Corlas Corinas is,' Naphur said, waving impatiently.

'– has this very afternoon walked back into the barracks as though he never left, and is down there right now talking to the gerent.'

'Well, get him up here talking to the Throne!' roared Naphur.

'Yes, lord!'

The messenger scuttled off down the red carpet, which ran from Borgordusmae's dais to a sunken stairwell at the opposite end of the roof. The Throne sat back as excited conversation broke out amongst the court. He put a hand to the Auriel, a habit of his when he was thinking. Many speculated that touching the sacred crown brought Naphur closer to Arkus, but in fact Naphur had always put a hand to his forehead when he was thinking and the Auriel merely got in the way.

He stood abruptly and walked from the throne. The court paid no attention, as Naphur never remained seated for long. As he moved towards the edge of the roof, only two pairs of eyes followed him. One pair belonged to Baygis Naphur, the Throne's only son. Baygis was eighteen. He had none of his father's build, but instead had a lithe, slender grace and a mischievously handsome face. His hair was a short and spiky brown, he wore an earring in one ear and the yellow robes of an apprentice mage. With his talent for magic, all Baygis's teachers agreed that the cloth would not remain that colour for long. Baygis caught Fahren watching the Throne too, and arched an eyebrow at the old mage. Silently the two made their way after their lord, to the edge of the roof where no wall or railing ran.

'I didn't expect I'd be granted a moment to think,' grumbled Naphur.

'You have been granted something better,' said Fahren, winking at Baygis. 'Counsel.'

'Pfah!' said Naphur, crossing his hairy arms. 'I don't know what makes you two believe you deserve such input. Especially you, young man!' He aimed his broad chin at Baygis. 'The Throneship has survived long without your *invaluable* advice.'

Baygis shot Naphur an exaggerated look of surprise, then proceeded to bow far too low. 'My lord Throne,' he said, the smile on his face sounding in his voice, 'it is only because I recognise my own inexperience that I am here. I simply wish to learn something of rule from watching you. If I offer my own views, it is simply to test them against one who is wiser and older. Much older.'

Naphur stared bristling at his son's exposed back, then at Fahren who was wrestling a smile without much success.

'Stop it!' he said.

'Stop what?' asked Baygis, rising with such a look of sincerity that it almost made Naphur grin. He squashed the impulse by spinning away from his son, red cloak swirling behind him, to stare out over the land.

'I really am interested in this fellow Corlas who vexes you so,' said Baygis.

'*You* vex me!' said Naphur. 'I was nowhere near this vexed before!' He rammed his hands down onto his hips and snorted loudly through his nose. 'And you, Fahren, stop strangling that laugh in your throat and pop it out before your heart collapses, you old bastard!'

Fahren hooted with laughter.

'Clowns for counsellors!' muttered Naphur. Then he glanced at their faces and couldn't help but laugh as well.

Those closest in the court turned curiously at the sound and saw the three most powerful men in Kainordas laughing together as they looked out over the realm. Somehow, they felt safer for it.

'Corlas was an excellent soldier,' said Naphur, now speaking seriously. 'He was already a cerepan when I first met him at the Autumn Games. I fought him there, actually, and we talked on a couple of occasions. I liked the man.'

'Did he beat you?'

'What?

'When you fought him.'

'Shush, Baygis. I thought you wanted to hear this.' Naphur scratched at the hair that crawled up the back of his neck. 'Anyway, he was promoted to commander and posted down to the Shining Mines, where men of his quality are always needed. The reports I had of him were good. The gerent down there was most impressed.' Naphur flexed his jaw. 'Then came the unexpected attack from Battu. It wasn't his full force, but it should have been enough to take the fort. It seemed inevitable that the Mines would fall. Then Corlas convinced the troops – against the gerent's orders, I might add – to leave the fort and take the battle out to Battu's army. The move, being thoroughly unconventional, saved the Mines. They say Corlas sat astride his war horse carving a path of death wherever he went, so charged with battle frenzy that none could touch him. He wounded the very Shadowdreamer himself.

'After the shadow receded, Corlas was found unconscious on the field, a wound on him to kill a lesser man. Instead he lived, and was taken from the fort into Erling's Vale where the best healers are. The reports I had were that he recovered slowly but surely . . . and then, after he'd almost fully healed, he disappeared. At first I thought he must have grown tired of sitting around mending, as many good soldiers do, and had simply granted himself permission to return to his post . . . but weeks went by, and it became clear that he'd really disappeared. I sent soldiers to search the land between Erling's Vale and the Mines, but they found nothing. Opinions formed about what had happened, but we never had any real information. Many thought the Shadowdreamer had managed to find Corlas and mete out revenge. Others believed that Corlas had deserted. All I know – I hate losing a Corlas.'

'Well,' said Fahren, 'we'll know what happened to him soon enough.'

'Ah,' said Naphur. 'There's the wise counsel I was kept waiting for.' He turned to Baygis. 'You would know of this man, son, if you had slept and eaten in the barracks as I did in my youth.'

'Father,' Baygis said, 'if we *must* have this argument yet again, I'll beg you to remember that it was at Mother's insistence I did not become a soldier.'

'Wilful bloody woman,' muttered Naphur. 'Just don't pretend you weren't happy with her intervention.'

'Actually, Father, I was quite disappointed by it. You know I've never been one to shy away from new experiences.'

Naphur eyed his son suspiciously for any hint of sarcasm. Before he could reach a conclusion, the messenger arrived back to announce that Corlas was on his way. As Naphur turned to stride back to Borgordusmae, Baygis added, 'And I doubt I'll ever grow tired of looking at soldiers.'

Naphur pretended not to hear.

The court fell quiet in anticipation as footsteps sounded on the sunken stairs. Gerent Rataacks emerged, and with him came Corlas. The court was silently impressed by the man. He was physically intimidating, tall and wide, his torso wrapped in powerful muscles. Although he didn't wear the uniform of a soldier, he walked with the same attention, his axe moving about his thigh like an extension of his body. His brown beard, moustache and hair were all thick, glossy and well groomed, and his features were hard, angular and proud. He strode towards Borgordusmae with assurance, ignoring the folk on either side, dropping to his knee when he got there.

'My Throne,' Corlas said. 'My name is Corlas, of the bloodline –'

'I remember you, Corlas Corinas,' interrupted the Throne, framed by the golden light of Borgordusmae. 'Do you suppose I'd forget the warrior who bested me at the Autumn Games?'

A few murmurs travelled about the court.

'Arise!' commanded Naphur, and Corlas straightened immediately. 'I don't feel like painting a rainbow here. Let's get to the point: where have you been?'

Corlas stared ahead. 'It has been very strange, my Throne,' he said slowly. 'I was at Erling's Vale, as you would know, healing from the injuries given me at the Shining Mines. Once I could walk again, I did – around the vale itself, the Grass Ocean and . . . near to Whisperwood.'

'Yes?' said Naphur.

'They say it is a place of Old Magic,' said Corlas, and now he did meet the Throne's eyes. 'I believe it, lord. I fear I strayed there once too often. One day I was sitting by a stream near the forest's edge when a magical creature came to me. A Sprite woman.'

Again, murmurs through the court.

'Even now I do not understand it. I was . . . entranced. She led me into the forest. I was held in thrall by her for many years. I forgot who I had been. I forgot where I had come from. I forgot my responsibilities.' Corlas shook his head. 'It is hard to recall now. It was like a long dream.'

'And never once did you *dream* about escape?' asked the Throne.

'I was bewitched, lord,' replied Corlas. 'It was not possible even to imagine escape. I did not desire it.'

'So what happened?'

Corlas shrugged. 'I couldn't really say, lord. I woke up one morning and she had gone. For a time I was confused, disoriented. Then I began to walk home. As I went, I remembered much that I'd forgotten. Now here I stand: returned and restored to your service, my Throne.'

Naphur leaned back in his throne, frowning. Then: 'High Mage!' he called, and Fahren stepped forward. 'High Mage, you have heard the man's story. Does one who understands *magic*,' he spat the word, 'believe this could be true?'

'My Throne,' said Fahren, 'it is true I cannot sense any enchantment about the man *now*. As for the story he tells, I have heard of stranger things where magic is concerned. It is also true that Whisperwood is an unpredictable place, seldom ventured into, about which we know little. There are many tales of strange happenings there. It is said the spirits of the Sprites live there still.'

Fahren nodded, so imperceptibly that only Naphur saw it, and they shared a private understanding. Fahren was an extremely intuitive mage, excellent at sensing lies (something which made him an irresistible challenge to Baygis) and if Fahren believed Corlas, Naphur was inclined to also.

'So, Corlas,' said Naphur, 'I suppose the question is, what shall we do with you? Your old post at the Mines is taken by a gerent to whom I do not begrudge the position –'

'Nor I, lord. Nor was I ever gerent.'

'– and I would prefer to keep you here at the Halls for a time anyway. We'll have to make sure this *enchantment* has really worn off.'

'If I may speak, lord?'

'Speak away.'

'I had not expected to be granted my old rank, nor do I wish for it.'

For a moment it seemed the light coming off Borgordusmae beamed a little brighter. 'Indeed?' said the Throne. 'So you've returned to tell me you didn't desert but that you now intend to?'

'No, my lord!' said Corlas quickly.

The Throne sat back, a stern expression on his face.

'I do not wish to desert,' reiterated Corlas. 'Only to request a new position. It will be soon enough that my hair runs grey, lord, yet I always wished to build a family. I have lost six years and now ... I wish to stay in one place.' He took a deep breath. 'I thought perhaps I'd have something to teach the young here. About battle.'

Naphur blinked as he realised what Corlas was asking. 'You want to be demoted?' he said incredulously. 'To *taskmaster*? You want to be a *teacher*?'

'I have fought well for you, lord,' said Corlas, 'in my day. Let me help others to do it in theirs.'

'You aren't that old!' said Naphur. 'And, by Arkus, if you are, that makes me old too – which I'm *not* – and I won't stop being the Throne when *my* hair goes grey, let me tell you!'

'My Throne –' started Fahren, but Naphur cut him off with a raised palm.

'I did not ask for your wisdom, High Mage,' he said, staring hard at Corlas. 'I can always use a good commander. I don't like to lose them. Especially not twice.'

Corlas's gaze returned to the middle distance. Naphur studied his unflinching features and received an inkling of how tired the man was. Maybe it was something in the grey storm of his eyes, or the lines on his face. If Corlas could inspire on the battlefield, maybe he could inspire on the training grounds too. Besides, Naphur would know where he was if ever he needed to call him to a greater duty.

'It will be an odd occasion,' he said eventually.

Corlas looked confused. 'Pardon, my lord?'

'Tomorrow night. In the barracks.'

Corlas continued to look puzzled, as did many of the courtiers. Fahren watched patiently, a smile darting around the edges of his mouth.

'Well, it will be a rather forked event, won't it?' continued Naphur. 'A feast in honour of a hero's return – and the announcement of his demotion.'

Corlas relaxed as understanding sank in. 'Thank you, my Throne,' he said gratefully.

Naphur leaned forward. 'Now on your way before I change my mind,' he growled. 'We will talk more later.'

Corlas bowed deeply.

Corlas was relieved he had managed to tell the truth, even if it had been a thoroughly misleading version. He well remembered Fahren's reputation for seeing through false claims and could not afford to be caught out at this crucial stage of the plan. As he headed down the stairs someone called him from behind, and his heart sank as he realised the High Mage bounced down the steps after him.

'Glad I caught you,' said Fahren, landing at his side. 'I understand why you wish to make a hasty retreat. You're probably exhausted.'

'I am tired,' agreed Corlas.

'Yes. I just wished to know a bit more of this Sprite woman.'

Corlas wondered how long it would be until his façade was shattered. 'Of course,' he said, knowing there would be no escaping this. Better to try to satisfy the mage's curiosity now and have it done with one way or another.

'Would you tell me about her?'

If you would listen, thought Corlas, *I could talk of her for hours*. Instead he shrugged. 'What would you know?'

'You said you were enchanted. I'm curious about what form this enchantment took.'

That was easy. 'I believed I loved her.'

'I see. And . . .'

'I thought her the most beautiful creature in the whole world, High Mage. I remembered no time before her and could imagine no time after. One day I woke up and she was not there. So I left. I don't know what else to tell you.'

'You were in that wood for years,' said Fahren, growing more forceful. 'Surely there is more?'

'That is the way I remember it.'

'Where did you live?'

'In the trees,' replied Corlas, lying outright for the first time. 'In a house in the trees.'

It was an image he remembered from stories of Sprites he'd heard as a child. If he told Fahren he'd lived in a little hut in a clearing, Fahren might start to ask difficult questions.

'There is something else,' said Fahren carefully. 'Some months ago, while you may still have been there, there were some very peculiar goings-on in Whisperwood.' The mage raised a wispy blond eyebrow. 'Do you know anything of this? Did you see anything strange?'

'The wood is a strange place,' rumbled Corlas. 'Often I believed there was more than trees out there. Is that what you mean?'

Fahren looked searchingly into Corlas's eyes for a long moment. Finally he frowned. 'No,' he said. His expression grew friendlier once more. 'Well then, Taskmaster Corlas,' he said, patting Corlas's shoulder, 'I should let you go. I'm sure you've much settling in to do.'

Corlas bowed his head. 'Thank you, High Mage.'
Fahren nodded. 'And, Corlas?'
'Yes, High Mage?'
'Welcome home.'

For two months Corlas took up the purposeful waiting that he was careful to disguise. It took great willpower to appear to be settling in and glad to be back. His welcoming feast had called for him to be jovial as he drank. In actuality the drink made his mood darker, and he found himself trying to chuckle with people he would have preferred to put an axe through.

One startling moment was when he saw the paintings made in his honour. He was especially interested in one tableau of the battle at the Shining Mines. It depicted him amongst raging forces of light and shadow, aiming a crossbow, his face fiercer than he'd ever imagined it. The target of the bolt was a dark silhouette all wrapped up in a billowing cloak, long cruel hands extended to the sky – the Shadowdreamer. Above was a vortex of dark blue energy, conjured by the Shadowdreamer, set to obliterate the both of them. Corlas had paused for a long moment before the scene and the disturbing memories it returned to him. It had seemed a lifetime ago, until right then.

As he'd requested, the Throne had made him a taskmaster. To his great surprise he discovered that he was good with students. It was only with the children that he forgot his simmering anger and disconnection from any kind of loyalty to the light. His troubles were not the fault of the young. What was more unbelievable was that the children, especially the younger ones, liked their big, gruff hero teacher in return. He felt conflicted about training them to serve those he no longer believed in, but as he kept telling himself, it was necessary if he was to achieve his end. The students would be the only ones he'd miss once he escaped with his son.

He'd seen the boy once. It had been a risk, but he had invented an excuse to visit the High Mage in the Open Tower. Under the guise of asking some questions about the 'enchantment' placed on him, he'd been able to sit and talk with Fahren while forcing himself to appear uninterested in the baby in the corner. He'd dared to ask casually about the lad, and Fahren had fed him some story about Bel being the orphan of two of the Throne's noble friends. Corlas didn't need any magical senses to know that Fahren lied. In those brief glances he'd recognised his own flesh and blood, even if the blue hair had been hidden somehow. As far as Corlas was concerned, Bel was not the child of power. Some kind of enormous blunder had been made, some superstitious folly. A fairytale from a hundred years ago was no reason to keep his boy cooped up in a tower.

Now, a month after that visit, Corlas made his way back to the Open Tower. He passed two of his students, a boy and girl, who smiled shyly at the fact he'd caught them holding hands. He chuckled to himself and silently bade them goodbye.

Arriving at the base of the Tower, he entered unchallenged and made his way up the spiral stairs. Here and there were doorways into libraries and mages' quarters and whatever else. It all seemed quite empty at the moment, in keeping with Corlas's timing. Many were at the Sun Court, where a meeting had stretched into the night.

It was a good distance to the top, but eventually he came to the landing before Fahren's door. Two guards stood there. They came to attention as they saw his uniform, and straightened even more when they recognised him – since his return, the Great Corlas had become well known around the Halls. It had made it harder that people wanted to befriend him all the time, necessitating more diligence in maintaining his mask.

'Sir!' One of the blades saluted. 'The High Mage is not currently in.'

'I know that, blade,' said Corlas. 'It was Fahren himself who sent me. You are aware of the boy he currently keeps within his chamber?'

'Sir?'

'There is some dispute over his lineage. The court wishes to see him, so Fahren sends me to fetch him.'

The guards looked uncertain. 'We aren't supposed to let anyone in, sir.'

Corlas tapped the insignia on his shoulder. 'Well, I'm not just anyone, lads. I'm the fellow who can assign you a hundred crawls through the mud in punishment for disobeying direct orders. And the way Fahren is getting worked up by Assicon Cydus, I wouldn't want to be in your sandals if he has to storm over here himself to see his will done. He is a man currently in dire need of taking out his anger on someone.'

The guards glanced at each other with obvious worry. Corlas was thankful they were so young, probably fresh out of peacekeeping; older guards might have stood their ground. He didn't want to use violence, especially since he had no idea what magical security measures Fahren might have activated. He was taking a huge risk as it was, but now it had begun he had to follow through.

In this moment he would put to use and simultaneously dispose of his good name as the hero Corlas.

'It's true I took on the Shadowdreamer,' he chuckled, 'but I would not like Fahren's gaze focused on me right now.'

The guards parted before him and he went to the door.

It didn't take long to bundle up Bel and leave, ordering the guards back to their posts as he strode down the stairs. If they were any good at all, they'd already be questioning whether or not they'd made a mistake. He'd blustered his way through with pure intimidation and might not have long. He couldn't believe he had his child in his arms again; it made him heady . . . then anxious, for he held a gift he hadn't yet won until he got clear, got away. Got back home to the wood. To Mirrow.

On the way down, Corlas encountered few people. A couple of times upon passing someone he tried to nod cordially, but felt gazes on his back. He held Bel closer, trying to enfold him from sight. Reaching the base of the Tower, he strode away into the gardens. Not far away was a disused shed in which he'd hidden a horse and supplies. As the shed came into view, Corlas sidestepped behind a tree and his heart sank. The horse was outside the shed and soldiers were standing around it. Maybe they'd heard it neighing. Of all the cursed luck.

Doubling back and moving wide of the shed, he headed towards the east gate. The portcullis was open and, as a taskmaster, he had no problem simply walking through, though the baby in his arms drew a few looks. He took the path down the hill, wondering how he would deal with the crippling blow of losing his horse.

As soon as he was out of sight of the gate, he moved off the path and started to run. If he could make it to a farm or village, he could steal a horse.

Over grassy foothills he went, until he spotted a wood that might hide his passage. It lay just beyond one of the faintly glowing ward stones that ringed the Halls. As he drew closer, he scanned the tree line, and something made him come up short. He'd learned to trust his instincts and something about the trees seemed not quite right. Branches and leaves rustled in the breeze, moonlight chasing over shapes as the canopy shifted. What had it been? He leaned on the ward stone, catching his breath. Just as he decided it had only been his imagination, errant moonlight stole over a branch that had hitherto been shadowed. For a second he saw red feathers and glinting blood-drop eyes. The bird cocked its head, seeming to realise it was visible, and the moonlight moved on.

Corlas stared hard at the darkness. Had it been Iassia? These lands were full of coloured birds, and why would Iassia sit watching him from the shadows? Why would any bird, for that matter?

From the trees came a fluttering and the bird broke free. 'Corlas!' he called. It *was* Iassia. 'I've been waiting, to help you escape!' The bird landed on the ground before him, just beyond the invisible threshold of the ward stone. 'Come!' he urged anxiously. 'We must be swift if we're to evade your pursuers!'

'Why were you watching us from the trees?' said Corlas. 'It seemed you didn't wish to be seen.'

'What?' exclaimed the bird in surprise. 'No! I was waiting for you.'

Still Corlas could not help but feel that Iassia had only flown out of the trees because he'd been seen. Why did he feel that? The bird's behaviour was suspicious, but this was his friend, wasn't it?

'I didn't think you were going to meet me,' Corlas said. 'It has been months since we parted ways.'

Iassia hopped about impatiently. 'We must hurry, Corlas!' he twittered. 'There are pursuers not far behind. All can be explained, but let us be away from here first.'

As Corlas watched the bird hop and twitter, he noticed something peculiar. It moved about frantically, yet it did not approach him. His eyes flicked to the ward stone between them – one link in an invisible chain keeping out the shadow. As his gaze moved from the stone back to Iassia, he found that the bird was staring at him silently.

'Why don't you fly up onto my shoulder here,' Corlas said, 'and say hello to my son?'

Iassia did not move.

'Shadow,' breathed Corlas.

Iassia chirped softly in amusement.

'But you . . . you helped me.'

'My enemy's enemy,' said the bird, 'is my friend.' He cocked his head. 'You haven't any allies in the Halls, Corlas. Come with me and we'll escape together. The Shadowdreamer doesn't care what happens to the boy, as long as Kainordas cannot set him against us. You can return to Whisperwood and hide, away from the light's clutches. Come, let us away!'

Corlas's brow darkened. 'Do you suppose that I still trust your words, little bird?'

Iassia fluffed his feathers in anger. Moments passed with neither moving. Then Iassia spoke with a menace

in his voice that Corlas had not heard before. 'So be it
then. You think you are no longer of the light, but it is
they whom you choose. And you can thank your Arkus
that I cannot invoke my bargain through this barrier . . .
but if you stray, Corlas. If you stray . . .'

The bird took off, a silent dart back to the trees.
Corlas gazed after it, a lump of ice in his stomach. It
seemed the shadow still hunted his boy, and he'd almost
delivered Bel into their hands. What 'favour' would the
bird have invoked from him? Deliver his son to Battu?
Kill him right here? It could have been anything. And
now he was trapped in the Open Halls.

He looked at the boy and the boy looked back,
smiling and aware. He did not seem like a normal baby,
that was true. Could he really be the child of power?
Everyone seemed so bent on possessing him. If it hadn't
been for the intervention of the Halls, perhaps Bel
would indeed have been taken to Fenvarrow. Confused
as his allegiances were, Corlas wouldn't have wished
that. Perhaps he did still prefer his homeland, despite
everything. The lesser evil.

He lost track of time standing there on the cusp of the
wards, wondering what to do. His boy chuckled cheerfully
as Corlas stroked his head. Everything else seemed to fade
away, and tears pricked the back of his eyes. They were
together, that was the most important thing.

'Taskmaster Corlas.'

The voice made him start. Fahren had come, though
no others were with him. They were alone in the moonlit
countryside, facing each other.

'Have you taken leave of your senses?' Fahren
said angrily. 'Why have you stolen this boy from my
chamber?'

'Stolen?' Corlas laughed bitterly. 'That is a very bold word for the likes of you, child-taker.'

Fahren's anger flickered, to be replaced by confusion . . . and, finally, realisation. 'By Arkus!' he murmured. 'You're Bel's father.'

'I have not decided,' said Corlas darkly, 'if that is to be his name.'

Fahren looked out into the night. 'Where were you taking him?'

'Home.'

'Yet I've observed you standing here for some time, Taskmaster. What has delayed you?'

Corlas tried to speak about the bird, but the words would not form in his mouth. That part of the contract held fast, it seemed. Instead he said, 'I grew worried for his safety beyond the wards. I did not believe until tonight that he might really be the child of the prophecy. But now . . .'

His heart sank as he realised he truly did believe it. What kind of life would that make for his son?

'Corlas,' said Fahren softly, putting a hand on his shoulder. 'I think you and I should go back into the Halls and have a long talk.'

A Name in the Ice

Heron shuffled out of the throne room into the corridor, the hem of her tatty grey skirt dragging behind her. Papery pale and pockmarked skin stretched over her creaking bones, and her flesh sagged in wrinkled bags. Her long grey hair ran in a ponytail down to the small of her back, when she wasn't clutching it to her chest and running her fingers through it. She was old now, very tired, and sometimes she went up to the higher balconies encircling the bulbous head of Skygrip to think about stepping off. She never had the courage, and there was always the possibility she'd be caught by a Graka patrol before she hit the bottom. Battu would not have been pleased.

All she'd wanted was to retire into a dark hole and drink herself to death. Instead the Shadowdreamer had forced her back to service. Now all she drank was what she could pilfer from the kitchens. The Golgoleth Ghost at the front entrance wouldn't let her leave the castle, and all other exits were guarded too. In her younger days escape would have been easier. Now she couldn't even escape sobriety.

It had been a horrible day when she'd woken up back in Skygrip, six years ago now. Her head pounding, her eye red-rimmed, she had stared about the bed chamber without memory of how she'd come there. To her dismay she could find no bottle to quell her cramps and shaking limbs. Curled into a wretched ball, soaking the sheets cold with sweat, she had lain in a disoriented haze for what seemed like hours. Eventually she'd managed to summon enough of her once formidable power to soothe the aching, and sat up woozily on the bed. She had stumbled to the door, only to find it locked.

Some time later the door had opened. Two female Grey Goblins had entered, carrying jugs of water which they emptied into a rusted bath in the corner. They had 'helped' Heron into the water, informing her that the First Slave wanted her clean before she was taken before Battu. Neither of them had answers to her questions. They'd left her feeling clean outside and rotten within, like an apple with a maggot in its heart. They didn't lock the door behind them, but it had seemed best to stay put. Tyrellan arrived and told her what was expected of her. He made her drink soup, and she'd managed to keep it down. The whole ordeal had been so terrible and foggy that she'd barely noticed the butterfly flapping around the room, and following Tyrellan as he led her to Battu.

The dark lord had been irritated to find her so reduced. Her once formidable power had been disused for years and her mind was still half-pickled. Battu had given her a week to sharpen up, not specifying what would happen if she failed. She thought she could guess. Tyrellan had watched her closely during that week. She had no access to drink, but he forced her to eat and walk. Her power grew again, more quickly than she would have believed. When she next came before Battu, she was more like the tutor he remembered from his youth. He had taken her to see the child she was to watch over and, eventually, teach. She'd been given chambers adjoining the boy's, and warned not to die from old age, else Battu would be forced to bring her back. If she was to escape him in death, her body would need to be destroyed beyond recognition, but she feared to fall, or burn in flames, and so she served.

As she retreated from the throne room, dead Shadowdreamers stared at her from their shadowy alcoves. She knew their faces well – not only had she passed them many times in her younger days, now her slow trudge gave her time to study them whenever she passed. There was Rassid, a strong-jawed Arabodedas, a great leader by history's account. Nim'rahl, a Black Goblin, her stone hair spilling from the pedestal down to the floor, who had presided over the genocide of the Green Goblins. Wide-eyed Timma, the trickster, who had caused an internal war in Kainordas through an elaborate deception. Skench the Builder, one of the few Graka Shadowdreamers, who had earned a reputation for fairness to all races, funding developments in each major city without prejudice. Telnuwind, a beautiful Arabodedas who had loved her land and whose people had loved her. And on, and more. Despite what they had in common, each was different from the last.

Heron wondered why she'd bothered to be nervous about approaching Battu. She had requested to speak to him about the boy, who had been asking to be told the story of his parents. Battu had displayed the same lack of interest he always did. She remembered well

the only other time she'd approached him uninvited to
discuss the child.

She had entered the throne room to find Battu standing
with his back to the long window, talking to Tyrellan.
Their gazes had turned to her as she approached.

'Yes?' Battu said without preamble.

'Lord Battu,' she'd said, bowing. 'I come concerning
the boy.'

'Yes, yes, Turry said. What is it?'

Heron raised her head. 'I feel it is time,' she said slowly,
'to consider his name. Not knowing whether my lord had
something in mind, I come seeking his wishes.'

Battu blinked. 'A name?' he said. 'Oh, yes. I suppose
he should have one.'

Tyrellan had shifted his stance, clawed hands
disappearing behind his back. 'An important matter,' he
said. 'It is a name the whole world will soon know.'

'Yes,' said Battu. 'It must be something befitting.'
He'd seemed to brighten and, in a voice that was almost
jolly, said, 'I'm sure you'll think of something, Heron. It
will give you a diversion as you while away the hours.
Let me know what you come up with and we shall see
if I approve. You may go.'

Heron had wondered why she was surprised. 'As
you say, my lord.'

She thought she saw Tyrellan glancing sideways at his
master, though it was hard to tell with his black eyes.
Still, it wasn't unexpected when he caught up with her
in the corridor. She'd noticed that the First Slave took a
very personal interest in the raising of the child.

'I take it my lord Tyrellan does not share his master's indifference to the naming of the boy?' she said, not turning to face him.

'Bite your tongue or I will bite it for you,' Tyrellan said. 'The Shadowdreamer does not tolerate such bold words.'

'And what if he did hear? He's already made it known that death is not an escape for me. And any other punishment he might inflict on this old body would be as good as death.'

'You are not as stupid as you sound,' said Tyrellan. 'There are many forms of punishment as you well know – why else do you linger here?'

Heron hoped she'd stopped shock from registering on her face.

'Oh, yes,' Tyrellan went on, reaching out a claw to scrape some lichen from the wall. 'Don't think I cannot see what is in your heart. You *would* escape that way, if you could. But to escape the Shadowdreamer in death, you must destroy your body beyond hope of being raised again. You would shatter it, then, from the parapets of Skygrip? Or maybe burn it? But you fear that, don't you? Fear the fall. Fear the pain of fire. You have no courage beyond a deadly herb brewed in a cup, a peaceful descent into sleep. Such an end would leave your body intact though, would it not?'

Heron returned his flat stare. 'It would. But there are other ways, Tyrellan. What makes you think I cannot fashion a spell for myself? Fire in the belly, as it were. An explosion from within, instant and painless, with nothing left behind but dust. Do you imagine that is beyond me?'

Tyrellan bared his fangs in a humourless smile. 'Then perhaps you are wiser than I take you for and know that the Dark Gods do not take kindly to those who return to them without fulfilling their obligations in life. If this boy has been born to carry out their will, they will be watching closely. Such knowledge will bind you to your purpose more strongly than any threat of Battu's. Otherwise you need the courage to face not only death, but what comes after, and you do not have either. You may return to the balconies freely, Heron, and continue to romanticise your own demise. I'm glad we had this talk. I will not fear for you any more.'

Beneath her anger, Heron felt sick.

They had arrived at the boy's chamber. It was large and circular, cut through with shafts of dim light from holes in the roof high above. Its lumpy stone walls were clear of adornment, besides a large iceplace in which glowed a slowly melting block. In the centre of the room stood a wooden cot, to which Heron and Tyrellan walked.

'His name,' said Tyrellan, looking down on the boy, 'is not something to be shrugged off lightly.'

Heron caught something in the goblin's gaze. Was it . . . ? No, impossible. Tyrellan was not *fond* of anything.

'What do you suggest?' she said.

It surprised her that he actually had some ideas. He muttered them as if self-conscious, and after a while she began to offer her own suggestions. He listened, seeming to test the weight of each one in his mind. Soon they were throwing names back and forth across the crib like some parody of parents.

A resounding crack echoed through the chamber, making them both start. The glow from the iceplace became brighter, blue light dancing across the walls. They turned to stare as fine threads of dark blue energy coalesced within the block, concentrating within the hairline split that had appeared through its centre. The threads twisted to form letters, electric and alive, and brief. The crack grew and the ice fell apart, letters gone.

'The gods,' Tyrellan had murmured in wonderment, 'take an interest.'

Suddenly Heron felt the cold touch of steel at her throat. 'You will not tell Battu of this!' Tyrellan hissed through pointed fangs, a strange gleam in his eyes. 'You tell him the name, but not its origin. Do you understand? You will never speak of this to anyone!'

'As you say, First Slave!' she'd choked, confused. What did Tyrellan fear? Would not Battu be pleased?

Tyrellan had pushed her away, giving her a hard look as though making up his mind whether or not to end her right then.

'I will not need the courage to jump from a high balcony if I have a dagger through my throat,' she muttered.

He'd scowled and left the room.

Heron had gripped the side of the cot to steady herself and looked down upon the baby.

Losara.

Heron entered Losara's chamber. It held an old cupboard full of knotholes, a low flat bed in the centre, a table at which Heron and Losara ate their meals in high-backed chairs, a board of slate against a wall where Heron drew with chalk when she taught him, and ice glowing in the iceplace. The few small oddments Losara had found for himself barely made an impression in the space.

It took her a moment to spot the boy. He was sitting half-submerged in the shadows that ringed the edges of the room. Naked and cross-legged with his back to her, he was sliding his hands along the stone floor. She raised a hand to her mouth when she realised that, as he withdrew his hands, the shadow came too, like melted toffee sticking to his fingers. Losara cocked his head to watch as it drained back through his fingers, though some flecks remained trapped under his fingernails. She had already guessed he had an affinity with shadows, but this, at such an early age?

The boy turned, regarding her with large, dark eyes.

'Hello, Losara,' she said.

Without speaking, he got up and padded over to the bed, spots of shadow shaking free of him to fly back to the edges of the room. He climbed up and sat, watching her, then patted the bed next to him. She smiled; despite his being the cause of her internment, she had grown fond of the boy. She sat, and he reached out to touch her hand.

A quiet child, he was strangely affectionate towards her – and, she had realised with some surprise, towards Tyrellan – whether it was a soft touch in greeting, or the gift of some small thing he'd found, or the look of acceptance in his beautiful ivory face. Although he rarely smiled, his face was full of expression: curiosity, compassion, sometimes something unrecognisable. His brown eyes had become almost as dark as the black of his pupils, and when he looked out from under his silky blue fringe, it was a gaze that seemed both full of depth and capable of seeing depth in what it looked upon. In a world of misery, he was the one thing that brought her comfort.

'What were you doing there?' she asked.

'Playing,' said Losara. He waggled his fingers at her.

'How long have you been able to do that?'

Losara looked at her as if the question didn't make sense. 'Where are my mother and father?' he asked instead, just as he had done that morning. Then he added, in a very un-childlike manner, 'I'll learn nothing else till I learn of this.'

She was taken aback by the command in his voice, and glad Battu had given her leave to tell him. She began to recount the story of his birth, on a stormy night six years past. She told it as best she could, not leaving out anything to do with the prophecy. When she finished, she expected questions, but the boy seemed to take the tale of his origins with calm acceptance. He stared into the distance with a thoughtful expression.

'Losara?' she said. 'Do you understand what I've told you?'

'Yes,' he said quietly.

'What are you thinking about?'

'Everything,' he said, then looked at her. 'My father, maybe. Does he love me?'

Heron faltered. It wasn't the first question she'd expected. 'I suppose so,' she said.

'But he hasn't seen me since I was born,' said Losara.

'That doesn't matter. There is a special bond amongst families.'

'Should I love him, then?' said Losara. 'I don't know him. He went to the Open Halls to look for the other part of me. Why doesn't he like this part?'

'My dear, I'm not sure he knows you even exist,' said Heron.

'Oh. But you said you supposed that he loved me. How could he if he doesn't know about me?'

'I . . . guess I meant he would if he did,' said Heron lamely.

'Sons are meant to be with their fathers,' said Losara. 'But if he doesn't know about me, maybe he's all right. I suppose I don't have to worry about him.'

Heron faltered again. Losara didn't have to worry *about* his father? He was asking these questions out of concern for the man, not for himself?

'I would like to meet him though,' Losara went on. 'One day.'

'Yes,' said Heron meekly. 'That would be nice.'

'Nice,' repeated Losara, as if testing out the word. There was a knock at the door. 'Tyrellan,' he said. He always seemed to know who was at the door. As Tyrellan entered, Losara slid off the bed. 'Hello, Tyrellan.'

'Hello, young master,' said Tyrellan stiffly.

'Hello, Tyrellan's butterfly,' said Losara.

Tyrellan gritted his teeth. 'Did Heron tell you about your birth?'

'Yes,' said Losara.

'And you are . . .' Tyrellan shifted his stance. 'Do you feel . . . confused?'

'Oh, no. Heron told it very well.'

'But . . . about what you must do. What you will be. It is a large task. An important task.'

'I guess that's why Heron is teaching me as much as she can,' said Losara. 'Everything makes more sense now.'

'I see,' said Tyrellan, his eyes shining strangely.

He glanced at Heron, and Heron couldn't help it – she shrugged. Losara reached out to tug Tyrellan on his trousers, not letting go when Tyrellan glanced down at his little hand.

'Yes?' said the goblin.

'Do you have a father?'

'I did.'

'What happened to him?'

'I killed him,' said Tyrellan, then blinked.

Heron didn't think he would have admitted that had he thought about it, but the boy seemed to bring out an honesty in the First Slave not normally seen. Maybe it was his innocent directness.

'Why?' asked Losara.

'He didn't want me to join the military,' said Tyrellan. 'He was a farmer.' The word twisted his lips. 'He wished me to stay on the farm, sought to stop me leaving and serving the shadow.'

'So you left your father to be what you needed to be?'

'Yes.'

'Then I guess we're the same,' said Losara, giving him a rare smile.

Tyrellan's snarl dropped instantly from his face; Heron had never seen him look so openly surprised. He covered it quickly, glaring at her with a hard look that dared her to remember.

'I have matters to attend to,' he said. 'Losara . . . Heron.' With that he turned and marched from the room.

'Well,' said Losara, 'it seems there are all kinds of fathers and sons.'

PART TWO

The Growing Powers

I am told that the time during which I grew up was uncharacteristically peaceful. Kainordas and Fenvarrow each knew that the other had a blue-haired boy, and each waited for theirs to turn into whatever it was he was destined to. In the meantime, strength was to be conserved.

The main difference was that Fahren decided to keep my presence a secret, giving the folk of Kainordas much less to hope for. They knew that Fenvarrow possessed a child of power, and believed it was the only child, which made them afraid the war was already lost. I'll always consider it a mistake that Fahren allowed such a dour mood to permeate, whatever his reasoning might have been. Although I shouldn't complain – it meant that when I was finally revealed, the people were all the happier to see me, all the more loyal to my cause. But I get ahead of myself.

As I grew, I began to feel some of the confusion that comes, you'll find, when your immortal soul has been torn in two. It wasn't pronounced yet, just beginning, gnawing away at my edges like a rat at a frozen corpse.

As if one does not have sufficient concerns merely from being eighteen years old.

Castle Captives

The blue hair that fell freely to his shoulders contrasted sharply with his porcelain skin, as did his eyebrows and eyelashes. He was slim of build, medium height, with a face that retained a soft boyishness. He wore a simple black robe, and under the fingernails of his smooth hands were trapped specks of shadow, which occasionally slipped free to zip back into whatever darkness was closest. He moved with a quiet grace, his bare footfalls making no noise on the stone, seeming to glide, and favouring areas where the shadows were deepest.

It was a long journey from the top of Skygrip to the bottom. The castle was almost immense enough to be considered a city in its own right. Here and there magical portal doors shortened the distance between points, but Losara avoided them to enjoy the walk instead. There were corridors so narrow that only one man could walk them at a time, which turned into wide pathways lined with carvings before constricting again. Passages could be straight, bent, or twisted like the insides of a writhing snake. In some places light was non-existent, in others nuggets of ice glowed softly in recesses along the walls, and in others windows or skylights let in the cold grey day. Sometimes the air blew sharp and fresh, sometimes old and stagnant. Walls were bumpy or smooth, crumbly or hard. There was no uniformity to any of it.

At one point he stopped to listen to two female Grey Goblins, who didn't notice his wafting presence. They intrigued him with their chatter, these simple creatures whose greatest concern was keeping abreast of washroom gossip.

Eventually he reached Skygrip's main entrance cavern. Skirting the edges of the circular chamber beneath the gaze of towering statues, he stopped inside the open double doors. Outside in the morning mist, figures moved about the castle fortifications. None came near the entrance unless they had to. Even the guards posted there tended to keep well forward of the doors. Losara could see them down the path: four Black Goblins who carried horns in case they needed to sound the alarm. Their breath steamed in the cold air, exaggerated by brittleleaf smoke.

Losara sank down into the archway. From somewhere came the smell of baking bread, which made him realise he was hungry. He produced a strip of meat from his robe, unwrapping the cloth that bound it. He chewed slowly, sucking the juices through his teeth. Heron had told him that in Kainordas it was common practice to cook meat. He'd enjoyed cooked meat on occasion, mostly for its ability to soak up other flavours, but he wondered why anyone would ritually burn all the blood and nutrients away. Those were the things that connected you most with what you ate, that made you realise it was flesh, that struck a primal chord.

'Me wonders who dares sit there eating such treats in front of Grimra.'

Losara tore a piece from the meat and tossed it up into the archway. The air around it thickened, there was an indistinct flash of white, and the meat disappeared. Losara continued to munch on the remaining piece.

'Not even a full bite for Grimra,' came the voice. It floated, sometimes high in the arch, sometimes next to Losara's ear, dry and hollow. 'Not big enough to get stuck in his teeth.'

'Haven't they fed you yet?' asked Losara.

'Theys be late,' said the voice. 'Or else Grimra is forgotten. If this be so, perhaps he takes a guard from up the path. Theys thinking Grimra cannot reach them way on up the path.' The air swirled and there was another flash of white. 'Theys be wrong.'

'I wouldn't take any more guards, hungry ghost,' said Losara. 'Tyrellan won't approve.'

At Tyrellan's name Grimra hissed, and for a moment Losara saw monstrous claws shining in the light. 'Perhaps Grimra eats Tyrellan then, next time he comes this way.'

'Only if you wish your amulet smashed,' said Losara.

This sent Grimra into a fury, churning the air so it rustled Losara's hair. Losara waited patiently as the Golgoleth Ghost worked off his anger. The entrance guards glanced back at the commotion, but quickly looked away again. Losara wondered if it was the angry ghost who made them uneasy, or him.

The air calmed, and some moments passed in silence. 'Grimra be glad Losara visits today,' said the ghost eventually.

Losara smiled. 'Why is that?'

The ghost didn't respond right away. It seemed to Losara that he was thinking. 'Grimra be glad whenever Losara visits,' Grimra concluded.

It had been three years before that Losara had first met this strange companion. Probably the ghost was his only real friend. As Battu's protégé, he was feared by all and consequently friends were hard to come by. The fact that the first thing Grimra had offered to do upon meeting him was slice his head off and drink the blood from his neck like wine from a glass made him stand out from the crowd. The only other people who spoke to Losara were Heron, who was miserable, Tyrellan, who was busy, and of course Battu himself, with whom his relationship was confusing. One moment Battu would be patiently guiding him through some basic magic; the next Losara would be lying dazed on the other side of the room with Battu shouting about some instruction he'd failed to follow. Often Battu would appear kindly towards him, with a voice calm and deep, a steady hand upon his shoulder. Yet for all the apparent goodwill, Losara had never felt any real love from the man.

The question was *why*? Why did a man as powerful as Battu care what Losara thought? The question had first occurred to him when he was six, the same day Heron had told him of the events surrounding his birth. Shortly after that, Battu had summoned him to the throne room.

Battu had turned from the long window. 'Ah, my boy,' he'd said, his voice soft and carrying as if it wafted on the breeze. 'Come stand by me.'

Losara went.

'Heron has told you about your birth?'

'Yes, master.'

'Good, good. As your understanding increases, so must your education. Now, you know that I am called the Shadowdreamer, but do you know what that really means?'

'Heron told me,' said Losara.

Battu did not seem to hear. 'I rule the land, that much is simple, but a Shadowdreamer is more than just a ruler. I am the shadow's servant in this world, its conduit of influence. Even now I can feel the shape of the land where the shadow falls. I'm connected to the Cloud, which comes from deep beneath us in the earth and makes its way up through the castle walls. It's all around us, above and below. The power of Skygrip is mine to draw on, the Shadowdreamer's right and privilege. Are you understanding me?'

'Yes.'

Battu smiled. 'Yes what?'

'Master.'

'Good boy. Now come. I will show you the Cloud.'

Battu had led Losara to Skygrip's roof, from which the stream of black and grey vapour curled slowly upwards. 'The Breath of the Cloud,' he announced. 'A gateway, for those gifted enough to survive it.'

'Where to, master?' asked Losara.

'A place where you can see the shadows of past, present and future. Like all shadows, these can be shifting or uncertain. Hence what we see are nothing more than dreams, yet the dreams of the whole world.'

'Shadowdreams,' said Losara.

'Yes. With the Cloud running throughout Skygrip, there isn't a night that shadowdreams don't visit my sleep – but they are strongest here, between earth and sky. Would you like to see?'

'Yes,' Losara had whispered, fascinated. 'Master,' he added quickly.

'Then come,' said Battu, leading Losara to stand before the Breath.

Losara had reached out to touch it, but Battu seized his hand. 'Stupid boy! You do not have the skill to do this by yourself!' Losara cried out at the Shadowdreamer's grip and Battu relaxed it. 'You must hold my hand as we go in,' he said. 'Don't try this by yourself, until I tell you otherwise. Are you ready?'

Losara nodded. Holding the boy's pale little hand in his own, Battu led him into the Cloud.

A fine sheet of moisture coated Losara instantly. He blinked, but couldn't see. Darkness moved against his skin like slow wind. It didn't occur to him to be afraid; instead, wonder filled him. So *this* was where the dreams came from. He'd always had them, as far back as he could remember in his short life. He'd always known them for what they were – reflections, half-truths, memories, possibilities, dim and half-remembered. How he'd known, exactly, did not seem to matter. Had someone told him, right at the beginning? He had an impression of whiskers and scales.

From somewhere beside him came Battu's voice. 'Breathe it in, boy.'

Losara breathed, and darkness suffused his body and mind. A moment later he could no longer feel his physical form, but seemed to float without a body. He spun, disoriented, but the presence of Battu hovered nearby, holding him steady against the tumbling eddies.

Somewhere Losara heard a tumultuous noise, far away yet all around, there, but impossible to listen to.

Do you hear that? came Battu's thought.

Yes.

It's the sound of the world from beginning to end. Don't listen too hard or you will be lost. Just drift.

A heady ecstasy coursed through Losara. Images rose out of the void to catch him, like bubbles. He shadowdreamed . . .

. . . he's older now, sailing alone across black waters. Ahead is darkness like a great cave mouth swallowing the sea. He rows towards it, the splashing of his oars the only sound . . .

. . . sharks are swimming side by side as they hurry after prey. One male leads, the biggest of the pack. A hunted serpent rounds on the male, flaring spiked frill and baring fangs. The male attacks, all snapping jaws and swiping tail, and soon the serpent is dead. The big male gorges himself on bands of its flesh while the other sharks circle uneasily. Their leader is strong, but he takes more than he needs, and he shares his mind with another . . .

. . . an old mage with golden hair stands above a gravestone, incanting uneasily, performing a spell that makes him afraid . . .

. . . a blond woman with pointed ears runs through a forest into a clearing. A man is there, tall and bare-chested, chopping wood with a huge axe. He drops the tool when he sees her and she runs happily into his arms. He swings her around, laughing . . .

. . . the city of the Graka, high in the Bentemoth Mountains where the air is thin and the temperature freezing. Graka emerge from caves onto stone platforms,

four of them carrying a casket between them, beating their wings to rise into the sky . . .

. . . a little boy with black hair runs through dry mud streets. Behind him come three older boys, chasing him with sticks . . .

. . . Battu, now the Shadowdreamer's Apprentice, raises a hand and points. Three men begin screaming, and die painfully . . .

. . . And then a scene of the present, of himself, of his other self . . .

Bel bounded down the Open Tower staircase three steps at a time. At six years old he was physically strong in a way that Losara had never been. His face was round and friendly with some slight freckling on his nose. His Sprite eyes were amber flecked with gold, sparkling infectiously. Losara had no such eyes, and circled closer with interest.

Bel ran to a log house, away a bit off the path between the trees. Was that where he lived? There were two other houses close by, and a leather ball lay on the grass. 'Hiza?' called out Bel. 'Vrymus! Are you not here, you lazy louts?' He kicked the ball.

He calls out to friends, thought Losara. Were there other families living in those houses? He pondered what it would be like to have friends his own age.

Bel ran on, until he spied another boy, who was sitting beneath a bush tugging up grass. 'Hello, Lyndal!' he said, jogging up. 'Having fun?'

Lyndal, slightly younger, regarded Bel suspiciously. 'No.'

Bel kneeled and tore up a clump of grass. He considered his handiwork briefly, then sprinkled the tufts on Lyndal's shoes. 'You're right,' he said. 'This isn't fun. Have you seen Hiza or Vrymus?'

'No,' said Lyndal, brushing the grass off his feet.

'Why are you so sour?' said Bel. He leaned closer, staring intently into Lyndal's eyes. Lyndal shifted uncomfortably.

'I'm not,' he said. 'Why don't you go away? I'm busy.'

Bel glanced at the severed grass, his fingers playing over it idly. Then he smacked Lyndal in the knee.

'Ow! What was that for?'

'Sorry,' Bel said jovially, standing up. 'Shouldn't kill the grass, Lyndal! But I guess we didn't all get the evil taken out of us when we were born.'

'What?'

'Never mind,' said Bel.

Losara felt a moment of sickness. Bel did know about him, but thought that he was evil. Was that true? Had Losara been a canker best removed?

Bel ran through scattered trees towards a high hedge. Children weren't allowed on the barracks grounds without an adult, but Bel and his comrades sometimes came here to climb a gnarled tree that grew next to the hedge. As he reached it he heard the clang of practice blades from the other side. He swung himself into the tree, eager to see the fighting. About eight paces up he found a branch well hidden within the foliage, which held a good view of the training ground.

A large man was advancing on a spotty youth, sixteen at most, batting his sword away while barking commands. Watching were a group of ten or so students.

One of them, Losara noted with interest, was a Saurian. The creature stood man-height but had lizard-like features and watched the fight through double-lidded eyes. It was a Ryoshi Saurian, Losara knew from his lessons. Not as dangerous as a Syanti Saurian, the Ryoshi's snake-like cousin.

Reptiles, thought Losara. *They need the sun. If the Cloud extended as far as their deserts, would they all die?*

The big man launched another attack and his student rallied, forcing him back a step. Some of the class gave encouraging claps. The man called for the lad to press forward with his attack – but it was too slow in coming. The man raised his sword to the boy's chest and the fight was over.

Bel shifted his weight, rustling the branch, and a few leaves shook loose. The man glanced up and Bel froze, not wishing to give away his secret vantage. The man seemed to smile a moment, then turned his attention back to his lesson. He called up another student, a stout young woman who walked with a roll to her shoulders and a proud air. She bowed to the man and a new bout began. She was a better fighter than her predecessor and the taskmaster laughed heartily as she forced him back under flashing whirls of dull metal. He announced he was going to try to disarm her and her expression grew more determined. It turned to surprise a moment later as, with a sudden lunge, the man jabbed his sword under the curved hilt of hers and flipped it from her hand. It spun up into the air and went sailing over the hedge, sticking into the ground at the base of Bel's tree.

'You have good technique, Gredda,' the man rumbled, 'but your grip requires attention.' The rest of the class laughed and the girl flushed angrily. The man placed a hand on her shoulder. 'Do not worry. You fight well. Now let us retrieve your sword.'

He turned towards the tree and seemed to look right at Bel. 'Ho, the tree!' he called.

Bel grinned. 'Ho, the ground!' he called back.

'Would you return Gredda's sword to her, young lurker?'

Bel swung from the branch to hang in plain view. 'With pleasure!'

'Oho!' said the man. 'I might have known!'

As Bel dropped to the ground to grab the sword and go running around the long way, Losara simply drifted over the hedge.

The man turned to his students. 'That is the end of lessons for today,' he announced. 'Gredda, wait for your sword. The rest may leave.'

The group broke up in different directions as Bel arrived, panting. 'Your sword, m'lady,' he said, going down on one knee and extending the sword towards Gredda. She snatched it back and strode off huffily. Then the gate soldier arrived behind Bel, red and breathing hard.

'I'm sorry, Taskmaster Corlas,' the soldier puffed. 'He ran through the gate before I could stop him!'

'Because you were asleep at your post!' piped Bel.

The soldier went even redder, and not from exertion. 'Why, you little cur! I ought to –'

'Be calm, soldier,' Corlas said. 'The boy is here by my leave. Return to your nap . . . I mean post.' He winked at Bel, who smirked.

'Right, sir,' said the soldier suspiciously, and turned with a frown to trudge back to the gate.

Corlas looked down at Bel. 'Your grip on Gredda's sword looked good,' he said. 'As if someone had taught you. But I know that *I* have never put a sword into your hands, my very young son.'

Son, thought Losara. *This man is Bel's father. My father.*

'The Throne once showed me how a sword is carried,' said Bel.

'Did he now?' Corlas's eyes narrowed slightly. 'Well, did you know that I once beat the Throne in a joust?'

Bel shook his head.

'I'd be careful who you get your advice from,' said Corlas, and ruffled Bel's hair. 'I am not supposed to teach one so young, but if the Throne himself deems you ready . . . Well, would you like to learn what to do with a sword once you can grip it?'

Bel's eyes shone, and Corlas chuckled.

Together they went to the armoury where, with the aid of an amused armourer, they found a wooden sword small enough for Bel to practise with. Back on the training field, Corlas began to teach the basics of swordplay. The boy learned quickly and well, seeming to have an instant affinity with the weapon. For hours they practised, neither growing tired. As the sun crossed the sky above, Losara wondered if there had ever been a deadlier six-year-old.

Yet I have no love for the blade, he thought. *Was I supposed to?*

The dream took him suddenly elsewhere, to a reedy river where frogs chirped, then a deep wood full of skeletal trees, then a mountain range on the edge of the world where rays from the rising sun shone between peaks like a bridge . . . Scene after scene came, flashing one after the other, blending into each other. The rush became overpowering and he reeled in the dark, his mind beginning to shred under the onslaught of *everything*.

A force had seized and contained him, halting his wild spinning. For a moment he felt squashed, then realised it was because he was inside his own body again. It was falling to the ground. He felt arms catch him, lift him and carry him out of the Breath. Looking up he saw Battu, with eyes like wells. He wheezed as air replaced the darkness in his lungs.

'You spread too thin,' said Battu gruffly. 'There is only so much one mind can take.' He kneeled by the gasping boy. 'This is why I was there with you, why you must never go into the Cloud by yourself. Rest a moment, boy.'

Losara did as he was told, quietly pondering what he had seen. Away in Kainordas, his father taught his other self and did it purely out of love. Meanwhile, he had the Shadowdreamer as a teacher. Battu wasn't his real father, yet he had taken Losara to raise as his own.

Why? he had wondered that day, for the first time.

The answer came to him on his twelfth birthday, when Battu had held a dinner for him and Heron.

'Try these, boy,' Battu had said, grinning sharkishly and sliding a bowl of quivering lumps across the table. 'Marinated anemones. Have to be served fresh. I sent a whelkling on a special trip to Afei Edres just for these!'

Losara was already full, but there seemed no end to Battu's appetite or his enthusiasm for seafood. Losara spooned a blob onto his plate and, with Battu watching intently, bit into it. The jellied flesh sliced cleanly into smaller pieces that slipped around his mouth, filling it with a briny taste. Losara found the meat unappealing, but he ate the whole thing.

'A delicacy, master,' he said.

'Have more,' said Battu.

'I am quite full, master.'

Battu scowled and shoved a whole anemone into his mouth. 'These are hard to come by, boy. I suggest you enjoy them while you have the chance. Not every day is your birthday. You may indulge yourself, I will not think less of you.'

Losara thought it best to eat another anemone, though he was careful to take more time with this one.

'Good,' said Battu. 'If you'd been brought up in that foxy little wood I rescued you from, there'd be no fine food like this on the table. You remember that.'

'Yes, master.'

Battu grew annoyed at this. 'What's wrong, boy? Is this meal not enough for you?'

Losara was confused by the outburst. He'd agreed with Battu, hadn't he? 'The meal is very nice, my lord,' he tried.

Battu visibly tried to relax his features, and pushed another bowl across the table. 'Spiced beef,' he said.

Losara dutifully took a handful of strips and tried to appear enthusiastic about forcing them down. The Shadowdreamer had something hungry in his gaze that had nothing to do with food. It struck Losara that while Battu didn't actually love him, the dark lord still sought Losara's love. Why would that be? Why would the Shadowdreamer seek such a thing from a young boy?

Loyalty was the answer. Battu was trying to raise Losara loyal, which meant making Losara love him. Everything became clear. Whenever Battu had been 'nice', Losara now realised it was for a purpose. Whenever Battu attempted to appear 'fatherly', he was motivated by his own concerns. Battu had grown angry now because Losara had given him an agreeable 'Yes, master' when he wanted adulation, not meek compliance.

'Wonderful,' Losara said, slurping noisily on the beef. 'Thank you, Father – I mean master.' He feigned concern over the slip, but Battu seemed extremely pleased.

With the mystery of the fatherly guise solved, Losara found the tyrant incarnation of Battu even more troubling. While most would be moved beyond terror at the slightest chance they'd displeased the dark lord, the trouble for Losara was that he did *not* fear him. Battu put Losara in mind of a snake that needed to be handled with utmost care lest it lash out in anger. Even through Battu's loudest tirades and harshest punishments, Losara had never truly been stirred. He'd learned to feign fear, especially if Battu was in a punishing mood, for he took no pleasure in pain and did what he could to avoid it. He often wondered what he'd lost in his division from Bel. Perhaps his ability to feel fear had been affected?

After careful consideration, he decided that was not the case. He knew what it was to be afraid, it was just that the dark lord did not inspire it in him. The punishments, though unpleasant, were petty and irrational and Losara could not respect them.

It was all quite confusing.

～

'Has Losara news?' asked Grimra, bringing him back to the present. 'Any enemies for Grimra to eat as they pass under his archway?'

'No, Grimra. Though perhaps soon enough. Battu is presenting me at the next meeting of the Shadow Council as his Apprentice.'

'What be "apprentice"?'

'An official title to acknowledge what I am already, but more than that. To be named Apprentice in front of the council is to be given a silent title as well.'

'What be the silent title?'

'Successor.' Losara stared into the distance. 'The Apprentice is marked to follow his master into rule. And he must also journey across the Black Sea. Apprentice can be a dangerous title to hold.'

'Grimra sees. Your shadow grows long.' A single claw the length of a sword materialised in front of Losara. 'Remember,' said the Golgoleth, 'enemies for Losara can be treats for Grimra.'

'Most gracious, greedy ghost.'

The claw faded. 'Do you be worried?'

'No. I am . . .'

Losara fell silent. How *did* he feel about the impending events? He knew there were many emotions another might experience – anxiety, fear, confidence – but for him, going before the council stirred up no more excitement than the prospect of a morning bath.

A high-pitched wail interrupted his thoughts. Behind him in the cavern, four Black Goblins were dragging a caterwauling Vortharg in manacles. Spittle oozed from her rubbery lips, spraying her tusks as she cried out in misery. She railed against the guards, trying to spring away on bandy legs. The leader lost patience and cracked her across the skull with his sword hilt.

'Me thinks it be dinnertime,' said Grimra.

The guards arrived at the doors, coming to an abrupt stop when they saw Losara sitting in the arch.

'Master Losara,' said the leader, bowing his head as the others watched with wary black eyes. Losara knew they were uneasy to stumble across him. It was a common theme. 'Er . . .' said the leader, unsure of how to proceed. Though Losara had no official title yet, most treated him with deference. 'Permission to feed the Golgoleth, sir?'

Losara rose smoothly to his feet. 'What is the Vortharg's crime?' he asked.

'Thievery, sir,' replied the leader. Losara waited long enough for him to realise something further was required. 'Er . . . she was a worker in the nursery, sir. Taking creeper saplings she was, to sell them on down in Mankow.'

Losara raised a blue eyebrow. 'A dangerous game, stealing from the Shadowdreamer.'

'Yessir.'

'You may continue. I would not stand between the Golgoleth and a meal.'

The leader nodded, and the guards dumped the groaning Vortharg in the middle of the archway. They all bowed to Losara.

'Permission to carry on, sir?'

'On your way.'

The goblins left gratefully.

Grimra drifted close to Losara's ear. 'Passed out she is,' the ghost whispered. 'Hungry as me be, me prefer meals awake!'

'I'll leave you two alone,' said Losara.

There was no response as he walked away and he knew the ghost was concentrating on its food. Glancing back, he saw blade-like claws hanging above the stirring Vortharg, working the air impatiently as if they already shredded flesh. A glimmer of a long-fanged grin appeared, insubstantial as smoke.

Losara kept walking. He had no desire to see Grimra toy with his food; he took no pleasure in the suffering of others. It wasn't that alone that turned his heels, however. There was something about the keeping and feeding of such an ancient spirit like a captive beast that didn't sit right with him either.

Losara arrived in the library corridor. Deep in the heart of the old mountain, he could sense the density of the rock around him. The statues along the corridor were amorphous and strange, like fonts of frozen lava. At the end of the passage was an intricately carved door covered with spidery runes. He opened it and made his way carefully down a steep set of steps, into the library. At the bottom, the stone floor was partially covered by a large rug that was frayed, faded and dirty. Rugs were a rarity in Fenvarrow, there being little liking for warm feet. He wondered how old it was. It felt prickly on his bare toes. Off to the side was a heavy oak desk. The librarian, Emepso, wasn't there at the moment, but scrolls and books strewn about were evidence of his continuing presence. All around, bookshelves stretched into the distance. The library had a low roof so it was hard to see how far back the shelves actually went. Hanging from the roof were steel lamps holding chunks of melting ice.

He moved between the shelves, pausing now and then to look over a book that caught his eye. Many were old, but had been imbued with preserving enchantments. Some of the truly ancient were kept sealed in glass cases, lest they collapse to dust in clumsy hands. Only the librarian had the key to those – not that keys were really a problem for Losara.

He heard a shuffling and Emepso appeared, clutching a couple of books to his brown robe. The little Arabodedas squinted suspiciously from under thick eyebrows. 'Master Losara,' he whined.

Losara moved past him and Emepso followed nervously at his heels.

'I thought perhaps you were one of those horrid goblin magelings,' chattered the librarian, wiping a wisp of grey hair from his forehead. 'No respect for the books, master. And there's nothing worse than goblin magic.'

'Is someone causing you trouble, Emepso?'

'No, master, no,' said Emepso quickly. 'Nothing I can't handle myself. Is there something I can help you with?'

'I'm meeting Heron here. Have you seen her?'

'No, master, no. But I'll tell her you're here if I do, master.'

Losara nodded, continuing on. During his infrequent visits to the library (Heron normally selected the texts for his study), he was always struck by how empty the place was. Only occasionally did he see another person here besides the librarian, and it made him wonder: with so many books and so few readers, how much forgotten knowledge was stowed away on these shelves? Perhaps the key to the destruction of Kainordas was in here somewhere, unread upon a faded scroll.

He came upon a clearing amongst the shelves. Another tattered rug covered the floor, with some tables and chairs standing atop it. He was surprised to see someone sitting at one of the tables. Her hair fell forward over her face to enclose her book in a prison of black tangled strands. From her mud skin he could tell she was a Mire Pixie, and he guessed her to be just over a pace tall. She wore a ragged green dress, low enough at the back for her crystalline wings to poke out and fold behind her. He remembered seeing her somewhere before. Years ago? In a dream?

He moved forward, deliberately making some sound as he went so as not to startle her if she looked up suddenly, but his effort had the opposite effect. Her head snapped up and he found himself staring into fearful blue eyes. She breathed in sharply as she realised who he was.

'Hello,' he said.

She flinched and he halted abruptly. She rose awkwardly to her feet, banging the chair as her legs pushed it backwards, and stumbled into a curtsy.

'Master,' she whispered. 'Forgive me. I didn't know you would need this space.'

She scrabbled for the book she'd been reading, closing it with a thump. Dust billowed out, causing her to give a little cough. Losara smiled at that, but she was already backing away.

'You needn't leave,' he said.

She moved into the shelves, hugging the oversized book to her breast with both arms. 'It's all right, thank you, I . . . I need to speak with the librarian anyway, master,' she stuttered.

Before he could say anything else, she'd disappeared amongst the books, her footsteps quickening as she escaped from view. He stood staring after her, sad that he'd frightened her away.

Later, after their lesson, Losara helped Heron back to their rooms. She clutched his arm tightly as they went, grateful for the support. She was over a hundred years old now, and she looked it.

'I saw a Mire Pixie in the library today,' said Losara.

'Did you, my dear?'

'I haven't seen many of them about the castle, besides the counsellors. I thought they preferred Swampwild.'

'They do, my boy, though some serve in the castle. It would have been a girl, I suspect, a few years older than you?'

'Yes, although I didn't see her face well. She was too busy curtsying.'

'Mmf. Sounds like Lalenda.'

'Lalenda.' He tried the name out.

'Yes. She's often found in the library. Battu's prophet, you know. She sees real things, not vagaries like in shadowdreams. She's the one who told Battu where you would be born. Poor little thing,' she added.

'Why?'

'At least when I served under Raker, I could come and go from the castle and experience something of youth! She hasn't been out since the day she was brought here.' Heron coughed wetly and spat phlegm onto the floor. 'No place for a Mire Pixie, that's for sure.' She coughed again. 'No place for an old woman either. Too many stairs.'

Losara patted her pasty hand. 'I'm sorry, Heron. I wish for your sake that you'd nothing left to teach me.'

'He should let me die,' said the old woman angrily. 'Look at me!' She pulled away, holding her arms aloft. They were like sticks. 'I should have died twenty years ago, curse him!'

Losara stared, seeing the misery in her faded old eyes. He felt pity for her, but she still had knowledge he needed. He took her hand and gently led her on.

Lalenda shut her door, breathing hard. She wasn't entirely sure what she was afraid of – there was little rumour around the castle about the blue-haired boy, for he kept mostly to himself. The reputation he had was built mainly on the prophecy – that surely a man who would destroy the light would be powerful and terrible indeed. One thing was certain – he was Battu's disciple, and if that made him anything like Battu, he was best avoided at all costs.

Still, as she sat on the bed clutching a book to her chest, she realised how much she had become invisible over the years, and how long it had been since anyone had really seen her, like he had.

Blade

'Whose damned chickens are these?' Bel demanded of the world in general. At his feet was a wire cage that had evidently fallen and sprung open. Chickens were running all over the street, getting in the way of carts and people.

'Settle down,' said Hiza, grinning at his companion's mock affront. 'They're only chickens.'

'That's right!' said Bel. 'They *are* only chickens! And I didn't spend years honing myself into a well-tuned, one-man fighting explosion in order to have to deal with damned chickens!' He flexed his arms. 'See these muscles? Do they look like the muscles of someone who spends his day picking up *chickens*?'

'Oh no!' A young woman darted between Bel and Hiza. She looked like a farm girl from one of Kadass's outlying areas. 'Excuse me, sirs! I'll have them all back in their cage in a moment!'

'These chickens,' Bel said, 'have been disturbing the peace.'

Hiza couldn't help but smirk.

'I'm sorry, sirs,' the girl said. 'If you'll just give me a minute . . .' She set about grabbing at bundles of feathers and stuffing them, struggling, back into the cage.

Bel gave Hiza a sideways glance as she pointed her posterior at them. 'I guess sometimes this work is rewarding,' he said.

A chicken flashed past him and he snapped his boot down on its tail. 'Here you go,' he said, handing the bird to the flustered girl. 'And next time, ma'am, make sure your cages are secure. Can't have these birds running about in front of carts and carriages.' He smiled and pushed back his curly brown hair. 'This your first time to Market Road?'

The farm girl seemed relieved by his friendlier manner. 'Well, no . . . my mother and I come every six months or so.'

'Ah,' said Bel, leaning casually against the stall. 'And where's your mother now?'

'She couldn't make it this time. She's in bed with a head cold.'

Bel's face became a picture of concern. 'What a pity.'

Hiza rolled his eyes. 'Come on, Muscles,' he said, grabbing Bel to pull him away. 'We can't stand around all day wasting our time on damned *chickens*, can we?'

The air of Kadass was thick and sluggish, muddying the constant murmur of activity – the shriek of children at play, the tapping of a blacksmith's hammer, the call of a street vendor, the music of a minstrel. There were parks and lakes where people swam, splashing and laughing. Traffic moved steadily along streets of orange stone between the city's neatly constructed buildings. On Market Road, the heat did nothing to slow the exchange of coin from hand to sweaty hand.

Bel and Hiza wandered the rows of stalls. At eighteen they were both new blades, seeing out their compulsory two years of service as peacekeepers. While many of Bel's friends had been posted elsewhere in Kainordas, he and Hiza had been assigned to Kadass. He would have preferred it if the choice had been his, instead of the precaution of keeping him safe behind the wards . . . but it wasn't so bad. Girls liked the uniform, and he enjoyed being able to swing his sword around sometimes. At least Naphur had made sure one of his friends remained with him. Hiza didn't realise there was a reason for their posting, as Corlas and Fahren had always advised Bel to keep his true identity a secret, unless he wanted to be treated very differently by everyone. Sometimes he wondered why he shouldn't be treated differently. Why shouldn't people know that their hero walked amongst them? At any rate, he was sure he wouldn't remain a simple blade for long. During training he had been a favoured student, and not just because his father was the great Corlas Corinas. Time and again he'd proved himself to be a master of weaponry and a charismatic leader. He didn't intend for that to be any different out here in the real world.

Somewhere, back the way they had come, a commotion broke out.

'If that's those chickens again . . .' said Bel.

'Thief!' someone shouted. 'Thief!'

The blades glanced at each other, then simultaneously broke into a run. It was a jeweller with a display of gaudy wares who was doing the shouting.

'Where'd they go?' Bel called to her.

'There!' she shouted. 'By the fountain!'

Ahead, a black-haired man was dodging between groups of pedestrians. Bel and Hiza pelted after him, calling out for people to stand aside. The thief tore down a side street. As they followed, a loose cobblestone shot out from underneath Hiza's foot and his ankle twisted with an audible snap. Bel skidded to a halt as Hiza cursed loudly.

'Keep going!' he muttered through gritted teeth. 'Don't let him get away!' Bel hesitated a moment, then started running again. 'By Arkus's great orange arse, this hurts!' shouted Hiza, and Bel knew the words were meant to spur him on, not bring him back.

The thief had disappeared, but Bel spotted a flight of steps up the back of a building with an open doorway at the top. From somewhere inside came the sound of glass smashing. He bounded up the stairs and through the door, into a low-roofed room full of crates. He guessed it was some kind of storage area for the tavern beneath. At the far end light came in through dusty windows, one of which was broken. Bel made his way between the crates, coming to the shattered window and poking his head through just in time to see a foot disappearing up onto the roof. He kicked out the remaining glass and clambered through the window, reaching up to grasp the edge of the roof. With a mighty heave he pulled himself up, flinging a leg over for purchase. On the roof, he took a moment to find his balance on the tiles then made for the peak. He saw the thief below him: a ratty little man with a gemstone pendant around his neck.

'Stay right there!' called Bel.

The thief screwed up his face in response, then stepped off the roof. Bel heard him land on wood and realised he'd jumped back down onto the stairs they'd both come up. He cursed and followed, coming down on the stairs as the thief was running up the alley. A few more paces and he would be back amongst the crowds, where he would easily disappear.

If I'm to bring down Fenvarrow, thought Bel, *I should be able to handle one thief.* He pulled out his boot knife and sent it flashing towards the thief, now some thirty paces away. It thudded into the man's thigh, bringing him down heavily. Bel trotted down the stairs, chuckling. *I'm impressive, no doubt about it. How many could make a shot like that?*

When he arrived, the thief was worming around on the ground, which made it difficult to retrieve the knife. 'Keep still, you rat-haired turd,' muttered Bel, cuffing the man over the head. He grabbed the knife and pulled it free, wiping the blade on the thief's shirt before sliding it back into his boot. He grabbed the little man by the collar and dragged him, protesting, back down the alley to Hiza. Hiza was propped up against a wall, being helped by a young couple who'd seen him fall. Apart from being pale, he contained his pain well. Bel dumped the thief unceremoniously on the cobblestones before him.

'How is it?' he asked.

Hiza winced. 'Broken, I think. Had worse as a boy, when at least I had gangly limbs to blame for such clumsiness.'

'You hear that, rat?' said Bel to the thief. 'My partner's injured because of you.' He kicked the thief in the ribs and the little man whimpered.

'Don't hurt me, sir! I ain't goin' nowhere!'

'How correct you are,' said Bel. He turned to the couple, who were looking on nervously, and shook his head. 'Some people just have to ruin it for the rest of us. Thanks for helping my partner.' He produced a gold coin from a leather purse. 'Take this, from Kainordas. If you would hurry and find a rider for us, you may tell them Bel Corinas said you're to have the same again.'

'Oh, no need to pay us, sir,' said the woman. 'We couldn't just leave your friend lying there.'

'Aye,' said the man. 'And we'll go and find a rider for you right away.'

'No, do take it,' said Bel, grasping the man's hand and pressing the coin into it. 'It isn't payment – it's thanks. Anyway, the Throne has plenty more.' He winked at the couple, who smiled. 'Please tell the rider we'll need a cart.'

The couple departed. Bel kneeled and took the pendant from around the thief's neck. He tossed it to Hiza.

'Pretty,' said Hiza, turning it in his hands.

'Not worth the trouble,' said Bel. 'Probably dyed glass.' Reaching down, he ripped cloth from the thief's shirt.

'Whatcha doin' now?' whined the thief.

'Trying to stop you bleeding, rat,' said Bel. 'Though Arkus knows why I'd be bothered.'

He wrapped the strip of cloth around the wound and pulled the knot tight. Again the thief cried out in pain, sickening Bel with how weak he was.

'Steady there,' said Hiza.

The fire faded from Bel's eyes and he shrugged. 'It has to be tight,' he said. 'To stop the flow.'

Bel sat alone in the Wayward Dog, staring into his mug. Normally he'd be having a drink with Hiza at the end of their shift, but Hiza would be in the Hospital of Arkus by now. At least that meant he had a friend in the Halls again. When he'd been assigned to Kadass, Hiza had moved his lodgings into the city. Bel, however, found himself ordered to remain in the barracks, where he was safer. He missed his old friends. There was still Hiza, but the rest of the gang had gone. The ring had left the ring leader and the Halls were much duller for it.

Sometimes he joined Corlas in teaching the younger students, where his sense of fun and fairness made him a popular addition to the class. The fairness came because he was conscious of the difference between him and his peers. Often he deliberately reined in his skill, having learned that no one liked to be outshone all the time. He knew he could beat them all anyway. Despite such distractions, he was beginning to feel trapped behind the ward stones, and had told Corlas as much. Corlas had said he understood better than Bel would ever know – whatever that meant – but he hadn't *done* anything about it.

There was a lot getting on his nerves of late. Sometimes he'd be walking along merrily then stop suddenly, feeling at a total loss for no discernible reason. Sometimes he heard echoes of strange thoughts or foreign emotions he could not quite grasp. They slipped away and he was left feeling disturbed, discordant. Often he thought about what he was destined to do, one day – but which day? When? Was he meant to sit around waiting until some event precipitated his greatness, or was he meant to go out and make it happen? No one had a good answer for him. They all told him to live his life, to try not to let it bother him – and yet they wouldn't even let him leave the Halls at an age when many young people went off to explore the world. He wondered vaguely about how his *other* self was faring, that dark slime that had dripped out of him all those years ago.

'Those muscles not strong enough to hold up the ends of your mouth, keeper?' came a woman's voice. 'You're staring at that beer as if it murdered your family.'

'Hmm?' he said, glancing up. And then both he and a strange girl he'd never seen before stared at each other in great surprise.

She wore a light green cloak with the hood back and dark green vestments underneath. Her nose was pointy and studded by a tiny emerald. Her forehead was high and proud, framed by red ringlets that escaped being pushed behind her mischievous little ears. She was a beautiful girl, but that wasn't why Bel stared; it was her eyes. They were green shot through with flecks of gold.

'Sprite . . .' he said.

'And you,' she replied.

Bel had to control an instinct to reach out and touch her, as if that would somehow prove she actually was a Sprite. He held out his hand, but forced himself to turn it into a gesture offering her the seat opposite. She sat, still staring.

'Did you . . . er . . .' Bel fumbled. Normally he was good at talking to women. He'd had practice: his mystical eyes and uniform had made sure of that. This time, for some reason, he felt odd and awkward.

'I was actually just coming over to tease you because you're a keeper,' she said suddenly, then seemed surprised at her words.

'Flattering,' he replied, though he didn't manage to inject any sarcasm.

'And also you looked so glum. But I didn't realise you were . . . I mean, I've never met anyone else who had Sprite in them. Oh, I've seen those poor children they cart around in the circus, but half the time they're the ringmaster's hatchlings with ears stuck on.'

'Well,' said Bel, 'I'm told we're rare. Not quite as rare as blue-haired babies, but rare nonetheless.' She looked confused and he waved the comment away. Searching quickly for something else, he found, 'So what work are you in, miss, to be in the habit of teasing keepers?'

'Oh,' she smiled for the first time, 'nothing I care to speak of. But I saw you chase down poor Jiggis before – quite an agile fellow, aren't you?'

'Jiggis?' said Bel. 'Oh, the rat who broke my partner's ankle.'

'Well, he didn't actually. It was your partner's ineptitude that did that.'

Bel felt his brow heat. 'I didn't notice you watching.'

'No,' she said. 'And you wouldn't have unless I wished it, unlike fools who snatch false gemstones in public. I had my own vantage. A lovely view, way up high.'

'Bold of you to admit such things to a keeper.'

'I've admitted nothing,' she said. 'Except to being in a tall building.'

Bel smiled. 'So this is how to tease a keeper, is it, oh unnamed thief? To hint at your profession and prove yourself uncaught?'

The girl took a swig of her ale. 'Mmm,' she said. 'That's good ale. I wonder if it's locally brewed.'

'I admire your spirit,' said Bel, 'but you should be careful which keepers you choose to tease.'

'Oh?' said the girl, arching an eyebrow. Her eyebrows were already naturally arched, so the result was pronounced. 'And you, sir, are one of those keepers best avoided?'

'I don't mind some friendly chat,' said Bel. 'But I'd steer clear of me out there,' he gestured at the door, 'while you go about your *business*, whatever it may be. I don't care what you say about vantages and such, I'm not an easy fellow to shake.'

'I believe you,' she said, and actually looked uneasy for a moment. 'Let's change the subject,' she continued, extending a hand with long, clever fingers. 'I'm Jaya.'

'Bel.'

When he took her hand his skin tingled and he instantly sensed their shared connection. He sometimes had a similar feeling around Corlas, but had always assumed it was the bond of family. She, too, looked affected by what she felt.

'Sorry,' she said, breaking into a grin. 'It's just . . . well, have you ever met anyone else like us before?'

'My father, maybe,' said Bel. 'My mother used to tell him he had the blood, but he doesn't really believe it.'

'So your mother?'

'Yes, she had it. Strong too, according to my father. I never met her; she died giving birth to me and . . . well, to me.'

'Lucky,' said Jaya. 'My mother lived.' She spluttered into her drink. 'Sorry, didn't mean that quite how it sounded.'

Bel smirked. 'I take no offence. I feel like I know her anyway, sometimes. Arkus knows, my father has told me much about her. I wouldn't be surprised if I'd been through every moment he remembers.' His cheeks went red. 'Apart from . . . well, you know.'

She laughed.

'But anyway,' he blustered on, 'a Sprite woman she certainly was. "Be careful if you ever meet a Sprite woman, son," my father sometimes says. "You . . . " . . . er . . .' Bel trailed off as he suddenly realised he *was* talking to a Sprite woman.

Jaya smiled. 'Forget I was here?'

'I just didn't put it together in my head before I started speaking.'

'Well, you *are* a man so that's to be expected. But do go on – what does your father say about Sprite women?'

'Um . . . I'd rather not say now.'

'You can't do that.' Jaya scowled at him. 'I'll arm-wrestle you for it.'

'What?' Bel glanced at her arms. True she was athletic, but there was no chance she would best him. 'Okay,' he said, and shrugged.

'I'm gonna win, you know,' she said, thumping her elbow on the table. He locked hands with her – again, a tingle – and 'Go!' she said.

She wasn't weak, but she was still no match for him. He didn't push her hand down immediately, but instead pretended to strain against her. 'Oh, you're so strong,' he said, which made her expression more determined. He gave way a bit, letting her force his arm down as if he were losing, giving mock grunts and saying, 'Oh no, you're winning.' As his hand came closer to the table he locked it up and held fast just a finger's breadth above the wooden surface.

'Pleased with yourself?' she said. 'Humouring me like that?'

Bel winked.

'Pride before a fall,' she said, and with sudden force that took him by surprise pushed his hand down the last little way to the table. She sat back, laughing. 'I win!'

'But –'

'You men, really. You love playing that "oh, you're so strong, you're beating me" game. Put yourself in the most vulnerable position, at the worst angle, then one little push and it's sneakiness beats muscles any day.'

'That's against the rules,' said Bel.

'Show me the rulebook.'

'Rematch?'

'I don't think so.'

Bel laughed. 'Damn it.'

'So,' said Jaya, 'I know any honest keeper would honour our agreement. What does your father say?'

'He says be careful if you ever meet a Sprite woman . . .'

'Yes?'

Bel sighed. '. . . because your souls might fall in love before they tell you.'

He feigned relaxation. From the sparkle in her eyes juxtaposed with an overly casual sip of ale, she was doing the same thing.

'So,' she said, wiping her lip, 'do you think that's going to happen to us?'

Bel shrugged. 'Not sure.'

'Want to hire a room upstairs anyway?'

Bel had never finished a drink more quickly.

～

Corlas made his way through the Open Castle, nodding to guards as he passed. It was almost as if he watched from outside himself, noting how much he looked as if he belonged. Sometimes he forgot to think about it and the mask seemed real even to him. Over many years his fakery had become habit. At the beginning, after he'd learned about Iassia, it had been much harder. In knowing that he couldn't leave lest the bird enslave him to some foul task, he had to appear as if the decision to remain were his own. He had talked at length with Fahren and Naphur and, admittedly, had found them more reasonable than anticipated. Naphur was a soldier at heart and right away spoke with Corlas as a familiar, cutting bluntly to the heart of any concern. Fahren assured him they had never deliberately separated him from his son, and backed up his words by giving Bel back to Corlas to raise. Perhaps all would have been forgiven if not for one thing. Even now, years later, he couldn't wrap his mind around the greatest violation he'd ever known, which he was powerless to set right: his child was not whole.

Fahren had not hidden the fact that part of Bel had been ripped away by cursed magic and taken to Fenvarrow. All Corlas's instincts cried out to do something about it, but what? He couldn't leave the Open Halls for fear of being caught by Iassia. Even if he could, what was he supposed to do – march to Fenvarrow, to Skygrip Castle, and snatch his child from the hands of the Shadowdreamer?

Fahren had tried to console him. 'Bel is healthy and happy,' he'd said. 'What crawled out of him was nothing but a dark worm, something he's better off without.' Corlas could see that Fahren was not as certain as he professed, but he'd pretended to accept Fahren's words. Meanwhile, he couldn't help but wonder, every single day, about his other boy. Did the Shadowdreamer care for him well, or was he being honed with harsh methods? What was he like; what did he look like? Did he look like Bel, or someone different? Did he know about Corlas? Did he despise Corlas for abandoning him?

When Bel was six, Corlas had listened to Fahren explain to him about the division of his soul. The old mage had simplified it for the young boy, making it sound as if Bel had been cleansed of an ugly ailment. 'Normal folk have to live with their dark sides,' Fahren had said. 'You are blessed to be rid of it.' It worried Corlas how Bel had taken that to heart – or perhaps 'let it go to his head' was a better description. More than once he'd had to explain to his boy that his transformation did not make him better than other people.

Corlas arrived in the personal chambers of the Throne. Time had treated Naphur well and, save some extra lines on his brow, he was the same man who'd strode into the Open Castle eighteen years before. Fahren, who stood smoking at an open wall, was a bit less sprightly these days, but everyone still thought he'd live forever. The Throne, who reclined in a voluminous red armchair with a glass of wine, now had streaks of grey at the temples and, though he was still stout and strong, had developed a paunch.

'Ah, Corlas,' he said. 'Have a seat and get some wine into the bloodline Corinas.'

'Thank you,' said Corlas, sitting. 'How was your trip?'

'Surprisingly pleasant,' said Naphur. 'Contrary to expectations.' He turned to Fahren. 'You know how I feel about the Trusted of Centrus –'

'You don't trust him,' said Fahren.

'– but Baygis was quite happy to lead the negotiations. That fox could convince the rain to fall sideways. Anyway, it gave me time to uncover a nest of huggers outside Kahlay and do the Trusted a favour by leading my personal guard against them.'

'A favour?' chuckled Fahren. 'I'd say it was the huggers who did *you* a favour by providing you with some sport, poor beasts.'

'Poor beasts, Arkus's arse! Rip your ribs out your back as soon as hiss at you. Anyway, I've decided to make Baygis my chief ambassador, which has inflated his ego even more. Just what was needed.'

'So he's giving up his duties as overseer?'

'He thinks he can do both and he's welcome to try. Maybe he'll be too busy with it all to annoy me as much.' He turned back to Corlas. 'On the subject of sons, we were just discussing your prodigy. I understand Bel's partner will be unfit to serve as a keeper for some time?'

'So I've heard,' said Corlas.

'Well, although it would be easy enough to assign him another partner, I've been debating about whether or not to pull Bel from the keepers entirely.' He sat forward in his cushions. 'I want to assign him to a troop.'

Corlas was surprised, though not displeased.

'A couple of days ago,' said Naphur, 'we received news of a hugger infestation near the forest town of Drel. You may have heard?'

'Aye.'

'The Drel soldiers are managing to keep the huggers out of the town, but they don't have the numbers to go into the forest and deal with the source. I'm sending a troop and I'd like Bel to be in it. The troop leader is Munpo, a capable man who's fought huggers many times.'

'I know of him.'

'So,' continued the Throne, 'I guess I want to know if you agree with this course of action.'

Corlas smoothed down his beard, taking a moment to collect his thoughts. 'As we know, Bel has always been extremely skilled with whatever weapon is put in his hands. There is little more he can learn from us without actually entering the fray. I also know he grows impatient with his confinement behind the wards.' The taskmaster shifted his weight. 'I would ask why you accelerate him, though. Others will wonder too.'

'Others will have to believe that it's because of his great skill,' said Naphur. 'The truth is, if Bel is to do the things he is supposed to do, he must have experience in the field. Fahren still harbours doubts about Bel following a warrior's path, but I do not. I wish to see how he fares in harm's way.'

The Throne seemed confident Bel would succeed easily, which made Corlas uneasy. The lad was untried in any real way, yet Naphur appeared to consider him an instant hero. The fact that Bel could swing a sword well in training was no guarantee of safety on the battlefield. Nothing was.

'I approve,' said Corlas, 'of Munpo's inclusion also. But . . .' He was troubled. The High Mage wasn't interjecting with his usual concerns for Bel's protection, so Corlas was forced to express them himself. 'Do you not fear for his safety?' he asked. 'By which I mean beyond the huggers themselves?'

'Indeed,' said Fahren. 'Of course.'

'So what are we going to do?'

Fahren shrugged. 'Be worried. Pray for his safety.'

Corlas must have looked confused.

'Corlas,' said Fahren, 'hopefully the shadow won't mark Bel's passing. There's no reason for anyone to think he is anything but another blade of the Halls. On top of that . . . well, if we don't give him some freedom soon, I fear he will shake us off. I don't want that. I've spent many years wondering how to shape Bel's destiny, but I have never found an answer. Perhaps he must be allowed to choose his own path. Certainly he must learn to fend for himself.' Fahren sighed. 'I don't like it, believe me.'

'Me neither,' Corlas said, then shot Fahren a gruff smile. 'But I think I like you more, High Mage.'

Bel ate with gusto, for after last night his appetite seemed without end. Never had he had such an experience, shared such a deep connection with someone . . . it hadn't seemed to matter that they'd known each other only hours. When they had touched, it was more than touch – it was like the very blood under his skin was drawn to her. What explanation was there? He did not care. He could barely wait to see her again in two nights' time.

'Bel? Bel!'

Bel stopped slicing his steak to find Corlas watching him ruefully. 'What?'

'That's a merry glint in your eye this morning,' Corlas observed, making it sound like a question.

'Hmm?' said Bel. 'What are you talking about?'

'And a wide grin on your face while you stare at something only you can see.'

Bel arched an eyebrow. 'A gentleman,' he said, 'does not kiss and tell.'

'Very well,' chuckled Corlas. 'But I need the gentleman to break his reverie a moment.' His expression grew more serious. 'They wanted me to be the one to tell you. You are being assigned to a troop.'

Bel stopped mid-slice. 'What?'

'You heard me.'

Bel put down his fork. 'Do they ever pull people out of the keepers early?'

'No. Not unless there is a great war.'

'So why me?'

Corlas finished chewing a chunk of meat, then wiped the juice from his beard. 'I won't bandy words,' he said. 'The Throne is grooming you for a military career. He thinks it might be part of this destiny of yours, and wants to test you. You are to be sent out on your first real assignment.'

Excitement shone in Bel's eyes. 'What is it?'

Corlas remembered his own enthusiasm for his first assignment, and chuckled. 'Huggers,' he said, 'coming out of Drel Forest. An unusually large infestation. The soldiers of Drel have asked for help, so the Throne is sending a hunting party.'

'And I'm to go with them?'

'Aye.'

This clearly appealed to Bel. 'When?'

'Soon. Within a couple of days.'

'Which troop?'

'Under Munpo.'

'Are you going?'

'No.'

'Why not?' said Bel. 'Don't you miss it?'

Corlas smiled.

'So why don't you come? Doesn't some time away slaying monsters sound like just the holiday you need?'

Corlas stared at his hands splayed on the mess hall table. The truth was, he was very aware of how long he'd been trapped behind the wards. For a moment he allowed himself to be swept along by Bel's enthusiasm ... then he remembered blood-drop eyes watching from amongst leaves.

'I cannot,' he said.

'But the Throne respects you. He'd let you go if you asked.'

'No. Do not try to convince me.'

'But –'

'No!' said Corlas angrily, startling Bel mid-chew. For a moment his shoulders rose and fell, but he mastered himself. Leaning back with a sigh, he met his son's worried eyes.

'I'd go with you, lad, if I could. But I cannot. Please don't ask me again. Now,' he stood, picking up his plate, 'finish your meal and then I'll tell you everything I know about huggers.'

Troop

'Now, Hiza,' said Bel smugly, 'I don't want you losing sleep over me – especially since sleeping is about the only thing you can do.'

'Very funny,' said Hiza. He lay in a bed in the Hospital of Arkus, the sun shining warmly into his open room. 'Is this what you came for? I thought you had your fill of gloating yesterday.'

'I had to say goodbye,' said Bel. 'And thank you once more for breaking your ankle.'

'Hmf,' said Hiza. He absently went to scratch his foot, discovered there was plaster in the way and scowled. 'Bloody hospital,' he said. 'What I'd give to be coming with you.'

Bel grinned. 'I know.'

'Oh, get out,' said Hiza. 'Get out before you float out. I can see how eager you are to be off.'

'I'll bring you back a hugger claw.'

'Don't bother. I'll be getting one for myself any day.'

Bel smiled at his friend and left the room. He strode along white corridors, manoeuvring smoothly around healers and patients. As boys, his gang had explored the hospital many times and any laid-up soldiers who tolerated questions and told war stories would find themselves with an eager audience. To get on the boys' bad side, however, was to run the risk of being mercilessly tormented. Many a healer had come running in response to shouts about mischievous children and caught nothing more than the echoes of laughter. Bel wondered if there were any bold scamps around to bother Hiza.

He left the hospital and headed for the barracks, a barely concealed bounce in his step. Hiza had spoken true: he was filled with excitement. Today he'd meet his new troop, and tomorrow they would leave for Drel.

News of his transfer preceded him. It was an unusual occurrence to be pulled from the keepers early and Bel's new comrades were highly curious about why the exception had been made. As Troop Leader Munpo introduced Bel to them at the barracks, the expressions on the assembled faces were varied – from friendly, to dour, to unreadable.

Bel met each pair of eyes, nodding and smiling no matter the reaction he received.

'All right,' finished Munpo in his dry, croaky voice. 'Let's take it out the back.'

The troop leader was a wiry fellow who constantly smoked brittleleaf rolls. His gnarled skin put his age anywhere between forty and sixty, he wore his lank brown hair slicked back in a ponytail, and craned his neck in a way that put Bel in mind of a vulture. His head bobbed up and down slightly as he led them to the training grounds, adding to the effect. Walking behind him in the group, Bel noticed a ropy blade called Hunna looking him over. Hunna nodded in acknowledgement.

'Howzit goin'?' he said.

'Good, thanks.'

'Yeah? You lookin' forward to killin' some huggers?'

'Absolutely, my man,' said Bel, knowing that others were paying attention to the exchange.

'You better be,' said Hunna. ''Cause these ain't no common browns, ya know. Green huggers are worse than browns.'

'Indeed,' said Bel. 'More intelligent, more coordinated, they stalk you through the trees and you never hear them coming.'

Hunna frowned.

'You fought huggers before, Blade Bel?' said a steely voice from his other side.

It was Gredda, Munpo's penulm, which made her second in command of the troop. She was a muscular woman of around thirty with mousy hair tied back in a ponytail. Bel wondered if she remembered him from when he'd been small and had brought her sword back into the barracks.

'Many times,' he said. Gredda raised an eyebrow. 'As a child, admittedly,' he continued. 'Equipped with only my trusty wooden sword, I kicked their hairy arses from one side of the Open Halls to the other. I wasn't allowed to fight them at dinnertime, though.'

A couple of chortles followed, but Gredda remained stony-faced. 'So you really don't know what you're in for,' she said.

'If you say so.'

'Some of us are curious, Blade Bel, as to how you came to be with us.'

'Oh,' said Bel, as if this was surprising news. 'You mean why was I pulled out of the keepers early? Well, that's no secret. My partner broke his ankle, and rather than have me sit idle while he heals his heels, they boosted me into a troop that needed an extra soldier. This one.'

Gredda scowled. 'That's horse shit. Why didn't they just assign you a new partner?'

'Yeah,' chimed in Hunna. 'Think no one's lost a partner in the keepers before?'

'We heard they moved you 'cause you're a favourite of the Throne,' said Gredda.

'Ah,' said Bel. 'So that's what you heard.' He smiled. 'Well, it's true I know the Throne, but that's not why they moved me.'

'No?'

'Nah. They moved me because I'm the *best*.'

Now he knew he had everyone's attention.

'Is that so?' spat Gredda derisively.

'Indeed.' Bel fired a wink at her. 'I'm surprised you haven't heard of me. I'm a master of the sword, a demon with the bow, as skilled a warrior as ever there was. Why, you'll never meet *anyone* with such lightning-fast reactions, such eagle-eyed accuracy, such sure-footed –'

Bel's foot hit a tussock of grass and he stumbled to fall on the ground. He rolled onto his back with an exaggerated look of surprise on his face.

'Arkus!' he exclaimed. 'They didn't tell me there'd be *grass* on this mission!'

The soldiers guffawed and Bel was glad his prank had paid off. Only Gredda marched on unimpressed.

'Why din' they just tell us they was sendin' a troop clown?' said Hunna, offering Bel a hand. Bel took it and they fell back into step. 'So, serious,' said Hunna in a low voice. 'Why *did* they send you over?'

'I've told no lies, comrade,' said Bel. 'I've told no lies.'

Together the troop trained, and Bel knew he was being watched. If his talents were on display, so be it. The troop would get their show.

Standing in a line of soldiers firing down the archery range, Bel notched arrow after arrow into his bow. Each shaft flew straight and true, hitting the target's red centre some twenty paces away. As he turned from the range he saw that he'd impressed his onlookers, one notable exception being M'Meska, a Ryoshi Saurian. She stood upright on powerful hind legs, reaching Bel's shoulders in height. Her body was covered in bright green scales and her tail was a pace long. Above her snout she had yellow eyes on either side of her head, and Bel knew she'd be a hard one to sneak up on. A row of spines ran from the crest of her head down the back of her neck, and rose in anger as she watched Bel sinking arrows into targets. M'Meska was the acknowledged champion bow of the troop and, as the line of archers switched over, she walked past Bel with a silent snarl, pointedly taking his former position in the line. She proceeded to fire impressively, though she hissed in anger as one of her shafts sank into the border of red and yellow, further from the centre than any of Bel's.

Swordplay was next, using practice blades. Munpo arranged the bouts in a tournament style, three pairs jousting at a time while the others watched. Bel's first match was against Hunna, which he won swiftly in two quick movements. Hunna was annoyed, claiming he'd not been ready, and demanded a rematch. Bel granted it to him, and again won swiftly. As he glanced towards those watching, he saw that their admiration for his skill was in danger of becoming begrudging. Perhaps he *had* won a little too easily.

He forced himself to draw out his second bout, against a well-muscled blade called Keit. Keit was a natural swordsman, flexible and strong, and far superior in skill to Hunna. Back and forth they went, swords flashing with speed and precision. For Bel it seemed like a dance, and he almost laughed with pleasure as his opponent forced him backwards under a barrage of blows. Cheers went up amongst the onlookers, and Bel realised with annoyance that they were barracking for Keit. Although he knew he should let Keit win, vanity proved more powerful than humility. As calls for Keit filled his ears, he suddenly found himself standing over the fallen man, his sword levelled at Keit's heart. The troop fell silent as Bel reached out to offer the man a hand up. Keit's hard blue eyes stared up at him, and for a moment Bel thought his offer was refused – but then Keit's hand caught his in a strong grip and Bel helped him to his feet.

'Well fought,' said Bel.

'And you,' said Keit. 'Corlas must be quite a teacher.'

'That he is,' came the dry voice of Munpo.

The troop leader removed a brittleleaf end from his chapped lips and flicked it away, then drew his sword from its frayed scabbard. He nodded at Bel, who realised he was being challenged by his commanding officer. Staring at Munpo, he resented the man for placing him in such an awkward position. He had no desire to show up Munpo in front of his troop, but he didn't trust his pride to let him take a fall to such a dilapidated opponent. Corlas had spoken of the man with respect, but even so Bel couldn't imagine the wiry little warrior posing much threat. Reluctantly he took up an answering pose, sword held ready. It was too much for the soldiers still jousting, who stopped to watch their troop leader challenge the new blade.

Munpo took a step back, inviting Bel to attack. Bel lunged and their swords clashed. Munpo's grip was surprisingly strong, his sword steady against Bel's blows. The troop leader edged backwards, blocking Bel's sword each time with understated moves, defending only a small circle around himself. He was quick, and Bel found his defence difficult to penetrate. He aimed a powerful swing, hoping strength alone would unbalance Munpo. Munpo simply lowered his blade, and Bel stumbled as his blow met no resistance. Munpo attacked for the first time, stepping forward to spike his sword, dagger-like, at Bel's stomach. Already off balance, Bel had to put more effort into his defence than he would have liked, batting away the attack gracelessly. Munpo pressed his advantage, little jabs and slices coming one after the other in quick succession. Such was the economy of his movement that he remained totally steady as he continued forward. Bel's defence was bigger by comparison and he knew he was expending more effort than Munpo. He tried to control his frustration at being pressed back by the quick little man, just as Munpo swung his sword back in a wide arc, leaving his left side exposed. Bel seized the opportunity, swiping quickly, but Munpo was already dodging away. Too late Bel knew it had been a trick, luring him to attack when he was already off balance. Munpo bounced forward to press his practice blade against Bel's rib cage.

As the troop applauded the victory, Bel stared at the older man. Munpo, who'd barely broken a sweat, nodded at him. 'We'll talk about this later,' he said.

Conflicting emotions fought in Bel. Although he had not wished to beat this man in front of the troop, he'd considered the choice of losing to be his. He knew he wasn't invulnerable – Corlas still beat him sometimes, but Corlas was a hero and his teacher besides. Against the spindly Munpo, Bel found it hard to accept defeat. Added to that, the rest of the troop was clearly glad that he'd been proven fallible. He understood this, of course, but he would have preferred to have secretly known that he could have won if he'd wanted to. It was a sobering blow to his ego.

Outwardly he took it with good grace. He nodded respectfully to Munpo and stepped back into the troop, where he received a few slaps on the back.

'Head up, blade,' said someone beside him, who turned out to be Keit. 'Munpo is wilier than a fox in a henhouse.'

'Indeed,' agreed Bel. 'Though such a fox would look better fed.'

Keit barked a laugh, and suddenly Bel was very thankful that Munpo had won.

After dinner the troop went to the Soldiers Bar, located next to the mess hall in the barracks. Being the only bar in the Halls, it wasn't just a meeting place for soldiers and so did a strong trade most nights. It was a long room, with squares cut into the floorboards through which trees grew from the earth beneath. Along the walls lanterns shone brightly, their heat rising up through the non-existent roof into a sky of twinkling stars. The bar itself ran the length of the far wall, while in the rest of the room attendants moved between tables taking orders. None of the noise travelled outside the bar due to the 'Essence of Walls', and thus didn't disturb sleeping soldiers elsewhere in the barracks.

Bel was waiting at the bar for his next drink when M'Meska stepped up beside him, a tall glass of bloodfire in her bluntly clawed hand. He noted that a tail was a handy thing to lean on when its owner had consumed too much bloodfire.

'You lucky today, Varenkai,' she said in a voice ill equipped for human language, rasping and full of odd clicks. 'Hit target good, yes?' She upended the glass of thick liquor down her throat.

'If anything,' said Bel, 'I'd say you're the lucky one.'

'What mean?' demanded the Saurian, slamming her glass down empty on the counter.

'Since I'm about to buy you a drink.'

He gestured at a bartender, and a moment later a mug of ale and another glass of bloodfire arrived. The Saurian grunted and took another large swig.

'You do know that's bloodfire, not water?' said Bel, counting out copper.

'I know,' said M'Meska, missing the friendly dig. 'Saurian blood not so thin as Varenkai, and sun not shine so bright in Halls as at Furoara Sands. I need warm my blood so far from home.' She gulped from the glass at a rate that made Bel queasy.

'Now,' said M'Meska, 'you.' She tapped the bar, summoning the bartender. 'Two,' she said, holding up two claws.

'Ah,' Bel began in protest, 'I don't think –'

'Warm your blood,' said the Saurian. She held up her claws again at the hesitant bartender. 'Two,' she repeated.

The bartender shrugged and soon two glasses of bloodfire stood before them on the bench. Bel stared at his with some trepidation.

'Drink,' said the Saurian, lifting her glass in a clumsy toast. Bel, not wishing to offend the strange soldier, lifted his too. They drank, Bel sipping and M'Meska swallowing greedily.

'Bah,' said M'Meska, licking her lips. 'You shoot like Saurian, but still drink like human.'

'Thank Arkus for that,' said Bel, coughing; his throat burned. He quickly drank some ale to wash it down.

'Be wary, Blade Bel,' came a creaky voice from beside him, and the smell of stale brittleleaf wafted past his nostrils.

'Troop leader,' Bel acknowledged.

'We have a long ride tomorrow,' said Munpo, 'and I've seen the aftermath when men try to match a Saurian at drink. It isn't pretty.'

'Bah,' reiterated M'Meska and moved away, bobbing birdlike on her hind legs. A barmaid with a drink tray had to sidestep quickly to avoid her swinging tail.

'Can I buy you a drink, sir?' said Bel.

'You may, soldier.'

Again Bel gestured to the bartender. Munpo took out his brittleleaf pouch and began to make himself a roll. 'What did you think of today?' he asked.

'Seems like a good troop, sir,' answered Bel. 'I'm glad to be part of it.'

'Mmm-hmm,' said Munpo, sealing the roll over his lips. 'And you did well in the bouts.'

'Sir.'

'But you lost to me,' said Munpo, putting the roll in his mouth and lighting it. Smoke issued over the counter. Munpo nodded to the bartender as his ale arrived. 'Any ideas why?'

Bel licked his lips. He was feeling a little foggy from the drinking, and the question irritated him. 'You're a quick man, sir,' he said after a moment. 'And a skilful fighter.'

'True,' said Munpo matter-of-factly. 'But those aren't the reasons. I saw you fight Hunna and Keit. I know, just as Keit does, that you could have beaten him sooner than you did. I imagine he's thankful that you didn't injure his pride as you did Hunna's, but he doesn't deceive himself. That said, I know he would not refuse you a rematch.' For the first time Bel saw Munpo smile, a dry enigmatic smile that tweaked the corners of his mouth then dropped away quickly. 'I almost thought you were going to let him win,' said Munpo.

'I thought about it.'

'Mmm. Now, why did you lose to me?'

'As I said, sir –'

'No, blade, that's not it. You lost because you under-estimated me. I'm not saying you would have won if you hadn't, but you certainly lost because you did.' He took a swig from his glass. 'You're not invincible, lad.'

Bel was openly annoyed by that. 'I never said I was, sir.'

'Your expression did, after I beat you. You couldn't believe it, could you? You, young and strong and full of juice, losing to a tired old scrap like me. Well, I tell you this, blade: you underestimate someone like me on the battlefield and you don't get to have an expression afterwards. You'll be face down in the dirt with your eyes seein' nothin'.' He stared Bel hard in the eye. 'Now you listen, lad. You're good, we can all see that. Corlas warned me, and now I've seen you for myself, I might just agree with him. But don't let your skill go to your head. The battlefield is no training ground. There's no one on one, no control. It's unpredictable and fast. You make one mistake out there and you're dead. You underestimate one opponent because you don't respect him and you're dead.'

He sucked his brittleleaf, letting Bel digest his words.

'You're young and untried in a dangerous world. I've seen skilful, brave and arrogant men die more often than I care to remember because they didn't keep their wits about them. Don't go letting someone like me rile you up so much that you fall for a simple trick. And remember, Bel, if a soldier is young, it just means he ain't been killed yet. If he's old, it means he ain't been killed a long time.' Munpo winked. 'But enough for now. You're doing well. Even M'Meska seems to have taken a liking to you. Word of advice though – don't accept any more drinks from her. It won't do my pontificatin' much good if tomorrow you fall off your horse and break your neck because you're still drunk.'

There was that fleeting smile again and Munpo moved away. Bel felt vaguely patronised, but he could see the point of what had been said. Nonetheless, he was bothered. How could he be expected to lead the light to victory if he couldn't best an old man? When he'd been young and they'd told him about his destiny, it had made him feel invincible. His was to be a life of adventure and greatness, and if he was to change the world, surely it was preordained that he would survive at least until then? Was any risk really a risk? Once he had stood at the edge of a building, wondering what would happen if he threw himself off. Would some miracle save him, ensuring he could go on to meet his destiny? He'd asked Fahren, who had said it didn't work like that, but couldn't really explain how it did work. The encounter with Munpo, while it hadn't been about life and death, had certainly showed him to be fallible. Feeling unsure of himself was an alien and unpleasant feeling. He took a big swig from the bloodfire, and spluttered immediately.

'That more like it!' said M'Meska behind him.

At evening's end, Bel glanced a final time towards the Soldiers Bar entrance. He hadn't really expected her to come, but had hoped nonetheless. They'd planned to meet in The Wayward Dog that night, before he'd received his orders for Drel. He'd left a note at the tavern asking her to join him here instead, but a criminal – and he was pretty sure she was one – would not lightly enter the barracks of the Open Halls. Yet excitement about the mission had not purged Jaya from his mind. The night they'd spent together had been something outside his experience. When morning had come it had been hard to part. He didn't want her thinking he'd abandoned their plan to meet. *Why hadn't she come to find him?*

Gods, he thought, *been waiting my whole life to join a troop; now all I want is something else.* Pushing back his seat, he rose from a table long abandoned by his comrades. *Ah well. Tomorrow is going to be a bright new day.*

Before the Council

Kakurd glanced around, searching for his friend Peasa. He spotted the old Graka about halfway up the throne room, standing next to the long window. *Typical of him to choose a place with the wind at his back*, thought Kakurd. He also spied the Arabodedas entourage, who were standing as close to Refectu as they could jostle. Kakurd had recently relinquished his title as Counsellor of the Arabodedas, and was now merely an advisor, like Peasa. Also like Peasa, he did not feel the need to stand with his main party, as there would always be time later for the younger representatives to haughtily discount what wiser old buggers had to say. As he made his way through the assembled council towards his friend, he wondered how long it had been since such a gathering had filled the throne room. Perhaps it had been when Battu had called them all together after the assassination attempt at the beginning of his reign, to let them see he was still in charge.

Peasa inclined his hairless ebony head as Kakurd arrived. 'His dark lordliness has not yet arrived,' he lisped quietly, forked tongue flicking out over pointy little teeth. 'Look, there's the boy, by Refectu.'

Kakurd followed his gaze. The blue-haired boy was standing by the dais, an empty circle around him into which no council member trod. The Arabodedas representatives were making a show of looking him over then talking behind their hands. The boy appeared not to notice and stood silent and still, his eyes moving about the room slowly, almost imperceptibly.

'You've heard the rumours?' said Peasa.

'Yes,' replied Kakurd. 'As have the rest of the Arabodedas. They aren't pleased.'

'Why not? The boy is a man, is he not?'

'Not an Arabodedas, Peasa.'

'He's as pale as one.'

'He is paler. And he was born in Kainordas. Most don't know what to make of him. They have no faith in the prophecy.' He considered the Arabodedas entourage from under grey eyebrows. 'Besides, they've already picked their favourite.'

Peasa ground his stony bat wings together. 'Roma?'

'Yes.'

'Good.' The Graka grinned. 'About time there was some excitement round here. I remember when the throne room was a lively place.'

'Before Battu,' muttered Kakurd.

'Speaking of the great one, I think he's arriving.'

The goblin aide Turry made his way down the middle of the room, snapping at people to clear a path. He arrived at Refectu and turned, adjusting his gold-rimmed spectacles. 'Welcome, members of the Shadow Council!' he called nasally. 'Prepare to receive the Shadowdreamer!'

The council fell silent as Battu appeared through the archway, followed closely by Tyrellan. The dark lord barely glanced at the assemblage as he made his way up to the dais, where he turned to stand before the ancient throne.

'Greetings, council members,' he said, though his tone did not imply much respect. 'You are called because I have an announcement to make. I would like to introduce to you my student Losara, who has recently come of age. Step forward, Losara.'

Losara did so, allowing everyone a good look at him. He even smiled politely at a few of them.

'As many of you know, I have seen to his care and tutelage since he first arrived at Skygrip,' continued Battu. 'He is the child of power, born of prophecy to overthrow the light.' Battu paused, casting his gaze slowly around his audience. 'I intend to name him Apprentice.'

Low talk broke out. Battu sat down on Refectu, his black cloak melting into its crevices, and smiled smugly.

'Look at him,' Peasa whispered. 'He *desires* a challenge.'

'It's better for the Apprentice if there is one,' said Kakurd. 'To display his suitability.'

Battu leaned forward and the scattered talk ceased abruptly. 'I will hear any discussion on this matter.'

From the Arabodedas camp, Counsellor Tysek cleared his throat cautiously. He was a middle-aged man with curly black hair, a bit on the tubby side. 'My great lord,' he said, bowing deeply.

'Counsellor Tysek,' acknowledged Battu.

'My lord, the Arabodedas are not convinced that this boy should inherit the mantle of rule.'

'The mantle of rule?' said Battu, raising an eyebrow dangerously. 'It will be a long time before *that* is passed on, I can assure you. Perhaps not in your lifetime.'

'Of course, my lord,' amended Tysek hastily. 'I only meant that it has always been understood by the council that the one named Apprentice is the Shadowdreamer's heir.'

'It still remains the council's responsibility to choose a new Shadowdreamer when the time comes,' said Battu.

When the time came, in fact, the title went to whomever had the strength to crush all opposition.

'The one chosen by you,' said Tysek, 'will be the one to journey across the Black Sea, my lord.'

Battu frowned vaguely, but nodded. 'As you say.'

Tysek continued. 'We feel, Shadowdreamer, that there is someone more . . . appropriate . . . to your tutelage, who would serve Fenvarrow better. And he is a native of our land, lord.'

'And he has courage, which I admire,' said Battu. 'It is not a faint-hearted thing to challenge the child of power.' He let his words sink in, then: 'He is here, no doubt?'

The Arabodedas called Roma stepped briskly forward – further forward than Tysek – and sank to his knee before Battu. He was a young man, Losara's age, wearing a black vest over a green shirt. His black hair was pulled back in a shiny ponytail and streaked with red dye, as was the fashion in the Arabodedas capital of Afei Edres. 'I am Roma, my lord,' he said.

'Roma, my lord,' echoed Tysek quickly, attempting to cover the youth's spirited forwardness. 'It is he whom we present to you. His talent for magic and his affinity with the shadow have been clear to all from an early age.'

'Who trained him?' asked Battu, staring hard at Roma.

'Memtas, my lord. She claims he is the most powerful mage out of Afei Edres in all her years of watching.'

'She has seen many years,' said Battu. 'I don't discount the opinion of Memtas lightly. Rise, Roma, and tell me why you deem yourself worthy to challenge my selected Apprentice.'

Roma rose, straight and proud, and spoke in clear and pompous tones. 'My great lord,' he said, and gestured to the silently watching Losara, 'forgive me if I doubt *this* to be the result of prophecy. We have all heard the stories of his miscreated birth. If they are true, then he is only half the man he was supposed to be.'

He made a show of staring down Losara, who held Roma's eyes calmly, his face a mask of neutrality.

'I do not doubt him to be a mage of ability,' Roma continued, 'otherwise a leader as wise as yourself would not vouch for him. I only ask to prove that I, of whom my lord was not previously aware, be allowed to prove myself better.'

Battu smiled. 'My young Roma, never presume to tell me of what I am aware. If I know how many pork pies the soldiers in the Open Halls eat each day, I can certainly find out what's happening in my own lands.'

Roma was sensible enough to look abashed.

'Your use of water in magic is particularly artful, I must say,' continued Battu. 'Some of your coastal displays have been very impressive. But are you up to the challenge so far from the sea?'

Roma shot Losara another malignant glare. He'd been taught to intimidate his opponent psychologically;

a lesson, it seemed to Kakurd, that Battu had not taught Losara.

'I am more than up to it, lord,' said Roma.

'Very well,' said Battu, clapping his hands triumphantly. He stood and, with great drama that he obviously enjoyed, announced: 'To the duelling cavern!'

Despite the passage to the duelling cavern being disused and cramped, the air that flowed through it was fresh and clean. This passage didn't divide into others, but led to only one destination.

The duelling cavern had once been a large natural cave, but when the sides of Mount Mokan were carved away during the shaping of the castle, the cave had been cut in half. Now it existed in the side of Skygrip like a puncture wound, its mouth facing south across Gravewood. In the centre of the chamber was a lowered square cut into the floor, thirty paces wide. Standing at each corner were columns carved with runes: once activated, they contained any magic cast within the square. Outside observers were protected, and the mages within could battle with all their strength. There was a faint sense of energy in the chamber, perhaps from the powerful wards in the columns, or the blood of many mages soaked into the floor.

The council filed along the passage and then moved towards the square. Some vied for the best positions, while others, less trusting of the protective columns, hung back. All were excited. Shadow magic was not a strong defence against shadow – there was none of the natural oppositional force of light – so fights between shadow mages were famously fast and brutal.

Battu strode to an elevated stone seat facing south across the square. Losara walked behind him with Tyrellan. On the other side of the square, Roma was leaning nonchalantly against a column, without yet having stepped into the depression.

'Be careful,' said Tyrellan quietly as he and Losara parted ways.

I'm going to build you a world of pain, came Roma's unbidden thought in Losara's head.

Losara knew he was expected to reply. Battu had given up trying to teach him posturing, but Losara felt that, in the spirit of any good fight to the death, he should try. *I'm* . . . It was no good. Threats were meaningless to him.

I'm going to build you a grand house, he sent instead.

Sensing Roma's confusion, he stepped down into the square, not pausing on the edge as Roma had. On seeing this Roma stepped down quickly too.

'Hold, mages!' called Turry. 'Do not start without the order!'

Battu waggled his fingers and chanted softly and the runes on the columns began to pulse blue. 'The square is sealed,' he announced. 'Neither magic nor mage will leave it until there is a victor. Begin on my mark.'

He raised his hand. 'Begin!' he said, his hand thumping down.

Roma attacked the moment the command was given. A flick of his fingers and a bolt of blue energy slammed into Losara's shoulder. Losara's cloak flapped around him as he sailed off his feet, arms flailing. He hit the ground flat on his back, the air audibly forced from his lungs.

Cheers went up from some of the council as Roma strode towards Losara's sprawled body. The mage raised his arms as he went and tendrils of darkness curled out of the ground around Losara, forming snake-like heads and snapping downwards. Losara screamed as one reared back with a hunk of bloody flesh and shredded cloth hanging from its shadowy mouth.

He struggled to sit, managed to raise a hand at Roma and send an energy bolt back across the square. Roma leaned sideways while *pushing* at the air and the bolt veered away, smacking into the invisible barrier between the columns and sputtering to nothing. Meanwhile, snake after snake darted in to bite Losara, each one pulling back with a mouthful of flesh. Losara screamed and struggled as snakes wound round his limbs, pinning him down. Roma made a snake shape with his hand, taking direct control of one of the biting heads. As he plunged his hand up and down, the shadow snake echoed his movements, plunging into Losara's neck, tearing loose trailing windpipe. Losara went still, though the snakes continued, and a giant pool of blood spread across the floor underneath him.

The council gave a great cheer and Roma turned to face them, smiling fiercely. Battu sat forward in his seat, staring shocked at the pulpy body of his Apprentice. Tyrellan, at his side, was still enough to be frozen in time. Roma forced the smile from his face and bowed low before Battu.

'As I thought, my lord,' he said. 'This was not even taxing. He was only half a man.'

'Not even that,' said Losara.

There were gasps as Roma spun, eyes wide. Losara stood in the shadow of a column, hands clasped before him. Roma glanced at the body on the floor, which was fading. As Losara stepped from the shadows, it disappeared completely.

'That was quite ferocious,' Losara said. 'I must admit, I was curious to see what you intended for me.'

'An illusion,' spat Roma. 'The stuff of street magicians.'

'I'm trying to find a level that befits you,' said Losara. He was quite proud of his attempt at ridicule.

Roma bellowed in anger, both hands extending towards Losara, crackling forth twin streams of energy. Losara made a small gesture and the streams slammed into a flat circle of rock hanging in the air. He had cut it from the ground and floated it in front of him like a shield, so quickly that none had actually seen it happen. He moved a hand forward and the circle hurtled towards Roma, who flung his arms over his head. An unseen protective wall went up around him and the rock smashed to pieces against it. Roma lowered his arms as the dust settled, glowering at Losara.

'Snakes, was it?' said Losara, and clicked a finger. A black tendril whipped out of the floor, knocking Roma from his feet. The next instant he was pinned to the ground by the same writhing shadow snakes he'd previously conjured. His hands moved in a flurry, disintegrating the snake heads one by one. More grew in their place, hovering over him, poised to strike, but waiting.

'I could have killed you by now,' said Losara.

Roma furiously channelled power. There was a blue flash around him and the snakes dispersed like smoke. He leaped to his feet again, summoning an attack.

'Looks like I'll need a bigger snake,' said Losara.

He raised both hands and a huge mouth erupted from the ground beneath Roma, seizing him by the waist as it powered upwards. Murmurs of amazement arose from the council. The huge shadow snake climbed twenty paces into the air, then looped back around itself to send its head slamming into one of the columns. The head broke to smoke against the stone, but Roma did not. He crashed against the column and fell, landing heavily on the hard ground, where he lay groaning on his side.

'Admit defeat,' said Losara.

A look of grim determination came over Roma's face and he uncurled a shaking finger. A blast of freezing wind hit Losara, instantly forming ice crystals on his white skin. His hair blew back and strands froze crazily in place. As he began to chant, crystals forming on his lips broke into dusty fragments. Frost covered his outstretched hands, hardening his flesh. With a wince, he clenched his fingers, cracking the ice from his skin and snapping the veins of frozen blood inside. He made a small batting motion and Roma went rolling violently across the ground. The freezing blast ceased and Roma lay on his back, blood oozing from his mouth.

'Admit defeat,' said Losara, almost sadly.

Roma tried to hoist himself up on unsteady limbs, defiance blazing in his eyes. 'To the death,' he spat, and began another spell.

Something grabbed him like an invisible hand, lifting him from the ground. The air began to move, and there was a rasping as dust took off from the ground. Pieces of the smashed stone shield began to bounce and roll, and soon they too were airborne, hurtling around a funnel that stretched to the roof. The wind howled, and the awe-struck crowd knew they were witnessing nothing less than a contained hurricane.

Trapped in the grip of Losara's power, Roma hung in the eye of the storm, struggling and cursing. Then Losara let him go and he was sucked into the wind like a rag doll. Up and down the funnel he went, round and round, twisting and turning, spinning and shrieking. Vomit joined the flying debris.

Losara's eyes went blank as he left his body, travelling into the shadow of the tornado itself. Inside the funnel his shadowform grew, billowing upwards to the tops of the columns. The giant shadow Losara reached out a black hand and snatched hold of Roma's limp body. Roma opened his eyes weakly, hiccupping another dollop of sick. Shadow Losara continued to grow, fifty paces up to the roof itself where storm clouds churned about his head. Rain began to fall and thunder boomed. Blue lightning forked downwards, striking the ground in many places, and the wind wailed high.

Shadow Losara spoke calmly in a voice that was somehow louder than the storm.

'KNOW MY POWER.'

Losara enveloped Roma's mind, letting the Arabodedas see him truly. Roma fell still with terror as he sensed the magnitude of Losara's power. It surrounded him like a great ocean, and he was but a speck floating on crushing waves. He knew in that moment that Losara could have destroyed him whenever he'd chosen. He knew that he'd never had a chance.

A world of pain, you said? came Losara's thought in his mind. Suddenly pain was everywhere, as though each tiny component of Roma's body was charged with it, as though there was nothing else in the world. His mouth opened in a wide O, but no scream could force its way out. The agony went on and on, into forever and back again, his tears beaten away by the rain. Then, just as suddenly, the pain was gone.

'Do you admit defeat?' echoed Losara.

'Yes,' croaked Roma.

Do you want to live, Roma?

Roma struggled to open his eyes to the monstrously looming silhouette. 'Yes,' he said.

You would serve me?

'Yes.'

Then, when the time comes, I will build you a grand house in Afei Edres and you shall rule the city as my loyal servant.

The rain stopped and the wind died. As Losara flowed back into his body, he set Roma gently on his feet. The mage immediately collapsed to his knees. Losara blinked, and turned to the council, who were watching with fear and amazement. Battu was unreadable, but there was something very intense about him as he sat tightly gripping the sides of his seat.

'I am victor,' Losara said. 'And though Roma's life is forfeit, I waive my right to it. He fought with passion and commitment, and I wouldn't rob our land of his skills. We will need mages of his quality once there is war.'

Roma raised puffy eyes to Losara and knew his lord. He would never fight Losara again.

Uneasy muttering broke out amongst the council. It was an unusual outcome, and the demonstration of Losara's power had shaken them. One day they would be ruled by this mage of whom they knew so little. Except that he was merciful. That was not a trait expected from a student of Battu.

Battu stood. 'The challenge is met, then,' he announced. He gestured at the columns and the glow faded from their runes. 'Losara is named Apprentice. It will be he who makes the journey across the Black Sea to Assedrynn's Isle. He will depart in three days.'

Losara was surprised at that. He hadn't expected to be leaving so soon.

It would be his first time out of Skygrip.

Visitations

The bolt flew true into the red centre of the target. In the dream, Losara watched his counterpart, that which he had been separated from . . . or was it the other way around? Losara didn't know how to think of Bel. He certainly wasn't a brother. He was an *other*. Another side of himself that Losara had never known. Bel seemed so different, but perhaps that was to be expected. Two sides to the coin? A coin cut in half, right down the middle. No wonder Losara sometimes felt so *thin*.

He tried to picture himself as he would have been whole, warrior and mage meshed together, and found it difficult. Instead, he decided to learn about what was real, and drifted closer. Bel was excited and impatient about the adventure ahead. Losara himself was to sail away across the Black Sea, to see if he could find Assedrynn's Isle. That would be an adventure too, he knew, but he couldn't help thinking his excitement was different. He felt the beckoning of the unknown, of the testing he'd experience, of the expansion of his knowledge. Bel had a louder, thrill-seeking reaction. It was purer, more extroverted, more consuming. It existed for its own sake, for the joy of it.

Another bolt flew, but before it hit the target the dream swirled. Losara found himself drifting through the throne room. Battu paced before the long window, frustrated, ranting to Tyrellan. 'When?' he demanded, spinning around. 'When will he emerge?'

'Your spies are no help?' asked Tyrellan.

'NO!' shouted Battu. 'It's impossible to get a bug-eye across the ward stones, and almost as difficult for the others. The High Mage maintains an admirable defence.' He turned to the window, glowering across Fenvarrow as though he could see the distant Halls. 'As for my operatives born of light, well . . . let me just say I hope you're keeping traitors out of Skygrip as effectively as they do it in the Halls. I have to rely on the shadowdream alone, and it shows me little of what I need to see!' This last he spat south, as if he were blaming the Dark Gods themselves. 'I have no idea how many pork pies the soldiers of the Halls eat each day. No idea! The average rate of pie consumption is highly guarded information!'

'Perhaps Corinas has told his superiors about Iassia?' said Tyrellan.

'No,' said Battu. 'The bird has bound him to silence. And if that bind was somehow undone, Iassia would know. No, Corlas is hiding. Coward! Does he plan to wait forever?'

The dream swirled again, and now he was in a tavern in Kainordas. The door opened and Bel approached the bar. 'I'm looking for a young lady,' he told the barman. 'Jaya, she was drinking here the other day.'

'I'm afraid I don't know anyone by that name,' the barman said, too quickly. Bel stared hard at him, making him falter. His hand went to his side and the barman quivered, but Bel was only reaching for a letter.

'All right,' he said. 'Well, I'm *not* supposed to meet her here tonight, so when you *don't* see her arrive, I'm sure it won't be difficult *not* to give her this letter. Okay?'

Swirl.

A beautiful girl with blazing red hair stood in a room with the letter in her hands. On the bed sat an older woman with black hair and dark eyes. 'So what does it say?' she asked.

'It says he's being sent to fight huggers in Drel Forest, but he shouldn't be away long. I guess he wanted to tell me he's not disappearing.'

'You're a fool, Jaya. The man is a peacekeeper.'

Jaya remained silent.

'Not exactly our kind of person.'

'He's a Sprite, Lerena. That's *exactly* my type of person.'

'Well, it hardly matters,' said Lerena. 'Tomorrow we leave Kadass. The road to Ismore is ripe with wagons.'

'Yes,' said Jaya. 'But he writes that I could meet him tonight at . . .'

'Where?'

'The barracks.'

'You would place us all in danger with such selfishness?'

'No,' said Jaya sadly.

So, thought Losara, *my* other *has a woman. Is that what the dream shows?*

～

Losara closed the door to the roof and produced a key from his robes. He had been told, of course, to return the key to Battu as soon as he was finished in the Breath. Placing it in the palm of one hand, he held the other above it. Darkness oozed from his sleeve to take on shape, forming an exact replica of the key. Losara smiled, and used the shadow key to lock the door. While he would not go against Battu's wishes, it was nice to know he could if he wished.

Reflecting on what he'd seen, he couldn't decide if the shadow had sent him a message or if the visions came simply at the whim of the dream. A part of him knew he should feel outraged that Battu was using his father in a plot involving his other self. His own coldness disturbed him. Where was his anger? Did he possess no passion? Deciding that he needed to think, he made for one of Skygrip's balconies.

The passages were quiet this close to dawn. Losara heard a couple of patrols tramping about, but didn't cross their path. He came to a passage where the air blew cold and fresh, and followed it out onto a stone balcony. Not far away someone was leaning against the wall, looking out into the night. It was the Mire Pixie, Lalenda. This time he could see her face clearly, her black tangle of hair swept back by the breeze. Long lashes curved from her cobalt eyes, and her mouth was downturned at the ends, as if the expression had etched its way into permanence there. Her lips were a darker brown than the muddy colour of her skin, as were her fingernails and the toes of her bare feet. Though she stood shorter, she had the proportions of a young human woman. There was a crystal shine to her cheek where a stream of tears had begun to dry. She was the saddest and most beautiful thing Losara had ever seen.

Without thinking, he stepped from the shadows. 'Hello,' he said, and she spun with a yelp of surprise. 'Please,' he said, raising his hands, 'don't be afraid. I won't hurt you.'

She stooped to curtsy, her hair falling over her face again. 'Master Losara,' she said, shaking. She was terrified, that was plain. Losara walked forward to rest his hands on the balcony wall, looking out over the dark expanse. Lalenda remained bowed, her eyes cast downwards.

'Please stop that,' he said softly. 'I'm only here to look upon the night, and I saw that you were doing the same. I thought perhaps we could both do with . . . company. Will you not come back to the wall, as you were before?'

'As my master commands,' said Lalenda.

Lalenda hardly heard what he was saying, so scared was she of Battu's Apprentice. When he'd come across her in the library, she'd considered it a grave misfortune. Now she feared she'd displeased him with her hasty escape and he'd tracked her down to punish her for her insubordination.

'It wasn't a command,' he said. 'Will you not look at me, Lalenda?'

She forced her head up and found herself transfixed by his dark stare. She was exposed, helpless, a mouse before a cat.

'It wasn't a command,' he repeated. 'It was a request. I'm *asking* if you'll stay a while.'

She was confused, but she couldn't do anything about it. She would simply have to obey, as ever. 'Yes, master.'

Losara gave a little sigh. 'You're free to go, if you want. I wouldn't keep you here against your will. On the balcony, I mean. I know you can't leave the castle.'

Her gaze faltered.

'Go, then,' he said, turning away. 'If I am so truly terrible.'

Despite her fear, Lalenda noticed his odd tone. He sounded offended, or, even more inexplicably, pained. She saw a sadness in his ivory face and for a moment was dumbfounded by it. Then she wondered if it was a trick. Battu could feign all kinds of moods, so why wouldn't his Apprentice be the same? One thing she did understand clearly, however: she would displease him if she left. Warily she said, 'I will stay, if it pleases my master.'

'I'm not Battu,' said Losara, as if he'd read her thoughts. Maybe he had? 'I don't kill people because I'm bored, or roast the cook who ruins my favourite dish. Have you ever heard of me doing anything like that?'

Lalenda stared, uncertain of what to make of this calmly expressed but seemingly heartfelt outburst. 'No, master,' she said.

'I do not mean you harm, Lalenda, please believe me. Stay if you wish. Go if you wish.'

She tried to seem, if not relaxed, then less afraid than she was. 'I will stay, master,' she said.

Losara was intensely aware of her standing so close, of the nervous intake of her breath. She hadn't run away this time, but he did not believe that she really wanted to remain. Now that she had, he found he didn't know what to say. There was a lot, of course, that he'd never told anyone, but they weren't thoughts to be shared with a frightened stranger. His mind raced over the castle chat he'd surreptitiously witnessed and grabbed the first thread that came to him.

'Have you . . . heard any of the washroom rumours?' he asked.

Lalenda gave him an odd look. 'No, my lord.'

Losara collected his thoughts. 'I heard Gedri soaked Counsellor Tysek's favourite underclothes too long, and sent them back too small. Apparently Tysek looked uncomfortable all day.'

He glanced at Lalenda and she quickly averted her eyes. She seemed confused by what reaction she was supposed to have, and Losara was confused too. When he'd heard the goblins in the corridor tell the story, they'd thought it was hilarious.

'Will he be punished?' Lalenda asked hesitantly.

'Who?'

'Gedri.'

Losara sighed and closed his eyes, feeling the breeze on his lids. 'I didn't think it was very funny either,' he said.

Some moments passed and she worried that she had offended him.

'I often enjoy silence,' he said, 'but I've never known it to be so uncomfortable.'

'My lord?'

'What do you think of silence, Lalenda?'

'Oh,' said Lalenda, her brow creasing. 'I . . . my part of the castle is very quiet, so if there's a noise it will usually startle . . . Silence is a companion you didn't know you had until it's broken . . .' She was rambling and she realised it. She tried to clamp down on her tongue, but it kept starting sentences she had to finish. 'Most of my companions are books, master, and they don't need sound to speak.' She managed to stop, and looked horrified with herself.

Losara raised an eyebrow. 'Books don't need sound to speak?' he echoed.

'I'm sorry, master, it was a stupid thing to say.'

'No, it wasn't.'

He's so calm, Lalenda thought suddenly. She hadn't seen it before as she was so frightened, but now, for a moment, she did. His voice was so even, his gaze so constant. The wind rustled the fine threads of his hair, and the folds of his cloak flapped about him, but he himself was as still as a statue. She felt as if it was the first time she'd ever truly seen him.

'I like books also,' he said. 'Though I don't read as many as I should. Always been a slow reader. Think too much as I go, you see.'

'I've read many, master. A word can paint a thousand pictures. And it's my only way to leave the castle.' On making this statement, she began to tremble. 'Forgive me, I don't know why I said that.'

'Probably because it is true,' said Losara.

'Master?'

'Heron tells me you've been kept a prisoner here since you were a little girl. I'm sure you hate it utterly.'

She was astonished by his words.

'I have also been here for as long as I remember,' he continued. 'Though I am luckier than you. I can go into the dream and visit other places, even if they are muted and cannot be touched. I suppose your books have the same effect. Worlds created insubstantial; a look through a window at other people's lives. Yes, we have that in common, it seems.'

Lalenda could not reconcile her assumptions of this man with the way he appeared to her now. Was he toying with her, or was this really him?

'While we're talking,' Losara said, 'there's something I'd like to ask you, you being the one who foresaw my birth. Will you tell me what you saw?'

Lalenda shifted her feet. If there was one thing she had no trouble with, it was remembering her vivid visions of prophecy, which stood out like lights in her dull past. If this was what her master wanted, this she could provide. She cleared her throat and spoke.

'It was not a universal vision, lord, but a vision had by me alone. I see a wood of grey trees and, walking through it, a strong man with a beard. He is looking for a special herb that his wife wants him to find. She has warned him not to pluck the stems, as the plant will not recover, but only to take its tiny leaves. He finds the herb, and fumbles at the leaves with big fingers, being very careful.' She paused, aware of the detail she was going into. 'Do you wish me to be briefer, master?'

'No.'

'Er . . . yes, master. Eventually the man has collected enough and goes home to a hut in a clearing. Inside is his pregnant wife, asleep. He brews the herb in a tea, and strokes her hair to awaken her. She drinks the tea, which is supposed to nourish and strengthen the unborn child. The herb is potent with an ancient magic, the wild magic that still lingers about the wood. In the dream I know this, because the woman knows this. The next day the woman awakes to find her hair has turned blue. The man is beside himself with worry, but she is not as concerned as he. I awoke from the dream knowing I'd seen Whisperwood, and that the woman would surely give birth to a blue-haired boy. Battu sent Tyrellan forth the next day to fetch you.'

'And a mage called Fazel,' said Losara.

'Yes, lord.'

Losara was silent a moment. 'Sounds like they loved each other.'

'Lord?'

'My mother and father. You know, Lalenda, what you've just told me is the most I know of them. Thank you.'

'You're welcome,' she said awkwardly.

'Let me ask you another thing,' said Losara. 'You used the term "universal vision"? I have little understanding of the art.'

'I shall explain as you wish, master. A universal prophecy is one that goes out to all prophets in the world. The foretelling of your birth was such a prophecy. That's why it has been common knowledge for the last century. More common is a personal form of prophecy, which more closely reflects the life of the prophet herself, or those around her. I have been known to dream of what I would have for breakfast the next day.'

Losara chuckled, and Lalenda found herself inexplicably flushing with pleasure.

'Occasionally,' she went on, 'we see greater events that others do not. So it was with your mother's hair turning blue.'

'A last question,' said Losara, 'and then I shall drop this subject, I promise.'

You need not promise anything to me, thought Lalenda.

'You did not experience that first prophecy that heralded my birth, but do you know what it was? I have asked Heron and Battu, but they only know what the prophets said of the vision, not the vision itself.'

'It has been described in various texts as the clashing of two armies, light and shadow. Under a setting sun they fight a great battle, a battle for the world. The vision closes on the victorious leader, who stands atop a hill with his sword raised high . . . and all that can be seen of him in the dying light is his long blue hair. The prophets knew that when a child with blue hair was born, he would be the one to defeat his enemy and so end the struggle between Fenvarrow and Kainordas.'

She stopped, suddenly aware that she might be talking about the very man who stood before her. He was too real to be the figure of this future legend.

'And the vision showed nothing of the split,' Losara said, almost to himself.

'No, master.'

Losara nodded, and Lalenda realised she had given him something to think about. She felt exhausted, however, and found herself wanting to be alone so she could sort through all the chaotic thoughts this encounter had bred.

'I'm becoming tired, master,' she said as politely as possible. 'I should get to bed. If you will excuse me?'

'Of course, Lalenda. Thank you for talking with me.'

Lalenda curtsied, deeply relieved. She walked away, careful not to rush. As she went, she was surprised by the realisation that perhaps she had actually wanted to stay. No one had really spoken to her in a long time.

Losara remained a while longer, troubled by the scene Lalenda had described. He pictured it again – the great commander holding a sword aloft in triumph – and looked down upon his own soft hands.

New Horizons

Battu sat on Refectu with his jaw on his fist, Heron and Tyrellan on either side of the throne. Before him stood the boy, dressed in green cloth with a satchel at his side, ready for his journey. He had a look of calm on his face that made Battu want to shake him. Instead: 'There's little guidance I can give you,' the Shadowdreamer said, as though he regretted it. 'Heron, please explain the old laws.'

'Master Apprentice,' Heron said, 'today you begin your journey to Assedrynn's Isle. At the village of Frake, the priests of Assedrynn will provide you with a boat. Though you have a starting point, the end remains uncertain. If the Dark Gods wish to receive you, they will. If they do not recognise your legitimacy, you may drift and find nothing. Be wary of the Boundary, for the Isle lies perilously close to it. If you travel across, you will be lost to this world.'

'I cannot share anything of my own journey, boy,' said Battu. He rose and stepped down from the dais. 'I can, however, wish you luck.' Awkwardly he clasped Losara's shoulder. 'I shall pray for your journey to be safe.'

'Thank you, master,' said Losara.

There wasn't much else to say. Battu watched Losara leave, escorted by Tyrellan to the aviary. Heron hobbled after them, taking an eternity to leave his sight. Finally only his goblin guards remained, silent and constant in their alcoves like statues. He was alone with his thoughts.

Memories of his own journey to the Isle had been stirred up, and an old anger came with them. How he hated the gods for what they'd commanded! How it frustrated him that he wouldn't know what they said to Losara! Would they tell the boy that Battu had disobeyed them? Thinking about it made him even more anxious – would he be punished when his soul reached the Well? Had he redeemed himself from that first rebellious act? There had been no further war since the Shining Mines, and his hunting squads roamed Fenvarrow exterminating the undead. Not to mention that he'd secured the gods their champion.

In his mind's eye Battu saw Losara again in the duelling cavern, a monstrous shadow encased in hurricane. Roma had been powerful, and at another time he could well have become Apprentice. It was unsettling that Losara had beaten him so easily. Battu had expected Losara to win, but he'd also expected some sweat and hard breathing. The real question that made him clench his fists: *Was Losara more powerful than he? The boy is a device*, he reminded himself. *If Losara is to lead our armies to victory, of course he must be powerful.* The trouble was, when Battu imagined that pale face and calm eyes, he could see nothing of what went on behind them.

Uncertainty grew.

~

Tyrellan had long ago perfected the art of staring at something while appearing not to, one of the advantages of having a pitch-black gaze. He now considered Losara from the corner of his eye as they walked down the passage.

All his life Tyrellan had felt little for those around him. Most were stupid or incompetent, and even the most powerful agents of the shadow usually put their own interests first. Battu especially was guilty of this indulgence. Tyrellan, on the other hand, was a true servant of darkness. He'd been born that way, bawling at his expulsion from the dark of his mother's womb. As a child he had skulked in the barn or the shade of trees, watching his brothers play in the open. His family had been nothing but dimwitted peasants, and he had never been bothered by the fact that he'd murdered them all.

Losara, however, was different. Tyrellan was sure he embodied the shadow's very will. Unfortunately, that fact was no protection against Battu, and for years Tyrellan had been a subtle protector, steering the dark lord away from dangerously fretful thoughts. He was thankful he'd managed to avoid having a bug-eye implanted in his skull, for sometimes small insubordinate risks were necessary, and it was bad enough knowing Battu could be lurking in any shadow. Of course it was the other problems with bug-eyes that had formed Tyrellan's basis for argument: sometimes a bug-eye became infected, or grew abnormally, and its host lost their sight or died. 'If it is my lord's wish that none of my daggers find the backs of his assassins,' Tyrellan had once said, 'then of course I invite him to ruin my depth perception right away.' The final reason Tyrellan didn't want a bug-eye was that if the Shadowdreamer died, all the bug-eyes connected to him also died. Tyrellan didn't see why he should be crippled in the event of Battu's passing. The end of Battu did not mean the end of Tyrellan.

Still, he would have traded the butterfly for a bug-eye in a flash. If Tyrellan had once been indifferent to his birthdays, now he hated them. Every day when he woke up and saw the butterfly, his hatred grew. It was a test, he told himself, a burden he must bear in service of the shadow. Sometimes, however, an interior voice whispered that even if every light went out in the north, and the sun sank into the sea and drowned, even *then* he wouldn't be rid of it. He was forced to do something he had never done before. He was going to ask a favour.

'My lord Apprentice,' he said.

'Tyrellan?'

'My lord. For two decades I have borne this insect that dogs my every move. I have asked the Shadowdreamer about it, but he has much to attend to. Perhaps this prevents him from seeing what an insult it is to have such a creature living freely in the castle, such a joke upon us by the light.'

'Upon you especially, Tyrellan,' said Losara.

Tyrellan's jaw tightened. 'Yes, lord.'

Ahead, their way widened into the grey light of a chamber. From within came the sounds of birds squawking and a deep-throated call like that of a cow.

'Heron has told me of legacy spells,' said Losara. 'She says they are impossible to undo.'

'So the Shadowdreamer has told me.'

'Would you have me ask the gods about it?'

Tyrellan dropped to a knee, effectively halting their progress. 'If anyone knows how to break such a spell,' he said, 'it must be them.'

'If indeed it can be broken,' said Losara. 'Not even the gods are all-powerful, I think.'

'If it can be broken, lord,' Tyrellan echoed.

Losara nodded. 'I will ask them,' he said, 'if I can. Now come. I'm eager to be on my way.'

The head of the castle aviary, a Graka, introduced Losara to the creature he would ride to Frake. It was called a whelkling, and looked like a hybrid of dragon and mammal. It was roughly the size of a cow, with stumpy legs and wide circular hooves. These were close enough to the body so they didn't drag in the wind, but made the animal very low on the ground. Of the dragon there was a serpentine tail and great leathery wings splayed out from its shoulders. Its face was long with a wide snout, a milky eye positioned on each side of its head.

Slapping it on the rump, the Graka said, 'Yep, these old sky carts aren't as common as they once were.' Staring at the ungainly, moronic-looking thing, Losara wasn't surprised. 'Be patient with this one, lord. He's getting on, which means he's even more stubborn. We don't send him out much these days, but he knows the way to Frake well enough. Does runs to get fresh fish for the Dreamer's kitchens, so you might have to forgive the smell. I've walked him around Skygrip a few times just now to loosen his muscles, so you should be all right.'

Tyrellan stepped forward and smacked the Graka across his ebony skull. '*Should* be all right?' he snarled.

'Is the beast sound or not? This is Battu's Apprentice, you snivelling streak of shit, not a sack of fish!'

Things did indeed seem a little shaky as they first dropped from the aviary cave high in Skygrip. The beast did not find its balance immediately, and Losara hung grimly to its neck as they plummeted. Then the great wings spread and the whelkling began to flap powerfully, giving its deep-throated call. They climbed southwards, passing over Gravewood. A fell cry went up at their passing, and though Losara searched hard for its source, the tops of the skeletal leafless trees formed a tangled and chaotic canopy. They rose until the Cloud was a few paces above them, and here the whelkling finally levelled out. Losara had never been so close to the Cloud, and could see sunlight shining in the upper reaches. He found himself disquieted that nothing separated Fenvarrow from the sun but this layer of suspended moisture. Far below the land spread out gloriously, blue with grasses, dotted with farms and woods. Snaking roads ran between towns and villages, and streams glistened like silver threads spilled from some celestial sewing box.

Losara had flown in the dream, but always in a sleepy, foggy state. Now the world was crisp and clear and tangible. The icy wind against his skin made him feel alive, and it was magnificent to be free of Skygrip. For the first time he could remember, he was cut off from the walls and floors of the castle, from proximity to the Breath, from the powerful shadows that had saturated him his entire life. Never had he felt more *inside* his own body, more awake. Surprisingly, he found himself thinking of Lalenda, still trapped in Skygrip without the space to fly freely. He knew she'd like to have been here too, and felt sorry that she wasn't.

Hours passed and they came within sight of the Black Sea. Where the Cloud met the horizon, it was like looking into the mouth of an immense cave. If the gods chose not to receive him, that was where he'd be left floating, and he knew a moment of doubt.

The Cloud dropped away above them as they began to descend. Closer to the land he spotted a bay that housed a town of rickety buildings. Boats were moored to jetties, and further out to sea were other vessels hauling their nets through dark waters. Blue pinpricks glowed, ice lanterns set against the dusk, and not for the first time Losara wondered about the deeper relationship between shadow and light. Shadow was not total darkness, and even the keenest night vision benefited from some light. Could shadow exist without it?

To the east of the village was a steep hill with a circular temple on top, and this appeared to be the whelkling's target. It hovered for a moment, then began to drop in jolts and spurts. It sent up a spray of dust as it neared the ground, then finally drew in its wings and simply fell the last pace, landing with a grunt. It draped its wings and hollered, and Losara knew he was being told to get off.

Sliding down onto the path on which they'd landed, he became aware of the stiffness in his muscles. Stretching, he glanced around at the temple grounds. They were earthy and flat, dotted by smooth trees hung with pale pears. In the distance he heard the crash of waves, the cries of sea birds, and activity in the village below. Then came footsteps and priests emerged from the temple. They wore long brown cloaks over bulgy bodies, with hoods hanging over their squashed heads. All had rubbery pebbled skin, though the colour differed from dull pink to brown, grey and green. Some wore ornate rings on their upward-curving tusks.

'Hail, Apprentice,' one of them gurgled, stepping forward. 'I am Head Priest Grepra. Welcome to the Temple of Assedrynn.'

These were the Vorthargs who would put him in a boat and watch him drift away.

The next morning Bel marched towards the stables with a spring in his step. Drel might be no further than two days' ride away, but it seemed like the other side of the world. The excitement even managed to dull the twanging in his heart, the disappointment that he had not seen Jaya last night as planned.

He arrived to find some of the troop already loading packs onto horses, and Corlas waiting. 'Where have you been?' said his father.

'What do you mean?' asked Bel. 'I'm right on time.'

Looking at Corlas's somewhat haggard appearance, he wondered if he'd experienced a restless night. He knew his father was worried – as were Fahren and Naphur – that he might face more than just huggers on this journey. What they didn't know was that he welcomed the chance to strike back at those who threatened him.

'Yes,' said Corlas, glancing at the sky. 'Munpo says you are getting along with the troop?'

'Most are friendly enough,' said Bel. 'Though I get the impression they'll reserve judgement until I've lived a day on the battlefield.'

Corlas nodded. 'Now,' he said, 'you remember what I told you? Green huggers are camouflaged amongst the trees. When the forest goes quiet you can be sure they are close. Birds and beasts catch their stink first, so they will be your early warning.'

'Yes, Father,' Bel said absently as he strapped a leather breastplate over his shirt. He'd been over this with Corlas already, and again with Munpo.

'Keep your eyes upwards –'

'Because they drop out of the trees,' finished Bel, and laughed. 'Father, I know this.' He put his hands on Corlas's shoulders. 'I'll be all right, old hero. You've taught me well. Of course, it helps that I'm damned good anyway.'

'Respect the danger,' said Corlas sternly. 'Huggers are murderous wretches. Do not be overconfident.'

'I won't have time to be overconfident. I'll be too busy filling the air with blood.'

'Bel . . .'

'All right,' chuckled Bel. 'I'll be careful, I promise. That's what you're trying to tell me, isn't it?'

Corlas grunted. Then he unbuckled the scabbard from his belt, which housed the shine-streaked sword he'd carried since his return to Kadass. 'Take this,' he said. 'It is a stronger blade than you carry.'

Bel was taken aback. 'I can't. It's yours.'

'It is a battle blade,' said Corlas. 'It lusts after the cut. A taskmaster does it no justice.' Without waiting for a response, he reached down to unsheathe Bel's sword and slide the shine blade firmly in its place.

'There,' he said. 'And yes, you be careful, soldier – the whole time.' He gave Bel's arm a hard squeeze. 'Now off you go.'

$\backsim$

Losara sat up in bed with a gasp. Blinking, he tried to focus on his surrounds, taking a moment to remember where he was. Normally, when he went to sleep in Skygrip, he would drift slowly away from himself, connecting through the castle walls to the dim awareness of the shadowdream. When he awoke from the dream, it was a slow and self-aware rise to the surface, and even as he opened his eyes he was not yet contained inside his own body. Thinking back on it, he realised how much he had taken to wandering the corridors still half in the dream. Maybe he had never really slept in Skygrip, and maybe he had never really been awake either.

Last night he had lain in the bed for hours, waiting for unconsciousness to seize him. It turned out natural sleep was a mystery to him and he'd no idea how it was meant to work. Obviously he must have achieved it, for he'd just become rudely aware of himself again as if born from a void. He tried to recall the point when sleep had taken him, and could not. It was very curious. Flipping back the bedcover and rising, he promised himself he would take more notice of how Skygrip affected him. Now that he was aware of it, he could control it more easily when he got back.

He dressed in black trousers and a dark blue vest, took a long drink from the water pitcher by the bed, picked up his satchel and left the room. Outside the priests waited, sitting cross-legged under brown cloaks, looking like ant hills.

'Ah,' said Grepra, rising smoothly. 'Come. Others are waiting with your boat.'

The priests led on, bobbing almost comically on their concealed bandy legs. They went through grey corridors and out of the temple, making their way down the hill. The hillside was soft and damp, peppered with spiky sea grasses and salt-encrusted bushes. The path levelled out into the village where it joined a muddy street. As they moved through clusters of buildings, villagers stopped to stare – mostly Arabodedas, Losara noted. One called out, 'Safe journey, lord,' as they passed.

It didn't take long to reach a pebbly beach where a simple rowboat was moored to the shore. It had a single wooden bar for a seat, two oars fixed in position, and was big enough for just one person. Grepra produced a cloth package tied with string. 'Provisions,' he said. 'It is some days to the Isle if you head straight and true. If you don't, who knows? Maybe it will take many days, or all the days left in your life.'

The priest held a suckered hand towards the boat. Losara waded into the chill shallows and stepped unsteadily into the rocking vessel. On the shore, Grepra untied the rope and threw it after him.

'The priests of Assedrynn commend you,' called Grepra. 'May he find and guide you, there and back.'

'There and back,' echoed Losara, turning to stare at the horizon. Black cloud and black sea.

'We will watch for you, Apprentice,' called Grepra. 'Now row!'

As the walls of his home disappeared behind him, the wind at his back seemed to urge him on. East they rode on powerful horses, across the grasslands of Borgordus.

'Come on, Blade Bel!' Keit called beside him. 'Last one to Drel eats goblin loincloths!'

Bel laughed, joy shining in his amber eyes as a wider world rose up to meet him.

Soon the coastline was a streak in the distance, only the cliffs visible above water. Losara rowed with the current, which gripped the craft so strongly that he couldn't have turned back if he'd wanted to. Finally the risks seemed real, yet he rowed resolutely towards the oncoming dark.

Good Spirit

'The town of Treewith,' called Gredda. The troop approached cross-country from the west and entered the town in fading light. It was a clean and orderly place, built in a valley between low hills, its houses painted green like the surrounding land. The Treewith Inn, where they were to stay, was three storeys high, with a warmly inviting glow in the lower windows.

'Stable's round the back,' Bel heard the innkeeper telling Munpo. 'It's not often we have so many horses at once, but I'm sure we'll manage.'

Bel slid from his saddle and led his horse to the stables, contemplating his own desire for sleep. Previously he'd only ridden short distances – how could he have done otherwise while confined to the Halls? – and the long day over hills and fields had given him all kinds of aches. Once his raging appetite was satiated, nothing would hold him from his bed.

From the eaves of a nearby shop, a pair of blood-drop eyes followed his progress.

~

Soon enough, Bel slept. In his dreams he was battling huggers, untouchable as they broke like waves upon him. For some reason Jaya was there, watching admiringly from a tree. Bel saved his troop mates time and again, including Munpo, who was suddenly not so deft with his sword.

In the rafters above, Iassia ruffled his feathers with pleasure. All these years Corlas had hidden behind the wards, making it impossible for Iassia to invoke his 'favour' and have the father kill the son. The weaver had been limited to hovering about the perimeter, questing into passing minds for any titbit of information – yet it seemed that finally Corlas had taken a risk. Did he think that Iassia had lost patience with his task? Twenty years was nothing to a weaver, and in fact Iassia had enjoyed his time in the region. The small settlements and villages around Kadass had proved entertaining, containing an abundance of weak minds to toy with. His favourite had been the old woman who'd fallen into a gully at the back of a farm and broken her leg. Iassia had hidden in the branches above her, deflecting the attention of her family as they searched, so that they could hear her yet not find her. Her misery had been sublime. It was good to have a holiday.

Today the waiting had paid off. A troop of soldiers thinking loudly about a controversial new recruit had led Iassia straight to Bel. Below him now, the boy lay unguarded and asleep, and Iassia worked through ideas as he watched him. He was loath to involve any of Battu's other servants, even if they were more capable of inflicting physical harm. This was his prize, long waited for! He staved off making a decision with a compromise: he would do a little reconnaissance, and if he didn't find a way of dispatching Bel easily, he would then contact the distant dark lord.

With Bel asleep, Iassia could attempt a total invasion of his mind, putting himself wholly inside it. He opened the gates that held his consciousness in and floated invisibly down towards the bed. Behind him a thread of awareness connected him to his own body, unfurling as he went. As he entered Bel's mind he became aware of the surface thoughts first. They had a certain texture to them – the man was confident, arrogant, vain. Iassia delved deeper . . . and suddenly knew he'd made a mistake. It was like stepping out expecting footing yet finding none. A void opened up beneath him and he fell, spinning wildly. He had to hold himself tightly to stop himself unravelling. What was this? Never before had he come across such a *gap* inside someone, a place where there should have been *thought*, *personality*, *soul* and yet there was nothing. He searched for a way out, but in the confusion his string of awareness had snapped. It was all he could do to move, struggling through the void as if trapped in tar. After what seemed like eternity he finally rediscovered the formed part of Bel. With his strength almost at an end and desperate to reconnect with his own body, he tapped into Bel's senses, and despaired.

Bel was riding through grassy fields surrounded by the rest of the troop. Iassia's struggle had lasted through the night and into the next morning, and now his body was leagues behind them, silent in the rafters of the tavern room – too far away for him to reach. Unwillingly he settled back into Bel's mind, waiting for strength to return.

 ~

Bel found the second day of riding harder than the first. He was on edge, and dogged by the oddest sensation – as if there was something almost audible just below other sounds, more sensed than heard. Several times he turned in his saddle thinking he'd heard a voice beside him, and found nobody.

Night had fallen by the time they reached Drel. The town lay on the edge of Drel Forest, surrounded by high walls of wood planking, with soldiers patrolling them on an inside platform. One wall bordered the forest, and there was evidence there that trees had been cut back recently, presumably to stop the huggers from swinging into town. Double doors as high as the walls swung slowly inwards as the troop approached, and a soldier came striding out to meet them.

'I'm to show you to the barracks, sir!' he called to Munpo. 'The town commander waits for you with the Citizen Prime.'

Munpo nodded, and the soldier led them into town. The main road was a wide dirt path lined by simple buildings of unpainted wood. Light came from the inn as they passed, but Bel heard nothing of laughter or song. The only sounds were hooves clomping and trees rustling in the forest outside. Even the draught horses penned in yards were strangely quiet. They passed many stacks of logs, timber being the town's livelihood. The few townsfolk on the streets were burly and strong, and they saw no children. There was an air of disharmony, and the wind blowing in from the forest seemed to carry the smell of menace. Bel rode his horse past a porch where two old loggers sat watching, glowing pipes hanging from shadowy faces.

   ...there is fear here...

He froze, blood cold, then reined in his horse. Behind him, M'Meska had to rein in hers abruptly or else run into him. She grunted in irritation.

'Why stop?' she demanded. 'Move on!'

'Did you hear something?' asked Bel. 'A voice?'

'No,' said the Saurian. 'Nothing but my stomach complaining, wanting not stand here chitty-chat. Move!'

Bel urged his horse on, glancing about uneasily. He could have sworn he'd heard words, soft yet unmistakable in the eerie quietness. They arrived at the barracks, where soldiers were waiting. The grounds were nothing but a field of dirt, the building itself tiny in comparison to the complex at the Open Halls. It looked as functional as it needed to be and nothing more. Munpo started talking to a tall, lean woman, while Gredda barked orders for them to dump their things and assemble immediately in the dining hall.

As Bel led his horse to the stables, Keit fell into step beside him. 'I don't care for those whispering trees,' he said.

'Would you prefer it if they spoke up?' Bel answered, and Keit shot him a smile.

   ...simpleton soldier...

Bel spun this way and that, again seeking the origin of the voice. Still, there was nothing there.

The dining hall was full of draughts that stole the warmth from its iron fireplace. The soldiers sat at parallel tables, smells from the kitchen making their stomachs rumble. The town commander of Drel stood before them, flanked by Munpo and Pelar, the Citizen Prime.

The commander was an athletic man called Rokinin, who had stringy brown hair and deep-set eyes. 'As I've told your troop leader,' he informed them, 'we don't know how big the brood is, as we've only seen their hunting packs. You may know that hugger broods can vary significantly in size, so I can't give you a total count . . . but with a large brood, which this looks like being, there may be over a hundred, which means up to forty male hunters. We suspect they were forced to move from deeper in the forest, for, some days before they arrived, we saw signs of a great fire at its heart.'

'How many have you killed?' asked Hunna. Gredda looked as if she might snap at him to be quiet.

Rokinin's eyes darkened. 'We don't know,' he replied, and raised a hand as muttering broke out. 'Please, soldiers, I will answer your questions as best I can. Two weeks ago, my own soldiers numbered thirty, almost two full troops. The outer regions of the forest are not usually hazardous and in the past we have easily dealt with any of the problems that arose. But two weeks ago came the huggers' first, and most successful, attack on Drel. Some of the trees had grown branches over the walls; foolishly, we thought nothing of it. One day, without warning, huggers dropped into our town. In the forest they stay in packs, but in this instance I think they were overcome by the amount of available prey. They spread to all parts of the town. There aren't many here who didn't lose a relative or friend.'

Bel remembered the grim faces he'd seen on their way down the road.

'To make matters worse,' continued Rokinin, 'six of my blades were in the forest at the time, searching for a woodsman who'd gone missing. When we discovered there were huggers about, I immediately sent others to fetch them back in.' He wet his lips. 'Of those six all we found were the signs of a fight. I have no way of knowing how many huggers they killed before they were dragged off. We never found the woodsman, and several other forest-dwelling families are also missing. All the others are now within our walls.

'The next day I took half my soldiers with me into the forest to find the nest. We were attacked a league in by some twenty, twenty-five males. It was too many, more than I'd expected. We must have been close to the nest, for there was a larger beast too, who looked to be the dominant male. We retreated. We killed some of them, but again, how many I cannot say.' He glanced at Hunna as he said this, then sighed. 'They got five of us that time, and the rest barely made it back alive. Perhaps I was foolish to take out so few soldiers, but I did not guess the size of the brood; nor did I wish to leave the town unguarded.

'Since then a hunting pack has attacked the town again, though no more townsfolk have fallen. Unfortunately a group of woodsmen snuck out one morning, led by one who had lost his young daughter in the first attack. They were stupid and angry and brave, and we mourn their passing. Again, I do not know how many they killed before they were killed themselves.

'Tomorrow I will lead you myself to where I believe the nest to be. I will bring four of my own soldiers, leaving only ten to defend the town, and that is not enough. I had hoped I'd conveyed the seriousness of our situation to the Halls so they might send more than one troop. That said, your troop leader assures me you are some of the best, and I am thankful indeed to have you.'

Bel wondered if it was unusual for a commander to be so forthcoming in a briefing. The man seemed to have been badly shaken by his experience here, though he was obviously trying to appear resolute. The actual effect, Bel thought, was that he seemed weak.

The Citizen Prime, Pelar, cleared her throat. 'I'm just as concerned as Rokinin that an extra troop is not enough,' she said. 'It simply brings us back up to how many soldiers we had here in the first place.'

'Before we were surprised and severely damaged, Pelar!' snapped Rokinin. It became instantly apparent that relations were frayed within the Drel hierarchy. 'I lost six blades before I even knew it!'

'Citizen Pelar,' said Munpo in his creaky voice, 'Commander Rokinin is right. He was on the back foot from the start. But now we can go in force together to hunt these animals, who have also been weakened by many attacks. Even if there were forty male hunters originally, which, frankly, would surprise me, we'll overcome them. I've some of the best archers in the Halls here, and experienced blades too. We'll free you of this menace, wait and see.'

Bel stripped off his soldier's garb, changing into trousers and a white cotton shirt. Keit and Hunna were going to the tavern, against Munpo's warning that they should take their rest. They wouldn't go for very long, and Bel knew he wouldn't be able to sleep anyway. Just a round of cards and an ale or two.

. . . drink won't fill the void in here . . .

Bel stood very still, a sheen of moisture prickling his forehead. There was no one else in the room, and the door was shut. This time he couldn't ignore what he had plainly heard.

'Who's there?' he demanded.

No one answered.

'I said, who's there?!'

. . . interesting . . .

'What?' Bel almost shouted. He restrained himself, getting his breathing under control. 'What's "interesting"?'

Another pause, then: *You can hear me?*

This time the voice was clearer, louder.

'Yes!' said Bel. 'I can hear you, you damned will-o'-the-wisp! Where are you?'

. . . so close . . .

Again the voice was muted, more of an *understanding* than a definite sound. Then it became clearer again.

I'm watching over you, Blade Bel.

Bel swallowed at the sound of his name. 'Are you a spirit?'

. . . no . . .

Yes.

Bel sat down heavily on the bed. What was happening?

Iassia struggled to shield himself against Bel's booming thoughts. It was difficult to cloak his presence; Bel had no actual psychic skill, but the proximity of their minds was letting him sense Iassia. What was worse, Bel heard not only those thoughts that Iassia directed towards him deliberately but also Iassia's private thoughts, albeit more dimly. It was like being trapped before a huge blind beast that swiped randomly with its claws – some blows connected, some missed.

It was all very ironic, Iassia reflected. As a result of entering Bel's mind to work out how to kill him, Iassia now needed to keep the man alive. If Bel was killed in Drel Forest, Iassia would be cut loose, a lost ghost. He needed Bel to make it back to Treewith alive, so he could reconnect with his body. In the meantime, the 'spirit' question had given him an idea.

Blade Bel, he directed. *You are the blue-haired child of power, destined to destroy the shadow. Is that not correct?*

'Nobody knows that,' said Bel.

Arkus knows it. Did you think Arkus would not send help to his greatest champion?

Iassia felt Bel register the words, which inflated his ego but did not dispel his doubts.

I am a good spirit, continued Iassia, *sent by Arkus to aid you in your coming trials. You journey to your first battle, do you not?*

'Yes,' said Bel slowly.

I will help protect you.

'How?' asked Bel suspiciously.

By warning you of danger. I can tell you what is around you. If there was a man hiding around a corner waiting to do you harm, I could tell you. And it works just the same with huggers in trees.

'Forgive me, oh disembodied voice,' said Bel, 'but this all sounds a bit strange.'

Yet you take it in your stride, said Iassia. *Because you've always known, haven't you, that you are special? An extraordinary man, Bel, will likely lead an extraordinary life.*

Again he felt that powerful ego, like a huge muscle flexing. Bel *wanted* to believe, and Iassia was winning him over.

Even now, when a lesser man would run shrieking from the room, you are not fazed.

'Oh, I'm very fazed, believe me,' said Bel. 'I just can't decide if you exist or not. But whether I'm mad or you're telling the truth, running isn't going to do me much good, is it?'

I suppose not.

'If you were sent by Arkus as you say, why have I been hearing you all day yet you only address me clearly when I demand it of you?'

Iassia faltered. It was a good question.

I had to wait until we were alone. If I'd announced myself sooner, your comrades would have wondered why you were talking to yourself.

'I see.' Bel considered this, and it seemed to make sense to him. 'My tutor was the High Mage,' he continued. 'He taught me much about the stranger creatures of the world. And while he said nothing of Arkus-granted ghosts, he did mention something of trickster entities who cannot always be seen.'

Ah, yes. That is a valid concern. Let me promise you this, then: I will never do anything without your permission or against your will. I won't suggest courses of action; only help you in those endeavours you choose to undertake. If ever you ask me to leave, I shall. It was a bit of a gamble, but Iassia knew he had no choice. *Would a trickster make such promises?*

'If he was being a trickster,' said Bel.

Would you have me leave, then?

'No,' Bel said quickly. 'Well . . . not yet. I must –'

There was a knock at the door. Keit opened it. 'You coming?' he said.

Bel glanced about the room as if undecided.

'Oh, come now,' said Keit. 'You aren't crawling off to bed early again, are you? You really think you'll get any sleep before your first true bloodshed? Come and sit with us a while, at least.'

If we go to the tavern, I can prove my worth. Then you can decide whether or not to keep me.

'Of course I'm coming,' said Bel. 'I just don't know where I put my money pouch. Ah – here it is.'

Bel, Keit and Hunna sat in the tavern by the fireplace, with mugs in hand and cards on the table. It was an old place with a low roof, the stuffed heads of animals hanging on the walls. Despite the dancing firelight, the atmosphere was sombre. The townsfolk present had glanced at the soldiers when they'd entered, raised their glasses in silent salute, then gone back to their hushed discussions. The blades had expected to find some of the town's soldiers here, but when Keit asked the barmaid where they were, she said they were either guarding or sleeping – there weren't enough of them for time off. So they sat alone, Hunna dealing out cards, Bel distracted by his ethereal new companion.

You can speak to me in thought, Bel. I will hear you.

What's your name?

Iassia.

*So how are you going to "prove your worth",
Iassia?*

*I can tell you what cards your opponents are
holding. It will then be your choice whether to win or
lose against them.*

All right, let's try that.

For the next several hands, Iassia whispered the value
of Keit's and Hunna's cards. Soon Bel had most of the
copper in front of him.

'Of all the luck!' complained Hunna, pushing the
last of his coins towards Bel. 'Hope you're as good with
your sword as your cards!'

*So Arkus has sent me a "good spirit" to help me
cheat at cards?* thought Bel.

Iassia chortled good-naturedly. *Just a harmless
example of greater powers, Blade Bel. Imagine being
able to outstep real opponents with such help.*

Iassia could sense that he'd succeeded. Bel had
been groomed his whole life to believe he was special.
Arrogance, vanity and ego combined to allow him to
believe Iassia's wild lies. If the situation had not been so
dire, Iassia would have been impressed with himself.

'Well,' said Keit, 'I think I've lost enough coin. And
we should all make it an early night.'

The soldiers rose and made their way into the
night. Somewhere nearby a shout went up, followed a
ferocious snarl.

'That way!' said Keit. They ran towards the sounds,
and as they neared the walls the shouting grew louder,
accompanied by a sound like a monstrous cat. 'Huggers!'
muttered Keit. 'I'd recognise that sound anywhere.'

They rounded a corner and arrived at the wall.
The commotion was coming from ground level, where

Rokinin was pulling his bloodied sword from the breast of a horrid beast. A bow lay against the wall clutching a slash wound in his arm. From outside the wall came a screeching in the trees.

They do not intend further attack, came Iassia's voice in Bel's head. *They are merely testing the town's defences.*

Soldiers on the platform above came running from both sides. Bows fired into the night, but there were no sounds of impact. The screeching died away.

'They're leaving,' Rokinin said. 'The leap from the tree line is too long for them now. Only this beast made it over the wall.'

That's untrue, said Iassia. *Many could have made the jump, but only one tried.*

Rokinin kicked the dead creature savagely, snapping its face towards Bel. Bel felt a chill as he stared into its eyes – yellow with tiny black pupils, hateful in death. It was one thing to hear a monster described, quite another to see one in the flesh. The body was the size of a large dog, though its limbs were long and ape-like, with retractable claws extended from the pads of its hands and feet. It was covered in mossy brown-green fur, which grew longer about its head. Its mouth was wide and lipless, an almost invisible line in the fur, and there were no nostrils in evidence. It stank of wet hair.

'I forgot how much I hate these filthy beasts,' said Hunna, prodding the corpse with his sword.

Keit grunted. 'Come on. There's nothing more to do here. Let's get some sleep.'

Drel Forest

All around, soldiers crept through the undergrowth of Drel Forest. Bel could only see a few of the others, despite how closely together the group was moving. The undergrowth was a verdant sprawl of ferns and shrubs, which shimmered here and there as someone knocked down a cascade of dew. To his left, Munpo disappeared around a mossy boulder at the base of a towering clawberry tree and Bel hurried to keep up. He had wanted to partner with Keit, but that morning Munpo had ordered him to stay close. He didn't feel he needed to be babysat by the leader of the group, but orders were orders. He pushed through entwining vines and found Munpo speaking to Rokinin. Both had their eyes turned to the trees above.

'Yes,' muttered Rokinin. 'We are close.'

Munpo gave a low whistle and Gredda materialised by his side. Munpo pointed through the trees. 'We'll make for that clearing,' he said. Gredda nodded and disappeared again. Munpo glanced around to make sure Bel was following.

'We're headin' for a clearing,' he said in a low tone, 'because we can assemble in collected force there, and watch each other's backs. The bows will have better shots without trees in the way, and they can stay in the centre firing outwards while the blades protect them in an outer circle. If we are near the nest, as Rokinin suspects, they should notice us here soon enough.'

Together they ducked beneath an overhanging branch covered in fungus.

'I thought huggers preferred an ambush,' said Bel.

'They prefer an ambush if possible,' said Munpo. 'But we'll be inside their perceived territory, so I reckon they'll come howlin' along pretty quick.'

Bel glanced around. No one else was close. Why was he getting this private explanation?

'I'll be all right, you know,' he said, managing to disguise his irritation as bland reassurance. 'I'll understand your orders once the battle starts, just like the others.'

'Good to know, laddy. That ain't why I'm tellin' you this.' Munpo paused in the shadow of a fig and sniffed the air. Birds sang in the canopy, an opera of melodic calls. 'If you're to be a leader,' he continued, 'and Taskmaster Corlas assures me that the Throne is takin' a personal interest in your military career, then the more you know the better. That's why I asked you to dog my heels today. You might learn somethin' about strategy and command. If you'd rather run off and play chasings with Keit, be my guest. Up to you.'

'Apologies, sir,' Bel said quickly. 'Just thought I was being spoonfed there.'

'You were,' said Munpo. 'It was just a bigger spoon than you thought.'

I sense an approach, came the voice of the spirit. Thrills went up and down Bel's spine, every sense alert.

Where are they?

To the east. Still some distance, but they know we're here and they are coming.

They arrived in the clearing, which had silently filled with soldiers. It was some fifteen paces wide, a mound of earth with stones peeping out of it like boils on a backside. From the centre outwards lay a fallen tree, its twisted roots exposed to the air. Above, branches from other trees were jealously vying to reclaim the gap left in the canopy.

Quietly Gredda spread the order that the blades were to stand in a circle around the bows, some of whom climbed up onto the log. Questing eyes went back and forth across the busy greenery. They'd barely got into position when Bel noticed that the birds had gone quiet.

They're close.

'They're close,' called Munpo. 'Be ready, soldiers! No need to be too quiet now,' he added to Bel, who stood next to him. 'Noise will draw them to us.'

In the upper reaches of the trees were plenty of shaded hiding spots. As the leaves moved in the breeze, roving patterns of light gave the illusion of movement. Taut bows swivelled to a rustling in the trees, but it was just a bird flying away. Bel turned his sword in his hands, waiting for the moment that was sure to come soon. His skin tingled with excitement and suddenly he knew with certainty – this was what he'd been born to do. He was a warrior. The truth of it shot through him, concentrating molten in his heart. Shaking himself, he told himself not to forget the danger, as Munpo had warned, but as he sensed the eyes of the enemy on him, he found it very difficult to keep a fierce grin from his face.

They're here.
Where?
All around.
I see nothing.
Look left. The palebark tree at the edge of the clearing. Halfway up.

Bel searched, his gaze falling on a spray of foliage in which yellow eyes glinted. 'There!' he said, pointing. 'In the palebark!'

The bows looked but did not spy the target. Impatiently, almost eagerly, Bel pulled a crossbow from his belt and loosed a bolt. There was a *thunk* in the shadows and a furry body fell from the tree trailing gangly limbs, to land somewhere outside the clearing. Bel notched another bolt in the crossbow.

A sound like cats in pain filled the air from all sides and the forest came alive. Shadows gave birth to snarling offspring. Growths of moss on trees became the hairy backs of monsters. Huggers ran out onto branches overhanging the clearing and dropped, their limbs stretched in oncoming embrace. Arrows whizzed upwards and beasts twisted in the air, screaming as their brown blood rained down. One fell past the wave of arrows and landed on a bow. The creature wrapped its limbs about her and gave a mighty *squeeze*. There came the sound of ribs snapping and the beast sprang away as she toppled, vomiting blood. Hunna thrust his sword towards it, punching into the creature's gut.

'Stand fast!' bellowed Munpo as more huggers bounded out of the undergrowth and swung through the lower branches. They were attacking on all levels, from all sides. 'Let them come to us! Don't break the circle!'

Bel found himself facing two of them on the ground, their baleful yellow eyes staring out from under tufts of brown-green fur, their wide mouths open to reveal rows of stubby little fangs. They prowled towards him, low to the ground.

The bigger one will leap first.

A moment later the larger creature sprang, a *schick* sounding as claws extended from its hands and feet. Bel slashed it to the ground, spilling its guts as the second creature darted in to swipe at his legs. Claws scraped the hard leather of his boots and it raised its head to snarl. There was a flash of metal about its neck and the head rolled away with snarl fixed forever. Munpo glanced at Bel, nodded, then called again for the blades to keep formation and protect the bows in the centre. Despite his shouts, the circle was breaking.

See the big male?

For a moment Bel saw it, stalking past a tree at the edge of the clearing, at least twice the size of the others. He pulled the crossbow free of his belt.

Watch out to your left!

Bel ignored the spirit's cry and went to squeeze the crossbow trigger. A hugger crashed against his shoulder, knocking the crossbow from his hand and pinning his sword arm to his side as it encircled his torso with its grip. He staggered backwards as the creature gnashed at him, its foetid breath making him gag. As he gagged, the hugger tightened its grip, forcing the air out of his lungs. Bel strained under the furry embrace and the creature snarled in rage as he started to loosen its grip. It threw back its head and howled, hugging with all its might, and Bel felt a sickening pressure on his chest.

Come on, man! Use your free hand!

Bel punched wildly at the hugger, bruising his hands on its muscular body. He tried to suck in breath and failed, unable to open his lungs wide enough. His vision dotted and the world swam. His free hand flailed, searching for the creature's neck, and found it. All his strength went into a squeeze of his own. The hugger's howl cut off abruptly as he crushed its windpipe, its eyes bulging as the light behind them went out. It dropped away limply, leaving Bel coughing and gasping as air gushed back into him.

The faintness passed quickly and he felt even stronger for the adrenaline hit. He bellowed and ran at three huggers who were bounding for a bow, swinging his sword about him with gathering momentum. He flew through the huggers like a metal wind, their screams filling the air along with their blood. One managed to begin a leap at the bow, but jerked backwards suddenly as Bel caught it by the leg and swung it around like a sack of potatoes to dash its brains out on a rock. Next to it, a wounded hugger opened its eyes just in time to see Bel's foot descending before its head was pulped.

Bel checked the ground for his crossbow and spotted it. He rolled towards it, coming up on one knee with the weapon in his hands, shooting a bolt into a hugger swinging from the trees. He slid it back into his belt and noticed Munpo, who had a gash in his arm but was otherwise unhurt. The troop leader was furiously glancing about for his next target. Around him soldiers were ramming their swords into the wounded or dying, but suddenly there were no fresh waves bounding in. The screeching in the trees began to dwindle – the huggers were retreating.

'The big male!' shouted Rokinin, pointing with one of the two longswords he carried. Bel saw the large hugger swinging away through the trees, followed by some of its smaller brethren.

'Follow it!' shouted Munpo, charging into the undergrowth. 'It'll lead us to the nest!'

Bel bounded after, slashing at plants in his way. Ahead he could make out the fleeing beasts, sometimes springing from tree to tree like cats, sometimes swinging like apes. He could hear other soldiers in pursuit and knew the troop had begun to spread out. Somewhere Munpo was calling orders – the nest had to be found and every beast there killed.

Bel stumbled over a hidden root, but caught hold of a branch and hardly broke pace. He heard a series of crashes to his side and saw M'Meska springing high on her powerful hind legs, spines raised along her back. Two bounds and she was away ahead of him. He rounded a boulder to see the Saurian sighting the big hugger with her longbow. Her arrow flew towards the beast, catching it in the backside mid-swing. It wailed and barely managed to catch its next branch. M'Meska sent another arrow and this one struck its shoulder as it was hauling itself up. It yelped and lost its grip, crashing to the bushes below.

Blade Bel –

Not now!

Bel found himself alongside Munpo, and together they approached the place where the big male had fallen. Somewhere nearby they heard Gredda calling for the rest of the troop to converge.

'Be careful,' puffed Munpo as they slowed. 'There may still be some fight left in it.'

Blade!

Quiet!

They came to a stop before the quivering shrubs where the big male had fallen. Munpo raised a finger to his lips and tentatively pushed aside a fern with his sword. The big hugger erupted, white mucus streaming from its wide maw, yellow eyes blazing with hate. Munpo and Bel each raised their swords, but the hugger jerked in-leap and fell, a final arrow sticking in its neck. They turned to see M'Meska on a log behind them, scaly lips pulled back in a snarl.

'Not even make good rug, smell so bad,' spat the Saurian. Her eyes flickered and her nostrils flared. 'Smell *very* bad here,' she said.

She glanced up, and the others followed her gaze. As they did, their knuckles whitened on their weapons. They were standing in the middle of the nest.

I tried to warn you.

In the trees above were row upon row of yellow eyes. Wide lipless mouths opened to reveal dripping fangs. Claws sheathed and unsheathed as the creatures began to hiss, the sound building as more joined in. Heads appeared from inside nest-like structures of twig and leaf as parents realised they had been invaded.

There were so *many*.

'Arkus,' whispered Munpo. 'I'm a fool. We only fought a hunting party. *This* is the nest guard.'

A hugger slid partway down a trunk nearby, lifting its head to howl.

'Come on,' said Munpo softly, backing away. 'We must regroup.'

As he, Bel and M'Meska began to move, more huggers descended. One landed in the undergrowth close

by, and the three broke into a run, heading towards
Gredda's calls.

'Regroup!' yelled Munpo as they went. 'Regroup!'

From all directions came sounds of soldiers blundering
through vegetation. Somewhere someone screamed.
They came upon Gredda and found her with half the
troop, still calling to the others.

'To me!' came Rokinin's voice, not far off. 'Face
outwards!'

'To Rokinin!' shouted Munpo.

To Bel it did not feel like his feet touched the ground.
As he barrelled onwards, the air sucked through his
flaring nostrils had never seemed so fresh. A hugger
dropped in front of him and he ran it through without
stopping, trampling its corpse beneath him. Faced with
death, he had never felt so alive. He burst into a patch of
ferns just in time to see a soldier falling beneath them, a
hugger wrapped about him and gnawing at his neck. The
plants swished and settled, the soldier disappearing as if
sunk beneath water. Rokinin and Hunna were standing
with their backs to a large clawberry tree, holding off
a seething mass of huggers under the ferns. Dimly Bel
registered that they were hopelessly outnumbered. Beasts
swarmed down the trees, and he heard them attacking
those who followed closely on his heels.

Even as Bel charged to help Rokinin and Hunna,
the huggers overpowered them. Hunna fell screaming
under a mass of snapping fangs, while Rokinin grappled
helplessly with a hugger wrapped around his chest. Bel
pulled out his crossbow, fired a bolt into the hugger as
it dragged Rokinin down. The creature twisted off, but
Rokinin was already on his knees, shaking violently as
he was torn at below the ferns, out of sight. Bel leaped,

stabbing and stomping his feet, but Rokinin was beyond aid. As the town commander gasped and died, the huggers turned their yellow eyes on Bel.

Bel whooped and swung his sword. 'Come on then!' he yelled. 'Let's get to it!'

Iassia had never been so afraid. Death was not usually something that concerned him, a clever weaver being practically immortal, yet now he faced a fate worse than death.

He had come across a lost mind once. A ghost thing it had been, mad and unpredictable, unseen and unheard by most. He had listened to it for a while and it made no sense to him, though it was obviously in great distress. He'd had some sport with it when it had weakly tried to possess his body. If this Bel died, the pathetic torment that had once amused him would become his own living nightmare.

During the fighting he had been helping Bel as best he could. At one point he had whispered in the mind of a bow that a hugger falling towards Bel wanted to kill her. Consequently she had shot at it instead of the hugger that *was* above her, to her detriment. He'd sent thoughts to the huggers too, helping them perceive other soldiers as bigger threats than Bel. These efforts were tiring, but the huggers were simple-minded creatures, easier to influence than intelligent beings.

Now, however, Bel was surrounded, and against such numbers Iassia's influence meant little. Bel was an impressive warrior, cutting bodies from the air and cracking crawling backs under powerful feet, but Iassia knew there were simply too many. In a panic,

the weaver cast around for the mind of Munpo, and
found him not far off. The man was standing with
the remaining troop, their progress halted at a wall of
snapping mouths. Frantically Iassia whispered to him
that more soldiers were available at Bel's location, that
if they could break through they would gain the upper
hand. The troop leader called out to those remaining
to follow him, and they fought towards Bel.

Bel felt almost meditative. His movements had slipped
into the pattern of the fight and he whirled like a leaf in
a howling wind. Stepping this way and that, his sword
was a streaking flash of light about him, carving huggers
free of their lives.

'Where are the others?' shouted Munpo, as he and
those with him fought their way into the knee-high
ferns.

'All dead!' Bel shouted back.

Munpo had seven with him, including Keit and
M'Meska. The Saurian hung back from the main fight,
sending off arrow after arrow in search of shrieks.

'How many?' called Keit.

'Must be over sixty adults!' said Munpo. 'Biggest
nest I've ever seen!'

He jabbed a hugger through its shrieking mouth.
Claws gouged at his side and he cursed, kneeing
away another creature. Two of the remaining soldiers
screamed and fell.

Bel found that he couldn't remain in a single place,
so couldn't stay with his companions. This was a dance
with death, and to survive it he had to lead. Time
seemed to slow as he felled beast after beast, hacking

paths through the brown-green mass. He heard a cry as another wave of monsters broke against his companions. A hugger dropped lightly from a tree onto Keit's back and slashed his throat open with its claws. Bel bellowed, limbs and lives flying away from him, a dervish of destruction. A fierce joy burned in his breast. He could *see* the pattern of the fight, *knew* the steps he needed to tread. Sword *there*, fist *here*, boot *now*, elbow *there* . . . on and on until he did not know how much time passed, nor did he care.

Finally he swung at a hissing beast only to see it turn and scamper away. He leaped at another, but it was gone already, ferns quivering in its wake. His head snapped feverishly from side to side. The only huggers left were dead or in pieces. He rubbed the sweat from his eyes. The fight was over.

He tasted something foul and realised there was hugger blood in his mouth. It dribbled down his face and coated his clothes. As soon as he became aware of it, the smell was repulsive. He bent over and retched.

Someone groaned, and he staggered to where his comrades had made their stand. He found them all fallen, and sank to his knees with exhaustion. 'Who is alive here?' he asked. Keit did not speak, the hole in his neck being answer enough. Of the others, only Munpo opened his eyes. The old warrior tried to sit up, but grunted in pain and slumped back against the tree. Bel reached out to help him.

'Don't move me,' said the troop leader.

For Bel, reality began to sink in. His friends were dead, his leader dying, and he had killed like one born to do so. He'd been consumed by the spirit of battle; meanwhile, his companions had been destroyed.

'I'm sorry,' he murmured.

'Not your fault,' managed Munpo thickly. 'Blade Bel?'

'Yes?'

'Roll me some brittleleaf. In my top pocket.'

Bel nodded, and removed the pouch. With shaking fingers, he rolled brittleleaf into a paper. It was difficult because blood had made his fingers sticky.

'I thought the hunting party was the nest guard,' said Munpo, smiling bitterly.

'I know, sir.'

'No wonder the big fellow was with them, with this many mouths to feed. Must have been a big fire.' He sighed deeply. 'What did I tell you, Bel – never underestimate your opponent. What a fool I am, scattering my troop to pursue one hugger, like silly children chasing . . .'

But whatever Munpo's children chased, Bel never knew.

He put the brittleleaf end in Munpo's mouth.

From the trees above came a mewling and Bel forced his eyes upwards. Over the lip of one of the nests poked the hairy faces of hugger kittens, calling for their parents. He blinked slowly and reached for his crossbow. Through clouded eyes he slid a bolt into it, but the pounding in his head became overpowering and he lost track of his target. Dropping the crossbow, he pitched onto his side.

The only other thing he remembered that day was the forest floor moving beneath him, a scaly tail swinging back and forth across it.

The Deep Dark

The eel wound lazily through the murky water, pale grey with a long snout and eyes like copper coins. From his wide mouth jutted fangs at angles as crazy as the pillars of rock that protruded from the ocean floor. His skin was mottled and tough, scarred in many places. Sometimes old pains flared up and the eel ground his fangs in frustration, but he always continued to hunt. To stop and wait for wounds to heal was to invite starvation, or other predators. Lately the pain had become more general, and persistent. The eel had raised many broods, eaten many fish, fought many fights. When he saw baby eels swimming frantically along the ocean bed, he knew that he must have been small like that once. He did not eat the young eels, as he might once have, but instead used their fear to steer them into safer waters.

His senses were duller than they used to be, making it harder to search out prey. Stealing surreptitiously towards a school of fish, he burst from between rocks at speed, but at the pivotal moment his body failed him. Once the cramping stopped and he could swim again, he settled for an algal colony on a rock tower, swallowing it in hope of energy. Flesh was what he really needed.

He happened upon an eel nest amongst a cluster of rocks. Young eels darted into the safety of crevices as he approached, and a lone female flashed out. As the old eel drifted closer in the current, she turned her head from side to side, showing him her fangs. He veered wide, knowing she wouldn't attack unless he came closer. He saw that she was young, but not healthy. Her stomach was sunken and she had a smattering of white discoloration. Where was her mate? Was he dead? She would have trouble providing for so many babies on her own.

As he drifted away, the female stretched out to full length and rippled her body towards him. The old eel wound to a stop, curious. Her mate must indeed be dead, for only brooding females without a partner would seek to entice another into the nest. Taking a replacement mate could be a risky business.

Salt.

The old eel was barely able to care for himself, let alone a brood of young. He sensed, though, that the mother was weak and desperate. If she didn't hunt soon she would die, and then all her young would die too. Instinct turned him back towards her and he began to swim against the current. The effort seemed more taxing than it ever had before. The female regarded him warily as he approached.

The taste of salt on his lips. The cold breeze through his hair.

The eel realised he was floating off course and tried to correct himself – but his body wasn't responding any more. He lost momentum, rolling in the current to drift towards the bottom. A cloud of sediment rose as he hit, a soft impact that he did not feel. He lay still as his heart slowed, his breaths coming further apart, until his gills stopped moving altogether.

This, then, was what he could offer. The young family would feed on him, drawing out the strength he could no longer use, and perhaps he would save them. It was better than waiting for the crabs, and the old eel only wished that he'd caught a fish and filled his belly with fresh meat for the young. As floating particles settled on his body, he died in peace. The mother drew closer, still wary.

Salt.

There was the taste of salt on his lips.

Losara licked his lips and found his tongue dry, and drifted back to consciousness. The salt crystals encrusted on his lids broke as his eyes opened. Above him the Cloud covered the sky more thickly than he'd ever seen it. The serenity that came from immersing himself in the shadows of the sea was replaced by the bite in his stomach. He empathised with the hunger of the old eel.

The boat rocked slightly as he rummaged through his supplies and drank what little remained of his water. He was close to the Boundary now, and before him the world opened like the mouth of an enormous cave, swallowing the ocean. He took hold of the oars once more and began to row. Weariness had become his waking world, having rowed for days with such limited rations. He had never done much physical work before and his slender frame had nothing to replace the energy he burned. He'd tried to use his powers to lure fish up to the boat, but discovered that something kept them away. He'd sniffed out an enchantment on the boat itself, old and subtle. He didn't know whether he could have broken it or not, but instinct told him not to try. If fasting was supposed to be part of this journey, so be it. He found that he kept drifting from his body, losing himself in the boundless ocean, riding with the strange souls that dwelled there. The shadow was so strong here, in both the air and the depths beneath, surrounding him on all sides. It was hard to keep himself contained.

He wondered if he was failing this test. If so, when he reached the Boundary, he would drift over it without finding the Isle. There were many theories on the Boundary and what lay beyond it. Some thought new worlds; some thought oblivion; others thought it was the home of the gods themselves, where they kept their Wells. Kainordas also had a Boundary, far out in the Shallow Sea. From what Losara had heard, as one went further and further out, the light grew brighter until it was blinding. He shuddered at the thought of such a place. Only one thing was certain about the Boundaries: no one who went over them had ever returned.

He didn't feel too unsettled, however. Somehow he didn't believe that being abandoned at sea was his fate. The fields of wavelets on the choppy waters, the fresh chill tingling his ivory skin, all the lives moving beneath the surface . . . He lay back down, dangled a hand over each side of the boat, and out he spread, into the sea.

. . . *a large sturgeon cruises along, a row of phosphorescent circles glowing on its cheeks to attract unwary prey. It swims around something that looks like a large rock, but as Losara drifts closer he sees the 'rock' is alive, a creature like a lump of flesh covered in tough brown skin. Vents open in its side and an*

*acrid excretion plumes out. The sturgeon is repelled
and darts away . . .*

*. . . a school of five jet-black shrimps fossick in a
silt valley. Their small claws work the sediment, but
one steps over a buried worm. The worm snaps up,
catching the shrimp and crushing it in the loops of its
body. The remaining shrimps flick off in alarm, their
sad school that much smaller . . .*

*. . . a thing like a sea urchin on long, stilt-like legs
moves haltingly across a sandy plain. A crab with
claws twice as long as its body scuttles beneath a
rock. A green and white jellyfish, with a body like two
circles spinning in opposite directions. Other things . . .
stranger things . . . older things . . .*

*. . . Tyrellan stands by a ditch with a reedy stream
at the bottom. With him is a well-muscled goblin and
Heron. Tyrellan nods, and the goblins go down the
embankment to the stream. Tyrellan lies on his back,
shoots Heron an intense look, then lowers his head
under the water. The other goblin holds him down,
muscles bulging as Tyrellan begins to thrash. Eventually
Tyrellan lies still. The muscled goblin drags Tyrellan
out of the water and up the embankment, laying
him before Heron. Heron kneels, putting her fingers
to Tyrellan's wrist, then his neck. 'Is he dead?' asks
the muscled goblin. 'Yes,' says Heron. She glances at
the butterfly, which rests on the bridge of Tyrellan's
nose, its colourful wings open so their false eyes cover
Tyrellan's closed ones. Heron extends her hand and
uses magic to draw the water from Tyrellan's lungs,
then shocks his heart into beating again. Tyrellan
lurches up, coughing violently. For a moment he's
dazed, then he looks around blearily and sees the*

butterfly. He scrambles to his feet and stumbles away, but it follows him as closely as ever. 'If death does not sever the connection,' he roars, 'will this vermin haunt my gravestone for all time?' . . .

He awoke to the oars straining in their holdings. How long had he been gone? The boat was now surrounded by a darkness he could not penetrate, and somewhere inside it was the Isle. There was no point rowing any more. The gods would guide him now, or not. Hours passed and he drifted, half-asleep, half-super-aware of the environment around him. Sea life dwindled, save for a few ancient presences that he felt cautious about approaching. As he dreamed he found himself looking down at the boat, which held a different passenger.

It is a young Arabodedas woman, her hair running in snakish dreadlocks, baring sharpened teeth. Losara knows her to be Assidax, the Shadowdreamer preceding Raker. He can see her clearly somehow, even though she sails through the same darkness he does. He can see everything, he realises . . . not as if it is being lit up, but just because it is there. He wonders if this strange sense is a result of the dream, or if it will carry into his waking state.

Assidax changes, and now it is Raker who sails to the Isle. A young man, he nevertheless looks as drawn as his bust in Skygrip. Many scars run across his face, and his eyes are afraid as he clutches a painful stomach and stares into the dark. He thinks that he has failed, that he will drift across the Boundary.

They were here, where I am, thinks Losara. They were here and they succeeded. I have not yet passed the Boundary.

Raker fades and a young Battu takes his place. Battu rows ceaselessly, his muscles bulging under his black robe, fierce determination on his face. Abruptly he lets the oars drop and stands up tall in the boat. 'Receive me, my gods!' he calls. 'Your servant is here!' Moments of silence go by and Battu's face twists in frustration. He sits down and begins to row once more.

Now his view is from beneath the waves, looking up at the boat far above, cutting across a roof of water. Ahead is a great undersea mountain, and Losara sees something climbing the slope. The sense of presence the entity exudes is awe-inspiring, and he draws closer in the dream, taking in the immensity of it. Colossal armoured legs rise and fall, sinking deeply into sand and rock with equal ease. Plates of exoskeletal armour as wide as villages creak against each other as it climbs, its cyclopean front claws opening like scissors. It is like a gigantean lobster, its horny black armour streaked with greens and reds, a being so enormous it could swat dragons like dragonflies. Slowly and surely it plods up the rise towards the boat.

Losara sees the hands of the boat's occupant trailing in the water as he sleeps. In a moment of cold clarity, he realises he is shadowdreaming the present, that the person in the boat is him, and the creature is reaching towards him with pincers that could crush towers . . .

Back he went, streaming to his body, rushing to contain his consciousness within it. At the very moment he arrived back inside himself, he heard a *snick* in the water beside him. The tips of the entity's claws appeared above the surface, razor-sharp points clicking together at the pinnacle of the great appendages. Losara sat up abruptly, raising his hands from the water to find them gone, sliced cleanly at the wrist. Twin fountains erupted from the stumps as his life pulsed out of him in a torrent. He wondered vaguely if the attack was over, or if the boat would smash around him as the monster finished its work. A moment later his eyes glazed over and he passed out.

Trickster

First came the birds, their songs competing sweetly. That was good – it meant there were no huggers nearby. Then came the sound of someone breathing, close to the . . . bed? Yes, he was in a bed. On the back of this realisation he became aware of his aching body. And then, distant echoes from the spirit . . .

. . . must get gone to Treewith . . . if someone finds it? . . . he's awake . . .

Bel certainly didn't feel awake. His eyelids were strapped down like saddlebags.

. . . he's listening . . .

When he recalled the battle, it was as if he'd been drunk. It had been intoxicating, mesmerising, how he had moved! But now, as with drink, his spirits plummeted in the aftermath. As he'd ridden a bloodlust high, his troop had been slaughtered and he'd managed only to save himself. Was that how it would be in the end? Was he to secure victory against the shadow even as his friends fell around him? M'Meska had lived, but something told him she would have lived anyway. In fact it was *he* who owed his life to *her* – she must have been the one to carry him back here after he lost consciousness.

Someone put a hand on his arm and instinctively he opened his eyes. For a moment he didn't recognise the lean woman sitting by the bed. Then he remembered she was Pelar, the Citizen Prime of Drel.

'Here,' she said, 'drink this.'

The liquid she pressed to his lips was bitter, but sparkled in his mouth and throat. Some sort of revitalising tonic?

'I'm in Drel?' he asked.

'Yes. Your comrade M'Meska brought you back from the forest. She says . . .'

'What?' said Bel wearily, closing his eyes again.

'That you two are the only ones who survived. That the nest was big, bigger than anyone thought it would be.'

'Must have been a big fire,' said Bel, echoing Munpo's words.

Pelar's brow twitched. 'Blade Bel? The Saurian says she didn't see Rokinin killed. Since we don't have any bodies, we've no way of knowing who we lost.'

Bel sighed deeply, remembering Rokinin shaking in the ferns. 'Everyone was lost,' he muttered.

'Are you sure? Did you see him die?'

Bel opened his eyes again, irritated that she pressed him. 'Yes,' he snapped. 'I saw him die! Horribly.' As tears formed in Pelar's eyes, he tried to control his annoyance. 'I'm sorry,' he said. 'Was he . . . dear to you?'

'It's a small town,' said Pelar. 'And he was a good man who'll be missed by many. I will be one of them.' She wiped her tears even as new ones formed.

'I am sorry,' said Bel, more sincerely this time. 'He died bravely, defending the people he loved.'

'Yes,' said Pelar. 'As did the others from Drel who were with him.' She rose. 'I'll leave you to get dressed. M'Meska will want to know you're awake. I think she's eager to be away.'

'How long have I been asleep?'

'Since yesterday afternoon,' said Pelar.

Outside it was a sunny morning, just like the one so fresh in his mind. Surreally, it felt as if no time had passed.

'Blade Bel?' said Pelar.

'Yes?'

'The town thanks you for your efforts. M'Meska told us how you fought. We are grateful you could free us from the threat in the forest.' She bowed her head in solemn thanks, then quietly shut the door behind her.

That's right, thought Bel. *We fought for the townsfolk. It is a victory, after all.*

The tonic was muting his aches and he no longer felt like going back to sleep. Sitting up stiffly, he swung his legs over the side of the bed.

. . . mad warrior . . .

What? he demanded suddenly, thinking in a shout.

Ah! came the spirit's voice, perfectly clear this time. *You're getting up?*

I can hear you, you know. I hear things I don't think you mean me to. What are you?

As I've told you, Blade Bel, came the quick response. *A spirit sent by Arkus to aid you in your battles.*

Aid me? What aid have you given me?

In answer Bel received a deluge of images from the previous day, showing each instance when the spirit had influenced the troop or the huggers. Bel somehow sensed that the spirit was trying to repress them, but they kept coming.

You used my comrades as monster bait? he thought angrily. *You made them ignore their own safety to protect me? You caused soldiers to die who might have lived? This is the work of Arkus?*

Blade –

Arkus would never send one such as you. What are you?

. . . betrayer . . . exile of the Garden . . .

WHAT ARE YOU?

'Awake, I see,' said M'Meska. 'Is good. The day run by. We must be gone.'

Bel hadn't heard the Saurian come in, but she was bobbing across the room to the bed. Gripping Bel by the shoulders, she hauled him unwillingly to a standing position. He realised, with some embarrassment, that someone had stripped him to his undergarments.

'Get dressed,' said the Saurian. 'No bashful. Your human parts mean nothing to me. Ugly as the rest of you.'

She started throwing Bel's things on the bed. Bel staggered to the window and looked out. He was in the Drel barracks.

'What happened?' he asked.

'You saw.'

'I passed out.'

'I know. Who lug you all way back to Drel, think you?'

He turned. 'Yes. Thank you for that, M'Meska.'

'Well, not going leave you there. You soldier of Halls.' The Saurian paused in attacking Bel's things. 'I in troop with Munpo lot of years,' she said. One of the spines on her head twitched. 'And some of others too. Other soldiers in troop. Many years.'

'I understand you.'

'Very bad, what happen in forest.'

'Yes,' said Bel. 'No argument there.'

'You fight very well,' she said. 'I never see like it. Like berserker, but more . . . art.' She looked frustrated. 'I have no way to say in Varenkai tongue. One man, how can take on so many huggers and live? Then but, you had M'Meska helping.'

Bel dimly recalled M'Meska leaping from rock to branch, plying arrows into shrieking huggers.

'I shoot down nests after too,' she said. 'No nest, no trouble for Drel.' She stood abruptly. 'Hurry up. I want get to Treewith tonight.'

. . . *Treewith* . . .

You and I are going to have words, said Bel.

Soon enough they were riding down the main road of Drel. Some of the townsfolk tipped their hats or called out thanks. Some remained silent. Bel knew the damage dealt to these people was ongoing. He was relieved when they passed out the gate into the green fields beyond. The day seemed sunnier as they broke into a gallop towards Treewith.

As they rode, Iassia could feel Bel listening for him. Try as he might to keep his thoughts shielded, this whole experience had left him weak and he desperately needed to be back in his body. Soon Bel would see through his lies as if they were made of glass.

What are you? came Bel's demand once more.

. . . a race once loved by the Sun God . . . now exiles from Paradise . . .

What? Why?

. . . because we betrayed Arkus . . .

Stay back, Iassia directed clearly. *Stay out of my thoughts.*

Your thoughts? Is that what I hear when I'm not supposed to?

. . . yes . . .

Why? How?

Our minds are too close. So close that if you continue to invade my thoughts, it will destroy us both.

I don't think so, replied Bel.

Foolish human, continued Iassia. *I am weak, and fighting you makes me weaker. Do you know what will happen if I expend my strength?*

Tell me, liar.

My mind will unravel inside yours and I'll never be able to leave. For the rest of your life you'll be haunted by echoes of me. Is that what you want?

Where did you come from? Bel demanded angrily. *WHAT ARE YOU?*

Iassia could not hold out against the force of Bel's will, and answering thoughts poured forth.

. . . I am a weaver . . . joined you accidentally at Treewith Inn . . . my mind was separated from my body when I entered yours . . . I became lost because there is something missing inside you . . . we need to get back to the inn . . .

A weaver? A weaver bird?

. . . yes . . .

So you are a trickster.

Yes, said Iassia. What did he care now? *I am.*

What did you mean there is something missing?

You aren't a whole person, Bel. You are forced together like the wrong pieces in a puzzle. Your components grind against each other like malfunctioning cogs.

He sensed Bel considering this.

Everyone has chaos inside them, Bel said eventually.

Not like this. You always believed, didn't you, that it was a blessing that the shadow part of you was expunged? You think you lost nothing. You think, in fact, that you are better than others because you have been cleansed of weakness. Well, it isn't true, Bel. You are less of a person than your other.

Your lies mean nothing.

But you'd be able to tell if I was lying, wouldn't you, Bel? You can hear my real thoughts. Listen to them now.

... empty ... shell ... half-made ...

You don't know what you're talking about.

The view is very clear from here, I assure you. You forget that I am privy to your thoughts, as well as you to mine, and your doubts betray you. You do not disbelieve my words in your heart.

You are nothing but a servant of evil.

And you, Bel, are a warrior. A killer. I have never seen a man fight like you.

Why are you telling me this? asked Bel, confused at the sudden change in tack.

You imagine yourself fighting on the side of right, said Iassia. *But in truth it doesn't matter who you fight for, because it's the fight itself that you love. I was there, Bel, along for that ride. How joyous you were amidst the ruin. Dancing, isn't that how you've been thinking about it?*

Shut up.

If it was you who'd been taken to Fenvarrow as a child, you would be fighting for us now, too stupid to know the difference. All you want is to be powerful, to be adored! Arrogance and vanity are not equal to fighting for one's beliefs, Blade Bel. There is no depth to you.

It is sickening to have such an insidious thing as you inside me, replied Bel. *Spinning your weaver's lies, no truth to their fabric. My father was born in Kainordas, and my family before him, yet you think me so mutable?*

You argue out of pride, said Iassia. *You have no true convictions. You simply love the thrill. And that, my dear, makes you shallow.*

Where is your body in Treewith? demanded Bel suddenly.

You couldn't destroy it even if you found it.

Where is it?

Don't force me to defend myself over this. I know you sensed the truth in the threat I made before, because I was telling the truth. It will not be pleasant for either of us if our minds become entangled.

Much to Iassia's relief, Bel fell silent.

Bel tried to keep his mind blank as they rode, not wishing to share his private thoughts with his invader. It was difficult – Iassia's words had shaken him, made him think again on his *other* self. That was just some dark, twisted thing, that was what Fahren had always told him. A worm of shadow that had crept away, which he was better off without. One day Bel would track him down and . . . what? He wasn't exactly sure.

Perhaps he did feel empty. Sometimes.

Time and again he found himself returning to thoughts of the fight, remembering the violent ecstasy that had fuelled him. He hadn't been empty then, of that he was certain. He found himself longing to fight again – surely that wasn't the right reaction? What had Iassia said? That he lived for the fight and not the cause. What did it matter, as long as the job got done? He needed time, he decided. Time to sort it all out.

When night fell, the Saurian asked if he wished to camp or push on. Bel opted to push on despite great weariness. A few hours later they saw the twinkling lanterns of Treewith in the distance. Bel sensed excitement growing in the weaver as they approached. He was loath to let the creature go free, but equally loath to delay its exit from his mind. They arrived at the inn and, while M'Meska saw to the horses, Bel went inside.

Where? he asked.

The same room you had before.

Bel spoke to the innkeeper and, thankfully, the room was vacant. He shouldered his pack and went quickly upstairs, pausing at the door to fumble with the key.

All right, you parasite, he said. *You'd better fly faster than my sword.*

There was no reply. Bel realised he could no longer hear the distant echoes of the weaver's thoughts. Pushing the door open, he pulled the crossbow from his belt.

On the windowsill sat a tiny bird like a colourful sparrow. A beautiful thing, yet Bel didn't hesitate to squeeze the trigger. The bolt flew across the room and bounced off some kind of invisible barrier.

'Mortal weapons?' chirped Iassia merrily, his blood-drop eyes glinting. 'How optimistic. And really, after all we've been through!' The bird gave a chirp that Bel knew was a laugh, and launched from the window into the night.

Bel ran to the window, but the weaver had disappeared. He closed the window and locked it, even though the night was warm. Still feeling disquieted, he collapsed face forward on the bed, exchanging worry for oblivion.

Iassia was joyous to be restored, savouring the air under his wings as he zipped through town. He was weary, but it wasn't the crippling weakness of the last few days. Dinner had been welcome too: a pigeon that had been roosting peacefully until his sharp little beak had stabbed into the main artery of its neck.

He landed on top of Treewith Inn, wondering what to do next. He would alert the Shadowdreamer to Bel's whereabouts, but doubted the dark lord's operatives would arrive before Bel made it back to the Halls. Battu would be angry, but Iassia wasn't worried. Even if Battu shadow-travelled to ask him questions, he would claim he'd only just stumbled across the lad tonight, and it was very sad there was no time left to take advantage of the situation.

After that, there was one more thing. He fluttered about the town, peeping through open windows, and soon found what he was looking for.

The small blond boy was stupid and easy to manipulate. He was also a clumsy writer and Iassia was growing frustrated. He hid it well, however, continuing to speak to the child in warm, soothing tones.

'Come now, young Meriwan,' he chirped from his place on the oak writing desk. 'Surely parents wealthy enough to own a lovely house such as this have also seen to your education?'

'Yes, birdy,' said the boy. 'Mr Neirdu is my tutor. He comes for lessons once a day, and I gotta practise an hour after too!'

'Well, that sounds like fun,' said Iassia.

Meriwan pursed his lips. 'It ain't,' he said. 'I hate it. It's borin'.'

The child stomped across the study, which was located on the second floor of a large house. The parents, who were downstairs with guests, were obviously well-to-do. Paintings and tapestries hung from the walls, and the ledge above the fireplace was littered with jade statuettes. The child Meriwan had been asleep in his upstairs bedroom when Iassia had spied him through an open window. It seemed, unfortunately, that the child's delight at meeting a talking bird was not enough to overcome his dislike of writing. Iassia was having to work harder than expected and he was getting a headache.

'Now, Meriwan,' he said, 'the sooner you finish the letter for me, the sooner I can give you your reward.' The child's eyes lit up with excitement. 'Just a couple more lines and then we can go. This boring work will be over very quickly if you just *sit down and finish*.'

'Allllll riiiiiight,' said the child, begrudgingly walking back to the desk and sitting down. He picked up the quill and dipped it in ink. 'What next?'

Iassia dictated the last lines of the letter and the child struggled onwards, sometimes stopping to sound out longer words. Iassia was sure there'd be spelling mistakes, but it hardly mattered as long as the message was clear. Finally it was written, and Iassia had Meriwan read it back to him. This also took a long time, and his anger with the moronic man-child grew, though he was the picture of patience as he listened. Eventually the child finished.

'That was very good, Meriwan,' said Iassia. 'Thank you very much. Now all we need is for the letter to go into one of these envelopes here . . . that's right . . . now a wax seal like you've seen Papa do, I'm sure . . . wonderful . . . and now we address it.'

Finally the letter was written, sealed and addressed. 'What a wonderful job you've done, bright boy,' said Iassia, making Meriwan beam with pride. 'You've certainly earned your reward!'

'It's time?' Meriwan asked with eyes alight.

'Oh yes,' chirped Iassia. 'It certainly is. Open the window, child.'

Meriwan went to the study window and creaked it open. Iassia felt sudden attention from downstairs. Someone had heard.

'Now, child,' said Iassia, 'I grant you the magical power of flight!' And he flew around Meriwan's head, singing a soft and lilting song as he whispered softly into his mind: *The power of flight is yours . . . the power of flight is yours . . .*

'That's it?' said the child excitedly. 'I can fly?'

'Of course you can,' said Iassia. 'What kind of magic bird would I be if my spells didn't work?'

He swooped down onto the desk and snatched up the letter in his claws.

'All right, my bright boy,' he continued quickly, hearing steps on the stairs outside. 'Let us go out together, soaring into the night! Think how jealous your friends will be!'

'Mr Neirdu can't teach me writing if I can fly away!' chuckled Meriwan.

'Indeed!' laughed Iassia. There was a footstep just outside the study door. 'Here we go, Meriwan! Follow me!'

As Meriwan's father opened the study door, he cried out in horror to see his son leaping from the window, laughing happily. The sound continued downwards, stopping abruptly as Meriwan hit the paving below.

What was Taken

Cold wrapped him like a second skin. Was he in the depths of the sea? Floating in the shadowdream? Both? How long had he been here? Hours, days... longer? Time had no meaning in this void. Sometimes he heard voices, and maybe he was spinning, as if being turned in huge hands... or claws? Then came one voice above the others, clear and silken.

'Losara.'

'Who is there?' he asked, not exactly with words.

'We are those who gave you your name. We are those who will ask you to serve.'

'You are the gods.'

'As you say.'

Something rose in the black and carried him along, though he could not tell where, or from where.

'What is this place?'

'No place. Between places. You are here while your body is mended. You are here to see.'

'See what?'

'What was taken,' said the voice.

Darkness turned to light.

He was in a forest, creeping through undergrowth. It was like being in the dream, but this time he was not a floating observer, nor even himself. He was someone else. He was seeing through another's eyes, running on someone else's feet, thinking someone else's thoughts. His own consciousness retreated into the background, a dim awareness only, as he *became . . .*

. . . Bel ducked under the frond of an enormous fern and glanced around through the trees. A tingle ran down his spine. Somewhere in Drel Forest there were huggers, and soon he would be fighting them. Here he was, on the cusp of battle – something he had imagined, played at and trained for almost as long as he could remember. Soon his sword would leap from its scabbard with real purpose, and perhaps it would never slide back in. Thrills went through him at the thought, every sense alert. He found, to his surprise, that he was not afraid. He felt like a boy again. He came upon numerous opponents, carved his way through, his blood firing at each blow landed, each attack dodged. He fought with sword and fist and bow, fought with rapture and a sense of purpose, until the battle was over . . . he put brittleleaf between Munpo's dead lips . . .

Losara floated free, himself once more, a rude shock. Gone was the body of Bel, the thoughts, emotions and memories, all at once and without warning. He felt as if he had been inverted. For a short time he had *been* his counterpart. He remembered Bel's feelings, but now only as words – they had none of their colour or taste. They were foreign, and he knew he could not manufacture them on his own. A sense of loss came over him, but his old calm returned and he put it aside. There was nothing he could do but seek to understand . . .

. . . *'If you're to be a leader,'* Munpo said, *'and Taskmaster Corlas assures me that the Throne is takin' a personal interest in your military career, then the more you know the better.'*

Leadership – there had been memories associated with that. Bel had often led his student peers to victory in mock skirmishes. He was popular and had become quickly respected within his new troop. The Throne himself had picked him out to lead. Losara knew that he too would have to lead one day. Did he possess Bel's qualities? Would he be able to inspire? Would soldiers follow him because they wanted to, or because they had to?

. . . *Bel felt as if he skimmed across the ground. He barrelled onwards, and the air through his nostrils had never seemed so sweet. A hugger dropped in front of him and he ran it through, trampling its corpse beneath him. Faced with death, he had never felt so alive . . .*

There was war in Losara's future, but he did not look forward to it, did not derive any satisfaction from causing harm. Bel, on the other hand, seemed well suited to the task. Bel would not shy from killing; he would seek it out. How did a reluctance to kill fit into Losara's future of conquering the world?

. . . *His movements slipped into the pattern of the fight and he whirled like a leaf in a howling wind. Stepping this way and that, his sword was a streaking flash of light about him, carving huggers free of their lives . . .*

A soldier, then, he might have been. The spirit of battle, dancing with death, instinctively able to navigate a fight. Instead, such a man was his opponent.

Lost in such thoughts, he rose above the forest until he could see only treetops.

He awoke.

He was on his back, staring up at the roiling darkness of the Cloud. The sound of lapping water came from all sides and a cold wind moved the blue hair from his eyes. He felt different.

He sat up. Beneath him, wet black stone ran down to the sea, which began just past his feet. Behind him rose a misshapen hill dotted with tiny blue flowers. He was on Assedrynn's Isle.

There was a splash at the water's edge as waves broke against the island. About a hundred paces out, something was rising from the sea. Spines pierced the surface, as tall as trees, and a huge bulk followed. Fibrous triple-pointed fins spread out flat over the water's surface, hauling up a bulging fish-like head. The head reared – thick rubbery lips and glistening black eyes, with whiskers that whipped like tentacles. There was no mistaking the being – Losara had seen him many times in carvings and paintings.

Assedrynn.

Losara rolled fluidly into a kneel. The water continued to bubble and then, to the god's left and right, others rose. Awe washed through Losara with each head that broke the surface. There was Elsara, the lionfish, all spines and stripes, sunset orange and blood red. Mokan and Mer, the twins, were like green-scaled Graka with fin-like wings. Lampet, the serpent, his long cobbled neck rising high above the sea, the oval eyes in his dragon's head glowing blue, then yellow, then red,

then green. Antennae and claws erupted upwards, and
Losara recognised Chirruk, the watcher, who had taken
his hands.

His hands?

Something stopped him looking. It felt like they were
still there, but lighter, like the rest of him. He felt as
if he could run a thousand leagues without drawing a
breath. He rubbed his fingers together – like silk they
were. What had changed? Still he did not look, not yet.
One thing at a time, and he was still marvelling that
the Dark Gods were just across the water. Should he be
afraid? Others would have been. The gods could grant
him favour or obliterate his spirit, but either way it was
their choice and he could do nothing but be himself.
Where was the fear in that?

'Losara.'

It was the voice from the void, but now it echoed
across the sea, rich and full. Assedrynn's voice.

'My masters,' Losara said. 'You honour me.'

Lampet's eyes flared blue and his head extended over
the sea until he was but paces away. His jaws opened,
revealing a crystal maw, stalactite fangs that glinted in
the light of his eyes. His voice rasped, and Losara felt
breath like the air of an ancient cavern wash over him.

'It is you who honour us, saviour child.'

Losara stared mesmerised into the pulsing eyes.
Sometimes he *could* understand fear.

'Recede, Lampet,' said Assedrynn. Lampet drew
back, the coils of his body slipping under the surface
until only his head remained. 'Your coming is welcome,
Losara,' continued Assedrynn. 'We had feared the
Caretaker might try something foolish.'

'The Caretaker?' asked Losara.

'The present Shadowdreamer. His pride has turned him against our will.'

'His greed!' howled Mokan, her voice like piercing wind. 'He spent too long with the sharks, the sharks!'

'Silence, Mokan,' said Assedrynn. 'There are many things to discuss and this is not the first. Losara.'

'Master?'

'We know you have not looked, but Chirruk is anxious. What do you think of her work?'

Again Losara rubbed his fingers. So smooth. Slowly he looked down . . . and gasped at what had been done.

The slice at his wrists was clean. Where skin ended there was shadow, as if he wore gloves made from night. But they weren't gloves, they were his hands. Shadowhands.

'Your mortal blood is drained away,' said Assedrynn. 'Our essence in its place. Shadow travels the winding paths of your body, feeds your flesh, moves your heart.'

Losara turned his hands, feeling nothing of the cold breeze. In the darkness, they were darker. They were beautiful.

'The world is changing,' said Assedrynn. 'Arkus seeks an end to the war between the gods. Your counterpart will side with him, and do much with what was taken from you. We need a champion, saviour child. Someone to carry our will to the world, to save our peoples, and us. Someone to serve as Shadowhand.

'Great power is yours, greater than the world has ever known.' The god rose further out of the sea, water rolling down his bulk. 'Will you serve us first and only, Losara Shadowhand?'

Losara looked north. Somewhere out there, the sun beat down on grassy fields and the enemies of his people plotted to conquer and destroy. His counterpart, turned against him, was waiting.

'Yes,' he said, as wind blew hair back from his midnight eyes. 'I will serve. But not first and only.'

Assedrynn stirred, and Lampet's eyes flared red.

'As well,' said Losara.

Lalenda gazed at the wall of her stark little room, thinking thoughts of home. Somewhere out there was Swampwild, and her mother, and others of her kind. They all seemed very far away, a dream from another life.

She went to her dusty mirror and regarded herself critically. She opened her wings, flexing them for the first time in weeks. She saw how creased and crinkled they were, and knew how weak they had become. She scowled at her reflection and walked out of the room.

Down to the base of Skygrip she travelled, heading for the entrance cavern – the only place she knew of that led to a cave complex beneath the castle. It took her some time to reach the bottom as she didn't know the route through the twisted corridors, nor the portal doors that would quicken the journey. She was careful to avoid patrols in case they took exception to her presence – she had no official reason to be so far down in the castle. Eventually she arrived at the entrance cavern and turned her eyes to the tunnel openings that lined its walls. Most led back up into the castle, but one or two, she knew, went down. Her eyes fell on a promising one and, after checking that the coast was clear, she circled the chamber towards it.

Voices floated into the cavern and she froze in the shadow of a towering statue. A cleaning squad of Grey

Goblins emerged from a tunnel carrying buckets and mops and, to Lalenda's dismay, set to work slopping water on the floor. She waited until they had settled into the task, then glanced over at the tunnel she wanted. It was only about twenty paces away.

'What does it matter if they see you anyway?' she whispered to herself. 'They're only cleaners.'

She skipped from the shadows, her wings spreading to make her lighter on her feet. She made little sound as she skimmed the floor and plunged into the enveloping blackness of the tunnel entrance. The Greys gave no indication they'd seen her. Relieved, she went further into the tunnel, which sloped downwards into dark. It took some moments for her eyes to adjust, and even then she couldn't make out much. The best night vision was not much use in absolute darkness, and she paused to reconsider her plan.

Icy fingers ran through her hair and caressed her neck, making her cry out in terror. The air around her seemed to move, there was a flash of white – and a gigantic, grinning maw of fangs appeared.

'What you be doin' down here, little tasty?'

Lalenda backed away, quaking. She'd never seen the Golgoleth Ghost before, but knew this must be him.

'Aren't you supposed to be guarding the front door?' she managed to stammer.

The grin widened and claws as long as swords flashed about her. 'Supposed to be, yes,' came the dry, hollow voice. 'But Grimra can go further from his amulet than most people be thinking. Why you be going into the caves, little flutterbug?'

Lalenda found herself backed against the wall. She

tried to inch her way back up the tunnel. 'Er . . . I'm just lost,' she said. 'But thank you for setting me right.'

'Lost?' The grin reappeared right in front of her, halting her progress entirely, turning her knees to water. 'Then no one is knowin' you be here?'

Lalenda plucked at the first thing she thought of. 'I'm on an extremely important errand for Lord Battu,' she tried. 'I'm his prophet, so if you eat me, he won't be very happy!'

A bark of laughter blew across her face. 'What change be that? Battu never be happy.' The mouth drifted away as if floating on a breeze. 'But wait,' said the ghost. 'You be the prophet?'

'That's right,' rallied Lalenda, sticking out her chin. 'Battu's best!'

'Lalenda,' said the ghost thoughtfully.

Lalenda was surprised. 'That's right. How did you know that?'

The Golgoleth snarled, a frightening sound. 'Losara tell me,' he said. 'Claw and tooth! Now Grimra not be able to eat you, little flutterbug!'

He moaned and circled the tunnel, sending up blasts of air as he went, slashing at nothing with claws that appeared as quickly as they disappeared. Still afraid, but growing bolder, Lalenda stepped away from the wall.

'Excuse me,' she said as bravely as she could, 'but did you say you won't eat me?'

'No,' said Grimra, settling down. 'Grimra not eat Lalenda.'

'Why?'

'Lalenda be Losara's friend. Eating her not be making Losara happy.'

'Losara has . . . talked about me? To you?'

'Stupid flutterbug!' hissed the ghost. 'Be you not listening? Losara speaks well of Lalenda, so Grimra cannot crunch her bones. No, no. Not suck her head dry neither, nor mince her bowels in his claws. Poor, poor Grimra!'

Lalenda didn't know what to make of this. She glanced down into the darkness.

'You be goin' to the caves?' asked Grimra.

'Er . . . yes.'

'Lalenda be careful. Not all ways be safe down here. Why should Grimra let Lalenda go into the darkness? Losara be angry if Lalenda is hurt.'

'I need a place to fly,' said Lalenda before thinking about it.

'Ah,' said Grimra, sounding surprisingly as if he understood. 'Yes. So you *do* be having hope.'

'Pardon me?'

'Losara say you be in Skygrip for many years. Wish to flutter free, but trapped, like Grimra. Easy to lose hope. But not Lalenda, she still wants to fly. She still has hope. Well, you be letting Grimra show you the way. He knows just the place – wide and safe.'

Lalenda found herself nodding to her strange guide. He floated off ahead, only visible as a single beckoning claw, pale and luminescent. She followed as he led her deeper. More than once the tunnel divided, and always Grimra chose the way, telling her to remember their route.

'Grimra not always able to come with you, flutterbug,' said the ghost. 'You bring an ice lantern next time.'

'I will,' promised Lalenda, growing less afraid.

Eventually the walls fell away around them and Lalenda knew they had stepped into a huge cavern.

'Here we be,' said Grimra. 'Here Grimra waits for you.'

'Thank you, Grimra,' said Lalenda, spreading her wings. It felt good. 'You've been kind.'

'Not kind!' hissed Grimra. 'Not tear your shoulders off as courtesy to Losara, that all! Don't you be telling no one Grimra is *kind*.'

Lalenda laughed and took off, flapping her dilapidated wings as hard as she could. They ached, but she didn't care. If she used them, eventually she would regain her strength. *Hope?* she wondered. Maybe the ghost was right.

She closed her eyes as she rose, reaching out hands to embrace the air. She couldn't see in the pitch black, but avoided the walls by listening for the echoed reverberations of her wings. In the vast cave it was simple enough. She rolled happily, exhilarated, not having flown in such a long time . . . and, strangely, found herself thinking of Losara. Of his calm face, his soft, dark eyes. He'd told the ghost that they were friends. Were they? Did she find the notion frightening or intriguing? Suddenly she felt sad that he was so far away.

'Maybe,' she whispered to herself, and laughed as she dived.

Mission's End

As Naphur and Fahren bickered, Corlas stood at the window watching the slow fall of evening. They waited in a hall in the barracks for the return of Bel and M'Meska. Yesterday a sundart had brought news from Drel: the huggers had been exterminated, but the only survivors were his son and the Saurian. Proud as he was, Corlas was anxious to hear the full report.

'Maybe we should send a welcoming troop to the east gate?' the Throne was saying.

'I don't think that would be appropriate, lord,' said Fahren, and Corlas silently concurred. 'These are lucky soldiers returning from a botched mission. There's no cause for celebration.'

Naphur frowned, scratching a hairy arm. Before he could argue further, a soldier entered and saluted. 'My Throne, the Drel survivors have arrived.'

'Not Drel survivors,' spat Naphur. 'Drel victors. Now send them in.'

Not long after, Bel and M'Meska entered. Corlas gave his son a smile and a nod, noticing dark circles beneath his eyes. Bel returned them both, looking relieved to see his father.

'Ah!' exclaimed Naphur. 'Well done, lad! And, er . . .' He peered uncertainly at M'Meska.

'Lady,' whispered Fahren.

'Never can tell,' whispered back Naphur. 'All right. Report!'

In the absence of the troop leader, Bel did most of the talking. Corlas noted that when M'Meska did speak, it was to praise Bel. It was obvious that he had impressed her greatly. Saurians weren't inclined to praise, but what she said of Bel made him sound like a special kind of warrior.

With the official report over, M'Meska was dismissed and Bel sat down. 'There's something else I haven't told you,' he said reluctantly.

'What's that?' asked Fahren.

'At Treewith,' Bel said, 'at the inn – there was a creature there. For some time I didn't know what it was, but . . . it was a weaver.'

Of the three older men, Corlas turned the palest.

'A weaver?' said Fahren. 'Did you make a deal with it?'

'No.'

'Thank Arkus,' breathed the mage.

'It could not be seen, filthsome trickster,' said Bel. 'Neither M'Meska nor the others ever knew it was there. It got trapped in my mind somehow. I don't pretend to understand. It tricked me, saying it was a spirit sent by Arkus.' He laughed bitterly. 'High Mage, I did not remember my lessons well enough.'

'Stupidity is not a prerequisite to getting tricked by a weaver,' said Fahren. 'But you must tell us what happened, Bel, and leave *nothing* out.'

Bel nodded and began a new version of his journey, this time including the weaver. Corlas listened intently.

He'd wondered for many years if Iassia still watched the wards, and now he had his answer.

When Bel finished, Fahren turned to Naphur. 'This should be taken care of as soon as possible.'

Naphur nodded, grim-faced. 'This creature will be destroyed, Bel,' he said. 'Have no fear of that. A job for Baygis, maybe.'

Hoped flared in Corlas. If Iassia were killed, he would be free! He could leave the Halls and . . . and what? Bel was no longer a tiny baby to be whisked away in the dead of night.

'In the meantime,' Fahren was saying, 'you must try to understand that the bird is a deceiver and you've no cause to feel guilt for its actions.'

Bel nodded blankly. 'I know.' Then: 'My Throne, I have a request.'

'Yes?'

'Restore me to the peacekeepers.'

Naphur looked genuinely confused. 'What?' he said. 'But you've already proved yourself. There's no need to tread backwards!'

'I don't really see it as backwards, my Throne,' said Bel. 'I did well as a keeper. I would like to finish my term.'

Naphur was stunned, and Fahren was quick to intercede.

'It is time you rested, lad,' he said, standing and placing a hand under Bel's arm to bring him to his feet. Naphur was clearly annoyed by the intervention, but Fahren held his gaze until he silently acceded.

Bel glanced from one to the other. 'I'm sorry, my Throne,' he said. 'I didn't realise my request would irk you.'

'You're tired,' snapped Naphur, 'and aren't thinking clearly. Go to bed. We'll talk more of this tomorrow.'

Corlas caught Bel's eye, wanting to convey that he, at least, was not angry. Soon the two of them would discuss this again in private.

'Oh, I almost forgot,' Bel said, producing the envelope from his trouser pocket. 'Someone left this for Taskmaster Corlas at the Treewith Inn.'

Corlas frowned as he took the letter.

'Good night then,' said Bel, bowing and leaving as Corlas thumbed open the letter.

'Well!' exclaimed Naphur. 'What was that foolishness?'

'It is as Corlas has said before, my lord,' answered Fahren. 'Bel's path may not be straight and narrow.' He glanced at Corlas, who didn't look up from the letter.

'Anything of interest, Taskmaster?'

'Just . . . tidings from an old acquaintance,' said Corlas.

His return to the Halls had forced him to become adept at hiding his emotions. Still, on seeing who had written the letter, it was a struggle to keep his features relaxed, to stop his hands from shaking. He couldn't afford the Throne and Fahren becoming curious about this missive. The sins of his past could yet do him harm, and silently he prayed that Iassia would be found and killed. In the meantime, he read on. The writing was messy, but the words were definitely the bird's.

> *Taskmaster Corlas,*
> *Greetings, old companion. How goes it with you?*
> *I'd ask you in person, but you seem to enjoy the*
> *Halls so much as to never leave, even to visit a*
> *helpful old friend. This is deeply hurtful, but I*
> *console myself by imagining how happy you must*
> *be, reunited with your boy. He's a smart little*

*soldier, just like his father. He's yet to murder
the innocent, but there's hope he'll follow in your
footsteps. Got a good head for bloodlust on him,
believe me. I've seen it close up.*

*I write to deliver a warning. You may consider
yourself safe, tucked up snug behind the wards,
but I am not without my options. I remember
who you killed, Corlas. I can shame you and
worse. What will your son think of that, and your
enemy friends?*

*By the way, I hear Losara is doing very well –
that's what we called your other half-son. Battu
has named him Apprentice, so you may yet meet
him again one day, perhaps when he leads the
charge against the light?*

Good luck, dear Corlas. See you again soon.

Your friend,

Iassia

Stiffly Corlas folded the letter. What did Iassia hope to
achieve? To scare Corlas from the Halls with threats?
Or coax him out in an attempt to find his other son?
Certainly it had been shocking to receive his first ever
news of Losara.

'Well,' he said, as if to himself, 'isn't that something.
I never would have imagined old Velmy as one to get
married.'

He needn't have bothered with casual lies, for he
wasn't being paid any attention.

'He can't accept responsibility for the entire troop!'
Naphur was saying. 'He's only one blade, not the troop
leader or even penulm! Corlas, surely you agree?'

'There's more to it than that,' said Corlas, thankful for the steadiness in his voice.

'What then?'

'It is his first taste of blood,' Corlas said. 'The first time he has seen comrades die. That is a change for any new soldier. Also he will be worried because ... he fears to lose control.'

Corlas found resonance in his own words.

'But he didn't lose control,' insisted Naphur. 'You heard the Saurian. It sounds as if Bel was perfectly in tune with his sword.'

'It sounds,' said Corlas, 'as if he went berserk. That can be a frightening feeling. To know that a battle can take you over, can drug you with screams, can make you forget your own senses ... It is ecstasy to be in that moment, and only afterwards that you feel the peril.'

'Don't forget that I was a soldier too, Taskmaster,' Naphur said. 'Hence I know the experience is different for all of us. I don't think you can assume to know what Bel is feeling.'

'With all due respect, my lord,' Corlas said levelly, 'I do not feel that my authority over Bel, or my understanding of his feelings, can be dismissed by any man.'

'Naphur,' said Fahren, 'we'd simply be giving Bel time to think things through.'

'Mollycoddle him, you mean,' said Naphur. 'Swords are forged in the fire, and he needs to harden up. No other soldier in the army gets to dictate his own placement.' He glared at them both, defying retort, but Corlas and Fahren remained silent. Finally, the heat went out of him.

'Oh,' he muttered, 'very well. I know that Bel is no coward. And it was not dictating, it was a request.' He scowled. 'He may have his way.'

Fahren leaned back in his chair and smiled at Corlas. 'It is amazing how wisdom will eventually show through,' he said.

With the distractions of the past few days dealt with, Bel found himself suddenly desiring Jaya sharply. It was as if he had put most thought of her aside, in order to concentrate on what had needed to be done – but now that he was back, and standing in The Wayward Dog, with no huggers to kill nor birds in his head, he remembered the smell of her, the sight of her moving above him, the way it had felt to lie together . . . There was nothing he wanted more in this moment than to be with her, yet she wasn't here, and he didn't know where she was, and he thought he might scream. He *deserved* to see her. What was the point of going off to be a hero if there was no girl to come back to? No wonder soldiers drank so much.

'Jaya,' he said, putting his ale down heavily on the bar and spilling froth. 'I left a letter for her a week ago. Don't pretend you don't know what I'm talking about, lest you want to make life difficult for yourself.'

'I got it to her,' said the bartender quickly.

'And?'

'And . . . she took it. I've not seen her since. Said she was going away for a while.'

'Going away for a while?' repeated Bel blearily. He took a big swig, then wiped away froth with the back of his hand. 'Going away for a while, she said?'

'Yes, sir.'

'Did she leave anything for me?'

'No, sir.'

'No, sir?'

'No, sir.'

'Right,' said Bel. 'Well, get us another ale then.'

'Excuse me for saying,' said the barman carefully, 'but sir seems very tired.'

Bel squeezed the mug and shattered it to pieces.

As the bartender stared at him like a cornered animal considering its next move, Corlas appeared by his side.

'Don't worry about my son, barkeep,' he said, making Bel start. 'He's had a dark day is all. We'll get a table out of the way.' He laid some coins on the counter, then put a firm hand on Bel's arm. 'Send over a jug, and the rest for your busted crockery.'

The bartender nodded in relief, and Corlas led a reluctant Bel to a table in a darker corner of the bar. Curious drinkers who had turned at the sound of trouble turned away again.

'Sorry,' said Bel distantly, not sounding as if he meant it.

'The Throne is not in his best mood tonight,' said Corlas. 'But he is going to allow your return to the keepers.'

'Ah,' said Bel. 'Well. Good.'

'He was right about some things though,' continued Corlas. 'You cannot take responsibility for what happened.'

'If I hadn't entered that . . . that *state* . . .'

'You probably would have died too.' Corlas shrugged. 'And then where would we be?'

Ale arrived, and Corlas poured it out. 'It is the nature of battle, Bel. People die. Others survive. There is no good reason for it.'

'I'm not pure,' muttered Bel.

'What?'

Bel met his father's eyes. 'All my life I believed what Fahren told me. About the dark thing which left me at birth. That I was better than normal people because I'd been *cleansed*.' He spat the word. 'That was why I was destined to lead the light to victory, I thought. But I am not pure, Father.'

'No,' agreed Corlas sombrely. 'None of us is that. The truth, son, is that I don't think anyone really knows what happened to you. But I do know this: I know you *now*. And I know something about what you're going through.' He took a deep breath. 'I think perhaps I should tell you about my time at the Shining Mines.'

Bel frowned, letting an unspoken question hang in the air.

'Not the fanciful way I told it to you many times when you were a child, overexciting you before your bedtime,' answered Corlas. 'Skimming the surface and sticking to the parts that make the eyes of young boys glow. I speak now of the full account – a man's account.'

Finally Bel seemed to leave his own thoughts and take an interest. Corlas noted with amusement that the glow he had spoken of was back just as he remembered it. He laid his hands palms flat on the table.

'Very well,' he said. 'This is what happened when the shadow grew long at the Shining Mines.'

The Tale of the Shining Mines

'In the year I turned thirty,' Corlas began, 'I was promoted from cerepan to commander and sent south to the fort at the Shining Mines. It was a posting desired by many young fools seeking the promise of battle. The fort, you see, has always been a tempting target for the Shadowdreamers. Not only is it the closest settlement to the border, but the mine itself is rich with the magical ore called shine. I, however, did not go there for glory. I simply went where I was sent.

'The fort lies in the barren lands of southern Centrus. Dust and rock piles and eroded trenches and little else. Flat too, the fort visible on the horizon from a day's ride away, atop the only hill for leagues around. When my troop and I arrived, we went up to the southern entrance, the only entrance – a portcullis cast of pure shine, my boy, is something to behold!

'We were greeted there by Gerent Ateppa, a ropy man as hard as nails, with a shock of white hair. He bade us welcome to our magnificent new home. Very soon I knew the fort inside and out, for in truth there wasn't much to know. Inside the towering grey walls the town was simple, nothing too fancy for us soldiers and miners, as dusty as the plains surrounding. In the centre of town, at the peak of the hill the fort was built around, was the entrance to the mine.

'I led many patrols, and within a month I oversaw my first shipment of shine. It was packed into a crate only a few handspans wide – maybe so big.' Corlas held out his hands. 'I was surprised to learn that the mine produced only three or four such crates a year, but that each could have financed the building of a castle.

'I quickly noted that many of the soldiers were uninspired by their long grey days of watching and waiting. I set about organising regular days of games and contests – must have been something of the taskmaster in me then too. I'm proud to say that for many they became the highlight of each month. The fact they gave soldiers extra reason to drill and train was merely a pleasant benefit.' He winked at Bel.

'My relationship with the gerent grew into friendship. Ateppa himself was a charismatic leader, tenacious . . . and perhaps occasionally overly excitable. Privately I wondered if serving at the fort for ten years had left him a little unbalanced. For the most part, however, he was well liked by his soldiers.'

Corlas leaned back and sighed, his eyes turning glassy as he stared into the past. 'I have always been sorry I had to turn them against him.'

Corlas stood on the parapets of the southern wall with the cool wind off Fenvarrow blowing on his face and the first rays of the rising sun warm on his back. The juxtaposition reminded him that he was wedged between two worlds, in a no-man's-land where even the weather was at odds. In the distance hung the Cloud, seething with menace. It too served as a constant reminder of their closeness to the enemy; although the fort walls were hundreds of paces high, it was the creeping darkness on the horizon that was truly daunting.

From his vantage he surveyed the morning activity within the fort. Everything seemed normal: soldiers marched along the walls, lookouts watched from the turrets, and below the miners trailed up the hill like a line of ants. Turning back to the land outside, he glimpsed a rare speck of colour far below. He squinted, trying to make it out. It was a tattered piece of red cloth, snagged in rocks, flapping in the wind and . . .

His blood ran cold.

A shout echoed from inside the fort below. Alarm rang clear in the cry, and Corlas turned from the grisly view, knowing in his guts that something was very wrong. He went to the nearest stairway and down the inside wall, taking the steps three at a time. When he got halfway he leaned over the stone railing.

'What goes, soldier?'

The soldier, who had been running towards the town, spun at his bellow, black braids swinging about her face. Even from this distance he recognised her as Adra, one of the younger penulms of the fort.

'Commander Corlas!' she called, relieved to see him. 'You must come quickly!'

Corlas continued down the stairs, and by the time he'd reached the bottom, Adra had rounded up a couple of blades. 'You,' she was saying, jabbing a finger at one, 'go and tell the gerent there's been an attack on the mages' quarters!'

'And you, blade,' said Corlas to the other, 'go to the cerepan on duty at the gate. There's been a death outside the walls. I want to know who, then I want an organised sweep of the fort and mine. Anything out of the ordinary is to be reported.'

Adra was waiting edgily for him to follow. She led him to the mages' quarters, which was a building separate from the main settlement and home to the fort's combat mages, the lightfists, whom Corlas had little to do with. They kept mostly to themselves when not on duty, and existed somewhat outside normal military hierarchy.

Adra led Corlas into the main chamber. Walls of pink-white marble were lined with elaborately carved bookcases choking with colourful spines. A spidery lantern hung above a majestic table long enough to seat two dozen. From skylights the sun's rays shone down on congealed pools of blood. Smashed glass covered the length of the table, and amongst the ceramic shards lay glistening lumps of flesh. At the far end a mage was sprawled back in his seat, his middle section gutted. On the floor, slumped against a bookcase, was the torso of a small boy, his eyes still staring in terror at whatever had killed him.

'By the light!' whispered Corlas.

'I had a look in the other rooms,' said Adra. 'They're just as bad. Many of the mages were in their beds. Did you hear that?' She cocked her head sharply, braids swishing.

Corlas stood still. 'No.'

Adra moved to the marbled arch at the opposite end of the chamber, drawing her sword. 'I didn't check all the rooms,' she said. 'Maybe someone's still alive?' She ducked through the archway.

'Adra!' shouted Corlas. He started to follow, but there came a clattering on the tiles outside and the gerent entered the chamber with six of his personal guards. Ateppa froze when he saw the scene, his face going almost as white as his hair.

'Ah,' he said.

From beyond the marbled arch came a stifled yelp and the sound of something smashing.

'Adra!' Corlas yelled, drawing his sword and moving to the archway.

'Wait, commander!' ordered the gerent, his soldiers fanning out beside him. 'Do not separate!'

'We already have,' growled Corlas.

'You will wait, commander!'

Adra stepped back into view, sheathing her sword. Her shoulder banged clumsily against the archway so that she half-lurched into the room. She straightened as she saw the gerent.

'What was that noise?' Corlas demanded.

'Oh!' she said, turning to him. She paused, seeming to consider something.

'Penulm!' growled Corlas, furious. 'We heard a cry, and a crash!'

'It was me,' Adra said quickly. 'It was so horrible in there, I gave a cry. I knocked over a vase.'

'Don't separate again!' said Corlas.

Ateppa was still staring at the carnage. He bent to his knees and ran his finger through a smear of mud on the ground. 'This has all the markings of a Mireform attack,' he said slowly. 'Everybody keep their weapons out.'

'A Mireform, sir?' asked Corlas.

'A terrible creature,' said the gerent, standing. 'Rare and terrible. A shadow creature, hard to kill; they are shape-changers. Fetch more blades,' he ordered one of his guards.

He approached Corlas as the remaining soldiers spread over the room. 'I was in a patrol that ran close to the border,' he said, loudly enough for all to hear. 'We came across a monster such as I've never seen. It killed twelve of sixteen, and the four of us who lived were lucky to escape. It followed as we fled, changing its shape, taking on the faces of our fallen patrol, mocking us.

'We returned later with mages who told us it had been a Mireform, a denizen of Swampwild far from home, on some errand for Raker most likely. They say Mireforms require a lot of power to control, but make powerful servants once tamed.'

Adra snorted, and Corlas gave her an odd look. Her face fell neutral.

'Did the mages kill it?' he asked.

'We never found it again. They're excellent at evading detection by magic, as you can see.' Ateppa gestured around the room. 'Making them perfect assassins for mages. Corlas,' he continued more privately, 'do you know what this means?'

'I don't like what I'm guessing.'

'Without our mages we're severely crippled, and that will be the point. Something is coming.' He fingered his sword. 'Might the mages on watch still be alive?'

'I'll go check!' offered Adra eagerly.

Corlas hushed her, remembering what he had seen from the walls. A shred of red cloth flapping in the wind – the colour of a lightfist's uniform. There were other things, too, amongst the rocks, and now he was sure the mages on watch had been the first to die, their bodies hurled from the parapets. He told the gerent what he'd seen and Ateppa raked fingers through his white hair.

'Arkus,' he swore. 'No mages at all.'

More soldiers arrived and the gerent divided them quickly into groups to search the building. As they moved out of the meeting chamber, Adra remained.

'Adra!' said Corlas. 'Attend us!'

She came reluctantly behind as they went further into the building. Each bedchamber was as gruesome as the last. Blood seeped from bloody beds. Dripping was the only sound besides footsteps. All the mages were dead.

'Those in their beds,' muttered Ateppa, 'are not as cruelly dismembered as those two in the main chamber. I suspect the sleeping were killed first, swiftly and silently. Once everyone else was dead, those last two, sitting up late into the night, could really be enjoyed.'

Corlas didn't hear, for he was staring in surprise at the floor. He went to tap his superior on the shoulder but Ateppa had moved away. Face down on the ground, partially hidden under the bed, was a head. A pool of fresh blood was engulfing the black braids that fanned out around it. Beside it lay the fragments of a vase.

A stifled yelp. A smash.

He looked up to see Adra watching him intently. A moment later her face split into the most malicious grin Corlas had ever seen.

They are shape-changers.

As the gerent brushed past her, Adra spun, raising her sword to plunge it into his back. Corlas yelled as he lunged, his own blade clattering against Adra's just in time. She backed away, her eyes darting between them both. Then, slowly and deliberately, she dropped her sword. Her expression, however, was not one of surrender.

'By Arkus!' called Ateppa. 'It's her! Blades! To me!'

In a voice like a sinkhole sucking down slime, the Adra-thing spoke. 'It was so horrible, I gave a cry!' she mimicked mockingly. Then her grin widened until it elongated her entire head, deepening to reveal rows of fangs.

'Hello, crow meat,' it said.

Soldiers spilled into the bedchamber, surrounding the thing with swords as it backed into a corner. It threw its head back and gurgled, a brown tongue tipped with barbed spikes slopping from its maw. When the head came down again, most traces of Adra had disappeared.

'It's changing into its true shape!' cried the gerent.

The creature's shoulders broadened and its arms lengthened. Muddy-coloured patches bubbled to the surface of skin and armour. Silver claws, thin and flat like knives, slid out the ends of its fingers. Its eyeballs shrank to white pearls sunk into deep sockets. The human nose collapsed in on itself, inverting into gaping nostrils. The thing grew taller on thick, bendy legs that were out of proportion to its small abdomen. Its brown flesh was moist and lumpy, peppered with moss-like growths. Holes opened up all over its body to sprout green tendrils. It was like some hybrid of mud, plant and beast.

'Kill it!' shouted Ateppa.

With a wet laugh the Mireform tottered forward in a way that might have been comical were it not so terrifying. It swayed atop its bendy legs, shoulders rolling, tendrils whipping so fast they put a *thrum* in the air. The tongue lashed out at the nearest soldier, sinking a barbed spike into his eye. The man gave a spasmodic jerk as the spike hit his brain.

'Attack!' shouted the gerent. 'Slice, don't stab – hack it to pieces!'

The soldiers attacked, spurred on by their leader and the death of their comrade. With the creature in the corner, only four blades could attack it at once, but those behind didn't have long to wait. Soldiers screamed as tendrils pushed into their bodies, or claws rent deep gashes, or the fearsome tongue spiked into hearts and minds. The second wave of blades advanced more warily, hanging back from the Mireform's ranging attacks. It gurgled, and again the tongue shot out, but this time a soldier was waiting. The soldier cleaved the tongue in half and the creature howled. The severed tongue splattered as it hit the floor, spikes and all, into something like sticky swamp ooze. Muck sprayed from the flailing appendage as the creature sucked it back into its mouth.

Seeing the creature wounded encouraged the soldiers to press on, and they sliced at its murderous curling tendrils. Each time a piece was cut from the Mireform, it too fell apart into ooze. Swords quickly became coated in brown. A knife spun over the fighting soldiers and sank into the creature's head, but this did not seem to bother it.

Ateppa, his face a mask of rage, moved to join the next wave of soldiers waiting for those in front to fall. Corlas also watched for any opening. A soldier screamed as she went down with a thick tendril wrapped around her neck. Another fell, his face in shreds. The Mireform roared, and those tendrils that had been severed suddenly grew afresh. The creature seemed to shrink a little with the regeneration.

'Keep at it!' screamed Ateppa. 'Hack and slice! Go for the larger limbs!'

A new tongue unfurled from the Mireform's mouth to strike a soldier full in the gut. Bellowing with rage, the gerent took the man's place. With a fast double slash he lopped off two squirming tentacles, and followed up immediately with a sudden lunge at the arm. His sword struck deep, lopping the whole limb from the shoulder. As it fell disintegrating to the ground, the creature shrieked, a sound that echoed as if it came from somewhere deep within the earth. The Mireform turned its full attention to Ateppa, its tiny white eyes flashing hatefully in their cavities. A tendril shot out to encircle his leg, but even as it tensed to yank him to the ground, his sword came down in a wild and powerful arc. It sank into the shoulder of the beast above the missing arm, carving away a whole piece of its side. The Mireform shrieked again and the tendril around Ateppa's leg jerked away. Other soldiers took the opportunity to hack off more tendrils.

The creature fell against the wall and shrank again. As it did, silver spikes protruded outwards through its cleaved side, then came the ends of fingers, then a hand and arm. Tendrils grew once more. In moments the Mireform was whole again, but now no taller than a man. Enraged by pain and fear, it leaped against them, a whirling mass of tendrils, tongue and claws. Three soldiers went down screaming, but the gerent fought on with eyes blazing. Corlas found an opening to join him, swinging his sword back and forth like a pendulum of protection. It protected well – squirming bits of Mireform flew about him like grass from a scythe.

Two large tendrils seized the gerent by the waist and lifted him into the air. Ateppa swung, but each time the tendrils bent out of his sword's path. The Mireform grinned and the pointed tips of the tendrils worked their way through Ateppa's skin. Corlas tried to reach him, but the tongue whipped out to keep him at bay. The tendrils squeezed and the gerent's cries halted as the air went out of him. As his eyes bulged in his head, it seemed only to strengthen the rage they contained. Leaning against the tendril that wormed into his side, he swung his sword at full arm's length. The blow struck the creature on the neck and sliced clean through. For a second the Mireform's face froze in mid-roar. Then the head collapsed into chunks of mud, slopping down its body. It dropped the gerent, who rolled away wheezing.

'Keep at it!' he managed.

A blade took his place, but the headless thing was folding over on itself. Its long legs twisted around each other and the body lengthened. Suddenly a thing like a huge brown snake was wriggling towards them! It barrelled through, knocking soldiers from their feet, slithering out the door and around the corner.

'After it!' shouted Corlas. He flagged down two of the soldiers as they passed. 'You two wait,' he said, then kneeled by Ateppa. 'Gerent?'

Blood oozed from Ateppa's side, but Corlas couldn't tell how deeply the tendrils had penetrated. Ateppa raised his face. 'Just need to get my breath back,' he wheezed.

'Blades,' said Corlas to the soldiers, 'one of you fetch a healer, the other stay with the gerent.'

'I don't want that creature leaving the fort!' yelled Ateppa, flecks of blood hitting his lips from within. 'Go! Kill it!'

As Corlas ran from the mages' quarters, he heard shouts at the fort gate. Ahead were several soldiers blocking the path of the snake thing, which was trying to circle around them. Those chasing it from behind were about to catch up. Just twenty paces past them was the raised portcullis.

'Lower the grate!' bellowed Corlas as he ran.

The Mireform twisted its snake head towards him, then turned back to the soldiers who barred its way and made a feint towards them. At the last moment it changed direction, knocking down one with a swipe of its tail. With its way clear, it slithered on towards the gate.

'Lower the portcullis!' Corlas bellowed again.

One of the guards at the gate finally heeded the order and yanked a lever. The portcullis creaked and fell, and the Mireform put on a final burst of speed. The pointed tips of the portcullis clanked into a row of slots in the ground, barely clipping the tail end of the fleeing Mireform. As it escaped the fort, a rain of arrows followed it harmlessly.

A shout of panic from the walls above curtailed Corlas's attention. The soldiers at the gate were also staring at something out on the plains. Further shouting rang from the walls. From behind him came the sound of a powerful impact, and he spun to see one of the town's houses with its roof smashed in, fire blazing through the windows.

What had happened?

His question was answered as a flaming ball plummeted from the sky and exploded on a street, sending out burning tar.

They were under attack.

At the gate, Corlas's spirits almost failed. On the grey plains before the fort stood an army of the shadow.

'How are they so close?' he demanded of a gate soldier.

'They just appeared, sir!' the blade said. 'There was a shimmer in the air and suddenly an army where none existed before! It must be magic, but why didn't our mages detect them?'

'The mages are dead, soldier.'

Fear blossomed on the blade's face. 'Dead, sir?'

'Yes.'

'S-sir,' the soldier stuttered, 'they shouldn't be here now!'

'What?'

'It's day, sir. The beginning of day, even. Ateppa always said a Fenvarrow army wouldn't attack in the day!'

'No,' said Corlas. 'Their magic is stronger at night. Sound the alarms.'

For Corlas, the enemy's entire tactic clicked into place. The Shadowdreamer had sent a deadly assassin during the night, an assassin that could take whatever shape it wanted. It could have posed as a soldier and come in the front gate, or climbed the walls as a spider thing, or . . . Whatever it had done, it had avoided detection by the mages. Then it had killed them, starting with those patrolling the walls, then the rest in their quarters. It had come at night so as not to be seen, and so that it had a better chance of finding all the mages in one place. Without the mages to warn the light of approaching magic, the Shadowdreamer had managed to cloak his troops from sight until they were within attack range. Battu needed to attack as quickly as possible after the assassinations, to press his advantage – hence here they were during the day.

As the shadow army's metal catapults launched another volley of fireballs, Corlas spied a group of Graka beating their bat wings and lifting something into the air. Then another group took off, and another . . .

The fort echoed with alarm bells. Archers swarmed up the stairs to line the walls and fill the south-facing turrets. Troops of blades assembled in the centre of town, and riders ran to the stables to ready their steeds. Corlas strode around shouting orders to all.

A wave of attackers, Arabodedas and Vorthargs, broke from the army to charge towards the walls. As arrows rained upon them, three Arabodedas mages stepped aside from the group. One summoned crackling power to his fingertips, while the other two protected him against flying arrows with magical deflection. The first mage's hands shot forth, sending a great bolt of blue energy roaring up the hill. It hit the wall at ground level, blowing out chunks of blackened rock. The mages swapped roles – the first added his efforts to defence, while the second began to charge up another attack. Moments later a second bolt of energy sizzled up the hill to explode in the same place, deepening the wound in the wall. The mages rotated again and a third bolt followed, this time bursting through the stone and creating a breach in the fort's defences some ten paces wide. With their powers depleted, the mages fled a safe distance from the archers. The Arabodedas and Vorthargs charged towards the opening.

As Corlas sent soldiers to defend the area, he heard 'Commander!' behind him. It was the gerent, white as a ghost and clutching a bloody bandage to his side. A worried healer stood next to him and six of his personal guards, who looked ready to support him should he stumble. Corlas reported quickly to Ateppa as another volley of fireballs plummeted around them, cracking buildings and spitting fire.

'All right, Corlas,' the gerent said. 'You take the walls. I'll see to the breach.'

Corlas jogged towards a stairway as, behind him, the gerent began to yell instructions. The situation was dire – without mages they were almost defenceless against any magic thrown at them. He glanced across the town as he bounded up the stairs and received a small boost of hope. The fireballs, while they damaged buildings, had not resulted in as many casualties as the enemy no doubt hoped. The fires did not spread well in the dry, stony town, so apart from those caught directly in a fireball's path, or who had been standing nearby as the tar flew out, all remained unharmed.

Reaching the top of the stairs, he saw a bow gesturing upwards. High in the sky, out of arrow range, clusters of Graka were flying. Corlas squinted to see what they carried – it looked like large cauldrons between groups of four. As the first group moved above the fort, they tipped their cauldron and liquid spilled downwards, glinting crystal in the sun's rays. It hit the ground and soldiers screamed. Corlas saw smoke rising from thrashing bodies as bones showed through ruined flesh.

'Acid,' he muttered to himself.

Below, the gerent was ordering soldiers to stay under whatever cover they could find. Corlas saw a group run into a house, narrowly avoiding an acid downpour. A moment later a flaming ball smashed through the roof. A foetid stench rose into the air to accompany the screams.

Fighting broke out as Arabodedas and Vorthargs reached the breach. Kainordan soldiers held them back easily, as the opening was only wide enough for seven or eight to get through at a time. Only a few Vorthargs managed to leap past the defence on their powerful hind legs. Like their smaller frog cousins, the mottled Vorthargs were able to jump long distances and cling to the sides of buildings. Their mouths were wide like those of frogs, though they had pudgy noses, ears like dried apricots and piggy eyes. More troublesome were their burning spit and large upward-curving tusks. Corlas saw a Vortharg spring onto a soldier, hang on with the slimy pads of its feet, and bite down on his head. Being so outnumbered, however, any Vorthargs past the line were quickly felled.

Above, the Graka were leaving with their empty cauldrons, no doubt to get another load. 'What I wouldn't give for a swarm of Zyvanix,' Corlas growled.

A second group of Arabodedas and Vorthargs detached from the army. Another volley of fireballs shot up into the air. The floor beneath Corlas shook as some smashed against the upper walls, one landing directly on a group of bows. As the Arabodedas and Vorthargs drew close, Corlas saw another three mages disengage from the group.

'Oh no you don't,' he said, and shouted, 'All bows, target the mages!'

Shouts came from taskmasters passing the order along the line, and the barrage of arrows pouring down shifted to concentrate on the three mages. As one began to summon energy, the other two found themselves facing an impossible number of arrows. Frantically they cast their deflection spells, but as the First Mage raised his hands to unleash a bolt, he fell screaming with an arrow in his heart. The bolt flew off randomly, hitting a place high up the walls without punching through. The other mages retreated.

Arabodedas and Vorthargs were again nearing the breach. 'Target the Vorthargs first!' Corlas shouted, for the Arabodedas were more easily held back. He frowned at these ground attacks, which were hardly effective. With a breach so small, and so many archers on the walls, each wave met death quickly. It didn't make sense.

In the distance he saw Graka taking off again. He squinted more closely at the Fenvarrow army. Minions of the dark lord ran here and there, attending to the catapults and large vats, which, Corlas guessed, contained the deadly acid. A good proportion of the army seemed to be focused on keeping the aerial attacks going, while the waves of ground attackers seemed almost a distraction. Suddenly Corlas knew what needed to be done. As long as they stayed within the fort, the Shadowdreamer could pelt down death from the skies. The fort had become a trap and they needed to get out.

He ran back down the stairs, at the bottom carefully avoiding ground where acid still smoked. At the breach he found a phalanx commander organising the defence.

'Where is the gerent?' he demanded.

'In the main square.'

Corlas covered the distance as quickly as he could. In the main square he found Ateppa on a stretcher, face drained of colour and set in a grimace of pain, blood trickling from his lips. Ignoring the healer's pleas, he was sitting up to shout orders. Troops had scattered so as not to provide large targets for the aerial attacks, and everyone looked edgy. There were more than enough soldiers at the breach to take care of the small waves of attackers, so a large portion of the fort's force was standing idle and useless.

'What are you doing here?' shouted Ateppa as he caught sight of Corlas. 'Get back to the walls!'

'Gerent Ateppa!' puffed Corlas. 'We must leave the fort!'

Soldiers nearby were paying attention.

'What?' said Ateppa. 'Are you mad?'

'If we stay,' replied Corlas, 'we will surely be defeated. Without mages to protect us, we cannot withstand these aerial attacks!'

'You talk of suicide!' said Ateppa. 'They cannot pelt us forever. We must hold, and wait for their main attack. They will not take us by ground!'

'This is their main attack, gerent!' said Corlas, flinching as a fireball slammed into a nearby building. 'We must leave the fort!'

'Get back to the walls!' screamed Ateppa, his ghostly pallor flushing red for a moment. 'Do as I command!' He slumped back onto the stretcher, moaning with pain.

Corlas stared hard at his superior. He needed to act, else the gerent was going to sentence them all to doom. Though it pained him greatly, he reached a decision quickly and turned to the gerent's personal guards.

'You blades take the gerent to his quarters and see to his safety. I am taking full command.'

'*What*?' screamed Ateppa. 'You dare to . . .'

'You are wounded, sir,' said Corlas loudly. 'You have lost too much blood and are not thinking clearly. If we are to win this battle,' he turned to the soldiers surrounding, 'we must *fight*. Soldiers – do you wish to be cooked here like crabs in a pot? Or shall we take this battle into our own hands? Shall we give the Shadowdreamer more than he bargains for?'

A chorus of assent went up. Already the soldiers had seen too much carnage as they stood powerless to stop it.

'You're relieved of duty, commander!' shouted the enraged Ateppa. 'Return to your quarters!'

Corlas stood, hands on hips, staring hard at the gerent's guards. 'We are dead if we stay,' he said.

One of the guards, an older man with a weathered face, looked from Corlas to Ateppa. Ateppa was writhing angrily on his stretcher, trying to stand up. The guard nodded slowly. 'Come, blades,' he said. 'Let's get the gerent to safety.'

Two men picked up the stretcher as the gerent shouted curses and protests and carried him from the main square. Corlas immediately sought out the officers in the crowd.

'Phalanx commanders, cerepans – I want all troops assembled at the portcullis before the next Graka strike.' He glanced around at the tense faces. 'We're abandoning the fort.'

Phalanx commanders and cerepans rode up and down the lines trying to organise troops of bows, blades and riders. The fort had only one phalanx of riders – that was, six troops – and besides this there were only horses for the officers. Corlas secured his own broad-backed war horse to cover ground more quickly. Armourers towed carts to distribute shields, armour and weapons, while soldiers at the gate stood ready to raise the portcullis. Corlas didn't want to give the enemy any early warning that they intended to leave the fort, so the portcullis would be left shut until the last moment possible. Behind them, fireballs thundered down on the nearly deserted town. Corlas glanced anxiously at the sky, knowing the Graka would be above them any minute. If soldiers were caught grouped together in the same place, the casualties would be devastating.

He reached a decision. The time was now.

'Raise the portcullis!' he commanded. 'Move out the troops!'

Taskmasters around him took up the call.

'Commander!' came a voice behind him, and he turned to see a burly man with a rough beard and dirty clothes. He rested a pickaxe over his shoulder, and behind him stood a hundred similar-looking men. Corlas recognised him as Brindle, the head miner.

'What is it, Brindle?'

'We will not continue in the mine while the very fort falls around us. Today we hew flesh, not rock.'

Corlas nodded. 'Very well. Find an armourer, or use your pickaxes if you will. Move it out, Brindle.'

'Right y'are, sir!' said Brindle fiercely.

At the gate, troops were streaming out and down the hill. Corlas glanced at the sky. The Graka should have been above them by now, but for some reason they seemed to be holding back. Then he saw why – the clear blue sky was no longer clear. High above, small pinpricks had appeared above the fort. As Corlas watched he saw them expanding outwards and his dread of magic grew strong. They were dark blue vortexes and, though small and distant, were as ominous as a knife glinting in the dark.

'Move it out!' he bellowed. 'Move it out!' The horse beneath him whinnied as he gave it a kick in the ribs, driving it along the lines of waiting soldiers. 'Move it out, soldiers! Magic they may have, but even a mage can learn the pain of steel! Target their mages! Make them *pay* for this! Make them learn what Kainordan soldiers are made of! Move it out!'

He raised his sword to the air, hollering war cries and driving soldiers before him. They spilled out through both the gate and the breach, heartened by the righteous rage of their commander.

Above, Corlas heard the warning crackle of magic approaching. Looking up, he saw lines of blue energy streaming down from the vortexes, straight and fast. As they slammed into the fort's centre, the ground shook. Where they hit, they obliterated, leaving deep craters in the ground and sending out shock waves that knocked flying anything in their path.

In the sky above, the vortexes faded. Corlas breathed out thanks to Arkus. The mages had obviously targeted the area where the Graka would have last reported the majority of soldiers to be gathered. As it turned out, the energy streams had destroyed a now mostly unpopulated section of the town. Corlas shuddered at how devastating the attack would have been had they not moved. He didn't know much about magic, but he knew that what he'd just seen would require a large amount of power, possibly many mages working together to create just one of those vortex things; and cloaking their army as they'd approached would have taken its toll as well. If Battu was tiring his mages, perhaps they had a chance.

As he rode from the fort, he saw the Graka flapping slowly towards his army, which was assembling again at the bottom of the hill. Corlas urged his mare down the slope and found more order than he had hoped for. In the distance he could see the Fenvarrow army milling about, preparing for a ground attack they hadn't expected. He came to a halt in front of the officers, many of whom met his gaze with fearful eyes. Glancing at the sky, he guessed they had about a minute until the Graka could bomb their present position.

'All right,' he said. 'I want to drive pronged attacks into their lines. If we are all mixed in together, their air attacks will be useless and their mages won't be able to target groups of us as easily. If you see a chance to take out a mage, take it, but not at too high a cost. We have to maintain our numbers.'

'The bows, commander?'

'They cannot attack from afar, they will only be killed from the air. They will be the heart of every prong we drive into their territory. Get them in and defend them.' He met each of his officers in the eye. 'There is no time for anything further. May the light be with us all. Do not despair . . .' He seemed to fumble for words, but then his eyes shone with strength. 'Do *not* despair,' he said.

He waited until the officers had returned to their troops, then drew his sword and spun it in his grip.

'Charge!'

Across grey, flat land the soldiers charged, roaring defiance at the black mass before them. Blades ran in groups around the bows, while the riders moved ahead with long spears lowered. The Graka let their acid fall, but most of the army passed under it unscathed, with only a few of the stragglers falling. Corlas found himself galloping past the miners, their grimy faces grim.

As they drew closer, arrows began to fall around them, but the dark lord had been complacent. Wrapped up in his plans for assassinations, aerial and magical assaults, he had failed to give proper thought to an unexpected ground war. While he had the numbers, his soldiers were not particularly well organised, and his archers were only now arriving behind the front lines. Kainordan bows returned fire as they ran, and screams rang out on both sides. Then came a clash of steel as blades drove attacks against the frontlines, wedging themselves into enemy territory. Within a few minutes, the Kainordan army was entrenched amongst those of the shadow.

Corlas rode tall, his eyes blazing with battle fury. Blood pumped hot in his veins and he whooped as he hacked and hewed from his horse. A joyous rage filled his heart and the very air around him seemed charged with energy. A Vortharg leaped at him only to fall away howling, guts spilling from its stomach. A dagger clattered against his shield and a moment later the Arabodedas who'd thrown it added his blood to the river that flowed from Corlas's sword. A Graka swooped out of the sky with claws extended, straight into Corlas's outstretched blade. The commander's arms bulged as he lifted the impaled Graka in the air, ignoring its scrabbling claws as it tried to free itself. He gave a roar as he flung it into a mass of Arabodedas, knocking some from their feet.

The display of strength lifted the spirits of those around him and they fought on with new ferocity. Corlas roared again and galloped through the Arabodedas, his war horse crushing skulls beneath its heavy hooves. He shouted encouragement as he passed his soldiers, stirring up his troops wherever he found them. Time seemed to slow, and he was able to avoid attacks on him easily with adrenaline-fuelled perception.

Scattered mages caught in the fray sent magic bolts at Kainordan soldiers, but fell as bows fired arrows in return. Other mages hung back from the fighting, but were unable to effectively target the enemy while it was so mixed up with their own forces. The bows turned their attention to the Graka, who had abandoned their cauldrons to fly low over the battle with spears. Their stony skin deflected most arrows, but well-placed ones sent the creatures wheeling towards the ground. Corlas ripped a crossbow from a dying Arabodedas and shot it at a Graka, which left behind a red mist in the air. Corlas put the crossbow, which still had one bolt left, onto his belt.

'See how easily cowards die!' he bellowed, and soldiers around him echoed the chant.

He spotted a group of Black Goblins surrounding a troop of his soldiers, closing in quickly and viciously. He hadn't seen many goblins up to this point – they seemed to be blessedly scarce – but now his soldiers fell screaming before their formidably fast blades.

'Trample the goblins!' he hollered at a nearby group of riders.

He himself bore down on them too, and many fell beneath hooves and blades. Soon the ground was rich with mashed black flesh.

Despite the tenacity with which his soldiers fought, Corlas could see they were failing in many places. Vorthargs spat poison into the faces of defending blades, then leaped over them to gore the bows they protected. Riders made easy targets for them too, standing taller than the rest, and Corlas had seen more than one go down screaming with a Vortharg on their back. The Arabodedas were skilled sword-wielders, but fortunately the blades had an advantage over their pale counterparts – many carried weapons or armour that contained shine. While the material was too precious to make entire suits on such a scale, a thin strip of shine reinforcing the right places could save a life again and again.

Corlas continued to stampede and stir his troops, but though they fought with all their hearts, his soldiers were being felled too quickly. With a snarl of rage he wheeled around, searching for some way to turn the battle. What he saw heading towards him made him throw himself off his horse with all his might. He heard a wet explosion, and chunks of steaming horse meat thudded down around him. He rolled to his feet, staring in the direction from which the huge bolt of energy had come.

On a slight rise, barely fifty paces away, stood the cause of all this bloodshed. Clothed in black, the folds of his cloak swirling about him, his recessed eyes turning this way and that over the battlefield, was the Shadowdreamer himself. Corlas hadn't realised how deeply they had driven into the shadow army. Too far, it seemed, which was why the tide was turning against them. He saw Battu gesture at him while speaking to a group of Black Goblins – an elite guard, by the look of them. Corlas had managed to bring himself to the Shadowdreamer's attention and the goblins would be coming for him.

'To me!' he shouted as the Blacks began to slip towards him through the battle. 'To me!' Nearby soldiers hacked their way towards him.

'Commander!' came the voice of a tall man on horseback. 'Troop Leader Murcoh at your service!'

'How many in your troop?' asked Corlas.

'Six remaining, sir! I think!'

'Black Goblins are coming this way,' said Corlas. 'Let's go and greet them.'

The troop leader smiled grimly and ordered his riders to drive a path ahead. They were veterans by the look of them, alive only for their great skill. The commander followed the horses on foot, towards the advancing goblins. About thirty paces from Battu, the two groups met with a clash of steel. One of the goblins sprang at a rider, bringing him to the ground in a struggling tangle of limbs. Another darted in at Corlas, but a rider sent his head spinning into the air. A third goblin appeared before Corlas and he swiped at it. The creature leaped backwards with a snarl, then darted forward again. Corlas swung again and again, but the goblin weaved and ducked and none of Corlas's blows found their mark. As he staggered from a mistimed swing, it lunged and he felt steel plunge deep into his side. He roared in fury and dropped his sword, grabbing the creature's neck as it tried to pull its sword free. With a sharp crack he broke its neck, then almost fell forward from the stabbing pain. He yanked out the goblin's sword and sent it spinning into another.

On the hill, the Shadowdreamer was looking agitated, shouting for more of his minions to attend him. Finding himself suddenly free of foes, Corlas stormed towards the dark lord. He forgot the fire that flared in his side, driven by the fire that blazed in his blood. On seeing Corlas approach, the Shadowdreamer narrowed his eyes and raised a hand to the sky. His face strained in effort as he conjured and Corlas looked upwards. Blue energy swirled as one of the vortexes opened above him. It hung lower in the sky than those over the fort, close enough for Corlas to hear its magic crackling murderously. Battu's intention was clear. He wanted Corlas dead, whatever the cost to his own troops. Corlas redoubled his efforts to reach the dark lord.

An Arabodedas leaped in front of him, punching him viciously in the face with the hilt of a sword. Blood spurted from his nose and his vision spun, but he managed to return the blow with a force that sent the man flying. He staggered onwards, glancing up at the spinning vortex. It was *following* him as it expanded, floating along in the air above. There was no question that it was locked onto him.

He broke into a run. Blood poured from his nose freely but was ignored, and any in his way were quickly felled. Putting on one final burst of speed, he found himself at the base of the rise, just ten paces from the Shadowdreamer himself.

Something smacked him across the back of his head and he pitched forward onto the rise. His assailant, a huge Arabodedas with a club, fell atop him. The weapon had only glanced him, but his head still spun as he grappled with the sweaty man. Above them, the vortex continued to expand. He managed to lock an arm under the attacker's throat and began to drag himself up the rise with his other, strangling the struggling man as he went. As he died, Corlas released him and continued crawling up the slope, breaking fingernails on the hard ground. At the top, the Shadowdreamer's face was writ plain with fear, but it was not directed at Corlas's approach. The dark lord was staring up at the vortex – having followed its target, it now boiled in the sky above both of them and Battu began to weave his hands frantically, trying to reverse the spell.

Corlas glanced around. He didn't have his sword, he realised, and couldn't remember when he'd lost it. His hand went to his belt and his fingers touched the crossbow that still hung there. Above them the vortex made a noise like thunder and suddenly blue energy streamed down from the heavens. Battu gritted his teeth, beads of sweat glistening on his forehead as he worked to undo his own magic. Grunting, Corlas slid his only bolt into the crossbow . . .

The crackling of power grew louder . . .

Corlas raised the bow . . .

Muscles bulged on Battu's arms . . .

The bolt flew from the crossbow, its metal tip glinting blue as energy blotted out the sky . . .

Above the hill, the energy sizzled away into nothing as Battu dispelled it, only a few thin strands hitting the earth and sending up tiny spurts of dust . . .

The crossbow bolt smacked deeply into the Shadowdreamer's side.

Battu screamed and toppled backwards, his arms still raised to the sky. He twisted a hand to point at Corlas as he fell, but nothing came out of it. All his power had been spent. He disappeared from view down the other side of the rise.

With a pained grunt, Corlas got to his knees and then, somehow, to his feet. With legs caked in sweaty grime, he took one more step up the rise before giddiness overcame him. All the pains of his body became real and he gasped. His legs buckled and he went sliding back down the rise, dust and pebbles bouncing before him. When he came to a stop at the bottom, against the body of the large Arabodedas, he was unconscious.

Of the battle he remembered nothing more.

He awoke sometime later to a darkening sky. Nearby were the sounds of footsteps and men talking.

'Well, find him!' said a voice. 'He must be here somewhere!'

'Troop leader!' called another, closer by. 'He's here!'

A silhouette loomed into Corlas's view. It was the tall troop leader, Murcoh. As Murcoh kneeled by Corlas's side, pain overtook him again and he faded mercifully into blackness.

Corlas set his mug on the table. 'And that was that,' he said. 'The day was won. Those of us left alive returned to the fort. It was badly damaged but it was ours. When I awoke there, I learned the wounded Shadowdreamer had ordered a retreat, spilling acid vats behind him to cover his escape. He left his war machines behind too, which were taken into the fort. They are still there now, in case he ever returns for them.

'The Shadowdreamer did not die from his hurt, but then again neither did I. Maybe both our gods were looking out for us that day.

'I heard that Brindle's miners matched the soldiers for ferocity – and also that their dark clothes and pale skin from days spent under the earth made them easy to mistake for Arabodedas. Perhaps that is why so many of them survived.

'The gerent and his guards were killed in the vortex blasts on the fort. I was sorry to learn he had died . . . but I will always be glad that we rode out of the trap and took the fight into our own hands.'

He flexed his hands as he stared at them, callused and coarse from the years they had seen.

'So you see, Bel . . . this blood frenzy you experienced is no stranger to our bloodline. I know how disturbing it can be to realise that you lost control. Even to realise that you *enjoyed* losing it, and enjoyed the death you carved out around you. But it has purpose: to protect us, and make our enemies quake. As long as you do not seek to feed it unnecessarily, it is not an evil thing. It allows us to do what is necessary . . . to survive and to *win*.'

He sighed. 'I took some time after that battle, just as you now seek to. In fact, I deserted my post. So I understand your desire to return to the keepers.'

Corlas felt suddenly tired, and realised his mouth was dry from an unaccustomed amount of talking. He raised his mug and downed his remaining ale. Bel sat silent, reflective, deep in thought – and, Corlas was pleased to note, calm.

Corlas rose. 'It's late. Time to retire, I think.'

'Yes, Father,' said Bel, and stood.

The Mocking Bird

Borgordusmae reflected the first rays of the morning sun, the Auriel sparkling beneath Naphur's hair. He'd come to sit and think alone on his seat of power.

Footsteps sounded on the sunken stairway that led up to the court. Baygis emerged to walk up the red carpet, his white-gold robe billowing around his feet. A year before his fortieth birthday, Baygis still looked youthful: the same slender build, the same twinkling eyes, the same mischievous face. He stopped before the towering chair and bowed lower than was necessary, as he always did. Naphur was too distracted to be amused.

'Long night, Father?' Baygis asked, arching an eyebrow.

'Long rule,' said Naphur, gazing off at the spreading light on the horizon. 'You know, Baygis, you were once so keen to sit where I sit.'

'I was younger,' said Baygis. 'The "trappings of power" did not seem such a literal definition. Anyway, I enjoyed making you watch your back.'

The Throne grunted. 'And you like your freedom too, don't you? Gallivanting about with your entourage of clever friends.' The Throne smiled then, at something remembered. 'I want to see the desert again, you know. Race some dune claws with the Saurians.' He broke his northwards gaze. 'Don't foul your leggings, son. There are too many things that need doing for me to retire anytime soon. But in a few years, Baygis . . . in a few years, I might give up the Auriel. I deserve some time to myself while I can still appreciate it.'

'What?' said Baygis. 'While you can still appreciate it? You're an ox, Father, who'll live another forty years at least, and I really will have to kill you if I ever want to warm my arse on Borgordusmae.'

The Throne smiled. 'Baygis, I'm being serious. When the time comes . . .'

'When the time comes,' said Baygis, 'then of course I'll take the seat. I don't know how you got it into your head that I didn't still want it. Of course I do. All that *power,* and the *women,* women who love *power* . . .' Baygis grinned.

Though Naphur knew he was being wound up, he couldn't help but react. 'Baygis! Being Throne is a difficult and serious task!' he snapped.

'I know,' said Baygis. 'Don't worry. I serve you well enough, surely, to inspire some modicum of faith?'

'And anyway,' said Naphur, 'I'm sure you already have more than your fair share of women. Many the poor servant girl, unmercifully seduced by his lordship on his travels. Oh yes – I know about you.'

'Servant girls?' said Baygis with distaste. 'Only if whichever Trusted I was visiting didn't have any virtuous daughters. Or happened to be the wrong species. The wasp Trusted's daughters, for example, are out of the question on a purely anatomical basis –'

'Baygis!' said Naphur, exasperated.

'I'm only joking, Father. Of course it's just servant girls. Well, maybe some minor ladies, but never – '

'Baygis!'

'Sorry.'

'Harrumph!' said Naphur. 'You do realise you are long overdue to be married!'

This time it was Baygis's expression that turned sour.

'Do you ever plan to produce any heirs?' asked Naphur.

'I'm sure I already have one or two I don't know about.'

The Throne went red.

'Like to change the subject, perhaps?'

'Perhaps,' said the Throne through clenched teeth.

'Very well. I got the morning missive saying you wished to see me. I assume it wasn't just to cover this old ground?'

'No,' said the Throne. 'There's a weaver out there, hanging around the wards.'

'A weaver? What do you want me to do?'

'I won't have the Shadowdreamer's eyes on my capital. Send yourself or your mages, I don't care which – just deal with it.'

'Very well, my Throne. Though I think I shall go myself.'

'There, at least, is a similarity between us,' said Naphur, causing Baygis to raise an eyebrow. 'Our love of the hunt,' he clarified.

'Ah, yes,' said Baygis. 'So it is.' He smiled at his father and left.

Naphur's eyes went north again and he thought about his brief youth, of battles and racing and travel, of the days before unending rule and responsibility. Baygis could take over once he'd sorted out this business with Bel. But how long would that take?

A while yet, perhaps, he thought.

Baygis hadn't hunted for some time and now he felt the thrill of it again. He'd been following a slight flicker of shadow *presence*, far off and possibly imagined, for many hours over hills and fields. The creature was fast when it moved, but then it would stay in the same place for a while, allowing Baygis to draw nearer. Finally, about a league past the ward stones, he'd crested a hill, seen a small wood and sensed that the creature was somewhere inside.

As an ambassador, Baygis had become highly adroit at going unnoticed. It often aided his purposes to overhear private conversations, or mingle easily in kitchens and barracks, the mixing pots of common gossip. As he covered the open ground towards the wood, he concentrated on making himself too inconsequential to notice, until not even the ants in the grass felt the vibrations of his steps. If the weaver happened to be watching from the branches, Baygis was confident it would not see him.

As he stepped into the wood, he relaxed a little, his physical presence being easier to hide amongst cover. He moved between trees like a floating ghost, questing out thinly with his senses, trying to detect the creature without it detecting him in return. Animals moved under bushes or along logs, oblivious to his presence. He paused in the shade of a big birch. He was close to the creature now, he was sure of it. There was a gap in his magical perception, something of the shadow that he knew was there but could not make out, a blotchy silhouette. Easing slowly around a tree, he examined the branches above. Perched on the branch of a clawberry tree, pecking at the corpse of a finch, was the weaver.

Its head snapped up, a strip of flesh dangling from its beak. Even as Baygis realised it had seen him, the bird was away, a bright flash through the trees. Baygis broke into a run, moving unnaturally fast.

Idiot mage, came the weaver's voice in his mind. *I am of the shadow, yet you stand in shadows to elude me?*

Baygis could sense the bird getting away and he burned magic for fleetness, tearing recklessly through the trees, so quickly that his feet hardly touched the ground.

The bird's voice came again. *Don't they teach you anything these days?*

They teach us not to prattle when we need to flee, returned Baygis.

Stretching out his hands as he ran, he conjured a sphere of light. 'Seek,' he told it, and it shot off into the canopy. Ahead of him the bird chirped in panic as the sphere caught up and suffused it, making it convulse and hurtle to the ground. It struggled to right itself, powerless against the gold bonds of energy that now pinned down its wings. As Baygis reached it, the effort of his run caught up with him. He sank to his knees before the prostrate weaver.

'What is your name?' he said between heavy breaths.

The weaver's blood-drop eyes swivelled to the mage who towered over him. 'Die screaming, Varenkai.'

Baygis waggled his fingers. Inside the bird's body tiny lines of fire ignited in pathways. It screamed, a sound like a kettle boiling. Baygis dropped his hand and the pain ceased. The weaver's yellow chest rose and fell with uneven gasps.

'What is your name?' said Baygis.

'Iassia,' said the bird.

'I'll have your true name as well. And it will depend entirely on you how long you must remain in pain before you speak it. If you answer my questions, release will come swiftly.'

Iassia's tiny head fell back against the grass. 'Release?' he said contemptuously. 'You think that is what such a death would bring me?' He twittered bitterly. 'It does not, I assure you. You'll never have my true name.'

'Are you sure?'

Baygis's fingers curled and the fiery pain spread again in myriad tiny threads that crisscrossed every part of Iassia's body. The mage waited patiently as the weaver writhed. His scream became soundless, his beak frozen open, his eyes bulging wide. Eventually Baygis dropped his hand.

'Your name,' he said.

Iassia didn't respond. His eyes closed and his wings went limp.

'I know you hear me, bird.'

Iassia opened an eye. His voice, when it came, was scratchy, ruined by the scream. 'You are a fool, mage. I will endure you forever before I speak my true name. Go ahead and convert all your power into pain. Once you are empty, let the other mages of the Halls work in shifts, burning me through day and night. I will still outlive you and all your kin. I can wait until Kainordas falls to time itself, and when the stones of the Open Castle lie in ruins grown thick with moss, *I* will emerge and fly away, and still you won't have heard my name.'

'There are other ways to find it, as well you know,' countered Baygis calmly. 'Perhaps I should try one of your own tricks.'

'What?' said the bird, but it was too late.

Baygis drove a mental spike into Iassia, entering his mind with stunning force. He knew he could not match the weaver in a prolonged test of psychic strength, but the suddenness and violence of his attack was enough to wedge himself inside. He felt Iassia's blocks go up, and raised his fingers above the bird once more, distracting it with physical pain. The blocks faltered and Baygis broke them down, swinging a hammer in Iassia's head, not concerned with the destruction he caused. Iassia screamed mentally as well as physically, and Baygis seized what he'd come for.

'Found it,' he said.

'No,' whispered the bird in true terror.

'Iashymaya Siashymor. A pretty name for such an ugly soul.'

'You have no right!'

'Wish to be sent back to Arkus, little one?'

'No! Please!'

'Perhaps you'll answer my questions now.'

'You'll kill me either way.'

'So you still want pain until the moss grows thick on the castle ruins?'

'No. No. Though, fortunately for me, I don't think I have to be that patient.'

'What do you mean?' demanded Baygis.

The bird raised his head. 'Behind you.'

Baygis heard the *whiz* a moment before the arrow's impact knocked him from his knees. Reflexively he rolled and sent a stream of liquid fire back towards the source of the attack. There was a short shriek as the fire hit someone, followed by a sizzling that was even louder. Baygis stumbled to his feet, throwing up guards against further attacks. He glanced to where the bird had lain and cursed to find his net had failed and it was gone. Sending out his senses with none of his former subtlety, he was just in time to feel Iassia flitting out of range of any useful spellcasting. Sharp pain killed his concentration and his hand went to his shoulder. He winced as his fingers closed about the shaft sticking out his back. Best to return to the Halls and let someone else remove it – healing was not one of his strengths.

He cursed again.

Trying to ignore the pain, he went to the body of his assailant. Smoke belched from the charred corpse and the smell of roasted flesh filled the air. It had been a Black Goblin, its lips melted away to reveal a permanent snarl. One of Battu's rogue archers? There'd been no sign of them for years. Perhaps the bird had managed to call it, but it had to have been very close.

One of its eyes rolled in the socket.

Baygis tensed, ready to attack – but there was no way the goblin could still be alive. He watched in disgust as an insect-like leg pushed from under the goblin's eyelid, hooking barbs onto the remains of the cheek. The leg tensed and the eyeball rose in the socket, other legs coming free beneath it, and clear wet wings. It was a bug-eye, Baygis realised, a creature that linked the sight of its host to the Shadowdreamer. Pulling a dagger from his belt, he stabbed the thing back down into the eye socket. Its legs whipped about frantically, lacerating the grilled flesh of the goblin's face.

Had the Shadowdreamer been watching?

He sighed at the failure of his mission, and turned to make his way painfully home.

Battu's eye refocused, joining his other in true sight. His link to the bug-eye had been severed.

The archer hadn't killed Naphur's boy, which would have been a pleasant bonus. At least the bird had escaped. Part of Battu considered Iassia's ordeal just punishment for not discovering sooner that Bel had been in the open. As it was, the assassins he'd sent into the area were too late – Bel had disappeared back through the wards by the time they'd arrived. He'd left the goblins there in case Bel became exposed again, but now the Throne would know there were Fenvarrow operatives close to the wards. They would have to withdraw.

Battu sank back in Refectu, the vision from other bug-eyes flicking through his gaze.

Quickly and painfully Iassia flew, shaken and angry and scared to his bones. No mortal before Baygis had ever learned his true name – the fate all weavers feared the most. He shuddered at the thought of what Arkus might have in store for any weavers who were returned to him.

He would bring destruction to these people, he swore it to himself. He would make them pay for what they'd done, for making him feel this way!

Fluid rose in his throat and he set down clumsily on a branch. The face of Baygis rose in his mind and he shivered and quaked and twittered in terror.

The Isle

From above Losara could see how small the Isle of Assedrynn actually was. It was smooth, flat black stone sitting low in the sea, apart from a small hill that rose at one end. For a traveller sailing dark waters under dark skies, it would be all but impossible to find without the help of the gods.

'South,' said Assedrynn, an unseen presence by his side, and they sped away across the water. Beneath, a white dot appeared and they dived towards it. Losara saw the white was foam turned up by the bow of a boat and that Battu lay inside, stretched out with his eyes closed.

'He dreams, as you did,' said Assedrynn. 'Of the depths. Riding with the souls beneath. But he does not move between them, he stays with one. Look.'

The sea rushed up to meet them and Losara braced himself – but there was no onrush of cold or wet as their ethereal forms plunged below the surface. Deeper they went, until the shape of the boat was a dot once again, this time above them. Rock pinnacles jutted out of the ocean floor, and long weeds waved in the current. Sharks emerged out of the black, matching the progress of the boat above. At the front swam the largest, its great bulk mottled with scars, skin straining as if it barely contained its flesh.

'Battu is there,' said Assedrynn. 'Inside. He drives the leader to hunt even when sated, to eat more than its share and leave the others hungry. Such is the nature of his greed. Power alone does not make him happy, only its assertion. That is why he has failed in his duty as Caretaker.'

'What is meant by "Caretaker"?'

'Come.'

The world blurred as they rose and left the sea. After a time Losara gained the impression of land beneath them, and soon they slowed. Ahead loomed the border of Fenvarrow, a curtain of light falling through the air, with bright Kainordas beyond. The Stone Fields crawled with movement. There were waves of Arabodedas, Vorthargs, goblins, low-flying Graka, and war engines burning. They clashed with troops of Varenkai, Saurians and Zyvanix wasps. There was no battlefront; all was muddied to chaos as the peoples of the world slashed and tore and broke each other.

'This was the failure of Assidax,' said Assedrynn. 'We named her Warmonger and gave her power, but she was beaten back from the Shining Mines and pursued into Fenvarrow.'

They circled closer towards a figure standing on a rise in the midst of the battle. Losara recognised Shadowdreamer Assidax, her tattered skirts whirling as she twisted left and right, screaming defiance and gnashing her teeth. A rain of arrows fell upon a group of Arabodedas nearby, and from those perished Losara saw something rise, like a black wisp of smoke.

'Souls,' said Assedrynn. 'Beginning their journey to our Great Well.'

Assidax raised her hands, weaving and incanting. The black wisps swirled as if caught in a gust of wind, and blew back into the corpses of the fallen. Limbs twitched and the dead rose, snapping the arrows off their bodies.

'Souls denied passage,' said Assedrynn. 'Denied death. And we, the gods, are denied the power we gain when they return to the Well. And this, also.'

A group of Saurians was being outnumbered by Black Goblins, who hacked resolutely at thick reptilian scales. Some of the Saurians managed to spring free, but many were slain. As they died, glowing globes of light rose from each and began floating towards the border. Again Assidax made her necromantic gestures and again the souls were pulled back to their bodies – blackening as they came, as shadow took them over.

'Born of light, but they will never find their way to Arkus's Well,' said Assedrynn. 'They are changed by Assidax, by her magic. They are ours now.'

Time began to pass more swiftly and the battle sped up to a crashing blur of shapes and colours. As it slowed again, the battlefield was emptying. Kainordans were fleeing across the border, beaten back by an army of the dead.

'They retreat,' said Assedrynn, 'but there is no victory. Assidax has used up much of Fenvarrow's army yet gained no ground. Worse, she does not release the dead, believing she can retain control of them. While they are lesser creatures than in life, they are hard to keep in such numbers. Most of these will wander and disperse. They will flee to the forgotten corners of the world, the edges of settlement, to forests and deep lakes. They will hide in holes and rot to unliving dust and still their souls will not return to replenish our Great Well. Thus *we*, the very gods, are weakened.'

The vision swirled and now they were inside Skygrip, and before them on Refectu sat Battu.

'*Caretaker* we named him, and Raker before.' Anger sounded clearly in Assedrynn's voice. 'Rebuilder. Healer. Keeper of Fenvarrow. Restorer of the shadow's might, that it may be ready for the prophesied child to wield. Hunter of the unliving, returner of souls to the Well.'

Gazing upon the hard face of Battu, Losara understood. The gods had charged him to be a peaceful Shadowdreamer, opposite to his desires and his very nature – and he had openly defied them. He'd attempted to storm the Shining Mines, depleting the very forces he'd been ordered to rebuild and strengthen *for Losara*. After his failure, Battu had carried out initiatives to cull Fenvarrow's undead, but always they had seemed half-hearted. Losara now realised that the dark lord only undertook these actions to redeem himself, not through any wish of his own.

'Caretaker in name no longer,' said Assedrynn. 'Nothing given in its place. Do you understand, Losara Shadowhand?'

'I do.'

Losara awoke.

He was floating in the sea, surrounded by the gods. As massively as they towered above him, and strange as they were, he felt safe. Mokan and Mir flew towards him, their feet dragging in the water as they beat their powerful wings. When they stopped, they sank into the sea up to their waists.

'You've seen?' shrilled Mokan. 'The failure of the Caretaker!'

'The sharks,' growled Mir. 'He swam too long with the sharks!'

'I have shown him,' rumbled Assedrynn.

Lampet's head appeared around Assedrynn's bulk, snaking along with his eyes flashing blue. 'The pilgrimage,' he hissed.

Assedrynn heaved a fin from the water and Lampet weaved out of its way. As it crashed down, Mokan and Mir howled laughter, while Chirruk opened and closed her claws with great cracks that resounded across the sea. Lampet gave a throaty chuckle and sank a little lower in the water.

'Enough,' said Assedrynn, and they fell silent. 'Losara, your time here is almost over. You know your ultimate purpose, but we offer a way forward. The dream has thrown up many possibilities, many futures . . . some a consequence of your next steps.'

'A pilgrimage,' hissed Lampet.

'A pilgrimage,' whispered Mokan and Mir together.

'The futures that hold the most hope,' said Assedrynn, 'appear to be born from the undertaking of a pilgrimage.'

It seemed a strange thing to be so important, but Losara said, 'As you wish.'

'Begin from Skygrip.'

'Any particular direction?'

'No,' said Assedrynn. 'Let curiosity lead you. Seek to know your land. One other thing . . .'

Elsara, the lionfish, had been sleepily submerged almost past her dark oval eyes. Suddenly she reared out of the water, her spikes sticking in all directions. She spoke in a rasping, echoing voice. 'Do not go alone.'

'Do not go alone,' muttered Mir, and a second later Mokan repeated it. 'Do not go alone.'

'Why?' asked Losara.

Assedrynn stirred. 'Because,' he said, 'it expands our understanding to see things through another's eyes. And company will make you travel true, not just whisk from place to place.'

'What do you mean, whisk?'

'Time to depart,' said Assedrynn, and Losara realised the great fish had been slowly sinking into the sea. 'Even at the world's edge we cannot long remain. Lampet will eke out a few more moments. Goodbye, saviour child. Carry our futures wisely.'

Silently the gods sank into the sea, all except Lampet. Once they were alone, the serpent's eyes flashed green. 'Return to the Isle, and up,' he said.

Losara swam towards the Isle and hauled himself out at the low end. As he walked up the hill, he noticed again the tiny blue flowers, growing not out of cracks but from the rocks themselves. Stooping by one, he turned its face gently towards him. Salt crystals glistened on dark petals, and it was so small and perfectly formed that it somehow seemed to stand out from reality.

'It would die anywhere but here,' came Lampet's voice over his shoulder. 'It is too used to salt and rock and hard and cold. If living were easy, this would die.'

'It's beautiful,' said Losara.

'First to go if the light triumphs.'

Losara continued to the top of the hill. In the sea surrounding were loops of Lampet's great body, but no boat.

'I don't see the boat,' he said.

'No more boat for you, Shadowhand.'

'How am I supposed to travel?' Losara asked, but he almost felt he knew the answer.

'Now that you are more shadow than flesh,' said Lampet, 'you need not anchor when you travel the shadowlines. You can simply go.'

Satisfaction suffused Losara at this confirmation – what freedom he now possessed. He could *whisk* anywhere in the entire world, and appear at the other side whole and complete. Unlike Battu, he'd never have to fear the path of shadows he travelled breaking or shifting behind him, cutting him off from his mortal body.

'You understand,' said Lampet.

'I do.'

'Anything more to ask? My time dwindles.'

Losara remembered his promise to Tyrellan to ask the gods about the butterfly. He described Tyrellan's predicament to Lampet and the serpent's eyes glowed red. There were answers given, but Tyrellan was not going to like them.

Lampet gave a great sigh and his eyes turned yellow. His head drifted backwards as his loops in the water began to sink out of view. 'Blessings upon you, saviour child,' he said. 'If not first and only, then serve us as well as yourself and our people.'

'As well as I serve any,' said Losara, 'that well I'll serve them all.'

As Lampet disappeared into the depths, the last thing visible was the yellow of his eyes.

Losara Shadowhand leaped off the hill, dissolving into shadow to speed across the sea.

By the time he'd wondered how fast he could go, Losara found himself the base of Skygrip Castle. Those parts of him that had physical substance whirled in the shadows, clinging to his core presence like moons circling a star. As he travelled up the outer walls, a patrol of Graka flew past. He leaped at one to land in the shade between its shoulder and wing. Riding with his unknowing host, he stayed for several passes around Skygrip, then sprang back to the tower. He reached the long throne-room window and slipped inside.

An unwelcome scene met his ethereal gaze. Battu was holding Lalenda aloft by a crystalline wing, his whitening fist threatening to snap it. His face was a twisted storm of anger, the black wells of his eyes expanding. Tyrellan looked as if he was trying to calm him, but the dark lord's shouting drowned him out.

'Why would *I* be walking through fields of grass?' he roared. 'Under the sun, by the Dark Gods! You must tell me, prophet – is it a dream, or will it transpire?'

'I have no answers for my lord,' said Lalenda, and Losara was surprised by a note of defiance in her voice. Battu began to shake her, making her wings rustle.

'Master,' said Losara. All eyes snapped to him. He hadn't even realised he'd stepped from the shadows, and quickly checked himself to make sure he was all there – and he was. He moved forward from the window, clasping his shadowhands together. 'I have returned from Assedrynn's Isle.'

Battu dropped Lalenda and she fell without a sound. The wells in his eyes did not recede, and for a moment he looked like a cornered beast. 'Apprentice,' he said, and glanced at the window, clearly wondering how Losara had come to be standing there so instantaneously. His eyes fastened on Losara's new hands and he faltered. 'They have blessed you mightily,' he said, attempting to force civility into his voice while everything else in his demeanour remained rabid. 'Well done, my boy.'

Tyrellan, his orb eyes wider than Losara had ever seen them, fell to one knee and bowed his head. Battu's anger flickered towards him, but was quickly contained.

'Did they . . .' Battu licked his lips. 'Is there any message they wish passed to me?'

'None,' said Losara, and Battu scowled. The Shadowdreamer stalked forward, falling just short of looming over his Apprentice. Losara did not think Battu would strike out, not yet, and watched him calmly. 'They only ask that you release me to a pilgrimage,' he continued. 'To travel Fenvarrow and know the land.'

'Of course.' Battu seemed relieved that Losara would be leaving again. 'If the gods wish it done, so shall it be.'

Losara arched an eyebrow as if to say, 'Oh, really?'

The expression was not lost on Battu. Not on Tyrellan either, and the Black Goblin's head turned slowly from Losara to Battu, registering something of the exchange.

'I am also in need of companions,' said Losara. 'The gods decree that I not travel alone.'

'Very well,' said Battu, his stance and face again completely contrary to the reasonable tone of his voice. Losara wondered if he even knew how he appeared. 'Who would you take?'

Losara glided around Battu so he could see Lalenda. The pixie had not moved from where she'd fallen, but sat sprawled with her hands on the floor. Though muck and tears stained her, she did not seem as tremulous as he remembered her. She stared at his hands, and then his eyes. Now that he thought about it, they had all looked at his eyes.

He smiled, finding he was genuinely glad to see her. The next moment he felt overwhelmingly sorry that she'd remained so trapped and abused in this place, while he had managed to soar free. *Why compare her feelings to my own?* he wondered briefly. *If I did that with everyone, I'd surely go insane.*

'Lalenda,' he said. 'I'll take Lalenda.'

'Lalenda?' echoed Battu quietly.

'Yes,' Losara said, and the pixie's eyes shone brightly. 'In fact,' he continued, 'that has helped me decide our first destination. We will travel to Swampwild.'

She stiffened at the word and half-choked a gasp. Losara turned and found Battu standing very close, definitely looming now.

'I will take Lalenda,' he repeated. 'It is the gods' will.'

'Yes,' hissed Battu. 'And who else will you take? Not Tyrellan, he is needed.'

He shot a meaningful look at Tyrellan, who returned his flat gaze to the middle distance. Losara frowned – he hadn't thought this far ahead. Who else indeed?

'My kind lord,' came Lalenda's voice, and he found her risen to her feet.

'Yes?'

'Might I suggest . . .'

'Yes?'

'Grimra, lord.'

Instantly the idea appealed. Grimra had also been trapped here too long.

'An excellent choice,' Tyrellan said. 'The Apprentice will need protection and I can think of none better.'

'Who's Grimra?' muttered Battu.

'The Golgoleth Ghost,' said Tyrellan, and Battu went very quiet.

'I shall be making preparations immediately,' said Losara. 'Lalenda, please ready yourself for travel. If she may be excused, my master?'

'Indeed,' said Battu, and waved angrily at Lalenda. She shot Losara a thankful look and fled happily from the chamber. They all heard her exclamation of joy as she entered the tunnel, which made Battu flinch.

The dark lord moved towards Refectu, but didn't seem to want to turn his back on Losara. He stopped just shy of the throne. 'Is that the extent of your list of companions?'

'Yes, master.'

'Then leave me be. I have some matters to consider.'

'As you wish.' Slowly and deliberately, Losara turned his own back on Battu without fear and walked towards the tunnel. 'Oh,' he said, stopping for a moment. 'I would see Tyrellan before I leave, if it please you, master.'

'It pleases me!' shouted Battu, no longer able to maintain his poise. 'It pleases me no end!'

'Thank you,' said Losara, and continued on, not pausing to see if Tyrellan followed.

∽

Together they walked, Tyrellan's cat-like padding matching Losara's fluid glide. Losara found himself heading
towards his quarters, though he didn't know exactly why.
There was nothing there he needed.

'You'll arrange for Grimra's pendant to be removed
from the archway?' he asked.

'Yes,' said Tyrellan.

He seemed withdrawn, and Losara wondered if
the exchanges in the throne room had put him in the
middle of things.

'Battu won't harm you,' he said.

'Mind your words,' growled Tyrellan.

'He isn't watching. I'd be able to tell.'

Tyrellan grunted and glanced away. 'You grow
arrogant, lord,' he said. 'It is not commendable.'

Losara felt the truth of the words, and nodded.
'Perhaps you're right. I am simply heady with my
change, Tyrellan.' He waggled his black fingers and
now Tyrellan did stare.

'You are truly blessed by the shadow.'

'Yes,' said Losara. 'And you follow the shadow
always, don't you?'

'Yes.'

'Battu does not.'

Tyrellan looked hard at Losara, the blue of an ice lantern
caught in his black eyes. 'You'll be taking action?'

'Perhaps.'

The butterfly flew from Tyrellan's shoulder, reminding
Losara of the conversation's purpose.

'I had a dream on the way to the Isle,' he said. 'You
tried to sever your connection to the butterfly by death.'
Tyrellan's gaze remained neutral. 'Is that something you
considered? Or did it actually come to pass?'

'I considered it.'

'Do not try it. I would save you from that dis-appointment.' He paused. 'I spoke to the gods on your behalf.'

Tyrellan bowed his head. 'I am honoured.'

'The news may not gladden you. The only way to break the legacy spell is to reunite it with the soul of Elessa Lanclara. There are two ways this can be done, and one of them sounds impossible.'

'Tell me that one.'

'Enter the Great Well of Arkus and find her.'

Tyrellan bared his fangs. *Well might he snarl at such an idea*, thought Losara. *All that light, coalescing – how to find one's way in such a terrible place?*

'What is the other way?' asked the goblin.

'Bring what is left of her back to the world. Reanimate her corpse and reunite her with that part of her life force trapped in your butterfly.'

'Not my butterfly,' muttered Tyrellan, and fell silent.

Losara knew he was thinking hard and deep about how insurmountable such a task would be – to penetrate the Halls, find Elessa's grave, perform the right rituals, and all based on a chance that some remnant of her floated intact enough in Arkus's Well to summon back.

'Maybe,' offered Losara, 'it will be a reward. When we stand there at the end, triumphant in the Halls, you will finally be able to rid yourself of the creature.'

It felt a strange thing to say, as he bore no real animosity towards the land of light. Nevertheless, Tyrellan seized on his words.

'It is gratifying to hear someone speak of progress.'

Losara knew the target of his frustration. 'Don't judge Battu too harshly,' he said. 'You don't know that he was ordered by the gods to avoid conflict. The action he took at the Mines may have damned him for all time.'

Tyrellan remembered . . .

When Battu was young, he was confident. After he had killed Raker, a conspiracy had formed against him. Tyrellan had put a stop to it, winning Battu's trust by becoming his confidant in that first and formative betrayal. After putting down the dissidents, Battu had immediately felt the need to consolidate his power and so he organised the assault on the Mines to prove himself. Tyrellan had been instrumental in encouraging it. This new understanding of why Battu had been loath to take further action against the light in all his years of ruling did nothing to improve Tyrellan's view of him. If anything it made him weaker, to have strayed so wildly from an explicitly laid-down path. Tyrellan would never have encouraged the attack on the Mines if Battu had simply told him it was against the Dark Gods' will.

He realised Losara was no longer beside him, and turned to find the boy staring at himself in a mirror-fountain.

'Had you not seen, my lord?' he asked.

'No,' said Losara.

There was nothing behind his eyes but shadow.

PART THREE

Of Purpose

I like to believe I'm not one to dwell on past possibilities. I know the roads that brought me here, and I cannot walk them again. And yet sometimes, in my quieter moments, I muse on what might have been. What if Corlas had been left alone to raise me himself, whole, in Whisperwood? Would it have been a peaceful existence, untouched by bloodshed and strife? Perhaps I wouldn't have escaped my fate at all, merely come to it by a different route.

It isn't for myself, I suppose, that I wonder these things. It could have gone better for my father, I think. Certainly he deserved better. Ah, well. It seems that compassion is not the currency of power.

But I digress. Let me return to our story, to a time when it did not seem there was any particular road in front of me. Or many, perhaps, crosshatched all the way to the horizon. Was it any wonder that I felt somewhat directionless? Part of me was, after all, on the other side of the world. A monumental task lay ahead and I had little idea of how it might be accomplished.

Stumble on, I supposed. Stumble on until I discovered the way.

The Streets of Kadass

Bel dropped to bended knee before the teary little girl who was clutching a raggedy doll tightly to her chest. Around them people bustled onwards, leaving peacekeeper and child an island in the throng.

'Hello there, princess,' said Bel. 'Who's that you've got with you?'

The girl's lip quivered.

'She's very pretty,' Bel went on. 'Though I can't see her face.'

Tentatively the girl raised the doll. Bel smiled a big, stupid smile, took the doll's limp hand in his own and shook it.

'Pleased to meet you,' he said.

'Her name's Shari,' said the little girl.

'What a beautiful name,' said Bel, and the girl looked pleased. 'I bet Shari's glad she has you to look after her. It can be pretty scary wandering around all by yourself.'

The girl looked worried again. 'We lost Mumma.'

'Well, that won't do at all. When did you last see her?'

'Over by the birds,' said the girl.

Bel looked about and quickly spotted a bench of caged birds amongst the other stalls that lined the Market Road.

Hiza appeared out of the crowd. 'The procession is moving,' he said. 'We should keep up.'

Bel nodded. 'Tell you what, princess,' he said to the girl. 'How about you get up on my shoulders and we go back to the bird stall? That way you and Shari will be up nice and high, and maybe between us all we'll be able to spot your mumma.'

Relief flooded the little girl's face. She took Bel's hand and he hoisted her up onto his broad shoulders.

Hiza shook his head and smiled. 'Always there for a damsel in distress, eh?'

'I think it was Shari who was really frightened,' said Bel. 'Lucky she had a brave friend to protect her.' He was rewarded with a happy giggle from on high.

They weren't long at the bird stall before the girl's frantic mother burst from the crowd. She thanked Bel profusely for finding her child, hugging her as tightly as the girl had hugged Shari. As they disappeared into the bustle, the girl raised a hand to wave happily at the blades.

'Come on,' said Hiza. 'The wasps are making good time.'

The two keepers began weaving through the crowd. People were milling around the market stalls, or gathering to stare down side streets at the colourful caravan that was passing along Kadass Road, a couple of streets over and parallel to Market Road. The caravan carried the Trusted of Cindeka and her entourage, who had arrived that morning at Kadass's western gate. They were going to the Halls to discuss a trade dispute with their neighbour state of Tria, but the curiosity of the general populace was in no way due to that. The people were out to see the only Trusted in Kainordas who wasn't a Varenkai.

The Zyvanix wasps were huge versions of their distant insect cousins, and not often seen in Kadass. Most of them lived in Cindeka, in towering hive cities constructed of earth. They had a reputation for arrogance, believing themselves to be the closest to Arkus of all Kainordas's races since they were blessed with the power of flight. It was only with a certain belligerence that they even recognised the Throne as their ruler.

Bel and Hiza caught glimpses of wasp warriors flitting about a lumbering caravan, their spindly arms clutching bows and barbed spears as they hovered in the air. The caravan itself was a sight to behold: huge and draped in the bright colours that the wasps favoured, pulled by the enormous draught horses of the western plains. The keepers were part of an unofficial guard for the arrival, dispersed amongst the watching crowds. It was a good thing they were there, Bel thought, for the Zyvanix warriors seemed to be enjoying the attention more than their duties. Still, it was unlikely there would be any trouble.

'You know she needs two translators?' said Hiza.

'Hmm?' said Bel.

'The wasp Trusted. She needs two translators.'

'Is that so?' Bel exaggerated his interest.

Hiza grinned at him. 'Yes. Zyvanix can't make human sounds with those weird mouths of theirs, and we can't make their sounds either. The translators can never talk in the languages they are trained to understand, so they need one wasp who can understand human speech to tell the Trusted what *we're* saying, and one Varenkai who can understand wasp talk to tell us what *they're* saying.'

'How interesting.'

'It *is*,' insisted Hiza. 'Imagine being the human translator! Stuck in Athika, surrounded by wasps, without even being able to talk to them! And a city built of mud beneath you – wouldn't you be afraid of the floors collapsing?'

'Not my choice of career,' said Bel. 'Excuse me,' and he stepped aside for a young woman carrying a basket of fruit. She blushed at his smile.

They approached another pair of keepers, one of whom was their captain, Hosarus. He was a man who had chosen to stay with the keepers instead of moving on to a career in the military. Was that a path for Bel to consider? Somehow he doubted it.

'Lads,' said Hosarus.

'Captain,' they chorused.

'I want you on Kadass Road.' Hosarus glanced around, chewing absently on a straw. 'Lovely day. Shouldn't be any hassle. Keep a lookout though. It's a big crowd, ain't it?'

'Sure is, captain,' said Bel.

Hosarus nodded. 'Off you go then.'

They obeyed, moving to the street of the procession. People were waving at the wasps, who stared back with multifaceted eyes, or waggled their antennae. For a notoriously bad-tempered race, it looked as if they were enjoying the fuss, Bel thought. He admired the dexterity with which they handled their weapons as they flew, using all six legs to manoeuvre them about. It would be impressive to see their archers in action, firing arrows from the quivers strapped to their stripy stomachs. No wonder his father had wished for a troop of them at the Shining Mines.

Something stirred in his blood and it took him a moment to recognise it. He spun around, searching the crowd, shoving through without regard for who he pushed. The feeling faded and still he searched, straining his neck for any glimpse of red hair. Eventually he gave up, with a dark glower and a heavy heart. He had been *sure* he had sensed her, if only for a moment. Had she really been passing nearby?

Bel sat in a corner of The Wayward Dog with Hiza as the afternoon light retreated over table tops like sunset. They'd been on their feet all day and the opportunity to sit peacefully was welcome.

'Looked like your mugs were close to empty,' said Corlas as he joined them, plunking three fresh ales on the table. Hiza and Bel tipped back their dregs in answer.

Bel raised his fresh mug in a mock toast. 'To the visiting Trusted,' he said. 'May she continue to sip on sugar water and never realise the joy of ale.'

'And to the shining sun,' said Hiza, 'for granting us a thirst worthy of such ale.' He grinned.

'And to your superiors,' added Corlas, 'for putting clowns like you in charge of our streets.'

They laughed and clinked their mugs together.

'Were you there to see the Trusted enter the Halls?' asked Bel.

'Aye,' said Corlas. 'I organised the ceremonious bowing of soldiers as she came through the gates. Your friend M'Meska was there, along with her standing order that you return to the military immediately.'

'Mmm,' said Bel, staring into his ale.

'She said that when she makes troop leader, she'll be hunting you down for her penulm,' said Corlas. 'I think she was serious.'

Bel forced a smile. The Saurian simply refused to understand his decision to return to the keepers. Not that he really understood it himself.

'At any rate,' Corlas continued, 'this is one engagement Naphur can't palm off to Baygis. Word is that the wasp Trusted refused to negotiate with anyone but the Throne himself. Personally I think Baygis would have done better. Relations with the wasps have always been difficult, but Baygis is as smooth as a river stone.'

'Did you get to see the Trusted herself?' Hiza asked.

'I thought I caught her peeking out of that ridiculous caravan,' replied Corlas. 'Who knows? They all look like bugs to me.' He took a swig. 'A couple of them put on an archery display for us.'

'Really?' said Bel. 'I'd have liked to see that. How was it?'

'Impressive. Very impressive. They shoot while airborne. With all those legs working, they can have another arrow ready as soon as the first leaves the bow. And their arrows look like wood replicas of their stings. I wouldn't want a swarm of Zyvanix on my tail, by Arkus.'

'Maybe we should see if we can "appropriate" some of their bows for the barracks,' said Bel. 'Another addition for weapons practice?'

'I'm sure it can be arranged,' said Corlas, returning Bel's smile. 'They *are* here on a matter of trade, after all. Perhaps if the barracks chef were to mix up some extra sweet sugar water?'

'Ah yes,' said Bel. 'That's good stuff, that sugar water.'

He screwed up his face in distaste and they all laughed again.

Night had grown old by the time Bel made his way home. Back in the tavern, a game of darts with some other keepers had blown out of all proportion, resulting in many rematches. Now he was glad to be free of the smoke, and savoured an unusually good mood that had come out of nowhere. He was awake, not drunk, and in no rush to be home. Instead he meandered, pausing on street corners occasionally to look up at the stars. He smiled as he recalled the little girl and her doll Shari. He realised he'd learned the doll's name but not hers.

Something seemed to be leading his feet and he allowed his course to come to him naturally. He entered a wealthy neighbourhood, with high walls enclosing houses and private gardens. The trees planted along the footpath were well tended, and flower gardens grew at their bases. As he walked, he thought of Jaya – where had she gone? Would she come back? Had he really sensed her today? He'd thought about her often after his return, and part of him wondered if he'd insisted on returning to the keepers just to maximise his chances of bumping into her again.

Suddenly, what he saw ahead made him slide into the shadows. By one of the high walls, a figure was swiftly climbing a tree. It swung nimbly off a branch and disappeared over the wall. Bel moved carefully down the

street towards the spot and stopped where the figure
had gone over. He thought he heard the slight creak of
a door closing. He went to the tree and hoisted himself
up, wincing as he made the branches rustle, but no
audible response came from over the wall. Climbing a
good three paces up, he grabbed the same branch he'd
seen the trespasser use and swung out over the wall. He
landed on soft grass and jumped behind a nearby bush,
waiting to see if he'd given himself away. He was in an
enclosed garden, about twenty paces square. Ferns and
small trees clustered about, and the outside wall of the
house ran with chains of ivy. Bel saw that the back door
was slightly ajar, and noticed scratch marks on the lock.
The intruder had picked it.

Bel went inside silently. He stood in a kitchen of pale
tiles, with a hardwood table in the middle and elaborate
lantern-holders in the walls. As he made his way into
the next room he was met by tapestries, paintings and
a polished dining table with an interconnected row
of candelabra running down its centre. With such
wealth on display, Bel guessed there would be privately
employed guards somewhere in the house. If he called
out for them, however, the thief would also become
aware of his presence. Instead he went from room to
room, skirting the walls and pausing at doors to peek
into the next before entering.

He came to a study with neat shelves of thick books
that looked clean and unread, and stole up to the open
door at the other end. Through it was a living room
– plush red carpet, deep armchairs and a huge metal
fireplace carved with flames. Around the walls were
marble pedestals on which rested various display pieces:

statuettes, carvings, a bust, and, on the one the thief stood by, a vase.

Moonlight crept through a window and Bel saw that the figure was hooded in a light green cloak and wearing black leather boots. She turned, revealing herself to be a woman as the moon chased the contours of her body. Of her face he could see nothing, for it was wrapped in strips of cloth, and the hood covered her eyes. As she lowered her head to the satchel, a lock of her hair came loose from under the hood and unravelled to full length, a dark red waterfall. She raised a hand to push it back into place with fingers long and clever. Bel froze, dumbfounded. It was Jaya.

She pulled something from the satchel and dimly Bel remembered that he was a keeper stalking a thief – a thief who was now behaving very strangely indeed. She held what looked like a water bladder, and unwound the cord that bound it closed. She upended the bladder and a black liquid poured out, filling the vase and spilling down its sides, staining it with dark streams. She slung the satchel over her shoulder and began to tread sound-lessly back towards the door where Bel stood hiding.

Bel flattened himself against the wall, his mind whirring. What was the purpose of her odd intrusion?

Instinct took over as her shadow passed through the door frame and his hands shot out. She gave a low cry of surprise, twisting immediately and with surprising strength. Bel came away with nothing but her cloak, ripped from her back. She turned into a fleeting shadow, darting away through the dark house. Stealth was forgotten as Bel chased after, desperate not to let her escape, and not because she had broken the law.

He entered the kitchen just in time to see her push open the back door. Into the garden they ran, her red hair streaming now that her hood was gone. He caught up to her as she started up a tree, catching her arm and pulling her to the ground. She rolled to her feet and Bel heard a rasping of metal as she produced a sword.

'Wait!' he said, but was forced to draw his own. From the house came voices, and lanterns were being lit. Bel deflected her sword, their blades flashing silver in the moonlight. 'Jaya, it's me!' he said.

'Bel?' she exclaimed in surprise. 'What are you –'

'There's no time,' he hissed. 'You must escape – but promise that you'll find me again!'

'I was going to,' she said. 'I promise.'

'Then go.'

She took a step away, turned to look at him again.

'Quickly,' he whispered.

She sprinted away into the garden as the door banged open. Four guards with swords emerged from the house and spotted Bel immediately.

'I'm a peacekeeper!' he called, tapping the badge on his shoulder.

'What goes on?' demanded one of them.

'There was a thief,' said Bel, 'in the house. I don't know where she went.'

'There!' shouted a guard, pointing to a silhouette that climbed a tree by the garden wall. As Jaya disappeared over the side, the guard ran to the garden gate, fumbling for his keys. Another guard gripped Bel by the shoulder.

'What's wrong, man? Are you hurt?'

Bel said nothing, just stared in the direction she had gone.

The man shook him. 'Why didn't you chase her?'

Bel looked at the man for the first time. What *was* he doing? As the gate opened and guards poured out, he realised he had better give chase as well, lest his actions look even more suspicious. He ran through the gate behind the guards. Out in the street, Jaya was hedged on both sides by high walls, without side streets to duck into. The guards in pursuit were catching up and Bel realised she was limping. She must have hurt her foot in the jump from the wall. Scant seconds later the guards had her, kicking her legs from under her so she fell hard on the cobblestones. One kicked her again so she rolled onto her back; another grabbed her hand as she went for a dagger in her boot. Swords levelled on her and she ceased all struggle, glaring up angrily.

'Search her!' ordered the head guard, and the others bent to probe her roughly. One emptied her satchel onto the cobblestones.

'Thieves' tools,' he announced. 'Nothing from the house.'

The head guard turned to Bel. 'Why didn't you call for help?' he demanded.

'What, and have her escape before I could grab her?' he shot back. 'I suppose, like you, I should have rampaged about the house like a pack of drunken mountain trolls, giving her ample warning of my whereabouts!'

The man scowled. 'Yes, you did so much better than us,' he said. 'Did you see her take anything?'

'No.'

The guard's eyes narrowed and he bent to Jaya, taking a shoulder to shake her roughly. 'What were you doing in the house?' he demanded.

Bel had had enough. He pushed the head guard away so roughly that the man fell on his buttocks. 'Back off, all of you!' he growled. 'This woman is a prisoner of Kainordas now. You may not touch her.'

'We will question her!' shouted the head guard, rising red with rage. The others took up dangerous postures.

'You will do nothing of the sort, *civilian*,' said Bel, moving between Jaya and the men, his fingers drumming the hilt of his sword. 'She will be questioned by an overseer, not subjected to thugs' justice. Lower your swords!' he bellowed, 'lest you all be charged with treason!'

The men glanced to their leader, who sneered and made a motion with his hands. The swords came down. Assaulting a keeper was a very serious crime.

'Well, then,' said the head guard, 'we will help you escort her to the holding cells – just in case you decide to *stand around* while she escapes again.'

His tone implied that he would back down no further, and Bel suppressed the urge to force him to. Little did these men know that, if he'd wanted to, Bel could have left them all in tatters. He nodded stiffly.

'Come, then. Help me with the girl, and that grip of yours better not be any tighter than it need be.'

'Nor yours any looser,' retorted the guard, and together they lifted the miserable Jaya from the ground.

Behind Bars and Beyond

'Where is she?' demanded Lord Cydus. He stood at the desk in the foyer of the keepers' headquarters, flanked by two of his brutish guards.

Captain Hosarus took a well-chewed straw from his mouth. 'In a holding cell, my lord,' he answered flatly. Bel stood behind him, glad his superior had taken an instant dislike to this man.

Cydus puffed up his already puffy cheeks. He was short and dumpy with a square brown beard and twirled moustache, both painstakingly well tended yet not managing to hide the pockmarked and blotchy skin beneath. His eyes were red-rimmed and his clothes looked hastily thrown on. He had obviously been asleep until very recently.

'I have some questions for her, captain,' Cydus said. 'You will let my men speak to her.'

'I'm afraid not, lord,' said Hosarus steadily. 'She will remain here until an overseer can question her. That is the law.'

'Don't play games with me!' spat Cydus. 'That little bitch came into my home and vandalised a precious vase! It was an intended gift, in fact, to the visiting

Trusted, and I will not go to her, having already pledged it, with nothing!' He stamped a foot, making Hosarus's eyebrows go up as it came down. 'She will pay, if I have to take it out of her hide, by Arkus!'

'I'm afraid my lord is overly upset,' Hosarus said. 'Perhaps it would be best if he returned home and finished the night's sleep.'

'I will see her!' shouted Cydus, his face bright red. 'She will learn she can't muck around with Assicon Cydus or his property!'

The man tried to go around the desk and suddenly Bel was blocking his way.

'I suggest you step back, Lord Cydus,' he said. 'You cannot enter here, nor your men.'

Cydus's moustache twitched about like a worm on a hook. 'The Throne will hear of this matter, and of your disrespect!' he said.

He spun and marched out of the building, snapping his fingers at his men to follow. They did so, after final hard looks at Bel and the captain. When they were gone, Hosarus sighed.

'Bloody lords and ladies,' he said, putting the straw back in his mouth. 'They think they own the place.'

'Excuse me, captain,' said Bel. 'But what will happen to her now? The girl, I mean.'

'Just what I said. Due process. Now you also go home and get some sleep. I don't want you snoring on your feet tomorrow.'

Bel paused, but his captain remained steadfast with hands on hips. Bel found that he, like Cydus, was forced to retreat.

'Don't worry,' said Hosarus. 'Cydus won't get near her.'

'Yes, captain,' was all Bel could think to say, and he stepped out again into the night.

Bel was face down in his pillow the next morning when a knocking sounded at his door. He woke reluctantly, sitting up to rub tired eyes. The knocking came again more loudly.

'All *right*,' he said. 'I'm not supposed to be up yet anyway!'

Sliding on a pair of trousers, he walked to the door. Upon opening it he blinked in surprise – his visitor was Baygis, holding a tray with a steaming pot and two mugs.

'Lord Baygis,' he said, becoming self-conscious of his near nakedness. 'I, er . . .'

'Never mind, Bel,' said Baygis, moving past him into the roofless living room, now lit up by the morning light. The bedroom was off to one side, with a ceiling to keep the sun from tired eyes. 'Sorry for waking you,' he said, smiling at the bleary Bel. 'I've brought tea as a gesture of apology.' He placed the tray on the table, swept back his white-gold robe and looked expectant.

'Have a seat, lord,' said Bel, searching around for a shirt to pull on.

'Thank you,' said Baygis. He sat and poured hot tea. 'Been a while since I had reason to visit the soldiers' quarters,' he said, and took a test sip. 'Mmm. Not bad for barracks brew.'

Bel had always liked Baygis, though he'd never had much to do with him. As an ambassador the man was a respected master of negotiation, and as overseer was reputed to be fair and even-tempered. He also had a charmingly mischievous side that created constant stress for the Throne and gossip for the court. Bel found it odd, and more than a little intimidating, to have the sleek, well-groomed lord sitting opposite him in his rooms before he'd even had a chance for bath or breakfast.

'What can I do for you, my lord?' he asked.

'Ah,' smiled Baygis, 'the obvious question. Fair enough, I suppose, when one is so rudely interrupted of a morning. I understand you arrested a thief last night, whom you caught breaking into the Kadass residence of the worthy and honourable Assicon Cydus?' There was only the sneakiest note of sarcasm in Baygis's voice.

'I did, lord,' said Bel, the thought of Jaya now truly waking him. 'What's happened?'

'Politics has happened,' said Baygis, spooning more sugar into his mug. He misread the look of concern on Bel's face and gave a reassuring smile. 'Don't worry, you're not in any trouble. One of Cydus's private guards complained about your conduct, but given your record, and his, we don't feel compelled to take him seriously. I always wonder about nobles who opt for hired swords over the trained soldiers they have every right to be allocated.' He swirled the spoon. 'So,' he continued, 'this is the situation: the only thing the girl did in the house, as far as we can tell, was pour ink all over a valuable vase that Cydus bought in Tulzan. You know of Tulzan?'

'A village in lower Dennali,' recited Bel, 'on the northern border of the Hinter Swamplands. They are noted masters of ceramics and use a special clay from the swamp.'

'Ah,' said Baygis, eyes twinkling, 'another casualty of Fahren's geography lessons. I suffered them myself for many years. Yes, that is Tulzan. It is also where Cydus holds his estate, and one of the reasons he graces us with his presence in Kadass so often – the insects bite like dragons down there and the weather is awful.' Baygis blew on his tea. 'Anyway, Cydus says the vase is an expensive piece from a master craftsman, and having seen it myself I tend to believe him. Probably worth a hundred gold at least . . . until it got stained by black ink. A strange crime indeed, and I'm curious to question the girl about her motives.'

'So you are the overseer on this?' said Bel, unable to keep tension from his voice.

'Yes, indeed,' answered Baygis. 'Cydus demands a fast hearing. He intended the vase to be a gift to the wasp Trusted, and now that it's ruined, he's embarrassed – having already bragged about the gift at the palace reception yesterday. He's been up at the Halls all morning, putting on a great display of anger for the Trusted's benefit, demanding that the Throne look into the matter quickly. Normally, of course, my good father would tell Cydus to go and soak his balls in hot water, or something equally incisive, but the Zyvanix are an odd people and the Throne is afraid to cause them offence. He wants to concentrate on the real matters at hand and hence is dealing with this distraction in the easiest way possible – namely, by dragging in his overseer son to deal with it. So,' he spread his palms on the table, 'what I'd like to do is hear your version of events before I go and see this girl.'

'Will you use magic?' asked Bel, managing to cover his anxiety. Baygis was famous for his ability to milk the truth from people using persuasive magic, and Bel was still sorting through the strangeness of the night before for himself.

'No,' said Baygis. 'Just tell me what happened. I only want your story to check against the girl's.'

Bel nodded. He recounted the events of the night before as though he hadn't known Jaya previously, and didn't mention his mercy in the garden, or the way he was stirred when he looked into her green flecked eyes.

Baygis was, thankfully, satisfied with Bel's version of events. After he'd left, Bel prepared for his day on patrol. He met Hiza in Kadass at the keepers' headquarters and together they set off into the streets. Hiza quickly discovered that his friend was in a contemplative mood, staring off into the distance and shutting down any attempts at banter with short, vague answers. When the patrol ended, Bel excused himself quickly and Hiza went off in search of livelier cronies.

Bel re-entered the keepers' headquarters. He made his way along cream corridors, heading for the holding cells where Jaya was being kept. He arrived in a room lit by fickle candles. Behind a desk sat Gint, a gangly old keeper who looked after the prisoners, hunched over in a comfortable-looking chair and reading a dog-eared book.

'Hello, Gint,' said Bel. 'Been busy?'

Gint glanced up. 'Ah, Bel. No, son, no traffic today. Not even a single rambunctious drunkard.'

'Thought you might like a pie,' said Bel, placing a cloth-wrapped pie on the desk. Gint's eyes lit up instantly. 'Mind if I go through?' he continued nonchalantly. 'I want to talk to the girl I brought in last night.'

'Go ahead,' said Gint, waving at the door behind him, clearly anticipating quality time with the pie. 'She's to the left at the far end. Key's in the usual place. Be careful of her, she's a bit feisty, I wouldn't go past the inner grille. Holler if you need me.'

'Thanks,' said Bel.

He entered the cells, closing the door behind him and taking down the set of keys that hung just inside. Before him was a passage lined with heavy oak doors, set with panels for observing the cells beyond. Bel came to the last cell and paused, attempted to collect his thoughts, failed, then opened the door. The room was divided in half by a grille of iron bars, creating a viewing chamber and the cell proper, designed so overseers could sit and question prisoners face to face in privacy and safety. In the ceiling was a grated skylight through which the moon dimly illuminated the cell and its occupant. She lay face down on a single bed pushed against the wall, one arm draped listlessly to the floor. Her clothes were the same as the day before – streamlined, body-hugging thieves' garb: a long-sleeved jade cotton shirt and black leggings. She raised her head.

'Who's there?'

Bel shut the door behind him and stepped into the shaft of moonlight. She sat up on the bed instantly, watching him. He felt exposed, for she could see him properly though her face was in shadow. Inexplicably, he didn't know what to do with his hands – just now there didn't seem to be any natural position for them, so he forced them stiffly down by his sides.

'Hi,' he said dumbly.

'Hi,' she replied.

Bel waited for something else to occur to him. 'You don't have any lanterns lit,' he said.

'There was nothing to see,' said Jaya. She moved forward along the bed, closer to the bars. 'Light one if you want.'

On Bel's side of the cell was a little desk where Baygis would have sat earlier that day. He found a lantern there and lit it. The shadows retreated and there she was.

'Nothing to see?' he echoed in wonder, and realised he'd said it out loud. She smiled at his alarm, and he smiled helplessly in return.

'Well,' she said, 'this wouldn't have been my choice of establishment for a second meeting. I don't really count last night, by the way. Or are you here on official business?'

Bel's eyes sparkled. 'No,' he said. He rapped the cell bars. 'So, this is where teasing the peacekeepers gets you. Who would have thought it?'

'Oh, hush,' she said. 'If it wasn't for *you*, I wouldn't even be here. Sneaking around in strange houses, leaping out of shadows to put your hands on a girl – *really*. You should be ashamed of yourself.'

'Me?' said Bel. 'By Arkus, it's *you* who was committing a clandestine act of vandalism. I was just doing my job. '

'So was I.'

'If you'd just come and found me at the tavern instead, all of this could have been averted.'

'Oh, really?' said Jaya. 'And how would that have worked? How would you have talked me out of . . .'

Her eyes screwed up and it took him a moment in the semi-light to realise she was trying not to cry. Without really thinking about it, he got up, unlocked the cell door and went in to sit on the bed next to her.

'That took you long enough,' she said, putting her arms around his chest.

'I thought you might be angry with me.'

'I *am* angry with you.'

'And upset, I think – about something else?'

She tried to hold him closer, but his leather breastplate got in the way. She knocked on it. 'Not very comfortable,' she said, and he laughed. All his doubts about her affection suddenly seemed stupid.

'Do you want me to take it off?'

'Yes.'

Things escalated quickly.

His desire might have been frantic after so many days spent in want of her, but instead he relaxed, as if he was finally coming home after years away. Around them, the rest of the world faded to grey unimportance, while she became so real it was almost overpowering. Again he felt that burbling in the blood, a fire that did not burn.

Some time later, he wasn't sure how long, they came to rest lying face to face with limbs entwined. He ran some of the hair off her face, and she kissed him.

'Strange girl,' he said.

'Why?'

'I thought you'd gone away. When I went to the tavern looking for you, they said you had gone.'

'I did go away. We were working the road to Ismore – there's plenty of caravans and such this time of year. Me and my partners, Lerena and Jeshun . . .' She trailed off.

'Will you tell me what happened to you?' said Bel. 'I don't care if you're a thief, Jaya, but I want to help you get out of this mess.'

'I doubt you can resolve this with a sword, Blade Bel.'

Bel thought about telling her then about his blue hair, about who he was. Perhaps the prophesied child of power would have more sway in getting her out of prison than just any old blade. He wanted to tell her, to reassure her, even just to impress her – but he bit his tongue, remembering Fahren's warnings. There would be time enough later, if he decided to. She wasn't going anywhere.

She sighed. 'All right. I may as well tell you – you could just go and ask your friend Baygis everything anyway. It's impossible to lie to that man. My secrets aren't my own any more.'

'Well, don't tell me if you don't choose to.'

'No,' she said, 'I choose. Just a bit annoyed about everything, that's all.' She gathered her thoughts. 'Lerena was in Ennoi village one day when she overheard Lord Cydus boasting tactlessly about his wealth – and about the Tulzan vase he was going to give to the wasp Trusted, who was soon to visit Kadass from my homeland.'

'You were born in Cindeka?'

'Yes, near Athika. My parents are farmers, raising cattle for the wasps, who are too lazy to farm for themselves. Anyway, Cydus's boasting was enough to tempt us, and we decided to rob his caravan once it got back on the open road. It was ambitious, but we love our adventures . . . or we did . . .

'We found their camp the night after they left Ennoi. Jeshun took care of the lookout with a sleeping dart and we crept up on the rest of them – they were all asleep. Lerena found the vase almost immediately, in Cydus's tent. Then a guard we hadn't noticed returned from relieving himself and sounded the alarm. We fled.

'They followed us on horses, and only I reached hiding in time. Lerena and Jeshun were caught and killed, in that order. I saw it from the trees. They were tied up, Bel, they could have been turned over to the keepers, but . . .' He felt her shiver. 'Cydus and his men are brutes. They may have been thieves, but that was murder. If you hadn't interceded when they caught me last night, I'd be dead too, I'm sure.'

Her voice grew hard. 'I decided that if the lives of my friends were worth a single piece of pottery, Cydus would pay for what he took. I came back to Kadass and waited for the Trusted to arrive, waited until the very day before Cydus planned to give her that accursed vase. I destroyed it when he would feel the blow the most. We may have wronged Cydus, but he wronged us back many times over, and he deserves what I did to him.'

She sighed. 'I know that doesn't make it admirable, and that these are the risks you take when you live your life cheating people.' Tears were running freely now, and he wiped her eyes. 'But he shouldn't have killed my friends,' she whispered.

'I'm sorry, Jaya,' said Bel. 'And you're right: Cydus had no right to execute prisoners.' He bit his tongue from reiterating, however, that this was the life she'd chosen for herself.

Some moments passed in silence.

'Bel?'

'Yes?'

'Why did you let me go?'

'What?'

'In Cydus's garden.'

'What of it?'

'It's not typical behaviour, you know. You're a peacekeeper.'

'I think you know why,' he said.

Hours later, Bel awoke. He sat up to see the grille door still unlocked and the keys on the cell floor. On the bed next to him, Jaya lay asleep, the morning sun falling on her peaceful face.

Swampwild

Together they sat by the iceplace in the small and simple inn. Losara, not wanting people to pay attention to him, had weaved a slight illusion about himself. His hands were returned to their normal pale tone, though some conceit led him to leave his fingernails black, and his eyes now appeared as their old selves, dark without being void-like. Opposite him, Lalenda sat in a dark green dress, low enough at the back for her wings to jut out. They'd bought it several days ago, a replacement for her worn-out rags.

Losara had imagined that the journey would be awkward, a prolonged version of that first conversation they had shared on the balcony. He had been pleased to discover this was not the case. She did not seem as afraid of him any more, and her great pleasure at being free of the castle was too pronounced to allow for many gaps in conversation. It filled each moment, either with words or without. Her shyness, Losara remembered, had never tempered her tendency to talk, and now that her fear was dwindling, that tendency shone.

'Did you notice that stormcrow a ways back before town?' she was saying.

Losara smiled gently in answer.

'It had a message tied to its leg,' she went on. 'Grimra was all for . . .'

Two mugs arrived, and Lalenda paused shyly in the presence of the barmaid. Once the woman departed, she continued.

'. . . Grimra wanted to snap it up, of course, just as he wants to do with everything.' She chortled. 'I tried to explain that if he did, someone somewhere would be bereft of correspondence and ever after doomed to wonder why their beau didn't write, or if their sister was still sick, or any of a thousand things. Of course he refused to understand any of it. In the end, the only way to save the poor creature was to convince Grimra it would be tough and stringy with filthy feathers that would get caught in his throat. I didn't hold out much hope, as he has no throat that I can see, but his food has to go somewhere, doesn't it? Anyway,' she blushed, as she often did at the end of a ramble, 'I'm sorry, lord. You're probably trying to sit in peace.'

She still apologised a lot, he reflected. 'I don't mind,' he said. 'It is peaceful listening to you talk.' That did nothing to stop her blush, which Losara also did not mind.

From outside the inn came a loud clucking, and the bartender cursed, grabbing a crossbow. As he opened the door, Losara raised an eyebrow at Lalenda. There was always a chance that the hens were simply being traumatised by a fox or some other predator, but more than likely . . .

'At least it's only hens,' said Lalenda. 'I'm surprised he hasn't gone for anything . . . or any*one* . . . larger.'

'Anyone that we know about,' added Losara, which made her frown with worry. He liked that she was concerned, but in truth she needn't be. He was quite sure the ghost was obeying *most* of his commands.

A low chuckling sounded from the floor and whiteness was momentarily visible swirling up through the floorboards.

'Grimra,' said Losara in a low voice, 'have you been attacking chickens?'

'Ah, yes,' said Grimra, and sighed in satisfaction. 'Grimra has.' The angry-looking barman re-entered with his crossbow unfired. 'So tasty and fat they be, Grimra gnash gnash gnash!'

Losara waved his fingers and erected a wall of silence around the table, lest other customers become aware that a large and malevolent spirit was in their midst.

'Not like stringy stormcrow – Lalenda be right about that,' the ghost continued. 'All stringy and feathery and *papery* . . . erch!' He made a spitting sound and for a moment his teeth flashed into view.

'Grimra!' Lalenda admonished. 'You ate the crow, after all?'

'Erch!' Grimra reiterated.

'I thought we agreed that livestock was off limits?' Losara said.

'Aye,' said the ghost sadly, 'but Grimra be Grimra. So fat and squashy, gnash gnash! How be Grimra resisting? If Losara doesn't want Grimra, why bring Grimra?'

'It wasn't my idea,' said Losara. 'In fact . . .' From his neck he lifted the pendant that bound Grimra to the world – a simple leather cord through a mottled stone. Reaching over, he dropped it around Lalenda's neck. 'It was Lalenda's idea to bring you, so it's only fair she bears the responsibility.'

Lalenda looked surprised, but not displeased. She held the pendant up for closer inspection.

'Lalenda bring Grimra?' said the ghost. 'Thank you, flutterbug! Grimra's favourite!'

He whooshed around, causing several guests to glance up to see if a gust had just blown open the door, and disappeared. Lalenda giggled and Losara gave a little sigh.

'Well, soon he'll have plenty of wildlife around him,' he said. 'Tomorrow we'll reach Swampwild.'

Mention of her home quelled Lalenda's laughter and he felt a twinge of regret at having brought it up. He knew she was tense about her return – she had said as much, if it hadn't been plain – and after almost two decades away she hardly knew what to expect.

'Praise be to Assedrynn,' she whispered, 'let her be alive.'

He reached across the table to pat her hand.

'It still feels like you,' she said.

Losara raised an eyebrow in query.

'The illusion – it doesn't change the way your hands feel.' She put her free hand on top of his, which was on top of hers, cupping it between. The sensation brought him right out of his head. 'Like silk,' she said. 'No. Smoother than silk.'

'And yours,' he said.

They made a strange group flying together. Losara lifted himself with power, tempering his speed to match Lalenda's. She flapped her crystal wings, and her endurance grew by the day. He was able to give her a boost whenever she needed one, letting the edges of himself partially tear away into a swirl of shadow that eddied underneath her wings to lift her. Sometimes the ghost would allow her to ride on his 'back'. Grimra was fast, and often shot off ahead or went about the land exploring. Often they would see a line of plants bending as Grimra tore along stirring up prey. Rabbits and pheasants would appear briefly, only to be seized in his invisible clutches and torn to pieces.

Losara began to appreciate why the gods had told him not to 'whisk about' with his new powers. There was something satisfying about journeying slowly, taking in the surrounds and learning the land. He knew that if he wanted to, he could be at Swampwild in the blink of an eye, but that did not bear serious consideration. For one thing, Lalenda was the reason they went there and he could not take her with him through the shadowlines.

The Ragga Plains, which filled most of the distance between Skygrip and Swampwild, were flat and fertile. Blue grasses grew lushly between groves of larger vegetation, giving the land a soft look. Prosperous towns spread lazily, and tended fields clustered in groups, a patchwork of green and blue and dark red crops and sometimes livestock. Shepherds guided flocks of horned beasts that Losara had not seen before, except, he was sure, in the form of meat. At one point he dived a little closer to inspect a Grey Goblin who wore simple cloth and culled his crops with a scythe. That was the life Tyrellan had escaped from, and Losara had trouble imagining him in it. The farmer chanced a look skywards and almost dropped his scythe in surprise.

Lalenda fell into a hover beside Losara. 'You'd think this was the first time he'd seen a man floating in the air,' she said, and giggled.

They journeyed on, and soon drew close to Swampwild. The land beneath grew wetter, and grass gave way to reedy ponds. Here and there ran raised pathways of compacted mud, slippery and hazardous. They reached the bog proper, where marshes were dotted by soft green hillocks. A rich and earthy smell rose to meet them – things growing, things decomposing, water full of life. An abundance of plants grew: willows and ferns, grasses and reeds, moss and free-floating tresses of weeds. The air buzzed with the sound of insects, and flecks of silver glinted as wings caught the light. Lalenda slowed, and Losara slowed to match her. He could sense her trepidation.

'Which way?' he asked.

'Deeper,' she said, and on they flew.

He stood, taking in his surrounds. The huts of the village Twir were built of dried reeds and mud, simple and hump-like. There was only enough room on each hillock for two or three, but most hillocks were connected by bridges in different states of decay, some as simple as toppled logs. Willow trees draped over the water and tangled with their neighbours, and a group of pixie children flitted about them, playing some kind of chasing game. The huts spread out around the base of an ancient willow tree, with a labyrinth of branches issuing from its thickly twisted trunk. It was full of wooden treehouses, more elaborate than those below, and a large town hall was the highest of all. It was here, on a landing, that Losara waited as Lalenda spoke to a wrinkled and grey-haired Mire Pixie mayor.

Grimra wafted by, rustling Losara's cloak. 'Grimra,' he said, 'go softly.' Grimra growled his acquiescence and eddied to a stop. Probably Losara need not have said anything. The ghost seemed to understand the current mood and had remained close and quiet ever since they'd arrived here.

'The flutterbug,' whispered Grimra, 'is not happy to be home?'

'It is not the homecoming she dreamed of,' said Losara.

The mayor turned and went into the town hall and Lalenda came to join them. Losara noticed that while her eyes were puffy, she was not weeping.

'She left a letter,' said Lalenda. 'In case I ever returned.'

Losara felt uncertain what to do. Should he embrace her? Or did she prefer to be left alone?

'I am sorry,' he said awkwardly.

'Sorry, flutterbug,' echoed Grimra. He swirled about her slowly, rustling her hair – his version of the embrace that Losara lacked the courage to offer.

What must it be like to lose someone? he wondered. He'd lost his mother too, but knew it wasn't the same. If he had known his mother before losing her, would he have felt more passionately? Maybe, maybe not. It was sad when life ended, perhaps, but there was nothing surprising about it. In a way, he thought, her mother's death meant that Lalenda was free. If her mother had been alive, Lalenda would no doubt have wanted to stay with her, who knew for how long. Meanwhile, he would have needed to press on with his pilgrimage and may have had to leave her here. That wasn't what he wanted. He realised a small part of him was relieved there was nothing to bind her to this place, and he wondered if that was selfish.

He found himself moving to embrace her, a natural thing once it started. As he reached around her, she moved against him, her head resting just below his chin. He stroked her hair, and for a moment she clutched his back and shuddered – but as she pulled away, he saw no tears.

'You do not weep,' he said.

'I've wept enough. And this sorrow is too deep and old.'

He wasn't sure that made sense to him.

The Mire Pixie mayor returned carrying a sealed letter. 'Here you are, child,' she said. She glanced furtively at Losara, whose presence had not really been explained to her. He got the sense she was holding something back.

'Don't mind me, ma'am,' he said reassuringly. 'You may say anything you like.'

'Well,' she said, and turned to clasp Lalenda's hand, 'it was only to say, we never did find out who . . . who told Skygrip about you. If we had, well . . . they would have been made unwelcome.'

Lalenda nodded blankly.

'If you wish to stay, I can arrange lodgings,' said the mayor.

Lalenda shook her head. 'I will visit my mother's grave and then we will depart,' she said. 'There is nothing left for me here save the distant echoes of what should have been.'

She spread her wings and glided from the landing, and Losara stepped out after her. She led the way to Twir's graveyard, and as they flew between trees Losara felt eyes staring at him. Being a human who could fly was no doubt responsible for the interest. Losara was glad they didn't know who he really was, or else there would have been fuss of some kind, and that would have overshadowed their real reason for being here.

The village fell away behind them as Lalenda followed some invisible route. Grimra disappeared as well, probably off to see which type of frog tasted the best. They came to an area where the willow trees grew thickly, and Lalenda brought them down on a hillock. Carved into tree trunks in spidery letters were names. She wandered slowly in a circle around the hillock's edge, examining them. The bog around them was still and thick, and Losara noticed that at the water's edge were luminescent red flowers with star-shaped petals.

'They are gravebloms,' said Lalenda, appearing beside him, 'planted around the ponds where we bury our dead.'

She sat down on the slope of the hillock and Losara joined her.

'This is where your mother's body went in?'

'Yes.'

'Did your mother's note . . . did it . . .' He struggled to phrase the question.

'It said that she loved me, and missed me, and was sorry,' said Lalenda. 'Simple things.'

'But important things.' Losara sighed. 'Battu was wrong to treat you as he did.'

They sat for a time in silence, staring into the muddy water. Occasionally a fat bubble would come to the surface, hold for a minute or two, and finally burst with a soft slurp.

'What was she like?' Losara asked.

Lalenda thought for a moment and a smile chanced across her face. Losara was relieved to see it, if only briefly. 'Stubborn,' she said. 'Kelan – the mayor – said she fought the wasting disease right until the end.'

Several bubbles broke at once.

'She wanted to see me again, you see, that's why she held on so long. I am too late by only a year. She was modest too. We lived in a mud hut, not in the tree. She wanted an ordinary life, I think. Probably she had one. Probably it is not unusual to lose one's family. Ills equal and worse befall many.'

'I expect so,' said Losara.

Something humanoid rose from the bog. Mud streamed from its misshapen head and off broad shoulders, running down root-like arms that ended in silver claws. Two pearl-like eyes appeared above a maw full of razor shards, and tendrils sprouted all over its body, grasping at the air. Lalenda hissed and leaped in front of Losara, her own retractable claws flashing out, low to the ground and ready to spring with her wings flat against her back. Losara could not say which surprised him more – the sudden arrival of the Mireform, or the way Lalenda instinctively protected him.

'Be at peace, Mire Pixie,' said the Mireform, its voice wet and gurgling. 'I do not mean your master harm.'

Losara put a calming hand on Lalenda's back. 'Rise, savage little,' he said.

Hesitantly, and not letting her eyes off the creature, she straightened and her claws withdrew – almost.

'Why do you come here?' asked Losara. 'Do you not know that this bog is a sacred burial ground to the pixies?'

'Their dead float high above us in the bog,' replied the creature. 'They do not disturb us.'

Losara wondered if he had been deliberately misunderstood.

'I come to recognise Losara Shadowhand,' said the Mireform, 'favoured by the Dark Gods. I come to pledge him the allegiance of the Mireform.'

Losara was pleased. Mireforms were rarely seen, and it took much power to summon one from the depths of the bog, let alone convince it into service. They were traditionally neutral, or perhaps apathetic to the worries of the world above. To have one appear and make such a promise was completely unexpected.

'Who are you to make this offer for all the Mireform?' Losara asked.

'I am Eldew,' it replied. 'And I am the biggest.'

'And why would you make it?'

'You are worthy,' said Eldew. 'And you will try to save Fenvarrow. Perhaps with the Mireform, you have a better chance.'

'I imagine so,' said Losara. 'I gratefully accept your offer. When the time is right, I may hold you to your word.'

'Return here to call for me,' said Eldew. 'I shall return.'

The Mireform sank away with a slurp, the mud settling after it. Losara turned to Lalenda and smiled.

'You tried to protect me,' he said. 'Thank you.'

She blushed.

Old Fire

It had been slow going and, although Iassia had seen the turn of many centuries, he'd found himself experiencing impatience. The blind woman was out of her element and did not move with the same sureness as she had back at the farm. Iassia remembered how, when he had first found the place again and watched her from trees on the hill above, he had not even realised her sight was gone. She had known the exact number of steps to the chicken shed, opened the gate without fumbling, collected eggs from familiar places. It had been as he'd swooped in closer that he'd noticed her eyes did not track, but simply stared into some knowable distance. It had made things a little trickier. Convincing commoners that he was a servant of Arkus sent to help them was not so easy, even with a little psychic nudging, but a blind woman was even more sceptical that she was really talking to a bird. Often when Iassia spoke, people did not believe their eyes, but she hadn't even had those to disbelieve with. Luckily the child, Essie, had been there too. While her mother, Frera, may have forgotten the burning need for revenge, in Essie he found it still ran hot, and she had been easier to steer. The girl lumped blame for her

430

mother's blindness at Corlas's feet, right along with the death of her father. Apparently it had not been long after Chavus's demise that Frera, weak with grief, had caught the wasting disease that clouded her eyes. 'Arkus is just,' Iassia had said to Essie, 'and desires that justice is delivered to his people.' The girl had looked upon him as if she'd been waiting for him all her life.

It had not taken long to convince her – a little longer for the mother – that they needed to follow him to the Open Halls and exact amends if ever they were to know peace. The road, however, had been ploddingly, maddeningly slow. Frera walked with a stick and was impossible to hurry, even though Essie tried, taking her by the arm to half-pull her along.

Iassia had decided he needed to take action. As he landed before them, the bag of coins in his beak jangled.

'Here,' he said, dropping it in front of Essie. 'When we come to the next village, we will hire someone with a cart to drive us.'

It would mean he'd need to stay out of view, or at least not talk, but it was better than spending a year on the road at a snail's pace.

Essie's eyes lit up as she spilled coins across her palm. 'Where did you get these?'

That was easy. 'Arkus will always provide what is needed,' he chirped merrily.

'Bless you, Arkus,' she said, holding the coins to her chest and looking to the heavens.

Bless you indeed, thought Iassia, thinking of the old couple further back down the road who would soon discover that their life savings were missing.

As Bel approached, he could see that something was happening at the barracks. There was a gathering by the archery range, and clothes of grandeur suggested a lordly presence. Black-and-yellow-striped Zyvanix rose in the air. Normally Bel would have been curious, but today he was too full of purpose and his eyes sought only the Throne. As he drew closer he spotted Naphur amidst a group of lords and ladies, looking uncomfortable in unusually resplendent robes. Next to him was the wasp Trusted, poised on two of her stick-like legs while the other four hung loosely from her abdomen. Her legs were decorated with gold and silver bands and there was some kind of pale substance encrusted in patterns on her body. Flanking her was a man and another Zyvanix, whom Bel guessed to be the two translators. As a cheer went up for a particularly good shot, Naphur said something to the wasp translator, who in turn buzzed and clicked it on to his mistress.

'Bel!'

Bel paused mid-stride.

Corlas arrived at his side. 'Where have you been? I've been looking for you all morning.'

'I was at the keepers',' said Bel defensively.

Corlas didn't notice. 'An archery competition,' he said excitedly, waving at the gathering. 'And the wasps are showing us up!'

'Well, they do have about a million eyes.'

'I want you to enter,' said Corlas. 'Let's stop those antennae waving about so smugly!'

'I don't feel like it.' Bel broke away to continue his march towards the Throne.

'Wait up, lad!' said Corlas, catching up again. 'What ails you?'

'I need to speak with Naphur.'

Corlas saw the look of determination in his son's eyes and immediately gripped his arm, halting his progress. 'Whoa there, lad,' he said. Bel looked down at the restraining hand in annoyance, but Corlas was unmoved. 'Bel,' he said, 'I can see you have something serious on your mind, but trust me – you should wait.'

Bel shot a glare at him and Corlas held it levelly. Eventually Bel gave in.

'All right,' he said.

Corlas let go. 'Naphur is very anxious when he's around the Trusted. Look at how he fidgets. He hasn't dealt much with the Zyvanix before. It's clear he's eager to please this beastie. The communication barrier is no help either. If you wish to talk to him, wait until the competition is over. Maybe then he can step away for a moment.'

'Wait until the competition's over, eh?' said Bel, eyeing off the range. 'Very well.'

Once more he marched towards the Throne and Corlas fell in at his side, now grinning. Naphur saw them coming and burst into a relieved smile. Bel bowed before him.

'My Throne,' he said. 'I am late, but I would still compete.'

Naphur clapped his hands in pleasure. 'Of course, Bel,' he said, and turned to the wasp translator. 'Trusted of Cindeka, this is Bel Corinas, one of my best soldiers.'

Again the translator clicked and buzzed at the Trusted, who waggled her antennae and clicked back. The human interpreter spoke: 'The Trusted is eager to see your man in action.'

Naphur nodded to Bel, who turned and made his way to the range. Wasp warriors were hovering in a row, firing off barbs towards the targets. As Corlas had said, they were extremely fast to notch new arrows and their accuracy was excellent. As Bel took up a position with the waiting contestants, he glanced over to see M'Meska baring her teeth at him in a lizard grin.

'At last,' she hissed. 'Some real challenge, yes? Now we truly see who is race superior on this range.' She bobbed her head and tapped her scaly chest. 'Saurian,' she added, for clarification.

The wasps on the range emptied their quivers and flitted back from the line. Scores were totalled and targets cleared. Stepping into position, Bel loosed off arrows in quick succession. They flew through the air shaft after shaft, each pounding deeply into the red centre of his target. The spectators watched in awe as he began to split arrows in a display of skill unmatched on the field. He swapped his grip on the bow to fire with his left hand and his accuracy remained unchanged. He lifted up a leg and shot from beneath it; pulled the bow over his head and shot that way; averted his eyes from the target to wink at the crowd as each arrow travelled a perfect course, not a single one falling outside the centre circle. Applause rose from the crowd. Bel hadn't shown off like this for some time and, despite his distraction, it felt good.

So it went for the last few rounds. Thanks to Bel, the Varenkai score quickly overtook the Zyvanix's. He looked over to see the wasp Trusted very still, Naphur looking uncomfortable and Corlas unreadable. The Trusted turned, clicked something to Naphur and took off without waiting to find out the final scores. Several of her guards rose to join her.

Bel bowed to the crowd and made his way back to the Throne, leaving behind a very sulky Saurian. As he arrived, the Trusted's human interpreter was finishing speaking to Naphur. 'Forgive my mistress – she desires respite from the sun.'

Naphur watched the interpreter leave, not seeming to know whether to be worried or pleased. 'Well,' he said to Bel, 'that was quite a showing. Quite a showing indeed.'

'Quite a showing *up*,' Corlas put in quietly.

'Thank you,' said Bel briskly. 'My Throne, I must speak with you about an urgent matter.'

Naphur was still staring after the wasps and seemed not to hear. 'Well,' he said, almost to himself, 'I don't know whether she's offended or not, but by Arkus it's a relief that she's gone.' Finally he smiled at Bel. 'Politics,' he said, shaking his head. 'I didn't become Throne to get mixed up in blasted *politics*, eh, Bel? It would all be easier if everyone just did what I said.'

'My Throne, I must speak with you.'

Naphur unceremoniously wiped the sheen off his brow with his cloak. 'Forgot to bring my poxy silk handkerchief,' he said. 'Now, what is it, Bel?'

Taking a deep breath, Bel launched into a somewhat confused yet passionate explanation about how Cydus had wronged Jaya. When he had finished, the older men both looked troubled.

'I'm sorry,' said Naphur. 'I don't see what I can do about it.'

'You're the Throne!' said Bel. 'Surely that counts for something!'

'I like to think so,' said Naphur, raising an eyebrow. 'But Cydus is a noble, and his complaints against this Jaya girl are real. I can't just disregard the laws our land is built on.'

'Why not? Cydus did when he murdered Jaya's partners!'

'Her *thieving* partners,' said Naphur. 'It's misconduct begotten of misconduct, and right now her word against Cydus's is not enough to have him questioned by an overseer.' He scratched one of his hairy arms. 'What is this girl to you, Bel? Why have you taken such an interest in her case?'

'She's . . .' began Bel, then shook his head in frustration. 'You wouldn't understand.'

'Oh, so it's like that, eh?' said Naphur. 'In which case I'm afraid I may very much understand.' He sighed. 'Please tell me you weren't mixed up with her before this crime.'

Bel remained silent.

'What is it, lad?' asked Corlas. 'Answer the Throne. How are you involved with this girl?'

'I love her!' yelled Bel, so loudly that some of the courtiers glanced over. He surprised even himself and fought to regain composure. 'I don't know how it happened, it just did.' He raked a hand through his hair and looked away, falling silent.

Naphur exchanged a glance with Corlas, then stepped forward to take Bel by the shoulder.

'My lad,' he said. 'You know I care about you, so what's important to you is important to me . . . but this all seems very sudden. A pretty girl can sometimes turn our heads so that we think –'

'No,' said Bel, the fierceness of his look daring Naphur to challenge his conviction. 'It isn't like that. Not wishing to be crass, my Throne, but I've had *plenty* of pretty girls, and I know I'm not mistaken in this. This is different.'

Naphur sighed. 'I see that it is. I believe you, Bel.'

'Then?'

'What would you have me do? Declare her innocent and set her free?'

Bel looked darkly at the ground. It was clear from Naphur's tone that this was precisely what he could not do.

'I'm sorry,' continued Naphur. 'I wish I could help, but I have responsibilities. The Thrones are not despots like the Shadowdreamers. Our land has laws so the people retain rights. I can't rise above that, lest the traditions of a thousand years crumble to dust. I cannot be seen to pervert the course of justice.'

'I see,' said Bel.

'Bel –'

'It's all right!' he said, trying to force calm into his tone. 'I understand, my Throne. You have your duty.' Anger scorched his voice, despite his efforts. 'I'm sorry for asking this of you. I must go.'

With that he bowed abruptly and quickly took his leave.

Naphur sighed. 'He asks too much, Corlas.'

'Aye, my Throne. But that doesn't mean you need do too little. Excuse me.'

Corlas followed his son, leaving the ruler of Kainordas looking perturbed.

'Where are you going?' asked Corlas, catching up to Bel with great strides.

'To see her. I promised I'd ask the Throne for her release, and I won't have her hoping in vain now I know that he won't help.'

'No, that wouldn't do,' agreed Corlas. They went in silence for a moment, then Corlas said, 'Will you tell me of her?'

Bel glanced at his father in irritation, but saw that the man was simply curious. The hardness within him mellowed.

'I would know,' continued Corlas, 'of the thief worthy enough to steal my son's heart.'

Bel tried to repress a smile.

'Indulge an old man,' said Corlas.

'All *right*!' said Bel. 'Stop it! I will tell you, if it will make you be quiet!'

He told Corlas the truth of how he'd met her and Corlas listened attentively . . . but when Bel began to describe her eyes, his expression turned strange.

'What is it?' asked Bel.

'She has Sprite blood.'

'Yes.'

Tears welled up in Corlas's eyes and he tried to hide them by looking away.

'Father?'

'You are lost, my son,' said Corlas. 'In the nicest way.' He smiled grimly. 'Your mother would have approved. Actually, I don't think she would have approved of anyone who wasn't part Sprite. In fact . . .'

Bel waited for him to collect his thoughts.

'. . . she would have called it a "soul kiss",' Corlas finished, and smiled.

'What's that?'

'Let me see if I can summon her words,' said Corlas. 'She rattled on about the Sprites quite often but not everything stuck. Hmm. I remember her saying a "soul kiss" for a Sprite was the most common and natural way to find a partner. Sprite souls are a lot more intuitive than minds and bodies, apparently. The best I can explain it is like this: two souls recognise that a capacity for love exists between them and bind themselves together without bothering to speak to their owners first. The two people fall suddenly and madly in love – an event celebrated by Sprites as we would celebrate marriage. In fact, experiencing a soul kiss was something of a rite of passage for young Sprites as they,' he looked fondly on Bel, 'grew up.'

Bel considered his father's words. 'Was it like this for you?' he asked quietly.

'Yes,' said Corlas. 'Very sudden. And very real.'

'Father, you told me that Mother always claimed you had the blood, but you never really believed her.'

'Yes,' said Corlas sadly.

'Well . . . since meeting Jaya, I think I am better at sensing others who have it . . . and I think that you do.'

'Bless you, boy,' Corlas said, and smiled. 'I think so too.'

On the road south of Kadass, the blind woman could hear the sounds of the city. 'How far to go?' she asked in a quavering voice.

'We're close, Mother,' said the hard-eyed young woman by her side.

'Yes, Frera,' said the colourful little bird perched on her shoulder. 'Almost there.'

Trial

Baygis elected to hold Jaya's trial in the Kadass courts, despite urging from Assicon Cydus to hold it in Arkus's Eye. For Baygis it was insult enough that he had to concern himself with a case of petty vandalism, but the idea of taking it to the Eye, the great court of the Halls where High Overseers presided over only the most important of trials, was appalling.

'If I were to try a vandalism case in the Eye,' Baygis had said to Cydus, 'I would be guilty of it.'

'Yes,' Naphur had agreed, then added, less diplomatically, 'Now please go away, Cydus, you audacious little peacock.' That had turned Cydus an interesting shade of pink.

Holding the trial in the Kadass courts meant that the wasp Trusted probably would not attend, which was ultimately the exact opposite of what Cydus had wanted – he had wanted to exonerate himself before her. It was beyond Baygis why the pompous ass didn't just buy her another present.

Baygis watched people filing into the court. He was just inside the entrance to the balcony from which he would preside – it overlooked a flat area of floor where the accused would stand. Tiered wooden benches around the walls formed a viewing gallery, and Baygis noted familiar faces there. Fahren sat with Bel and Corlas opposite the balcony. Baygis gave his hearing a magical boost and tuned into their conversation.

'If she's found guilty, the term won't be especially long,' Fahren was saying. 'And I'm sure that the Throne won't stop you visiting her in Kadass Jail.'

'Is that supposed to be reassuring?' said Bel. 'And what do you mean *if* she is found guilty? You need not soften your words for me, High Mage.'

'Don't call me that,' said Fahren anxiously. 'And worry not so overly. Cydus's power in this matter is transitory, and exists because the wasp Trusted is in Kadass and Naphur is afraid to agitate her.'

'Naphur should show some backbone,' said Bel. 'The Trusted is his subject, just like everyone else.'

'A very *powerful* subject, my boy,' said Fahren.

'Well, don't forget who amongst us is really the *powerful* one,' replied Bel. 'Perhaps it would be best not to get the future saviour of the realm *agitated,* or does that count for nothing?'

'Bel! Just remember that when the wasp Trusted leaves, Naphur won't be so worried about Cydus kicking up a stink. Who knows how long Jaya will remain in jail – especially if she marries a peacekeeper.'

Bel turned to Fahren wearing an expression of such alarm that Fahren's eyes crinkled in amusement. Baygis also smiled – he well understood Bel's reaction to marriage. He continued to look around the court. At the front, of course, sat Cydus with a couple of his friends, speaking loudly and laughing. Baygis noted a few other courtiers scattered about, boorishly interested in the slightest of scandals. Behind him an aide cleared his throat and Baygis turned slightly in acknowledgement.

'High Overseer,' said the aide. 'The accused has arrived. She waits with the other witnesses.'

'No other witnesses will be necessary.'

'Very good, lord. Shall I announce you?'

'Please,' said Baygis unenthusiastically.

The aide walked to his own small desk on one side of the balcony. He cleared his throat and a murmur rippled through the crowd as they realised the trial was about to begin.

'Silence, please!' called the aide. 'This is the trial of Jaya Kincare, charged with unlawful entry into the house of Lord Assicon Cydus and reckless damage to his property. Presiding is High Overseer Baygis Naphur.'

Baygis entered the balcony and took his position on a high bench at the front. He flicked his white-gold overseer's robe out behind him as he sat, and nodded to his aide.

'Bring in Jaya Kincare!' called the aide.

A guard appeared leading Jaya, who was shackled at the wrists. Baygis glanced at Cydus, who was waiting greedily for the girl's humiliation. He would not be sorry to disappoint him, or the other scandalmongers sitting in the viewing gallery.

'You are Jaya Kincare?' Baygis asked in a carrying voice.

'Yes, High Overseer.'

'I have already had your admission. Is there anything else you'd like to add?'

'No.'

'Good,' said Baygis. 'Then you are guilty as charged and sentenced to two years in Kadass Jail.' He rang a brass bell that stood on the bench. 'That's it, everybody. Off you all go.'

Cydus was clearly outraged at being denied seeing Jaya chewed up by the court and Baygis gave him a little smirk. Then Baygis glanced across at Bel and the others, and his amusement faded as he saw Bel's expression.

Bel barely heard Fahren speaking to him.

'. . . am sure we can work out some kind of . . . visitation rights . . .'

Let the old man waffle, thought Bel. *I'm not going to settle for any kind of compromise.*

As the woman he loved was led away, she looked back at him and an understanding passed between them – he would fix this, somehow. She disappeared, and he fell to wondering how. He briefly imagined storming into the jail and freeing her no matter who was in his way and hang the consequences – what could they really do to the blue-haired boy? *Man,* he corrected himself. *Blue-haired man*. The other way, though, was to simply demand it. Would they really refuse him? Would they dare?

'Come, Bel,' his father was saying, taking him under the arm. Bel blinked – the courtroom was emptying. He rose and allowed himself to be led out. Baygis appeared in the corridor outside.

'Bel,' he said, 'I am sorry. If there was another way –'

A commotion broke out at a nearby doorway. A young woman ran into the corridor, her curly hair wild and her eyes wilder. She was followed by a nervous peacekeeper who kept ineffectually trying to grab her wrist.

'. . . can't come in right now, miss!' they heard him say.

'They said he was here!' insisted the young woman, knocking the keeper's hand away.

An older woman appeared at the door behind the young woman. This one was obviously blind, as she was leaning on a stick and holding the door frame. 'Essie?' she said, but Essie – Bel assumed Essie was the young woman – wasn't answering. As Essie's head turned, her eyes fixed on a point and blazed.

'There!' she shouted, pointing at Corlas. 'There he is, Mother! He's there! It's him! That man!' she screamed, ignoring the peacekeeper trying to quiet her. 'That's the swine who murdered my father! HE KILLED MY FATHER!'

She screamed it again and again, stabbing her finger like a dagger of justice. Her blind mother called plaintively from the door frame, and everyone else stood and stared.

'Oh, yes!' shouted the woman. 'I recognise you, you swine, you dog, you filthy, murdering –'

'Enough!' roared Bel, stepping forward. 'Cease this slanderous outpour lest I choke it to a stop! This man is Corlas Corinas, the hero of the Shining Mines, a soldier of Kainordas! Who are you to dare sully him with these baseless accusations?'

'Do you deny it?' spat Essie, still staring at Corlas.

'Of course he denies it!' shouted Bel, and whirled to his father.

Corlas stood frozen, staring at Essie, his expression ashen. Bel blinked, not understanding what he was seeing.

'Father?'

More guards appeared. 'Seize her,' said Baygis. Essie continued to scream and claw at the keepers who held her, while her mother sobbed. 'Take her to a holding room, and see the blind woman is given a place to wait.'

'What madness is this?' said Bel.

'That,' said Baygis calmly, 'is exactly what we shall find out.'

The hatred from this young woman is astounding, sent Fahren.

Yes, replied Baygis. *She believes it so vehemently.*

They were in one of the rooms used to house prisoners before trial, featureless but for a table at which the girl Essie sat. A guard behind her forced her down each time she tried to rise, to shake her fists in anger, to scream and yell. It took time to get any sense from her.

It was over twenty years ago, said Baygis. *And she remembers only a big man with a big beard. Many fit that description. A man with a similar beard and build to Corlas would be easy to mistake.*

But his name, said Fahren. *She knows his name.*

'How did you learn the name of this man?' Baygis demanded.

'What?'

'His name, girl! You knew the name Corlas. Did you learn it during the attack?'

Essie stared back defiantly. Baygis laid his hands on the table and leaned in close, piercing her with power-filled eyes. She faltered before them, her gaze flickering downwards.

'You didn't, did you?' said Baygis. 'Even insane murderers usually don't leave their names behind for witnesses to remember.' He sent magic into her, slipping around her tongue and vocal cords, making them pliable to the truth. 'How?' he asked. 'How did you learn the name Corlas?'

Essie gulped. Only the strongest of wills withstood Baygis's ability to force out the truth.

'Arkus,' she gasped.

'What?'

'Arkus sent us a messenger!' she said shrilly. Again she tried to stand, but the guard behind placed strong hands on her shoulders. 'He said we deserved justice!' she shouted. 'He said that the crimes against our family had gone unpunished long enough! He said that the Sun God himself had deemed us worthy to know the name of our transgressor!'

'A messenger?' prompted Baygis, raising an eyebrow.

'Iassia!' shouted the girl. 'I promised I wouldn't tell!'

Iassia? came Fahren's thought. *The weaver you caught?*

Yes. He obviously has some dark purpose in this.

'Essie, listen to me,' said Baygis slowly. 'That bird is a manipulator of minds. Do you understand? He is no servant of Arkus. This name he gave you means nothing.'

Essie shook her head miserably. 'I know him,' she said. 'I'll remember his face till the day I die. He killed my father. He ruined everything! After he came, the farm fell to dung around us. My mother could hardly get out of bed. It is no lie. *It is no lie.*' She fell back, exhausted by her struggles.

What could the bird want? asked Fahren.

I don't know. But we cannot trust this girl.

Her conviction is powerful, though, said Fahren. *For all their skill, I do not think weavers can reinvent memories. Baygis, she truly believes that Corlas murdered her father.*

Do you?

There was a pause. *No,* said Fahren. *Not yet. But I find it worrying. Weavers are extremely intelligent. I don't think this Iassia would have underestimated our ability to discover he'd played a role here. And . . .*

What?

Weavers have the power to silence those they enter into a bargain state with – yet Iassia didn't invoke that power here. If he'd made a deal with this girl, we'd never have discovered his involvement. Yet he didn't block us from finding that out.

What are you saying?

That weavers are magnificent engineers, Baygis. Right now, we might be doing exactly what Iassia wants.

You mean he wants us to question Corlas?

Yes.

We must still question him, said Baygis.

Yes, said Fahren, his face growing worried.

I cannot see Corlas's hand in this, said Baygis. *The man has been a faithful servant of the light for as long as we've known him. He fought the Shadowdreamer himself, by Arkus!*

Let us see him.

They went to the next room. It was just like the first, except Corlas sat at the table, his expression unreadable.

'Taskmaster Corlas,' said Baygis, drawing up a seat. Fahren did the same.

'High Overseer. High Mage.'

Baygis glanced at Fahren. *Do we mention the bird? Not yet.*

'These are troubling accusations, Corlas,' said Baygis, and his face indeed was troubled. 'What do you have to say about them?'

Corlas stared back from under bushy brows. 'I do not know this young woman, nor her mother,' he said. 'I did not kill their kin.'

'You were in that area, though, around the time of the crime,' said Fahren. 'Were you not? On your journey between Whisperwood and the Halls?'

'You know that to be the case,' said Corlas. 'I would not deny it.'

'And you never stopped at the farm where these women lived?'

'No.'

He has always been difficult to read, said Fahren. *When he first returned to the Halls and explained absconding from the army with a story of enchantment, I could not fault him. It was a version of the truth, however, and . . .*

You sense a lie in this?

Yes.

I shall ask about the bird.

When Fahren raised no objection, Baygis went ahead. 'Have you ever had dealings with a weaver bird, Corlas?

The one called Iassia, perhaps, whom I tracked down outside Kadass?'

Corlas opened his mouth, and paused. Then he said, 'No.'

'Corlas,' said Fahren, 'please – we are not your enemies. We don't think you're a murderer, but there is something more to this, something beyond mistaken identity. Those women were coaxed here by a weaver – a weaver who knew your name.'

Corlas's brow furrowed and he seemed about to say something. The look changed to frustration and he remained silent.

Baygis sighed. 'I'm afraid I must question you again, Corlas,' he said. 'Under the influence of magic. I'm sorry.' He sent magic into Corlas, lubricating his throat so the truth would slide out. 'Now again,' he said, 'tell us everything you know of these events.' Even as he intensified his truth-coaxing magic, Corlas kept his mouth firmly closed. 'Corlas?' he said forcefully. 'What can't you tell us?'

A fine sweat broke across Corlas's scalp but, in a remarkable display of will, he remained silent.

'This taciturnity does not aid you!' said Baygis, growing angry.

He has a will of iron! he sent to Fahren.

'Corlas . . .' said Fahren pleadingly. 'What can't you tell us, my friend?'

Eventually, exercising an enormous amount of control, Corlas opened his mouth. 'I am sorry, Baygis, Fahren, but I will not answer your questions.'

Baygis stood angrily, and Fahren looked dismayed.

'So be it then!' exclaimed Baygis. 'If only you would speak with me, I'm sure we could work this

out! But if you'd rather remain under suspicion, then
congratulations, for that is what you have achieved!
Guards!'

Guards appeared at the door.

'Take the taskmaster to the holding cells! He hasn't
left me any choice!'

Corlas stood, huge in the small room. He did not
look into Fahren's hurt eyes as he walked, haltingly,
out the door.

'I must speak with the Throne,' said Fahren.

'What are you thinking?'

'I felt a block in his mind when you asked about
the weaver. It's part of why he could resist telling us
the truth.'

Baygis raised an eyebrow.

'Corlas has made a deal of some kind,' said Fahren
sadly, 'with the enemy.'

Corlas sat in his cell wondering how it had come to
this. His hate for the bird, which he'd thought could
not possibly grow any stronger, grew stronger. In the
years since his crime, Corlas had hoped Frera and Essie
would have got on with their lives, eventually putting
behind them the tragedy that had befallen them. If it
hadn't been for Iassia, that might have been the case.
He could picture the bird stirring up old emotions,
opening old wounds, reawakening old nightmares and
spurring his wretched puppets into a journey of revenge
that benefited nobody.

Much as he hated the bird, however, Corlas knew he
could not absolve himself of blame. He *had* committed
the crimes he stood accused of. The man he'd killed

had been a peacekeeper whom he'd refused to obey, and that was a serious charge no matter his state of mind at the time. With a cold acceptance that grew lump-like in his gut, Corlas knew he would be found guilty. Iassia had successfully engineered his downfall, though to what spiteful end Corlas couldn't guess. Maybe the bird simply sought revenge for the years spent waiting for him beyond the wards. Or maybe, with a creature like that, evil was its own reward.

He knew he couldn't withstand another bout of Baygis's questioning. Answers had been creeping along his tongue, knocking on the back of his teeth. It had taken all his will to remain close-mouthed, and he suspected that next time he would not even try. He decided he'd rather make his admission willingly than have it forced out of him, to tell it in his own words. If only they'd never come to take his child all those years ago. Damn Kainordas and Fenvarrow both! If they had *both* just left him alone!

'Mirrow,' he whispered. 'Forgive me that I will come to you through shame such as this.'

Would they execute him? He wasn't sure. If they did, what would happen to his soul? Would Arkus even accept him into his Well? The thought came suddenly: would *she* be there if he did? Her soul had been commended to Whisperwood. He hadn't really thought about it before, but now it hit him with force. He could not be executed in Kainordas! He had to get back to Whisperwood, lest he spend all time separate from her!

There was a click at the door; Corlas knew who it was.

'Father!' said Bel, rushing into the room. Corlas stood and they embraced, arms locked, chests crushed against the columns of cold steel that ran between them. Bel pulled free with angry eyes. 'How can they charge you with these crimes?' he said. 'How do they dare it?'

'My boy,' said Corlas, his eyes dropping to the ground. 'I will not lie to you.'

'What?' said Bel. 'What are you –'

'Bel,' said Corlas, so wearily that Bel fell silent. The resignation in his father did not speak of innocence, and he took a step back when he saw it.

'Yes, son. I am guilty.'

Bel stared at him disbelief.

'It was just after your mother died.' Corlas sighed. 'I was angry. When I met the peacekeeper, he challenged me. I tried to leave but he attacked. I did not mean to kill him, only to defend myself. Then . . . well, you know what happens to the likes of you and me in such circumstances. He brought out the blood fury in me.'

'Then it was his fault,' said Bel darkly.

'He was a stupid boy indeed,' agreed Corlas. 'Bel, listen – they must not be allowed to execute me here.'

'Execute?' repeated Bel, eyes blazing. 'Execute? No, I think not! Not unless they want me to execute *them*!'

Bargain Fulfilled

Rage coursed through him as he strode along. It boiled and bubbled, filling up the spaces within him where his *other* had been stripped away. Even his eyeballs felt hot.

The guards who tried to bar his way found themselves lying on the floor with heads throbbing. He burst through the doors into the Throne's chambers with a crash. Naphur and Fahren, who had been talking at the edge of the room, looked up in alarm. Guards rushed in behind Bel, drawing their weapons.

'No!' said Naphur, raising a hand. 'It's all right, soldiers! Stand down!'

The soldiers glanced from Bel to the Throne and, although they didn't like it, backed away rubbing their bruises.

'Close the door!' ordered Naphur. When they did, he stepped forward. 'Now Bel,' he said, keeping his voice calm, 'Fahren has just told me about your father. I don't know what these charges are, but –'

'Quiet,' said Bel, and struck a nearby statuette off its pedestal, shattering it to splinters. Naphur stopped short at the display, shocked. 'There is talk of execution,' Bel went on.

'I have given no such order,' said Naphur. 'And I will not. We don't even know if the charges –'

'They are true,' said Bel. 'My father has admitted it to me himself. He met the keeper on his journey here, to find me. The man tried to stop him, attacked him without real provocation, and Corlas gave him the death that he deserved. So, what do you say now? I have seen how reluctant you are to intervene when it comes to this land's precious laws. If you will not bend them for a thief, will you break them for a murderer?'

Naphur and Fahren glanced at each other uncertainly.

'Do not even *consider* execution as an option,' said Bel. The fire in him was daunting, even to these two powerful men. 'Mark me well.' With that, he stalked out, almost ripping the door from its hinges as he slammed it open.

A hesitant guard peeped around the creaking door. 'Is everything all right, my lord?'

'Leave us!' snapped Naphur. 'Close the door!'

The guard quickly obeyed.

'Corlas,' muttered the Throne. 'I placed great trust in him. I tried to repay the wrong that was done to him. Arkus knows, I did what I could! Now he throws it back in my face. Murdering, and striking bargains with weaver birds . . .'

'My Throne, we don't know the nature of his bargain,' said Fahren, trying to maintain calm for them both. 'We don't know if he is in the process of fulfilling it, or if it is yet to occur. He probably didn't even know Iassia was the enemy when he made it.'

'It is precisely the uncertainty that is troubling,' said Naphur. 'You say you cannot break the block that would allow him to speak?'

'No.'

'Then he is an enemy in our midst. For all we know, the deal was to *pretend* to be the boy's father, entrench himself in the Halls and wait for the best moment to bring us all down.'

'That seems overly elaborate, even for a weaver.'

'But it's possible, isn't it? You yourself have said how inventive they can be. It could be anything – maybe Corlas is to wait until the very deciding moment, when the armies of shadow and light clash for the last time, then stab Bel in the back.'

'Then why would Iassia give him away?' said Fahren. 'My Throne, I don't think Corlas is a willing agent of the shadow.'

'Perhaps not,' growled Naphur. 'I also would not have thought him capable of the crime he's accused of. Even if he was, I would have listened to his explanations; I would have helped him if I could. But he has lied to us before, and now he lies to us again!' Naphur began to pace. 'I did as right by him as I could, did I not?'

'Yes, I feel that you did.'

'I was sorry for what he went through. I tried to make it up to him. I respected his counsel where the boy was concerned. I did not send him away, or cut off his access from Bel. We were *friends*. I bent to his will as no ruler is obligated to, even when it was against my better judgement, and this is how he repays me!' Naphur came to a stop at the edge of the room, glaring out across the Halls. 'What shall I do?' he asked. 'Even now, I would not see him executed.'

'No, my lord, that would be most unwise.'

Naphur spun around – Fahren had seldom seen such a fierce expression on his face. 'Banishment,' the Throne said. Fahren raised an eyebrow, but let Naphur continue. 'Banishment from Borgordus. I cannot kill him, but I cannot allow his presence when he could be working against us. He must leave. Today.'

'My Throne, please stay this action a moment longer.'

'Why? I am in no mood for advice at this time, High Mage.'

'Naphur,' said Fahren steadily, holding the Throne's gaze, '*I* have not betrayed you.'

Naphur's eyes flashed, but a moment later he breathed out, and some of the redness faded from his cheeks. 'Very well, Fahren. What is it?'

'Do not forget that Bel is our primary concern in this. Any action must take him into consideration.' The High Mage lit a brittleleaf roll with a spurt of flame from his fingertip, which was shaking slightly. 'Right now Bel feels that it is *we* who are the enemy. If we send Corlas away, who knows if Bel will remain in the Halls afterwards, or ever listen to us again?'

'I cannot let such crimes go unpunished,' said Naphur.

'I agree,' said Fahren. 'And Corlas is lucky you have chosen so mild a punishment. He cannot stay in the Halls, but neither can we afford to have Bel go chasing after him. We must work hard, and immediately, to re-establish his trust in us.'

'What do you suggest?'

'Think of it from his perspective. We are about to send away his father, and we have just put the girl he loves in jail. He's been robbed of those he holds dear, and you and I will receive the blame.'

Naphur sighed. 'When did my Throneship become all about this boy?'

'He is potentially the most important person born in millennia,' answered Fahren. 'We need him. We need to prepare him, and he still needs our protection. We cannot afford to make an enemy of him.'

'So what do we do?' asked Naphur dully.

'We let the girl go.'

Instantly Naphur became angry again, opening his mouth to object.

'You are the Throne!' interrupted Fahren. 'You've been a just and fair ruler for decades, and you do this thing now for the good of the land! Not because of a personal desire, not because you are corrupt! The girl's charge is small, and not important in the scheme of things. We can deal with Cydus, get him out of Kadass, order him back to that swamp he presides over.'

'I don't need a lecture on what I *could* do,' said Naphur. 'I *could* have done a great many things that I never chose to, and no one could have stopped me.'

'I know,' said Fahren. 'And Kainordas is lucky to have such a leader. But this will not be an abuse of power, Naphur. It is necessary, believe me. If we don't do it, Bel will have no reason to stay here and we will lose him to the world. Then, maybe, we will all be lost. You can never forget the shadows in the south, lord.'

'I never do,' said Naphur. 'You know that.'

'I do. So don't let an ink-stained vase determine the course of our fate.'

Naphur stood silently, his mind ticking over.

'Very well,' he said eventually. 'The girl will be freed – but Corlas will leave this very afternoon.'

'You are charged with the murder of a peacekeeper,' said Naphur through the bars.

To his left stood Fahren, looked perturbed, and to his right Baygis wore a steely expression. Corlas sat wearily in the cell on a wooden chair. He hadn't bothered to rise when the three powerful men entered the cell, which he knew had not gone unnoticed.

'What you are certainly guilty of,' continued Naphur, 'is consorting with the enemy. I treated you with respect, I tried to be compassionate. I thought we understood each other. Yet for any wrongs we may have done you, you wronged us in return twice over.'

'I doubt that,' said Corlas, scowling openly.

Baygis smacked the bars of the cell, making Corlas start. 'If you show this disrespect to my father,' he said, 'because you imagine you are to be executed and therefore have nothing to lose, then cease to make such assumptions!'

Corlas was surprised by that.

'I don't know for sure if you are guilty of the murder,' said Naphur, 'but there will be no investigation. Your accusers will be told they were mistaken, and Baygis will not question you again.'

'Why?' asked Corlas, dumbfounded.

Naphur sighed. 'For the sake of your son.'

'For the sake of your *control* over my son,' corrected Corlas, scowling again.

'Are you saying you don't wish to be set free?'

Corlas couldn't believe his ears.

Naphur's voice hardened. 'Free to leave.'

'Leave, Throne?'

'My men will take you to your quarters to get your things, and then you will leave the Halls forever. You are banished from Borgordus, and if I ever see you here again, it will *not* be forgiven. Since we do not know the nature of this bargain you made with the weaver, and you cannot tell us what it is, I have to assume you are a threat. I don't care where you go, but it had better be somewhere far enough away that I never hear of you again. And Bel will not know where you go either. You will not see him again, ever.'

Finally Corlas stood up. 'You cannot ask that.'

'I'm not asking,' said Naphur. 'And if you do not comply, I will have Baygis tear your mind apart in search of the truth. There will be a public trial, and a public execution too. All the good you have done in your life will be erased, and your name will be sullied forever. Shame will mark your passing. Go now, salvage some of your dignity, and leave Bel with the better memories of your time together.'

Corlas bared his teeth. Angry though he was, he thought of the trial and the admissions he would have to make. He thought, too, of his other son, that other part of Bel whom he'd never sought out. Perhaps now was the time to try. Finally, he thought of Iassia. Would the weaver be waiting outside the Halls, ready to ask his 'favour', whatever it may be? If only he could speak about it, tell them the bargain was not yet in effect, but would be if the bird found him. The words, as ever, would not form in his mouth. It seemed he would have to take his chances.

'You leave me scant choice,' he muttered.

'I would ask you to swear,' said Naphur, 'but I've learned how little your word means. I leave you, then, with threats instead. Do not return, Corlas. Blades!'

Four large blades entered the cell, moving to unlock the grille.

'Take him quickly,' Baygis instructed. 'Speak of this to no one. Do not shackle him, but if he tries anything, kill him. He is to be led past the wards and then turned free. Make sure he puts down some distance before you return.'

The blades nodded, and ushered the big taskmaster out of the cell.

'Goodbye, Corlas,' said Fahren sadly.

Corlas stared ahead with glazed eyes, silent as he was escorted from the cell.

'Where is he?' Bel demanded. 'Where have you taken him?'

He'd caught up with the three men at the entrance chamber of the Open Castle. Baygis stood straight and tall, his face neutral. Naphur's eyes were troubled, and Fahren's more so. The old mage had been like a grandfather to him and Bel couldn't believe that he would hold back at a time like this.

'Fahren?' he said.

'He's gone,' said Fahren hesitantly.

'Gone?' said Bel. 'What do you mean?'

'We did not want to see him answer those charges,' said Naphur. 'None of us wish your father executed. Better that he disappear, as quickly as possible, before it gets too difficult to . . .'

'To cover it up,' said Baygis flatly.

Bel fell silent for a moment, remembering his father's admissions in the cell. Corlas had not been at fault – that damned peacekeeper had brought his fate on himself. How could these three fail to see that?

'It's for the best,' said the Throne, placing a hand on Bel's shoulder.

Bel glanced down at the hand, then pushed it away. 'I want to see my father. Where is he?'

'There is good news with the bad, Bel,' said Fahren desperately. 'The Throne has reconsidered your request about Jaya. She is to be released.'

'Jaya?' said Bel, momentarily distracted. 'But she's been sentenced.'

'Well . . . we'll see about that,' said Naphur. 'If you love her, she's almost family – and perhaps she had a good reason for her crime. If Cydus is guilty of wrongdoing . . .'

His words did not have the calming effect they'd hoped.

'That is well!' spat Bel savagely. 'Very well indeed, though it could have come sooner. Now tell me where my father is, or I will consider him murdered, as I have no evidence to the contrary. I will be forced to search the Halls for his body, dig up every grave, violate every tomb!'

'You will do no such thing,' said Baygis levelly. 'Do you imagine that your anger grants you ultimate authority?'

'*After* I am convinced that his body isn't here, I will search for him outside the Halls,' continued Bel. 'I will search until I find him and know that he is safe, that he has left of his own accord – which I find hard to believe, given he bade me no farewell.'

'It is a delicate situation,' said Fahren. 'He had to leave as quickly as possible.'

'And we never claimed he left of his own accord,' added Baygis. 'He failed in service to his Throne, and still my father did not wish him dead. He is exiled.'

Suddenly Bel drew his sword, the shine flashing silver along its edge. Baygis raised a protective hand. 'Bel . . .' he warned.

Bel grinned madly, raised the sword to his own breast and slid it between a join in his leather armour.

'Bel, no!' said Fahren.

Bel tightened his grip. 'Where is he?'

'Lower that sword!' commanded Naphur.

'Don't move,' said Bel, 'unless you want me to skewer my half a heart.'

'You're bluffing,' said Baygis.

'Am I? How can you be sure what I'm capable of? You know that I'm unbalanced, you know that part of my very soul is missing. Oh, I know I've been told that all I lack is some dark thing that crawled away – that I am the good it left behind. Nice to believe in such convenience, isn't it!' He screamed the last, and tensed his hand.

'Steady,' said Fahren. 'Don't do anything rash . . .'

'Don't tell me what to do,' said Bel, backing further away. 'I'm the one *you* need. I am your *saviour*. But I can't be a saviour if I'm dead, can I?'

The three men looked at each other, knowing they had no choice.

'The east gate,' said Naphur quietly, and sighed. 'That was where he was taken out. The soldiers he was with have not yet returned. Hurry and you will catch him.'

Bel rushed from the hall.

'This doesn't bode well,' said Fahren.

'I'd better go after him,' said Baygis, 'and make sure that he comes back.'

He glanced at his father, who nodded.

'Be careful.'

'I will.'

Baygis left swiftly. It was but a few moments later that Naphur and Fahren realised there was nothing else for them to do but follow.

Bel rode hard through the east gate, his sweaty palms slick on the reins. Outside, he cast feverish eyes about the hilly grasslands. White ward stones shone softly in the distance, and he spotted soldiers coming towards him, a group of four on horseback.

'Have you been with Taskmaster Corlas?' he called.

The blades looked uncertain about how to reply, which was all the answer Bel needed. He kicked his steed sharply and away he went, riding in the direction the soldiers had come from, following a trail of trampled grass. He passed the wards at speed. The sun was close to setting and orange light coated the hills. Cresting a hill, he spotted movement against a line of trees. Hope flared and, as he drew closer, he saw it was a man on a horse with a pack on his back and an axe at his side. Corlas.

'Father!' Bel shouted. Corlas turned in dismay at the sound of his son's voice. Bel almost fell from the saddle and rushed towards him.

Corlas jumped from his own steed. 'Go back!' he shouted.

Bel hardly heard him, and a moment later the two smashed into each other in a brief embrace.

'Do not leave,' said Bel. 'Return with me, and together we will change the Throne's ruling.'

'I think not,' said Corlas, his face stormy. He glanced around uneasily. 'You must not stay here, Bel. It is not safe.'

'I'll ride with you then.'

'No,' said Corlas. 'It's too dangerous. The Shadowdreamer hunts you still, that you *must* believe. You must return to the Halls at once.'

'I do not quail before the Shadowdreamer,' said Bel. 'Let him come and face me, and I shall cut off his lips and feed them to him.'

Corlas felt tears filling his eyes. Despite all his anger, he knew that Bel still needed the protection of Naphur and Fahren. 'Your woman is there,' he tried. 'And you will love her in a way you won't believe possible.'

There was a soft chirping from the tree line. Corlas spun, drawing his axe. 'You must away from here!' he shouted to Bel. 'Now!'

Out of the trees flew a little bird, flashing prettily in the dying light. Corlas bellowed in alarm, raising his axe.

Your weapon is no protection against me, Varenkai, came Iassia's voice in his head.

Corlas swung as the bird flew over, twittering with laughter as the axe swished uselessly through the air.

I'm so glad to finally see you past the wards, said Iassia. *And with your son as well. Too perfect.*

The weaver circled them as Corlas stood frozen, all the blood draining from his face. Bel looked on in confusion. 'What is going on, Father?'

Finally our bargain can be fulfilled.

'No!' shouted Corlas.

Oh, yes. Say goodbye to your son, Corlas.

'Run!' roared Corlas, grabbing Bel by the shoulders and pushing him violently away. 'Run, damn you, boy! Trust me now if never again and run!'

This is what you shall do for me.

Something in Corlas's mind began to unfurl: the bargain planted years ago, binding him to the bird's will. He felt the *command* of Iassia's words as they began to form, and knew he had no choice but to carry out whatever the bird willed.

Corlas, you will kill . . .

Unwillingly Corlas's grip tightened on the axe. 'No!' he screamed. 'No!'

. . . your . . .

'Bel!' came a cry. It was Baygis, riding full pelt towards them. He reached out a hand as he leaped from his horse, and Iassia shrilled as he was pulled to the ground, seized in Baygis's power. Somehow Corlas felt his terror through the link between them.

Kill the mage! the weaver screamed. *Kill him, Corlas! Kill the mage who knows my true name!*

A consuming purpose took hold of Corlas and he strode towards Baygis. There came the sound of more horses, and over a hill appeared Naphur and Fahren, riding hard with soldiers at their heels.

'Corlas,' said Baygis, breathing hard as Corlas strode towards him. 'What – '

His eyes opened wide as the axe head whooshed towards him, and froze in a surprise that remained on his face as his head hit the ground. A river of red flowed from his severed neck as his body collapsed to his knees, then forward.

Naphur roared. Corlas blinked in confusion, staring at the bloody axe in his hands, then at Bel, who watched in disbelief. Finally he saw the approaching horses, and soldiers drawing their swords.

'By Arkus!' he cried. 'It was the weaver, Bel! The weaver! I had no choice!'

He stumbled away, shedding his pack and dropping his axe as he broke into a run towards the trees. 'Tell Naphur it was the weaver!' he called.

'Father!' Bel shouted, but Corlas disappeared into the trees.

'Kill him!' Naphur screamed, and the soldiers rode after Corlas. 'Kill Corlas! Kill him a thousand times!'

He leaped from his steed to fall by the body of his son, his face unbelieving as he clutched at Baygis's chest. 'Not my son!' he cried. 'By Arkus, no!'

'Bel?'

Bel blinked, stunned by what had happened. Fahren stood beside him, speaking softly. 'What went on here?'

'I don't know,' said Bel, shaking his head.

Nearby on the ground, the weaver lay pinned, watching them balefully. Fahren had managed to trap him anew even as Baygis's magic had faded.

'You,' said Fahren to the little bird. 'You had a hand in this!'

'Or a wing, to be more accurate,' cooed Iassia. He struggled feebly against the glowing net. 'A shame,' he continued, 'that your ruler's son had to die instead of Bel here, as I had intended.'

Fahren's gaze was icy cold. 'I know your name,

weaver,' he said, and instantly the bird fell still. 'The mage you killed – he told it to me.'

Iassia squawked as he struggled against Fahren's power, his blood-drop eyes bulging in fear.

Fahren raised his voice skywards and threw out his hands. 'I call your attention, Arkus! I call on you to reclaim your servant, *Iashymaya Siashymor*!'

Although the sun had almost set, suddenly a column of light was shining brightly upon them. At their feet, the bird opened and closed his beak in soundless terror as the light shone on him most brilliantly, picking up the colours of his beautiful plumage. It grew stronger until it hurt their eyes and they could no longer see anything of the world outside.

'What is this?' whispered Bel.

'I don't know,' said Fahren in wonder. 'But I don't think we need be afraid.'

Even the ground beneath seemed to be nothing more than light itself. Ahead of them the light blazed and they covered their eyes. When the flare faded, and they lowered their hands from their faces, a magnificent being was standing before them. A colossal helm on its head was covered in spikes that seemed to change at a point from metal to light, becoming like rays of the sun. In the eye slots, fires blazed and danced, and the armour was made from great plates of gold. Slowly the warrior reached out a shining gauntlet, opening it over the struggling bird.

'No, my lord!' squeaked Iassia. 'I beg forgiveness! I never wanted to leave you; it was the others who made me!'

Iassia fell still, and from his body rose a glowing

form, flapping piteously and calling soundlessly. The giant's fist closed on the spirit, enveloping it utterly.

'Arkus,' whispered Fahren. He fell to his knees, while Bel stood and stared.

Arkus's head turned, creaking, and flames spurted from the eye slots of his helm. When he spoke, his voice crackled, as if the words themselves were on fire. 'My thanks to you,' he boomed, 'for the return of my servant.'

'Praise be,' murmured Fahren.

'It is good,' said the god, 'that you have unwittingly opened this pathway. I have words for you both.'

'For us?' said Bel dumbly as he gazed up at the breathtaking entity.

'Yes, Bel Corinas. Even my fate depends on you now. You are the one who will upset the balance.'

'But, great lord,' stammered Fahren, 'what of the other?'

'It is true the one called Losara grows potent with shadow magic,' rumbled the god. 'Soon none will be able to match him.'

'Are we lost?' asked Fahren.

'The solution lies with the Stone of Evenings Mild.'

'I don't understand,' said Bel.

The fires flared. 'Bel Corinas, you were born with the blood of the Sprites, with both light and shadow. That is why the Stone ripped your soul asunder. The mages who warred over you did not know the power of the gateway that splits light and shadow. He who was one now stands divided. Balance will continue until you are combined again.'

'Combined again?' echoed Fahren.

'Yes. If Bel and Losara return through the gateway of the Stone, to emerge as the individual soul they once were, we will have won.'

'How?' asked Bel.

'Because you are stronger than Losara,' said Arkus. 'The shadow in the child you once were was never as strong as the light. It came from the Old Magic in your Sprite lineage, and your parents were not even full-blooded. You are born of Kainordas, and Losara is only a small residual part. If he is drawn back into you, he will become that small part once again.'

'But how can he be small?' asked Bel. 'If he's as powerful as you say?'

'His power with magic is but a single trait. *You* are the governing personality, Bel. You are more complete than he.' The god seemed to shimmer, like a mirage in a heat haze. 'I cannot remain long. Hear me well. To stop the threat against us, Losara must be merged once more with Bel. You must find the Stone of Evenings Mild.' Arkus's voice became more distant. 'As before, two mages must work the Stone – one of shadow, one of light. Only through such a combination will the Stone function. Only then can you undo what has been done.'

The world began to appear again, the same as before Arkus came to them: Naphur slumped over his dead son, the soldiers calling to each other in the trees, evening falling. No time had passed.

'Only then,' came Arkus's final words, 'can Bel lead us to victory.'

Then the god was gone and Fahren and Bel were kneeling on grasses that rustled gently in the wind. After the warmth of Arkus, the world seemed very cold.

⌒

'Well, well,' said Lady Vyasinth. 'Wherever did weavers inherit their penchant for lying, I wonder?'

She sat back from the still pool, pondering what she had seen. She had chosen a good time to watch, it seemed. Often when she tried, Arkus blocked her sight; and if she looked southwards, Assedrynn did the same. This evening, however, Arkus had been preoccupied, filling the boy's mind with strange directives.

He can't possibly know that bringing Bel and Losara back together is the way for him to win. Nobody knows the way for sure, except perhaps cursed fate. So why claim it?

Maybe, she thought, *not because he knows it is the only way he* will *win but because it's the only way he* can *win.*

She rose into the air, a swirl of twigs and leaves.

And maybe the same goes for me, she thought merrily.

Pilgrimage

They did not tarry long in Swampwild, for Lalenda found it difficult to be there. Although she still had not wept, neither did she look back as her home fell from the horizon. In the days that followed, she was quiet, speaking only to thank Losara for setting her free and taking her to Swampwild. She had regressed almost to the Lalenda he knew from Skygrip, except that her sadness was deeper and less fearful. He grew more and more annoyed with Battu for having caused this. It would have been a simple matter to allow Lalenda out of the castle to visit her mother, or at the very least fetch her mother to her, but that would never have crossed Battu's mind.

South they flew, and soon came to frosty plains sparse of vegetation. Ahead lay the towering Bentemoth Mountains, a range like shards of broken glass, ancestral home to the Graka. The journey to the top was arduous, for swirling winds flung snow and ice at them, and the peaks were almost as high as the Cloud itself. Losara had to cloak Lalenda in his power to protect her as they buoyed upwards, while Grimra laughed and raced around, snapping his fangs at the tails of lightning bolts.

Losara noticed that finally Lalenda seemed to be taking in the world around her, her eyes gleaming with reflected lightning, her black hair flying wildly about her head. She grinned fiercely.

'You're keeping me safe, my lord?' she said, and somehow the question didn't seem to be just for there and then.

'Yes,' he said.

They arrived on a high plateau where a Graka funeral was taking place. A wiry old Graka with a chin sharp enough to cut bread was presiding over a corpse, chanting and making signs in the air. Four others pulled the coffin along with ropes, two at the back and two at the front. As they reached the edge, they beat their wings and carried the coffin out over the leagues-long drop. A group of mourners standing further back began to sing a funeral dirge.

'Back to the rocks!' wailed the elderly Graka.

The four flying Graka released their ropes and the coffin disappeared into the swirling white.

'No good for meat,' Grimra informed Losara and Lalenda. 'Graka be hard, 'specially when dead. That one be nothing but pebbles and dust by the time he bounce all the way to the bottom.'

Losara landed on the ledge and presented himself and Lalenda to the surprised Graka, who never saw outsiders this far up the Teeth. They were welcoming enough when he told them who he was, and together they went into the mountains, where he saw elaborately carved halls full of statues, and an ice mine where glowing blue veins rippled the rock.

After that they flew west, all the way to the Midgeon Hills. The hills themselves were low, uniform, pale and dry, with orange grass as patchy as the scalp of a burn victim. Clumps of stone congregated here and there, and sometimes it was hard to tell where these ended and the ruins began. Some forgotten people had lived here once, but now there was little sign of civilisation save a lonely winding road. As Losara and Lalenda landed atop a hill, Grimra's skull became visible low to the ground, as if he sniffed after something.

'What is it, Grimra?' asked Lalenda.

The skull faded. 'Grimra be living here before Tyrellan be catching him,' the ghost said. 'Long hunts along the funnels between them rises, Grimra had.' He seemed to be having trouble remembering. 'In them ruins, that was where Grimra's pendant be, buried or hidden . . . or Grimra forgetting. Not good eating round here . . . plenty of dead things, scarce of the living. Travellers sometimes, but they learn where Grimra can reach the road and leave it to circle wide!'

This particular memory seemed to enrage Grimra and he flew straight up into the air, howling. Losara decided they had best not tarry.

North they flew, following the coast, to where the Nyul'ya River met the sea under the harbour city of Afei Edres. The Cloud above seemed thinner, and the light that shone through it showed off the colour and style of the city. A high stone wall ran around it, enclosing it against the sea, while the river ran through the centre under a gaping arch with raised portcullis. Inside the walls were blue stone buildings of many floors, with curly-topped turrets painted yellow. These seemed to be home to many people, putting Losara in mind of ants' nests. The streets were a network of wharves, bridges and platforms elevated above the tide line and the river, and often there was the sound of water underfoot. There was a sense of cleanness and wealth to the place – the air was fresh and crisp, there wasn't filth lying about, and the people were well dressed and industrious. The Arabodedas capital did its people proud.

'I wouldn't mind staying here for a day or two,' said Losara as they strolled along.

'Me either, lord,' Lalenda said. 'Let's.'

They ate and rested and walked about. No one paid them much mind, as the city bustled with all kinds of folk. They visited markets, where Lalenda was fascinated by so many things that Losara offered to buy her a gift. She took enthusiastically to the task of choosing one, but, after frowning at this and frowning at that, she simply took his hand and kissed it.

'Thank you, my lord, for your kindness,' she said, 'but I simply cannot decide.'

Such an odd girl she could be.

They walked along the docks and watched fishing boats coming and going. Further on they saw some of the city's famous water magicians who could manipulate the sea, conjuring up waterspouts and carving them like clay on a potter's wheel. Soon they came to a place where the coast jutted out from underneath the walkway. Below, on an outcrop of rock that overlooked the ocean, a small crowd had gathered around a water mage dressed in a green robe, with a red streak in his ponytail. The mage reached out and pulled a jet of water from the sea. With a twirl of his fingers he set it spinning on its axis, then plucked away at it, sending off sprays of water to reveal the shape beneath. A fish flew out and plopped back in the water, and the people laughed. The mage's hands conjured frantically as blobs shifted position, a furious look of concentration on his face. Finally the crowd gasped – rotating before them was a watery carving of Lampet. The serpent god's curves shimmered in the light and Losara almost expected to see his eyes flash different colours. The mage wasn't done, however – his arms shot out and the serpent came to life, his body unfurling as he 'swam' over their heads, dripping salt water as he circled upwards. High in the sky, he exploded into a fine mist. The mage bowed, the crowd clapped and tossed coins into a wooden box at his feet.

'Come,' said Losara. 'I wish a word with him.'

They made their way through the dispersing crowd, towards the outcrop, where the mage still stood. As the mage saw them approach, a strange look came over his face.

'That was a beautiful display,' said Losara. 'Lampet himself would have chuckled to see it.'

The mage inclined his head. 'Thank you, my lord. I am sure by now you know that for a fact.'

Losara was pleased that he did not detect any jealousy in the remark.

'Performing these tricks is the main source of my income,' the mage continued, 'now that my old mistress Memtas has cast me out for my failure. So it is gratifying to learn that my new master approves.'

Lalenda looked from the mage to Losara, confused by the exchange.

Losara smiled. 'I would not worry overly, Roma,' he said. 'I told you I would build you a grand house . . . and I will. The time to serve me is coming.'

Roma bowed low.

The next day, before they left, they called Grimra back from the sea. He'd been spending all his time there, as he had never seen the ocean before. Enthusiastically he told them that 'floating meat be everywhere'.

East they flew, past Fort Logale, to the southern edge of the Stone Fields and the ringlet of the five goblin cities. There was Trelter, smoky grey and awash with industry. Smalt was orderly and metallic, and they saw open areas where war engines were being assembled and furnaces glowed red in the night. Barramoor was the city of the Greys, clean and poor, but somewhat colourful. Froxen was the capital, densely populated and teeming with trade, livestock, markets, gambling dens, taverns and at least three of everything else ever seen in a city. Finally came Childris, the city of teachers, with academies and schools and an enormous barracks.

From there they went north, out over the Stone Fields. Although rocky, it was not a barren region. Moss grew, streams ran full of fish, spindly trees pushed their way up from beneath, and insects lived in stone mansions.

At the border they landed to look out over Kainordas. It was daytime and a bright wall of sun fell right at their feet.

'Can I put my hand out?' asked Lalenda.

'I don't see why not,' said Losara.

Carefully, curiously, she reached out into the sun and held her hand there for a few moments. Then she withdrew, shivering. 'Prickles,' she said.

'Grimra does not like it here,' whispered the ghost. He flashed white along the border. 'Too much warmth . . . but hello? What is this?' Fangs flashed over nothing.

It took Losara a moment, but suddenly he was aware of the shadowy souls that floated listlessly all around them. He remembered hearing about the Trapped – undead without bodies, who wanted to return to the light but could not. Undead whose souls were now of shadow, whom the gods wanted sent onwards to the Well. He watched as Grimra shredded one to pieces and it faded away in relief.

'Bah,' said Grimra. 'No good for eating. All show and no taste.'

Losara felt sorry for the poor creatures. They needed to be put out of their misery, and indeed the gods had ordered it so. Why had Battu left them to drift?

'I'll be back shortly,' he said.

He dissolved into the shadows and stretched out until he was weblike. Then he rushed along the border, catching the Trapped in a net of himself. At the edge of the Stone Fields they petered out, so he changed direction and rushed the other way. Bundled against him, the souls were barely able to struggle, but he could feel their terror. Best to end it for them quickly. At the western end of the Stone Fields, he came to a stop, a swag of the undead souls wriggling in his grasp. As he gathered his power, finally they seemed to understand what he offered them. They became still, eagerly awaiting, and he let his power ripple through them. There was a collective sigh as they disintegrated.

'Safe journey to the Well,' Losara whispered, and sped back to join the others. Lalenda gave a little start when he solidified out of the rocks.

They wandered along the border, though there wasn't much to see – the land was barren on each side. One creature interested Losara – the shadowmanders that darted out over the border to kill anything born on the other side. They seemed to possess such instinctive hatred of the light, and reminded him of Tyrellan. Losara knew he must learn to be like the shadowmanders if he was to succeed, but how? He didn't want to kill something just because of what it was.

They went east along the border, and eventually the land on both sides became fertile once more. Where the Dragon's Sorrow River crossed into Fenvarrow, it became the delta that surrounded the Dimglades, and here they stopped.

Losara sat by the stream with his legs tickled by reeds, careless of the moisture that soaked his robe. Frogs croaked, and dragonflies chased each other across the delta. The air was temperate and still, as lazy as he felt.

A fluttering of wings heralded the arrival of Lalenda. She touched down lightly and sank to her knees.

'Hello there, Miss Pixie,' he said.

'This is a strange place,' she said. She took hold of a reed by the water's edge, pulling its puffy white end up towards her. 'Of all that we've seen, this one makes me uneasy.' Her finger curled and a single claw flicked neatly in and out, cutting the head from the reed with a quiet *snick*.

'Is that because it reminds you of Swampwild?' he asked.

'No, my lord,' she said, and he believed her.

'Why then?'

'Because it is so . . . between.'

Losara knew what she meant. Here on this fertile borderland were creatures that lived happily in both shadow and light. The frogs did not seem to mind whether they hopped about on the Fenvarrow or

Kainordas side. Amphibians were used to living in two worlds, Losara supposed, but four? Water, air, shadow, light? Birds from the Dimglades flew down to catch insects in Kainordas, and fish swam the channels and ponds around the entire circumference of the delta. These were lives on the edge of two places, and they didn't seem to notice or care.

'Why cannot light and dark exist like this?' he wondered aloud. 'Living side by side without discernment?'

'I don't know my lord,' said Lalenda quietly. 'I only know that they can't.'

'Why?'

Lalenda struggled to find an answer. Perhaps she felt it instinctively, he thought, like those shadowmanders. She was born of shadow, after all. He was not – he had been born in a between place too, he realised, in Whisperwood. Did he therefore not possess the hatred of the light that would carry him to victory? Perhaps there was another way. But how could that be the conclusion of his pilgrimage? Why would the Dark Gods, who wanted only triumph, send him to learn such a lesson?

'My lord?' said Lalenda.

He stirred from reverie and turned to look at her. She didn't seem to realise, but there was a silver-winged fly tangled in her hair. He reached up to offer it his finger and it pulled itself free.

'Will you punish the creature for sullying my hair, my lord?' she asked, a playful note in her voice.

'I think you know me a little better than that by now,' he said.

'I do.'

What a beautiful thing she was, he thought. He had seen plenty of beautiful things on their journey, but this . . . this was different. Why had he brought her with him? It wasn't just that she'd needed rescuing, it wasn't just compassion. He knew the answer, dimly, far back in his mind. He knew why most men would ask a woman to accompany them.

'My lord?' she said. 'You're . . . well, you're staring at me. I don't mind, of course, it's just . . . well . . . are you . . . that is to say, I've been wondering –'

'Lalenda,' he interrupted, 'I wonder if perhaps . . . the time is long past that I should have attempted . . .' He felt the sentence growing long on his tongue, clunky and awkward. These were not the right words, he knew, but could not stop them. '. . . to make known my admiration of you. By way of some . . . action, perhaps. With your permission, of course.'

She stared at him in a way that made him feel strangely uncomfortable, then shifted towards him a little. 'You've never needed my permission for anything,' she said. 'But you gave me back my permission to give . . . and I do.'

Clumsily he put an arm around her, hesitantly, lightly. 'Lord,' she whispered, 'I will not break like glass.'

The realness of her penetrated his calm exterior, awakening something inside him, bringing him out of his head. He kissed her, and felt her lips soft, and her cheek too. As he ran his shadowy hands over her skin, she gasped and he pulled back in concern.

'Your touch,' she said. 'It's truly like no other.'

She pulled him back to her, and he let the shadow spread out from himself over her, caressing her, exploring and, as they grew more entwined and her cries of pleasure became more insistent, seeking out the shadows within her.

Losara had never had fewer thoughts in his head.

When he became aware of himself once again, he was lying on his back with her small form slumped across him, her lashes tickling his chest as she dozed. He didn't feel like moving, so he closed his shadowed eyes and joined her in sleep.

The dream he dreamt gave him the reason for his pilgrimage.

A Few Drops

Losara floated, disoriented for a moment, uncertain of where he was. He steadied and turned to see the Throne standing silhouetted by the open end of his quarters, a glass of bloodfire in his hand. The sun was low in the sky to the south, and the liquid caught its rays brightly, casting a red wash over the rest of the room. The Throne did not turn as Bel and Fahren entered, and waited in silence. Losara drifted backwards to take it all in, losing himself in the flow of the dream.

'Are you not to blame?' muttered Naphur eventually. 'If you had not pursued Corlas, Baygis would still be alive. It was you who placed my son in harm's way.'

He raised the cup and drank deeply. Bel opened his mouth, but Fahren caught his eye and shook his head.

'Fahren has told me of the bird Iassia,' said the Throne. 'Of the part he played.' His tone grew resentful. 'You should know, then, that I have called off the hunt for your father.'

A moment of relief passed over Bel's face, but he quickly returned to his stony demeanour.

'As long as he flees far,' added Naphur, 'and stays a horizon's length from my sight.' He turned, but the glaring sun behind him still hid his face. 'But that does not mean I am not angry.'

'Naphur,' began Fahren.

'Enough, High Mage!' said the Throne. 'I've heard you speak, and granted the mercy you begged me for. But now I will have my revenge.' He stalked forward, revealing the dark belts under his eyes. 'We attack Fenvarrow with all possible haste!' he said. 'And you, Bel, will lead. The child of power will fulfil his obligations.'

'My Throne,' Fahren tried, 'I have told you that Arkus charged us to find –'

'Curse Arkus!' shouted Naphur. 'I am old, heirless, and done with waiting.' His look to Bel became almost imploring. 'If I must not blame you, Bel, nor your father, then help me attack those I can blame. We must let Kainordas see you, rally to you, as we march to crush the dark. I have already sent out word, on wing and hoof in every direction. I promise that war is coming, with or without you, and on this I will not be dissuaded. But will you help me, Bel? Will you help me cut down those who have brought such ruin upon us?'

Fahren cast Bel an alarmed look – it was obvious he didn't agree with such action – but Bel didn't care. Ever since Arkus had spoken to him, his destiny had felt like a crushing weight across his shoulders. It wasn't a burden he'd chosen to bear, and Naphur was offering a chance to be rid of it. Why did he need to join with Losara if he could just kill him? Without its champion, the shadow would fall.

'I will,' said Bel. 'The sooner I have something to kill, the better.'

The Throne's eyes gleamed. 'We're of like mind,' he said, and gave a twisted smile.

The dream swirled.

Losara found himself floating high in the sky. Though the bright sun shone upon him, he felt no heat from it.

Beneath, from the Halls, a great force set forth, the morning light streaming at their backs. Bel sat astride a white war horse, his blue hair gleaming for all to see. On one side rode Naphur in ornate golden armour, and on the other rode Fahren, with expression dark and brooding. Behind followed the soldiers of the Halls, tromping the grass flat. Jaya broke from the mob to speed forward on a sleek stallion, laughing as she reached out to grip Bel's hand and hold it high.

Word had spread throughout Kainordas that the blue-haired child had announced himself and was leading the charge of charges to defeat the shadow once and for all. To rally to him was to secure one's place in history. Every day the army grew as troops arrived from all directions. Folk who had never touched a sword before fell into step, from nobles and their entourages to farmers and beggars. In jails across the land, prisoners were offered the chance to fight in exchange for pardon of all but the most heinous crimes.

Of the non-human races, the Saurians were the first to arrive. They made a fearsome sight to behold, approaching quickly over the Grass Ocean. The lizard-like Ryoshi Saurians, like monstrous pale scorpions, rode hulking dune claws. Their cousins, the Syanti Saurians, were more snake than lizard, with legless serpentine bodies and yellow slit eyes, and carried cruel-ended whips and impossibly thin swords. As the army reached the Great Rass River, a swarm of Zyvanix descended, their collective buzzing loud enough to vibrate teeth. They were a welcome addition indeed, and there was much celebration that night in the camps.

The army slowed as it grew, and at Kahlay Bel ordered them to stop, to allow others following to catch up. Naphur, unable to rest, it seemed, took to riding around the sprawl of camps. He preached like a prophet about the blue-haired boy, about victory and revenge on Fenvarrow. Those priests amongst the ranks took up the Throne's words, speaking of the champion Arkus had delivered. Losara watched Bel listening in on the words with gleaming eyes. *Do they give him strength?* he wondered.

When the army left Kahlay a week later, it was greater than any Kainordas had ever seen.

One night, as they camped, Bel found Fahren smoking a brittleleaf roll and gazing with concern over the red glow of many fires.

'Old teacher,' he said, 'I know you disagree with this action.'

'I'm trying to accept it,' said Fahren. 'I've seen there's no talking you out of it.'

'What do you think about so deeply then?'

'If this is indeed the war to end all wars,' said Fahren, 'as our poor lost Throne calls it, then I think about the only thing that bears thinking about. How to win.'

'Ah,' said Bel. 'I've been giving that some thought myself. I don't think we can simply march into Fenvarrow and expect to sweep through.'

Fahren cast a glance at him. 'I'm glad to hear you say that, for it's precisely what Naphur intends. We are in need of a better plan.'

'Have you thought of anything?'

'Nothing to speak of.'

'We'll make final camp at Holdwith,' said Bel. 'I understand there are many mages there.'

'Yes,' said Fahren. 'Lightfists are trained there. It's a good place, so close to the border, to sharpen their skills.'

'Perhaps they'll know some spell to help us.'

Fahren shook his head sadly.

'Come now,' chuckled Bel. 'Don't be so defeatist. Surely you don't think you've seen everything under the sun?'

After many weeks of marching, they arrived at Holdwith. Built on the edge of fertile lands, the farms on the north side were well tended, yet seemed somehow makeshift and temporary. To the south, battlements overlooked dusty plains that ran all the way to the border. Here the Cloud was so close that after midday the sun moved behind it and the light grew dim.

As the army set up camp around the fort, Bel, Naphur and Fahren rode to the gates and entered. The walls of Holdwith fort encircled a large town that seemed to contain more buildings than people. From the town centre rose a cobblestoned tower, higher than the surrounding walls. The Throne immediately headed towards it, saying he would speak to the local gerent, not pausing to see if the others followed.

'We should visit the Lightfist Academy,' Bel said. 'See if there's some spell, or idea, or magical artefact to give us an advantage.'

Fahren looked miserable and Bel knew he didn't think searching would bear any fruit.

'High Mage,' he tried, 'you always lamented my lack of magic, but don't let that stop you from *being* my magic. This is the path we are on.'

Fahren blinked, and his jaw tightened. He considered Bel for a moment, then nodded. 'You are right. I must stop this moping. Come, we shall see what we can find.'

They made their way to the Lightfist Academy. In a cobbled courtyard they found students wearing red and yellow robes unleashing fireballs at dummies of Black Goblins. A pair of Lightfists, dressed in pure red, walked back and forth instructing them.

As the High Mage entered with the child of power, all turned to stare.

'We need to see Methodrex immediately,' bellowed Fahren.

A Lightfist apprentice, about the same age as Bel, frowned deeply in concentration. From the air he conjured a translucent sunwing that beat large butterfly wings. It strung an arrow to its glowing bow and loosed it at a distant target. Next to him, another student held out a flaming torch and waggled her fingers at it. Each time a speck of ash fell from the torch, it was caught by an invisible force and hurled expanding and fragmenting across the courtyard to pelt the dummies with scattershot fireballs. The next student in line held the end of a fiery whip, which lengthened and retracted as he lashed with stunning precision and considerable devastation. The dummies flew to pieces faster than they could be magically reassembled.

Losara watched the display with interest – it was impressive; and so hot – he was grateful he felt nothing as he drifted along. Was this the extent of what he'd have to face?

High Overseer Methodrex, a short old man in white-gold robes, turned away from the target range. 'You can see we have some fine students,' he said, as yet more dummies exploded behind him. 'But I doubt they display anything the High Mage has not seen before.'

Fahren grunted agreement.

'If these spells are commonplace,' said Bel tersely, 'where are the rarer ones? What of those that can only be achieved when many mages work together? What of the spells that set student apart from teacher, mage apart from High Mage?'

'There are many spells, lad,' Fahren said. 'Not all are easy or safe to demonstrate in such confines. Of those that have merit in war, there are none the enemy cannot match.'

Bel scowled. 'What of the library here, Methodrex? Has it been scoured for every strange and remote possibility?'

Methodrex drew himself up straight. Losara noticed the man treated Bel with reverence, perhaps rightly so. 'It could perhaps stand further investigation, my lord,' he said.

'Then by all means investigate!' said Bel, and waved a hand dismissively.

It took Fahren a moment to realise he was being included in the instruction, and he looked taken aback.

'It shouldn't surprise you that I give you orders, old friend,' Bel said. 'After all, you and Naphur raised me to be a leader.'

He held Fahren's stare until the High Mage nodded and joined Methodrex in departing. Bel stalked off along the line of students, further inspecting their spells. Lava bubbled out of the ground, vines twisted to follow their caster's wishes, white light crashed in waves and golden bolts of energy shot forth. It was all very impressive . . . and ultimately useless. With a stormy expression, Bel left the academy and walked out onto the cobblestoned street. Naphur was coming towards him, along with Holdwith's gerent and several officers.

'There you are!' called Naphur. 'We must make ready – the longer we wait, the longer Fenvarrow has to prepare!'

'No, Naphur,' said Bel, quite clearly. 'We must wait. There are others still journeying to join our army, and it will take time to outfit them all. We must pool our resources.'

'Bah,' said Naphur. 'You sound like Fahren, always wishing to delay. What do you seek in the academy, Bel? Magic? I thought we were beyond that, you and I.' He drew the sword from his hip and ran it over his gauntleted palm. 'I thought we believed in steel.'

'If I say we wait,' said Bel, 'we wait.'

'How dare you give me commands!'

'You asked me to lead this army,' said Bel, 'and lead it I shall. The many who have joined us – some no more than peasants – why did they so readily leave behind their homes, their families? Because of a promise given, Naphur – the promise of me. You gave it yourself many times as you rode amongst them, and now you must reap what you have sown. They follow me, Naphur. And I say we wait.'

Naphur's eyes blazed and for a moment the sword was stationary across his hand. Then he slid it into its scabbard and gave a curt nod. The gerent and other officers present witnessed the Throne of Kainordas bow to the will of the blue-haired man. It was a story that would spread quickly.

A booming cry echoed around the fort, full-bellied and animal.

'What was that?' Bel demanded.

'Nothing to worry about, lord,' said the gerent. 'We captured a whelkling a short while back – must've got blown off course somehow. We've just been working out what to do with it.'

'A whelkling!' Bel recalled the creature from his lessons with Fahren.

'It were carrying supplies to Skygrip,' continued the gerent. 'Overburdened, so maybe that's why –'

'Enough!' said Bel. 'Did you say it was bound for Skygrip?'

'Yes, lord.'

'So if it were released with someone on its back, it would bear them to Skygrip Castle?'

'I suppose so,' chuckled the gerent. 'But that particularly insane person would meet a very nasty end, I'm sure.'

Bel stood in silent thought for a moment, then walked away.

'Well,' snapped Naphur, 'don't just stand there like hair stuck on shit. You heard him – we have to see to the arming of the army!'

The town's inn had a 'garden' comprised of large pots and long stone trays. These housed plants from the surrounding plains, unspectacular yet somewhat pleasant. This was where Bel found Jaya, lazily twirling a knife as she sat on a bench. He sat down next to her and she rearranged herself against him.

'Any luck?' she asked.

'I know little of magic,' he replied. 'Fahren and the head of the academy are searching for something to help us, but they don't seem optimistic.'

Losara watched them curiously – they were so easy with each other, so naturally entwined. Would it be this way for him and Lalenda? Did he love her as these two clearly loved each other? And what if Losara had met Jaya – would he have fallen in love with her? Would Bel have fallen in love with Lalenda?

'You are worried that your other has such great magic at his disposal?'

'I'd be a fool not to,' Bel said with a sigh, and she kissed his neck. 'It is well and good to be a great warrior, but a man is still just a man. What can one man do?'

'The answer will come,' she murmured. 'It has to – fate got you this far.'

The door to the inn opened and a willowy girl in a red and yellow robe emerged. She went to an urn of water, then spotted them and gave a start.

'Forgive me,' she said, trying not to stare at Bel's hair. 'I didn't see you there. I'm Gertrum, the innkeeper's daughter . . . I was just going to water the plants, but I can come back later if I'm disturbing you . . .'

Jaya giggled softly. 'What a sweet girl,' she whispered sarcastically.

'Go ahead,' said Bel with a wave. 'Water the plants.'

Gertrum nodded and turned back to the urn. She put her hand in the water and a hissing began. The water bubbled and boiled, and vapour rose rapidly from its surface. Gertrum waggled the fingers of her other hand, magically collecting the vapour into a ball. After a couple of minutes, she had created a dense little cloud.

'Well,' said Jaya, 'I'd been wondering why there wasn't a watering can.'

Bel watched with interest as the girl walked around the courtyard with the cloud. She would wave it into position above a plant, then mumble something and rain fell.

'That's nothing,' said Jaya. 'Back in Athika, our family sometimes paid for the services of a weather mage. Dry plains out there, sometimes too dry for the crops we planted. I've seen a mage gather moisture from a cloudless sky and make it storm . . . if only for a moment.'

Bel's gaze turned slowly from Gertrum's little smudge of vapour to the grey mass of the Cloud that loomed above them. Suddenly he leaped to his feet. 'You there!' he exclaimed, so forcefully it made Gertrum jump. He strode over and took her by the arm. 'This spell you're casting – what is it?'

'Um . . . er . . .' She glanced at his hand but did not pull free. 'It's just a rain spell my lord. Most mages can do them – it's just basic magic.'

'And it affects the whole cloud on which it is cast?'

'Um . . . well, yes, lord.'

His hand shot up to the sky, finger pointing at the billowing darkness. 'Could it be cast on a cloud like that?'

'I . . . I don't know,' the girl stammered. Jaya stood and gently prised Bel's unthinking grip from her arm. 'Maybe. If you were close to the heart of it.'

'The heart of it,' repeated Bel, as the cry of the whelkling boomed off the walls.

The Storm

Suddenly Losara was himself in the dream, watching Battu striding back and forth and shouting orders at the troops.

Let him, he thought. He was certain that he was meant to eventually supplant Battu as Shadowdreamer, but the gods had not specified a time frame, and there was no point making trouble with Battu before a battle. They needed all the strength they could muster.

He dissolved into shadow and travelled swiftly to the border to look upon the growing army of his other. It was an impressive force, many tens of thousands strong, and each race was fierce and determined. He wondered if the great power he felt inside himself – as yet not truly tested – would be able to hold them all back. Certainly thousands would fall to him, but would it be enough? He didn't like to discover himself thinking this way – loss of life on such a scale brought him no joy.

Meanwhile, the Fenvarrow army was growing larger by the day, but the gods had been right – the population had never grown back to its full force under the Caretaker. They had a greater diversity of soldiers, that was true, with Arabodedas, Vortharg, Goblin, Graka and Pixie.

The Mireform too had kept their word, and though only eight had met Losara's summons, the arrival of such mighty allies had boosted morale considerably. It was interesting that the Mireforms answered only to him, refusing even to speak with Battu – a fact that Battu glowered over but pointedly failed to mention.

Somehow it all felt wrong. It was happening too fast. It didn't feel as if he was treading the right path.

Suddenly he was wrenched free of himself as the dream swirled again and thrust into his other, into Bel . . . and it was as before, when he had seen through Bel's eyes in Drel Forest . . .

The whelkling grunted as it dropped from the top of the cobblestoned tower and Bel knew he accounted for most of the weight. Fahren, behind him, was as light as thread and sinew, but Bel was broad and wore steel bands on his legs and arms, along with sword, boot knives, steel skirt and chest piece. Fahren had promised that he could give the whelkling a helping boost and, as they plummeted downwards Bel prayed he would be swift to do so. A moment later he felt an upsurge of warm air and the whelkling suddenly gained height. It began flapping heavily, bearing them up towards the Cloud. He dared to glance downwards, saw those on the ground watching, saw the worry on Jaya's face as she faded into a pinprick far below.

The whelkling climbed until the Cloud was but paces from their heads. Beneath them sprawled Fenvarrow, dark and unwelcoming. The temperature was dropping rapidly too, and Bel shivered.

'Look!' he shouted over the rushing wind.

Some few leagues back from the border, a vast army of shadow creatures camped upon the Stone Fields. There were raised stone paths along which moved war engines and wagons. One, carrying an entire load of dark ice, glowed eerily.

'You are certain they won't see us?'

'No, our invisibility spell is cast.'

'Good!'

'Let us just hope that Battu and Losara are both down there seeing to their minions, far from Skygrip.'

Bel felt as if he'd dived into cold water. They were high above and well inside enemy lands, with no turning back. His blood began to tingle.

For hours they flew, passing thousands of shadow creatures below. The glowing lights of the five goblin cities lit up the horizon for a time, blazing against them as they passed over. Bel couldn't help but feel exposed, despite Fahren's assurances. Soon the cities fell behind and Skygrip loomed on the horizon. Bel had seen pictures, but he was still awed by the towering fortress of twisted rock and the great spikes of its sceptre head.

'This is total madness,' came Fahren's voice in his ear. 'Good luck to the both of us!'

The whelkling began a slow decline, which seemed to Bel to stretch an age. Skygrip was so massive that he kept thinking it was closer than it was. They circled about the sceptre head, then angled towards a cave mouth that opened in its side. The whelkling gave its booming cry as they swooped.

A patrol of six Graka appeared around the tower, moving to intercept the whelkling. Angry shouting erupted as they spotted the intruders on its back. Fahren sent crackling bolts of energy at them, and three fell

screaming. Two wheeled towards Bel, and he felt a
zing through him as he instantly plotted the necessary
movements of his sword and saw them transpire a
second later. The two Graka shrieked, each missing
a wing, and began spiralling like leaves towards the
ground. The one remaining Graka turned and dived,
managing to dodge Fahren's bolts. The whelkling flew
on obliviously, its course unaltered.

'They'll know we're here!' Fahren yelled.

'Let them come!' screamed Bel.

The cave mouth swallowed them suddenly and they
landed in darkness with a heavy thud. It took a moment
for their eyes to adjust, aided when Fahren conjured a
glowing ball of light to see by. They were in a large
cavern populated by stalls of whelklings and cages of
birds. Several Grey Goblins stood frozen in surprise,
and gasped as Fahren's light found them. Bel slid from
the whelkling and moved forward with a slash and a
stab, cutting them down without resistance.

'Come when I call you,' whispered Fahren in the
whelkling's floppy ear and pressed his fingers to the
side of its head.

'There,' said Bel, pointing to a staircase heading
upwards. Together they ran towards it.

Skygrip was a maze, but Bel was sure they would find
a way to the roof if they kept going up. At the top of
the stairs they ran along a tunnel, and heard the sound
of running feet echoing behind them. They turned into
a wide corridor with a mural of the Dark Gods cut into
the wall and came face to face with a goblin patrol.
'There!' barked the leader, and without another sound
the goblins charged.

Bel rushed to meet them, feeling as if he overtook even himself, and clattered against their knives as a blur. The goblins were faster and more conniving than any hugger, and the path his sword had to travel to keep him alive was less tight and strict than before. He swished at one hissing face that ducked, but others that rose against him met with steel. The fury overtook him and he laughed as he rent limbs asunder and spattered the walls with black blood. He spun as the last goblin fell and saw that others had caught up from behind. Fahren was backing towards him, one hand holding the glowing sphere that blinded the goblins and made them curse, while his other pumped back and forth sending fireballs that burst messily against whatever they hit and ran like liquid. Bel heard himself yell as he charged past, crunching over sticky charred remains to hack at any who still stood. From somewhere lower down in the castle came wails of rage and the sound of many, many feet.

'Hurry, Bel,' shouted Fahren, and they dashed along the corridor and up another flight of stairs. At the top they found a thick wooden door with a lock that Bel's sword couldn't smash.

'Let me,' said Fahren, pushing him aside with a nudge of power. The mage focused on the lock, which glowed briefly in his hand and clicked open. They toppled out onto the roof, where ahead of them rose the billowing Breath of the Cloud.

'Close the door!' Fahren yelled. 'There are too many for you to fight them all!'

Bel bellowed his indignation and swung his sword. There could never be too many. He slammed the door shut nonetheless.

'Stand back!' ordered Fahren and Bel stalked away. The mage made a circular action with his hands and there came a great grinding noise. A disc of rock lifted from the roof, cracking to pieces as it did. Fahren's hands shot forward and the pieces hurled against the door, driving it into its hinges and piling up against it. Almost immediately came a thumping on the other side.

'It will take me some time to channel enough power into the spell,' called Fahren as he moved towards the Breath. 'I must not be interrupted. You must protect me.'

He fell to his knees before the great spout, raising hands that glowed white as he built up power. Bel strode to stand over him, watching the skies and the door, his sword jumpy in his hand. Pebbles on top of the rock pile wobbled as those behind the door strained to open it.

'Get axes!' came a muffled shout.

A group of Graka appeared at the edge of the roof. They spotted him and Fahren immediately, but did not yet swoop towards them. Another pair appeared, beating their wings more heavily, and after a moment Bel saw why – each had an arm hooked under that of a Black Goblin, who hung between them in the air. As soon as they brought him over the edge, he twisted free and landed lightly on all fours like a cat. Astoundingly, a butterfly sailed after him to land on his shoulder. He rose smoothly to his feet, revealing a sword and a brace of daggers hanging around his waist.

'My my,' he said in a dusky voice devoid of emotion. 'Long time since I clapped eyes on you, my boy.' He padded forward, the sword leaping into his grip, and arched a hairless eyebrow at Fahren. 'What's your mage doing there?'

'Destroying you and all your people,' said Bel.

Tyrellan bared his fangs. 'Get him!' he shouted, and the Graka dived.

Bel held his ground, knowing he could not leave Fahren exposed. He drummed this fact into his head repeatedly, forcibly stopping the path of his sword as it tried to lead him away, resisting the urge to dance amongst the whirling bodies. Instead, he rooted his feet to the ground and let them come to him, each breaking against his steel. As the last Graka fell into the pile of bodies before him, Tyrellan watched him, still and silent.

'Knotty fellows you have around here,' Bel said, and poked a dead Graka with his sword. 'I guess they mark the line. Step over them and die.'

Tyrellan padded forward, halting just shy of the heap of dead Graka. 'Here?' he asked. 'Here is as far as I may tread? Very well.'

His hand moved deceptively and suddenly a dagger flashed towards Bel, heading between his legs towards Fahren's back. Bel flicked his sword, managing to swipe it out of the air, sending it clattering away over the stone. He lashed out, but Tyrellan didn't move, and the sword passed a hair's breadth from the tip of the goblin's nose.

Tyrellan sneered. 'Seems you were right,' he said. 'That is indeed the line.'

He turned his back and walked casually across the roof to retrieve his dagger. Behind Bel, Fahren's mumbling got louder and energy crackled.

'Hurry up, High Mage,' Bel hissed.

Tyrellan stooped to pick up his weapon, then was suddenly charging with daggers flying. Three points of steel and a sword tip came at Bel as Tyrellan leaped. Tyrellan managed to turn all three daggers aside with a well-timed arc, while catching Tyrellan's sword on his breastplate with a juddering clang. Tyrellan hit the ground and rolled, his sword flashing at Bel's feet. Bel jumped and slashed, but confusion seized him. He could not find the right path for his sword to travel and kill this target, only to defend himself. Another dagger came from a new angle and he kicked it, with his boot just a handspan away from Fahren's face. It spun into the Breath and he didn't hear it land.

Tyrellan came at him again, slashing and then darting away, staying out of Bel's self-imposed reach. After the fourth pass Bel roared, 'You're not one with time to waste, goblin!'

'It is done!' cried Fahren. 'The spell is cast!'

Bel felt a wet spray hit his back. *Now*, urged his frenzy, *you no longer need to protect the mage.* With a roar he charged forward, his sudden change in tack catching Tyrellan off guard. The goblin was smashed backwards as blades fell so thickly that each combatant seemed to possess more than one. The butterfly fluttered between them, and Bel's blade rebounded from it as solidly as if it hit iron. He took no time to wonder at such strangeness, and a moment later their swords locked. Bel reached out with his free hand, seized Tyrellan under the arm and hurled him away across the roof. The goblin landed not far from where Fahren lay, exhausted. He raised his orb eyes to the funnel of the Breath, blinking as raindrops fell on his face. Above them, the Breath seemed to be misting away, losing its shape.

'What have you done!' howled Tyrellan, leaping to his feet.

The rain grew heavier, a sheet of water expanding outwards, while torrents of water began to cascade off the roof. Lightning cracked, making Tyrellan's fangs gleam as his face twisted to pure hate.

'In a storm you were born,' he hissed. 'In a storm you will die.' He sprang towards Bel.

Time seemed to slow and, finally, Bel could see the path. Calmly he bent his knees, then brought his sword up to meet the goblin's. As soon as he felt the downward pressure of Tyrellan's blow, he pushed upwards from the ground, lifting his opponent. As the goblin passed overhead, Bel pushed up with his sword and simultaneously punched a hand into Tyrellan's stomach. The goblin turned head over heels, his sword falling from his grasp as he reached to snatch at a spire as he sailed past – but he was too far away. He made no sound as he travelled out over the edge of the roof and disappeared into the downpour.

Bel stared after him for a moment, finding it oddly bittersweet that such a challenging fight was over. Then he shook his head and started coming back to himself.

'Fahren!' he called, running to the mage's side. 'Are you all right?'

There was a crash from inside the doorway – those on the other side had managed to pull down the door. Rocks began to shift from the top of the pile.

'I will be,' wheezed Fahren. 'Just have to catch my breath.'

'Call for the whelkling,' said Bel. 'Do it now.'

Fahren smiled. 'Already did.'

A booming sounded out of the rain and the whelkling skidded to a stop on the wet roof.

'Good man,' said Bel, and hoisted Fahren onto its back. 'Now tell it to take us back to Holdwith.'

The whelkling clumped to the edge of the roof and slipped off just as the last rocks fell free of the doorway. It dropped sickeningly and Bel felt his gizzards rise into his mouth. He clutched desperately to the harness as they scythed downwards, the rain hammering them solidly. In his hands the leather was slick, and Fahren had a grim grasp around his waist that dragged at him. The onrushing wind sprayed water in his eyes, and he only just managed to keep his grip as they levelled out and began a broad curve upwards. Ahead he saw the wall of advancing rain, moving too quickly for them to overtake it. A moment later the water thickened and he could see nothing at all. He knew that this time Fahren might not have the strength to magically aid the whelkling's flight, so he wrenched off his chest piece and let it fall. After that, there was nothing to do but hunker down, grip the harness as tight as he could and pray that they would make it back to the border.

Losara broke free, himself again, spinning in the air, feeling faintly sick, watching his other disappear. The dream swirled again.

He was himself once more, although not quite – rather some future possibility of himself, whose emotions he experienced as he had done with Bel, but whose actions he was powerless to direct. He settled back behind his own eyes, watching, becoming . . .

Lalenda trailed along after him, chatting away happily about something wholly unrelated to their present situation. He heard her words on the surface somewhere, but mostly her voice just pleased him as a reminder of their companionship. It was amazing how her mind could wander, how she could talk about some silly story she'd once read about a woman who fell in love with a statue, when their situation was so serious.

They walked along a raised ridge that overlooked the Fenvarrow army. More had arrived, but still Losara wasn't sure it was enough. At least they could choose to fight in their own land, where his – and the other mages' – power would be stronger. Even Battu had the sense not to be goaded into crossing the border.

He stopped suddenly, causing Lalenda to bump into him. She giggled and put her hands around his waist. He stood very still, sensing something.

'My statue,' she whispered.

The wind picked up, rustling his cloak, and it was a cold wind indeed. Something was wrong.

'There's a storm on the way,' she said, snuggling against his back.

He turned to look south, where the horizon was darkening. He stared at it until he realised it was a great fall of water, blocking out everything beyond. Something was very wrong.

'Losara!' came Battu's bark, and Lalenda yelped. From the rocks billowed a shadowform, which seemed for a moment like a shark, but wavered and resolved into the silhouette of Battu. 'Can you feel it?' asked the dark lord.

'Yes,' said Losara. 'It is as if the shadow has ... weakened.'

'Something has happened at Skygrip,' said Battu distantly.

The rain came faster than any natural storm. In moments it was falling on them like a great wave breaking, and moving on towards the camps.

'This is our enemy's doing,' said Battu. He sounded groggy, as if he had been dealt a grave blow. 'Hmm,' he said. 'My body's going to be all wet when I get back to it.'

Losara turned to shadow so quickly that Lalenda, who had been clutching him, almost stumbled off the ridge. Up he went, streaming through the raindrops, up and up into the Cloud. He sensed the spell immediately, permeating in all directions, cancerous, reaching through the Cloud like myriad bright fibres. A sort of dazed wonder came over him, and he thought vaguely that perhaps he was missing a reaction that his other would have felt in this situation.

Without hope he attacked the spell. He let his shadow self spread thin, wiping out bright fibres with his darkness. He rushed through the Cloud as broadly as he could, leaving cured paths behind him . . . but the spell seeped back in. There was no heart to it, nothing central that he could target. Worse, the spell drew power from the light above the Cloud, where the sun shone unhindered. All his mighty power was not enough. It could not even buy moments.

What should I be feeling? he wondered. *Despair?*

The dream swirled.

The goblins standing guard atop Skygrip felt the rain beginning to ease, and the flood that poured off the roof slowed to a trickle. From the sky came a lightening, and they cursed as they covered their eyes. Rays of sun hit the roof, bathing its glistening tar skin in light, warming the exposed black stone from which the Breath of the Cloud had once issued. Feeling a horror that ran to their bones, the goblins quickly fled from the roof, back into the darkness of Skygrip.

By the edge of the roof, a small shape rose. It was a butterfly, with wings of pure white edged by sky blue. It set down, and a moment later a clawed hand reached from below to hold it tightly. Sunlight touched the claw and it stopped moving. As the hole in the Cloud above expanded, the light found Tyrellan hanging by one hand from the edge of Skygrip Castle. He stared dully over Fenvarrow, seeing other spots where the rain was clearing and rays of sun were falling upon land they hadn't touched for a thousand years. Light reached Mankow and, even from this distance, he heard a collective wail of disbelief. For a time he could not seem to find the will to pull himself up the last short distance to safety.

He cannot stand to see Fenvarrow like this, thought Losara sadly. *Does he consider letting go?*

'No,' growled Tyrellan, as if in answer to the question. 'Not until an end finds me.'

The butterfly flapped its wings and rose, pulling Tyrellan up into the light.

The dream swirled.

At the top of the Teeth of Grakvak, the snow stopped swirling. On the peaks, ice began to melt. The Graka shrieked and retreated to their caves, which would soon begin to warm. Their leader told them they would be safe here, high as they were, even if the rest of Fenvarrow fell. He was later proved wrong, when Zyvanix wasps took a fancy to the elaborately carved caves.

∽

In Swampwild, Mire Pixie children turned to stare at the sun. Even so young they instinctively feared it, crying as their parents bundled them up and dragged them inside huts. As they stared out of windows and through doors, the full light of day made Swampwild look strange and alien. It wasn't their Swampwild any more.

The mud began to dry.

Deep in the mud, Mireforms grew dimly aware that something above was wrong. They buried deeper and hid for years, until all the mud above them had hardened; dim presences trapped in the earth.

The army of Fenvarrow fell in to chaos. Battu strode high and tall, bellowing orders and trying to keep order. Much as his people quailed before him, they quailed even more as the sun shone upon them. Even the steely Black Goblins quivered as heat touched their skin.

The Kainordas horde came charging across the Stone Fields, light glinting from swords and axes. At their head rode a blue-haired warrior, and, though Fenvarrow had its own blue-haired champion, he was nowhere to be seen.

Battu knew desertions would start soon, if they hadn't already, and he raged at all to stay focused on their purpose. He could not instil as much fear as he once had, however. His connection to the power of Skygrip was broken and the strength of the shadow was fading.

It was something Losara felt as well, as he sped back to the army, travelling less easily now that sunlight shone everywhere. He erupted into form next to Battu, and even that small effort drained him.

'Where have you been, you fool?' growled Battu. 'The troops need to see you, lest they break in all directions!'

Battu pushed him and he stumbled forward, dazed. He had burned so much of his power chasing the spell hopelessly through the Cloud, and now there was little shadow in his surrounds to draw on. He wandered through the ranks, letting the soldiers see him . . . but could think of nothing to call out, no encouraging words to give them hope. He stared blankly at them and they stared blankly back, their eyes hooded against the blazing light.

As the Kainordas army came onwards, Battu screamed for aerial attacks to begin. Graka rose from the ground carrying cauldrons of acid, and war engines hurled rocks and flaming balls. Archers rained arrows as the enemy got closer, and then the armies broke against each other. Losara knew a moment of pride as brave Fenvarrow folk threw themselves screaming into the fray.

He led his mages in a charge. He tried, time and again, to summon the great power he'd once possessed, but he couldn't seem to find it anywhere. It felt as if he was missing a limb. Around him his mages fell screaming to yellow bolts or fireballs.

Scores of Fenvarrow soldiers were breaking ranks, fleeing back across the Stone Fields. Swarms of Zyvanix buzzed overhead, culling the skies of Graka and peppering the ground with needle-like arrows. Just ahead of him a great scorpion burst through a line of Black Goblins, its huge stinger juddering back and forth to spear them through, while the Saurian riding it loosed off arrows. Mireforms raged with flying tendrils and stabbing claws, and he knew that they, at least, would fight to the end. He chanced a sight of his other – the muscular man moving with amazing agility, ducking and weaving and hacking and slashing, forever untouched by blows aimed at him.

Nearby, the Shadowdreamer sent out blue lightning, frying whole troops of Varenkai, sizzling the wings from Zyvanix, melting scorpions inside their exoskeletons. The light mages turned their focus upon him, advancing and beating back rippling waves of his power, suffusing him with light. He screamed as it came from all sides, and caught fire. Losara shuddered.

Lalenda, came a thought, and he collapsed forwards to spill into shadowform. He moved through cracks in the ground while soldiers fought above him, winding around bodies and pools of blood. He forgot about the raging battle – all that mattered was finding her. He searched and searched, until he found her shape in a corpse on the ground, and trickled around her, unable to believe. A mighty sadness welled up inside him and he pooled beneath her. He lost track of time.

He came back to himself suddenly when he realised there was silence. The slaughter had subsided and there was no doubt within him who had won the battle. Nearby came a crunching of feet and he turned his shadowy gaze to peer up from Lalenda. A short distance away stood a man in gold armour and his other. The man took off his helm and Losara recognised the Throne.

'Cowards,' spat Naphur. 'To flee in such numbers.'

'Let them flee,' said Bel. 'Soon there will be no corner left in this land to hide in.'

The Throne grunted in satisfaction. 'So, we continue?'

'Yes,' said Bel. 'We continue.'

In the following weeks, the sun wrought many changes on Fenvarrow. In Swampwild, humptoads died in dry stream beds. The blue grasses that had grown so widely lightened as they withered, and green invaders took over. The Vorthargs retreated deep into their underground lakes, where one day they would be found and cornered. Shadowmanders along the border grew disoriented, wandering from their homes until they were too weak to go on. Even on the Isle of Assedrynn, light found the tiny blue flowers that grew out of the rocks. Their petals began to curl.

Losara never returned to his physical form, for he feared the tears that would fall. As a shadow thing he wandered, slipping quietly from place to place, watching his people suffer as their homeland faded away. The slaughter wherever the light's forces found them was complete, regardless of sex or age. After a time he could stand it no more and he dwindled away to the delta at the Dimglades, where he recalled that things lived in harmony. There he waited, until the war was truly over and the Dark Gods were no more. He felt the moment when their Great Well broke – the end of shadow magic, and the end of him. On that day, in the comfortable shade of a willow tree, he too faded away.

Off in the east, Bel stood over a fallen Arabodedas with his sword raised to kill, while behind him Afei Edres burned. It was one of the last cities to stand against him, and had fallen too easily to truly excite him.

As Losara died, the sword fell from Bel's hand and he dropped to his knees with empty eyes. Their soul, divided in life, was united in death.

It didn't matter. He had served his purpose.

The light had won.

Losara awoke with a start. Snuggled at his side, Lalenda stirred but stayed asleep. Carefully he disentangled himself from her. Around them the delta was loud as the sun set, full of frogs and insects chirping. He looked up to the Cloud and there it was, high in the sky. He breathed a deep sigh of relief.

'What is it, my lord?' came Lalenda's sleepy voice.

'I know the reason for my pilgrimage,' said Losara. 'I know why I needed to see the land, the beauty that will be destroyed if they triumph. I appreciate now the price of failure. I understand that there can be no peace. I must fight my other and I must win.'

She was sitting up now, her eyes glistening in the dark. He bent down and cupped her cheeks in his hands. She smiled.

'I have something to do,' he said, 'but I'll be back before you know it. Sleep, my flutterbug.'

She closed her eyes and his touch evaporated. In shadowform he sped towards Holdwith. There, in the cobblestoned tower, he found a whelkling chained to the wall.

'Fly home with a lighter load,' he told it, and disintegrated the chain.

From there he went north, through Kainordas and all the way to the Open Halls. He circled around the wards to find the point closest to the Open Castle, then broke through the resistance. He knew somewhere alarms were sounding and mages and soldiers would be rushing to find him, but they would never be fast enough. He sped to the Open Tower and up to the Throne's chambers.

It was a familiar scene. The Throne stood silhouetted by the open end of his quarters, a large glass of bloodfire in his hand. The sun was low in the sky to the south, and the liquid caught its rays brightly, casting a red wash back over the rest of the room. Losara knew Naphur waited for his other, was going to give him the order to charge, to put him on the path.

Gathering himself into physical form, Losara stepped from the darkness and placed a shadowy hand on Naphur's chest. Naphur gasped as Losara froze his heart.

The door to the room opened and Losara turned to see Bel and Fahren enter. At the sight of him, Fahren's hands shot up, suffusing himself and Bel in a defensive light.

'You!' said Bel, his jaw dropping open.

For a moment the two of them stared at each other. There came the sounds of other feet and Losara knew he had best not tarry – he was not at the height of his powers here. He pulled his hand back from the Throne, who slid lifelessly down the wall. Bel's cheeks heated and he drew his sword.

Losara smiled thinly. 'I think perhaps you'd best check the path before you strike me,' he said.

He watched as Bel's expression grew confused, then horrified with realisation.

Losara chuckled. 'The way to defeat me – it would not be to strike yourself down, would it?'

With that, he dissolved and fled.

Epilogue

Little Kaja peeked around the rock again, but there was still no sign of the other children. That didn't mean they weren't there, hiding or hunting through the wood. Her older brother, Duri, was excellent at playing the hunter, and Kaja knew he could be sneaking up on her at this very moment. The thought of it made her blood tingle, and with an excited giggle she jumped to her feet and ran further into the wood.

She spotted a large bush and, knowing it would make a good hiding spot, wormed her way amongst the branches, positioning herself to look back the way she had come. Duri and the others would have a hard time finding her here! Minutes passed and she remained silent. Soon she began to grow bored. Where was Duri? She hadn't heard any gleeful shouting as other hiding children had been discovered, or seen any hunters running through the trees after fleeing quarry. There were no sounds in the wood except the flapping of wings in the canopy and rustling in the undergrowth. Maybe the others had gone home without her?

She crawled out of the bush and got to her feet, almost hoping that Duri was going to erupt triumphantly from somewhere nearby. 'Duri?' she called. 'Are you there?'

When there was no reply, she began to tread her way back to the forest's edge. After walking some way, she stopped and looked around. She should have been able to see the edge of the trees by now, and the tended fields that lay beyond. She realised with rising panic that she had somehow become lost and was way beyond the bounds her parents had set.

She continued walking, telling herself that everything would be all right. If she really was lost, her father and mother would soon come looking for her, and there was nothing in the forest to be afraid of. Still, now that she was alone, Kaja began to imagine all kinds of ferocious beasts lurking amongst the trees. She quickened her pace.

As time passed, it became harder for her to remain calm. She suspected she was walking in the wrong direction, and that it would have been wiser to stay put as soon as she'd realised she was lost. She was just about to turn around when she spotted an open area through the trees ahead. Breathing a sigh of relief, she made her way towards it. Relief was short-lived, however. As she came to the edge of the tree line she saw not fields, but a clear area of grass some twenty paces wide, ending in a rocky cliff face. She'd heard her father talk of the higher ground in the middle of the wood and now she definitely knew she'd walked in the wrong direction. Tired, frustrated and afraid, she sat down heavily on a root to catch her breath.

A sudden noise made her start, and she scrambled behind the root to lie as flat as she could, her heart pounding. About halfway up the cliff face was a dark hole, which, a moment before, had been empty. Now, at the mouth of the raised cave, a figure stood, stooped in an enveloping robe that shrouded its face.

Kaja raised her face above the root – she had to know if the figure had seen her. For a moment it stood as still as the rock that surrounded it. Then it moved forward, and Kaja had to suppress a gasp as it stepped into the air and floated slowly down from the high cave to land softly on the grass. There it paused again, and she had the most horrible sensation that it was searching for her. She stiffened, ready to jump and run the instant its shrouded face turned to her . . . but the hidden gaze passed on.

There was a rustling in the leaves by her side and a tiny mouse appeared. It seemed unafraid as it came to a stop on the root just in front of Kaja's peeking eyes. *Go away,* she willed it miserably. Instead the mouse sat up on its hind legs, twitching its nose at her. It gave a soft squeak and bounded down the other side. Kaja watched as it raced into the clearing, heading straight for the figure. The figure's head snapped over and the mouse came to a stop. The little creature began to squeak again, waggling its whiskers, apparently unworried by the cloaked figure. The figure whispered back, and with a terrifying certainty Kaja knew that the mouse was betraying her presence.

The figure reached down towards the mouse, and this time Kaja could not help but gasp. The hand it held out was black and skeletal!

After her gasp, the thing most certainly knew she was there; it turned its head right to her. A moment later Kaja was on her feet, dashing away through the trees, squealing uncontrollably in panic. Faster and faster she went as she imagined the creature coming after her, floating through the trees, its skeleton hands reaching for her. She screamed out to anyone who might be searching for her, ignoring the burning pain of her breathlessness, the branches that scratched her as she went.

Back in the clearing, the figure stared after her. Eventually it turned back to the mouse, stroking it behind the ears with a bone finger. The mouse squeaked approval.

'That was clumsy,' said the figure in a voice that echoed.

He drew back his hood to reveal a charred and blackened skull beneath, cheekbones rough and crumbling away, teeth like charcoal blocks, eye sockets empty.

'Well,' he said, 'I suppose it's time to move on again.'

The mouse squeaked, leaped free of the hard palm and raced away into the wood.

'Goodbye to you too,' said Fazel, and sighed.